From grandmother to mother, from mother to daughter, the joy and emotion of motherhood are things to cherish . . .

A HOMESPUN MOTHER'S DAY

A breathtaking collection
of stories celebrating motherhood—
by three outstanding
Diamond Homespun Romance writers . . .

It was strictly business when Lydia Turner sold her father's drugstore and soda fountain to a handsome doctor. But she found herself caring for his young son with a tenderness she'd never known . . . when motherly love comes *before* marriage in *"Twice Blessed" by REBECCA HAGAN LEE*

A grandmother protects her young grandson from the stranger who drifted into their barn seeking shelter from a storm and a good night's sleep. But can Emma Parker protect her compassionate heart from stirrings of love? *"Emma's Day" by JILL METCALF*

Rachel Cameron didn't know if her grandma's Ozark Mountain sayings were sage or superstitious. But she couldn't deny the handsome lover who suddenly appeared in her life—just as the ring at the bottom of her coffee cup predicted—in
"Coming Home" by TERESA WARFIELD

A HOMESPUN MOTHER'S DAY

By Rebecca Hagan Lee –
Jill Metcalf –Teresa Warfield

DIAMOND BOOKS, NEW YORK

This book is a Diamond original edition,
and has never been previously published.

"Twice Blessed" copyright © 1994 by Rebecca Hagan Lee.
"Emma's Day" copyright © 1994 by Jill Metcalf.
"Coming Home" copyright © 1994 by Teresa Warfield.

A HOMESPUN MOTHER'S DAY

A Diamond Book / published by arrangement with
the authors

PRINTING HISTORY
Diamond edition / May 1994

Diamond Books are published by The Berkley Publishing Group,
200 Madison Avenue, New York, NY 10016.
DIAMOND and the "D" design
are trademarks belonging to Charter Communications, Inc.

PRINTED IN THE UNITED STATES OF AMERICA

10 9 8 7 6 5 4 3 2 1

CONTENTS

TWICE BLESSED

by

Rebecca Hagan Lee

ONE

As always she was perfectly prepared.

Lydia Turner tucked a stray lock of light brown hair back into the Gibson-girl bun on top of her head and carefully repinned it. She pulled on her best visiting gloves and picked up her handbag, checking one last time to make certain she'd put the calling card, with the train's arrival time carefully written on the back, inside her bag along with her handkerchief and leather change purse. She straightened, drawing herself up to her full height, and fastened the gold-braided frogs on the front of her military-style jacket. Lydia adjusted the high ruffled collar of her blouse just so and ran her hands over the front of her skirt, smoothing invisible wrinkles. *"Control,"* she whispered to herself.

Control and Lydia's attention to details gave her the false courage she needed, helped her to focus on what she was going to do. In the past four weeks, her world had been turned upside down and Lydia had found herself in the unaccustomed situation of feeling like a small boat adrift on the wide, vast sea—anchorless and without direction.

And she knew the feeling would continue. Although her meeting at the Eden Point depot was necessary, even if it turned out to be successful, she'd be at a loss. Lydia would finally have a tidy sum in her bank account, but she'd lose the only job and the only home she'd ever known.

She glanced down at the delicate gold watch pinned to her jacket. Ten-fifteen. His train was scheduled to arrive at ten forty-five. Thirty minutes to walk to the depot and await Major Sullivan's arrival. Only thirty minutes.

Control. Lydia took a deep breath to steady her nerves, then walked to the big yellow-tinted, plate-glass window and straightened the hand-painted sign. She pulled the shade down on each of the front doors, stepped out onto the crushed-shell sidewalk, then closed and locked the doors to Turner's Drugstore behind her.

Lydia allowed herself one backward glance at the red-brick building with the large window as she headed down Front Street toward the depot, but all she could see was the white sign with the big black letters proclaiming her father's drugstore FOR SALE.

"Major Sullivan?" Lydia addressed one of the passengers, a middle-aged man with frown lines and thinning hair, disembarking from the train.

The man shook his head.

She approached another male passenger. "Major Sullivan? Major Thomas Sullivan?"

"I'm Thomas Sullivan."

Lydia turned.

A tall black-haired man, in his late twenties or early thirties, exited the depot office and hurried toward her. He carried a black leather physician's bag and wore civilian clothing—a well-tailored black suit—instead of the uniform of an army surgeon. He wasn't what she had expected. And he wasn't alone.

He carried a child, a little boy of four or five. The boy had his face pressed against the major's chest. As Lydia watched, Major Sullivan hefted the sleeping child a bit higher.

"Lydia Turner." She stuck out her hand.

Major Sullivan glanced at it and nodded. He couldn't accept her handshake. His hands were already full.

Lydia's cheeks flamed with color. Struggling for something to say to ease the awkwardness, she looked up at him and said the first thing that came to mind. "You're not at all what I expected, Major Sullivan."

"It's Dr. Sullivan now, Miss Turner. I've resigned from the army." He met her gaze.

Lydia couldn't seem to stop staring at the man. His eyes were the most extraordinary shade of green. "Please, call me Lydia."

He smiled down at her. "What exactly were you expecting, Lydia?" He emphasized her name and found himself liking the way it sounded. It was soft and gentle to his ears.

Lydia blushed again, but managed to find her tongue. "Someone different. Someone in uniform, older." She shrugged her shoulder. "More—"

"Experienced?"

"—like my father."

They spoke at the same time.

"Ladies first," Thomas said, urging her to continue.

"I . . . please, let me apologize," Lydia stammered, feeling all of sixteen instead of a mature twenty-six. She cleared her throat, straightened to her full five feet four inches, and tried again. "I know you're an experienced physician, Dr. Sullivan, I've read of your record."

"How?"

"What?"

"How did you know of my record? I've only written you the one letter stating my interest in purchasing your father's practice."

Lydia's cheeks reddened again. "Well, after I received your letter, I wrote to a few of my father's colleagues asking about you."

He frowned.

"I had to know if you were the kind of doctor Eden Point needs." Lydia hurried to explain. "You see my father was the only physician and pharmacist in Eden Point for years. When he died"—she paused—"I felt I had to find the right man to take over his practice. It was my duty as his only child."

Thomas nodded, somewhat somberly. As if he understood duty all too well. "What did you find out from your father's colleagues?"

She decided not to be embarrassed about her nosiness. "I learned you were stationed in Panama and later volunteered to serve as a doctor with the Army Medical Corps in Europe. You stayed in France even after your term of duty expired a couple of months ago. I know you're the most fully qualified doctor to express an interest in coming to Eden Point—a doctor more qualified than I'd ever hoped to find—but your civilian clothes and your"—Lydia toyed with the gold braid on her jacket—"well, I didn't expect—" She stopped abruptly. She'd read his record, knew he'd graduated from college and medical school at the top of his class, knew the year of his graduation, knew that he'd spent years in the Panama Canal Zone and four years caring for the troops in France and Belgium, but still she'd expected . . . something, someone, different. Someone balding, with a paunch around his middle from too little exercise, and dark circles under his eyes from too little sleep. This man, this Dr. Thomas Sullivan, was tall and lean, and gorgeous. How could she explain that she'd never expected him to be so young and handsome or that she would respond to the sound of his voice like a twittering schoolgirl? "Control," she whispered again.

"What?" Thomas asked.

Lydia felt the color rise in her cheeks as she fought to control her reaction to him. "I didn't count on having the train arrive ahead of schedule. And I didn't expect . . ." She clamped her mouth shut to keep from making an even bigger fool of herself.

"My son, Robert." Thomas studied the woman standing before him. He'd expected someone different as well. Someone older, a spinster—tall, spare, and as tough as old leather. He'd done his homework and knew almost as much about the late Dr. Josiah Turner and his very efficient daughter as she knew about him. But none of Dr. Turner's medical-school colleagues had thought to mention how young—or how pretty—Lydia Turner was, and the sight of her had set him back several paces. She wasn't very tall—didn't even reach his shoulders—and Thomas suspected that was part of the reason she carried herself with the stiff comportment any soldier would envy and dressed in a severe fashion. She probably thought it made her look taller, older, and more businesslike. But she was wrong. Several strands of baby-fine hair had come loose from her topknot, ruining the severe look of her high-necked military jacket and the crisp white ruffle of her blouse, emphasizing the delicate beauty of her oval face. And the dark jacket and skirt accentuated, rather than concealed her slight figure. Though she tried to project a no-nonsense image, Thomas got the feeling she wasn't as straitlaced or rigid as she appeared. At least he hoped not. But she didn't seem thoughtless, or scatterbrained, either. He knew a flighty, carefree, society miss when he saw one and Miss Lydia Turner simply didn't fit the bill. But she was definitely flustered. Thomas liked what he saw. His instincts told him she'd be like a shot of adrenaline to his war-weary brain. He smiled at her. "Am I making you nervous, Miss Turner?"

"No, no, of course not." She pulled a gold thread loose from one of her jacket frogs. "What makes you think that?"

Thomas bit the inside of his lip to keep from smiling at her again, then spoke in his best doctor's voice. "I seem to have that effect on people. I'm afraid my height is intimidating."

"Not at all," she said, speaking the truth. Lydia didn't find his height daunting, though he stood head and shoulders above her. It was his face and his youth, and his warm, wonderful, baritone voice that had her babbling like an idiot. Lydia glanced up to find him looking at her, but she couldn't quite meet his gaze. "Shall we go?" she invited. "The store is just a short walk down the street." Feeling more in control, Lydia turned to the porter. "Amos, we're going on ahead. Please send Dr. Sullivan's luggage to the store." She started down the platform steps.

"Yes, Miss Lydia," the porter answered.

"I planned to stay in a hotel, Miss Turner," Thomas said as he followed her down the steps onto the sidewalk.

"Eden Point doesn't have a hotel, just Casey's Boardinghouse. But its clientele mainly consists of railroad employees and traveling salesmen." Lydia explained. "It's a male establishment—lots of rough language and drinking and"—she blushed—"fancy women. I don't think you'd find it suitable for your son."

"I see," he said, taking careful note of the fact that she had definite ideas on what was right or wrong for small children. "What about the summer visitors? I understood Eden Point to be a resort town." He could hear the roar of the surf and the shrill cries of the seabirds in the distance, and taste the tangy salt on the breeze. "I admit I've been looking forward to treating nothing more serious than an endless stream of sunburn and jellyfish stings," Thomas joked. He studied the layout of the town as they passed and the businesses lining both sides of Front Street. "So where do all the vacationers stay while they're in Eden Point?"

"In the cottages on the beach."

"Oh," Thomas said. "Where is the beach?"

Lydia stopped in front of a glass-fronted, two-story building and pointed to her left, across the street, down a narrow path between two buildings. "A hundred yards or so, beyond those dunes. You can see part of the roof of the pavilion from our . . . um . . . the store window." She retrieved the key from her purse. "Here we are."

Thomas noticed the carefully painted For Sale sign in the window as Lydia unlocked the door. Moments later she pushed the door open. A brass bell announced their arrival as Lydia turned to Thomas. "Welcome to Turner's Drugstore," she said proudly.

TWO

Thomas stepped inside the drugstore, then paused a moment to look around, to absorb the feel of the place.

"Come on inside," Lydia urged, "and I'll show you around."

Thomas followed her to the back of the store, then waited as she opened a door to her right.

"This was my father's examining room. There's a cot behind the screen." She pointed to the fabric-covered screen on one side of the room. "You can put your little boy down there if you like."

Thomas nodded his agreement. He set his doctor's bag on the side table and eased Robert's arms from around his neck.

Lydia crossed the room and quietly moved the screen aside.

The cot was small, and only a few inches off the floor. The sheets were amazingly white against the dark wool of the blanket, fresh smelling, and cool to the touch. Thomas noted the crisply folded hospital corners and smiled. He leaned over and Lydia rushed forward to pull back the covers. Thomas gently placed his son on the cot, tucked the blanket up around Robert's shoulders, and planted a kiss on his cheek. Straightening, he turned to Lydia.

The front of his suit was wrinkled and pressed against his skin, damp in places from holding the child's warm body throughout the long train ride. He tugged at the hem of his jacket, then glanced down at his son. "He was exhausted by the trip and fell asleep just as we pulled into the depot. I didn't have the heart to wake him."

Watching as the little boy slept, Lydia understood why.

Robert seemed small and delicate. His face was pale and his features pinched with fatigue, but his cheeks were flushed with color. His chest rose and fell in a rapid cadence and dark rings formed half-moons beneath his eyes. "You can wait here until he wakes up if you'd rather. I can show you the rest of the store and the clinic later," she offered, starting toward the door.

"I think he'll be fine if we just let him sleep." Thomas's chest seemed to puff with pride at the sight of his son sleeping soundly. He reached down to touch his son's forehead. Robert was another reason Thomas felt he'd needed to leave France and return to the States. He didn't want his son growing up surrounded by the memories of war.

"Do you think he's feverish?"

Thomas heard the edge in Lydia's tone of voice and recognized her fear. He knew from her letter that she'd lost her physician father to the influenza epidemic. And his death had forced Lydia Turner to put the drugstore up for sale. She couldn't continue to operate the store, dispense, or purchase drugs without a doctor or a licensed pharmacist on the premises.

"No," Thomas told her. "His temperature is normal." He shrugged his shoulders, and a bittersweet smile tugged at the corners of his mouth. "I like to touch him when he's sleeping," he admitted, a bit sheepishly. "He doesn't allow it when he's awake."

Thomas ushered her from the room, but Lydia placed her hand on his as he started to close the door behind them. The contact jolted her. She snatched her hand away, but she couldn't remove the feeling of warmth his touch had given her, or the slow the rapid beating of her heart. She turned and looked at him over her shoulder. He seemed embarrassed, as if his demonstration of love for his son had left him vulnerable somehow. The picture of Thomas Sullivan kissing his little boy as he tucked him into bed popped into Lydia's mind and the memory wrapped itself around her heart. "Leave the door open," she whispered. "You'll be able to hear if he wakes up."

* * *

"The pharmacy contains the latest prescription drugs available," Lydia explained as Thomas removed a bottle from the shelf and stared at the label in wonder. "Though we're practically out of quinine and several other drugs necessary for the treatment of influenza. I wasn't able to reorder the stock. The pharmaceutical companies are working day and night to meet the demand, but"—she faltered—"with so many people ill with the flu . . ." She let her words trail off, then she recovered. "There's only so much anyone can do. My father prided himself on keeping in step with the times. He studied the latest medical techniques and researched the uses of all the newest drugs. His office library is nearly filled to bursting with medical books and journals. And the clinic"— Lydia opened the door to the clinic attached to the back of the store, then stepped back to let Thomas enter—"contains ten beds and the latest in hospital supplies and equipment. You won't find anything like it this side of Tallahassee."

Thomas didn't doubt that a bit. The Turner Clinic was the cleanest, most well-equipped small hospital he'd ever seen— this side of Tallahassee or beyond. It was a far cry from the converted houses, churches, basements, and field hospitals he'd operated in during the last four years. He studied the hospital beds neatly aligned in two rows of five, the two oxygen canisters on the back wall awaiting use, the sparkling enameled surfaces of the instrument trays and tables, and smiled. He could work here, Thomas decided, he could help people heal. And maybe, just maybe, the people of Eden Point would do the same for him and Robert.

"You'll find everything you need in the cabinets. They're locked right now, but I can get the key for you from my father's office," Lydia said.

"No, please, I'm sure everything is in order. You and your father have done a remarkable job." Thomas shook his head in wonder, then glanced around again to make sure it was real. The medical practice, the office, the clinic—even the drugstore—all seemed like a gift from heaven, and Lydia Turner the angel sent to deliver it.

"Maman!"

The child's frightened cry echoed through the store.

Thomas ran from the clinic, down the short hallway, back to the examining room, and Robert. Lydia picked up her skirts and followed close on his heels.

"Maman!" Robert cried out again as Thomas crossed the room in two strides and enfolded his son in a protective embrace.

"It's all right, son, Papa's here." Thomas sat down on the cot, held Robert in his lap, and rocked the little boy back and forth. "Papa's here."

Robert opened his eyes, looked up and recognized his father, then pushed away out of Thomas's arms.

Thomas let him go. He turned and found Lydia Turner standing in the doorway, watching. His eyes met hers.

Lydia saw the flicker of raw pain in the depths of Thomas's green eyes and knew he was struggling to hide the hurt. She walked over to the bed and stood before Robert Sullivan. "Hello," she said.

Robert stared up at her. He didn't return her greeting and his big brown eyes mirrored his wariness. Dismissing her with an arrogance Lydia hadn't thought possible in a child so young, Robert lowered his gaze and studied the hardwood floor.

"It's rude not to speak, Robby," Thomas said softly. "Say hello to Miss Turner."

Robert glanced defiantly at his father, then at Lydia. *"Bonjour."*

"We're in America now," Thomas reminded his son, "Please speak English."

"Bonjour, mademoiselle," Robert replied.

Thomas took a deep breath, then expelled it, in one long frustrated sigh.

"I think French is a lovely language." Lydia attempted to bridge the gap between father and son. "If you prefer French, I'll do my best to follow along. I guess I can use the practice. But don't say I didn't warn you." She smiled at Robert. "Are you thirsty?"

He nodded.

"Well, come along"—she offered him her hand—"and I'll take you to the soda fountain and show you how to make a chocolate malt."

The little boy's eyes lit up.

"So, you like that idea, eh?"

"Oui." He reached out and clasped Lydia's hand.

Her heart seemed to skip a beat at the contact, and instinctively, Lydia looked up to find Thomas watching her.

"Okay, Monsieur Robert, let's go."

"Ro-bear," Robert corrected as Lydia led him from the examining room to the marble-topped counter that ran the length of the drugstore.

Thomas stood quietly and watched Lydia Turner create a chocolate malt for Robert and another one for herself. She topped the drinks with a froth of whipped cream and plopped a long-stemmed cherry on top, stuck a long straw in each of them, then slid one of the malts across the counter in front of Robert.

Robert marveled at the beverage, but made no move to taste it.

"Don't you like chocolate, Robert?" Lydia asked.

Thomas walked over to the soda fountain. "I don't think he really knows what it is. Chocolate was unavailable during the war, and the inflation in France has made it so costly, I doubt he's ever tasted it—especially in malted form."

"Try it," Lydia urged the little boy. "Do like this." She picked up her malt and drank from the straw.

Copying her actions, Robert took a sip of his drink. His brown eyes widened in wonderment. *"C'est bon."* He took another sip, then a larger one.

Thomas leaned against the countertop.

Robert turned, saw his father, then favored him with a rare smile. *"Ça, c'est bon, Papa."*

Thomas's green eyes brimmed with emotion. He glanced at the young woman standing behind the marble counter enjoying her own chocolate treat. She fished the long-stemmed cherry out of the whipped cream with a spoon and popped the sweet fruit into her mouth. A speck of whipped cream clung to her upper lip. Thomas stared at Lydia, swallowed hard, then cleared his throat. "What does a man have to do to get a drink around here?"

Lydia laughed and set her glass aside. "Ask," she told him, "then name your poison." She pointed to the chalkboard listing the available treats.

"I'll have what you're having," Thomas said. He smiled down at the top of his son's head as Robert sucked the last bit of froth up his straw. "I've heard chocolate malts have magical healing powers."

"It isn't the chocolate," Lydia confided, "or the malt." She stared into Thomas's green eyes. "It's the place. Turner's Drugstore is known for its magical healing power. Ask anyone. They'll tell you. The magic is everywhere—especially the soda fountain."

Thomas suspected the magical healing powers were confined to the woman working the soda fountain, but he kept that thought to himself. "Well, if that's the case, I have no choice except to buy the soda fountain, too."

"Do you mean it?"

Thomas nodded. "Name your price," he said.

THREE

Lydia opened her mouth to speak, not quite sure at the moment if she'd heard him correctly. There was something about his tone of voice, something about the look in his deep green eyes, that made her question her hearing. Maybe she didn't quite understand what he meant, but she didn't get a chance to ask him.

The bell over the front door jangled merrily as Amos, the porter from the depot, opened the front door and wheeled a handcart containing an army footlocker and two small leather suitcases into the drugstore. "Where do you want these, Miss Lydia?"

"Upstairs, Amos."

"What's upstairs?" Thomas asked.

"The living quarters." Lydia met Thomas's gaze, but did her best to downplay the fact that the upstairs apartment had been her home for the past twenty-six years and still contained most of her mother's furniture. "There's a three-bedroom apartment, a living room, a small dining room, bathroom, and a kitchen. Plenty of room for you and Robert." She glanced down at her shoes to keep him from seeing the how much it hurt her to have to sell the store and her home.

Robert stared at the porter.

"Would you like to go upstairs and help Amos?" Lydia asked.

Robert nodded, then turned to Thomas. "Papa?"

"If Amos doesn't mind."

"It's fine with me," Amos said.

Robert hopped down from his barstool and followed the porter up the stairs.

15

Thomas couldn't help noticing that Lydia refused to look at him, or the fact that she was pulling at the loose thread on her jacket again. "Where do you live?" It didn't take a genius to figure out that Lydia Turner was selling her home along with her father's business.

"I . . . um . . . used to live upstairs, I don't anymore." She stumbled over her words, trying to explain. "I've moved into the carriage house next door. I didn't think anyone would want to buy it." Lydia looked up at him. "You see, the carriage house is old and the apartment isn't much. It's only one room and a bath. And there's no kitchen, not even an icebox or hot plate."

Thomas shook his head. "I don't understand. I thought you were moving away from Eden Point, yet you're living in a carriage-house apartment next door."

"I haven't decided what I'm going to do once I sell the store," Lydia admitted. "This has all been so sudden. I didn't have time. . . . In a few weeks I'll probably go to Tallahassee and try to find work."

She ended the conversation by saying, "I'm sure you and Robert will be very comfortable until Mrs. Sullivan can join you."

Thomas finally understood. He glanced toward the stairs to make certain Robert couldn't overhear him, then took a deep breath. "I'm not married. Robert's mother, Françoise, is dead."

"I'm so sorry." Impulsively, Lydia reached out to touch his sleeve. "I didn't know. I just assumed your wife had stayed behind in France until you were settled."

Thomas's startling green eyes clouded. He tried again. "I don't have a wife. Robert's mother and I were never married."

"What?" Lydia took a step back. "You don't mean . . ."

"Yes, I do." Thomas nodded. There. He'd told her the truth. Regardless of what she'd learned from her father's colleagues, he'd been honest with Lydia Turner. Thomas just hoped she wouldn't send him and Robert packing now that he'd admitted his son had been born out of wedlock.

He glanced down and met Lydia's wide-eyed stare. Once again, he hoped she wasn't as straitlaced as she appeared to be. He needed this job—this quiet, normal town. He needed stability for himself and for his son. "Robert's mother died over a year ago," he continued when Lydia didn't reply, "and he hasn't forgiven me for it. He thinks his *papa,* the American doctor, was too busy saving the lives of the American soldiers to save his beautiful *maman.*"

Lydia recognized the note of bitter regret in his voice. "Were you?" she asked softly.

"I tried to save as many lives as possible," Thomas answered honestly. "In a way, I guess I did concentrate on the soldiers."

"If she was ill, why didn't you . . ."

"Spend more time with her?" Thomas met Lydia's intense hazel-eyed stare. "Cure her?" He paused, then fixed his gaze on the marble counter. "I couldn't. No one could." He broke off and ran his fingers through his short-cropped hair. "I regret not having been able to cure her. But," Thomas asked, "how can I regret having Robert? Having a son? And how can I explain to him that he . . ." He glanced back at Lydia, studied her, willing her to understand. "She never recovered from Robert's birth. She grew weaker instead of stronger. There wasn't anything I could do."

"Except allow your little boy to think you cared more for the soldiers than you did for his mother." Lydia's words weren't an indictment, just a fact.

"I never meant for Robert to think I didn't care. But I was away so much—at the front—in the field hospitals. I wasn't able to get to Paris as often as I wanted. One visit Robert was a baby, and on the next he was a little boy walking and talking, so happy and full of life. Then his mother died."

"And he changed."

Thomas reached up and rubbed at the aching spot on the side of his neck. "For a long time Robert didn't speak at all. Now he speaks when he has to, but only in French and never to me, if he can help it."

Lydia looked puzzled. "But he spoke to you a moment ago."

"Because of you," Thomas said, "and Turner's Drugstore, and the magical elixir you created."

"There's nothing magical about milk and malt and chocolate," Lydia reminded him.

"Then it must be you and Turner's," he said simply. "I'll buy the store, Lydia. I'll pay any price you name. But only if you'll stay and run it."

Lydia gasped. She tugged at the loose thread and half of a gold-braided frog came away in her hand. "I can't."

"Can't or won't?"

"I can't." She tucked the portion of her jacket closure into her pocket, then unconsciously began pulling at threads on the other half. Lydia turned around.

Amos, the porter, stood in the doorway. He cleared his throat nervously. "I put the luggage in the big bedroom for you all to sort out later."

"Thank you, Amos." She walked to the other end of the counter toward the cash register.

"I'll take care of it," Thomas told her, and handed the porter fifty cents.

"Thank you, sir," Amos replied. "Your little boy's upstairs, sir. I helped him unpack his toy soldiers. He was playing with 'em on the floor when I left." He smiled at Thomas, showing a white toothy grin. "Nice young man you got there, sir. Quiet. Don't talk much." He tipped his cap in Lydia's direction, nodded to Thomas, then left the drugstore through the backdoor.

"I'll need help," Thomas said once the porter had gone. "I can't see patients all day, run a drugstore, and keep an eye on a five-year-old boy."

"I'm sure my father's nurse would be happy to return to work. She can help you with the practice and catch you up on all you need to know," Lydia replied.

"What about the store? And Robert?"

Lydia hesitated at the thought of her beloved drugstore and the grieving little boy upstairs.

Thomas saw her hesitation and pressed his advantage. "You could stay here instead of going to Tallahassee. Haven't you thought about it? Don't you want to stay in Eden Point and continue to work in the store?"

"Of course I've thought about it," Lydia replied. "When I got your letter, I thought about staying on to run the store while you took up Daddy's practice. For a few days I even thought that having a new doctor here would make things almost like they were before. But I was wrong. Things are different."

"What's different?" Thomas wanted to know. "I'm a doctor ready to open a practice. You know all there is to know about running a drugstore." She was wavering. He could see it in her eyes—in the wistful expression on her face. Though he'd planned to purchase the medical practice almost from the moment he'd stepped off the train, Thomas hadn't been so sure about the store. Now he wanted it desperately. But not without Lydia Turner standing behind the counter. Somehow he couldn't picture Turner's Drugstore without her. "Do you really want to leave Eden Point right away?"

"I stayed in Eden Point after my mother died because it was home. My father was here and he needed me to help him. But now he's dead. And I'm leaving for Tallahassee as soon as Daddy's estate is sold and settled, as soon as you go talk to the banker."

"I won't talk to the banker unless you agree to stay on and teach me how to run the business."

"You're a doctor," Lydia said. "You know how to practice medicine. And you're smart enough to learn how to dispense it without me."

"I've never had a practice of my own," Thomas reminded her. "I've always worked for the U.S. Army."

"I've never been on my own," Lydia countered, desperately fighting her desire to stay. "I've always lived in Eden Point and worked for my father. Maybe it's time for me to test my wings."

"I could run the place into the ground. For all I know, the store could be bankrupt in six weeks."

Lydia moved from behind the counter, but Thomas caught her arm, gently wrapping his fingers around the delicate bones of her wrist. The touch of his fingers sent shivers up and down her spine.

"Stay, Lydia, teach me."

The earnest expression in his green eyes and the pleading tone in his deep voice was impossible for her to ignore. Suddenly she realized that Thomas Sullivan was asking for more than help running a drugstore. Somehow, in some strange way, he needed her. And she knew he felt Robert needed her.

"But I planned to go to Tallahassee." She hung on to the idea like a lifeline. She'd lost her mother and her father. She didn't want to stay in Eden Point and risk forming an attachment to two strangers—a man and a little boy—just to lose them to someone else. Thomas Sullivan was young and strong and handsome. He wouldn't remain unmarried for long. He'd find a wife and Robert would have a new mother.

Thomas seemed to sense Lydia's need to keep her distance. "We can make it a temporary arrangement," he insisted, "until I get used to the practice and learn the operation of the store."

"How long?" Lydia needed a number.

"Eight weeks?"

Lydia shook her head. Eight weeks was a long time. In eight weeks, she could be firmly entrenched in the running of the store. Thomas Sullivan might come to depend on her, expect her to be there. Robert might get used to having her around. No, eight weeks was too long. Much too long. "Two."

"I can't learn all I need to know in two weeks' time," Thomas said. "I'll need at least six."

"Three."

"Five."

"Four," she countered.

"Four," he agreed.

Lydia stared at Thomas Sullivan's outstretched hand. "Well," he asked, "do we have a deal or not?"

She placed her hand in his. "Four weeks."

"If things don't work out . . . If you decide you don't want to work for me, if you can't give me the entire four weeks, I'll understand," Thomas offered.

"We agreed on one month," Lydia told him. "I'll live up to the terms of our agreement."

"Good." Thomas nodded at her. "Let's go find Robert. And after you show me the apartment upstairs, you can teach me how to make a chocolate malt."

FOUR

Lydia couldn't stop thinking about their agreement as she led Thomas Sullivan upstairs for his tour of the living quarters. What had possessed her to agree to stay in Eden Point and help him learn the business when all her instincts urged her to run? She didn't want any more emotional attachments. She didn't need any more people to worry about. And if she stayed in Eden Point, she wouldn't be able to help caring for the Sullivan males.

It was already impossible for her to look at Robert without feeling a tug at her heart. He was so small and fragile and lost. She watched as Robert lined his rows of tin soldiers into two opposing armies—one French and the other German. He suffered the loss of his mother, and separation from everyone he knew and loved except the near stranger who was his father. Those losses were more than any child should have to bear.

And what about his father? What about Thomas Sullivan? He was different from any man she'd ever known. He understood honor and duty, yet he failed to marry the mother of his child. How could he fit into Eden Point society? He was a man with a scandalous past. Lydia looked at him now, studied him as he went about the business of inspecting the apartment's furnishings. He stood in the hallway and reached for the doorknob to the nearest room.

"Are these the bedrooms?"

"Y-yes," she managed. "That room belonged to my father."

Thomas opened the door, then sighed in relief. "At last a bed built big enough to fit me." He turned to look at Lydia. "You wouldn't believe how torturous it is to try to squeeze six feet four inches into an army cot."

Lydia stared at a spot on his chest above one of his shirt buttons.

"This is great." Thomas crossed the room to sit on the side of the massive bed. "Mind if I try it?"

Lydia's breath caught in her throat. It was all she could do to utter the words, "Go ahead."

Thomas took off his suit coat and folded it across the foot of the bed, then stretched out and grinned up at her. "This is heaven. Pure heaven."

As she looked down at him lying on the bed, Lydia imagined a woman curled up beside him—a beautiful woman who shared Robert's delicate, aristocratic looks. Lydia pictured Françoise tilting her face up toward Thomas's, awaiting the pressure of his lips on hers. Embarrassed, Lydia felt the color rush to her cheeks at the thought, and quickly glanced down at the toes of her shoes.

"Lydia, are you all right?" Thomas sat up.

"I . . . uh . . . I'm fine." She met his concerned gaze. "It's just hot up here. Don't you think?"

As a matter of fact, the heat upstairs had been turned off, and now that he'd removed his jacket, Thomas found the apartment a bit chilly, but he refrained from commenting on it. Lydia was stammering again. Something he noticed she did only when she was nervous or embarrassed. "Are you sure? You don't look fine."

"I am."

"Come here," Thomas said in his most authoritarian tone. "Let me see." He didn't really think she was sick, but he couldn't dispel the need to touch her.

Lydia moved toward him.

Thomas reached out, took hold of her hand, and pulled her closer until she stood just inches from him. He let go of her hand and moved to her wrist, gently feeling for her pulse with one hand while he reached up and brushed his other hand against her forehead. "No fever," he said.

Maybe not, Lydia agreed, but her pulse was racing at his touch. She tried to pull away. *Control.* She had to regain control of herself.

Thomas kept a light, but firm grip on her arm. "Your face is flushed, your heart is pounding, and you keep looking down at your feet." His smile was as warm as the sun on the white sandy beaches. "Is it me?"

Lydia raised her head and met his probing gaze. "I have to go."

"Do you?" Thomas continued to smile warmly at her. He held her hand in his as he caressed the vein in her wrist with his thumb.

"It's nearly lunchtime and—" She bit her bottom lip. His hand was warm and big, nearly twice the size of hers. She liked the feel of it.

"And you don't have a stove in your apartment, remember?"

She'd forgotten mentioning that to him.

"Have lunch with us," he offered. "I'm sure we passed a café on the way here."

"No, really, I—"

"Robert and I are strangers in town," Thomas insisted. "We don't know anyone except you. Won't you have lunch with us?"

"But there are things I need to do," Lydia protested. "Business to take care of."

"We won't keep you long, I promise. Just lunch. Robert would like it," he said quietly. "*I* would like it."

Lydia sighed. "All right. I'll have lunch with you at the Eden Point Café."

Thomas let go of her hand. "Thank you." He got up from the bed. "I'll get Robert and then we'll freshen up and meet you downstairs."

Lydia blushed again as mental images of Thomas washing up rushed through her mind.

Thomas couldn't help himself. He reached out and tilted her chin up with the tip of his finger so he could see the expression on her face. "I understand how you feel, Lydia," he said. "I know it's sudden and completely unexpected, but it might interest you to know my pulse is racing, too." He unbuttoned his shirt sleeve and pushed it up his forearm as he extended his hand to her. "See?" He guided her hand to his arm and placed her fingers on his wrist.

Lydia felt the strong, rapid thump of his heartbeat beneath her fingertips and jerked her hand away from his arm. "I . . . I . . ." She couldn't put her thoughts into words.

"It's all right, Lydia. Nothing to fret about. It happens sometimes." Thomas leaned down and gently covered her lips with his own. "We're attracted to one another."

"I can't stay," Lydia blurted. "I can't work for you."

"You promised a month to help get me acquainted with the business," he reminded her.

"But it wouldn't be right . . ." she began.

"Who says?"

That stopped her.

"Who says you have to go to Tallahassee? Who says you can't live next door and continue to work in the store? Where is it written that Lydia Turner has to leave everything she's ever known and cared about?" He leaned down and kissed her again. "Stay, Lydia. Stay with Robert and me and explore life's possibilities."

Lunch was a quiet affair. Robert refused to speak and Lydia hadn't attempted any conversation beyond ordering her meal and performing the necessary introductions for the curious townspeople.

Thomas didn't miss the fact that Lydia chose not to single him out. She introduced him to Marjorie Eddings, the owner of the Eden Point Café, and to the customers who came in the restaurant as Dr. Sullivan, one of the prospective buyers for her father's business—not *the* buyer. He wasn't surprised. Thomas knew he'd frightened her with his declaration, but there didn't seem to be a whole lot he could do about it now. Though he hadn't planned to announce it the way he did, he wasn't going to apologize for being attracted to her— for discovering he still had desires. He suddenly realized he hadn't felt the sharp, overwhelming desire for a woman since Françoise. And after Robert's birth . . . It had been a struggle at times, and he had been forced to suppress his natural desires, but he'd remained faithful to the mother of his child. His attraction to Lydia Turner was sudden and unexpected, but as he'd told her, sexual attraction sometimes happened that way between a man and a woman. It sort of sneaked up on them when they least expected it.

He wanted to kick himself for changing right before her eyes from Thomas Sullivan, the doctor—the safe, impersonal doctor—to Thomas Sullivan, the man, but there wasn't anything he could do about that, either. It had happened. He had no excuse, except that he was weary, tired of ignoring his most basic emotions, tired of pretending he didn't have any. So he had acted on impulse, laid bare his soul, and kissed her. And he knew immediately that he'd made a huge mistake. It was all right to think about kissing her, as he had since he met her at the station, but actually tasting the sweetness of her lips— not once, but twice . . . *that* was a mistake.

How was he going to pretend ignorance? How was he going to manage to look but not touch? How was he going to sleep at night, now that his dormant desires had roared to life like a hungry bear in springtime? Thomas studied her as she sat stirring her soup. She'd barely said a word to him since he'd kissed her, but that kiss—that innocent kiss had tapped a well of emotions Lydia kept hidden. He had tasted the hunger, the wonder, the desire, and the hint of desperation in her kiss— and reciprocated. For whatever reason, Lydia Turner touched a chord within him, and his response had been immediate. He wanted her. It was as plain and simple—as complex and convoluted as that. But he should have kept his knowledge to himself for a while longer—until she got used to the idea of him buying her father's practice, of having him and Robert constantly underfoot. Until she got used to the idea of . . .

Thomas shook his head as if to clear it. It was crazy. No, really, it was absurd even to consider such a thing. And yet the idea had merit. . . .

"I'm ready to go home now." Lydia pushed her bowl of seafood chowder out of the way. She wasn't hungry and hadn't managed to swallow more than a few spoonfuls of Marjorie's delicious soup. "And Robert"—she was careful to give the little boy's name the French pronunciation—"is practically asleep at the table."

Thomas set his cup of coffee down in its saucer and glanced over at his son. Robert's eyelids were slowly closing. Any minute now his son was liable to fall asleep on his plate. Thomas took out his wallet, removed enough money to cover the cost of lunch and a tip, and placed it beside his plate, then he shoved his chair away from the table and leaned over to lift Robert from his seat. He pulled the little boy into his arms and cradled him against his chest as he stood up. "He hasn't recovered from the long journey." Thomas smothered a yawn. "And neither have I. In Paris, his grandmother would be getting him ready for bed. He's exhausted. I need to take him home and put him to bed."

"That would be best," Lydia agreed. She rose from her chair and picked up her gloves and handbag. "We can work out the details of the sale and my . . . uh . . . temporary employment tomorrow morning. Good day, Dr. Sullivan." She didn't offer him her hand to shake this time, but simply nodded in his direction, dismissing him.

"I'll walk you back."

"I've lived in Eden Point all my life. Just about everyone knows me on sight and no one is going to accost me in broad daylight." She gave him a polite, impersonal smile. "You don't have to worry about me, Dr. Sullivan."

"I'm not worried, Lydia," he said. "I know you're perfectly capable of taking care of yourself, but I think I'll walk you home just the same."

Lydia looked up at him and found him studying her, his dark green-eyed gaze unreadable. "Why?" she asked. He knew she didn't need an escort, yet he insisted on accompanying her two short blocks up the street.

Thomas shifted Robert's slight weight in his arms. "Because I want to."

Suddenly Lydia couldn't resist the unfamiliar urge to flirt. When she spoke, her usual businesslike tone sounded husky and seductive. "Do you always get what you want, Dr. Sullivan?"

"Almost always," Thomas answered truthfully.

"What about today?" Lydia persisted. "Are you going to get what you want this time?"

Thomas couldn't take his eyes off her. Ten minutes ago he'd have sworn she didn't know the first thing about flirtation; an hour ago he'd have sworn she'd never been kissed before; but now he didn't know for sure. In the space of a few seconds, Lydia Turner had transformed herself from innocent to bewitching. And Thomas found her desirable in both guises. "I think it's possible," he replied.

FIVE

"Lydia has a beau." Marjorie Eddings cranked the handle on her Sears and Roebuck Improved Long-Distance Battery-Operated Telephone and gave the news to Georgia Murray at the Eden Point Telephone Exchange over in the office of the *Eden Point Gazette* within five minutes of Lydia and Thomas's departure from her café.

"Well, who is he?" Georgia demanded more details. "Anyone we know?"

"*I* know him," Marjorie replied. "I only just met him, but it's the new doctor."

"What new doctor?"

"The one that's come to town to buy Doc Turner's practice and Turner's Drugstore from Lydia. Dr. Sullivan, she said his name was. Dr. Thomas Sullivan."

"How do you know he's her beau?"

"Why, Georgia Murray," Marjorie replied in an exasperated tone, "I'm old enough to recognize a couple making calf's eyes at one another. You should have seen the way those two carried on in the café. The only time he took his eyes off Lydia was when he was tending to his little boy." Marjorie paused, drew a deep breath, and continued, "Yes, he has a little boy about five or six. But I don't think it matters much to Lydia. You know how she dearly loves children and she's getting a mite old. . . . Of course I'm positive about this. Lydia was watching him as much as he was watching her, but she did it only when she thought nobody else was looking. He has to be her beau. I heard Amos Brown say she met him at the depot when his train arrived this morning. Now, don't tell me they aren't sweethearts because you know as well as I do, Georgia,

29

that Miss prim-and-proper Lydia Marie Turner is not the kind
of woman to moon over a man she just met. There isn't a
foolish bone in her body. She's been down-to-earth since the
day she was born. She'd never fall for a stranger in two hours'
time. Never in a million years."

"Where's he staying? One of the cottages?"

"Oh no." Marjorie couldn't wait to relay this juicy bit
of gossip. "Amos said Lydia told him to take the doctor's
luggage upstairs—above the drugstore. He's planning to stay
there with the little boy and Lydia."

"How did Amos know that? If the new doctor plans to
buy the place, I'm sure he'll want to live upstairs. She must
be moving out," Georgia replied reasonably, not wanting to
believe Lydia Turner would risk her reputation in so flagrant
a manner.

"Well, if she is," Marjorie crowed, "she's not planning to
take anything. She hasn't moved her clothes. Amos peeked
in her closet to check. And all her mother's precious furniture
and china are still upstairs."

"I never would have believed it," Georgia breathed, "Lydia
Turner inviting a man to share her living quarters. And her
father dead only a few weeks."

"Believe it," Marjorie said. "It's true. And that's not all,"
she continued, unwilling to share Georgia's qualms regarding Lydia's reputation. She and Lydia had been rivals since
first grade and Marjorie couldn't hide her glee when sharing
gossip about Lydia. "Lydia's beau didn't marry the boy's
mother."

"What?"

"You heard me. Dr. Sullivan's son was born out of wedlock."

"How do you know that?"

"Amos heard the doc tell Lydia."

"Lydia knows about the boy?"

"She sure does," Marjorie confirmed, "and she's romancing
the doctor anyway. It seems prim-and-proper Lydia Turner
isn't so perfect after all. Her beau is a man with a scandalous past."

"Wait until Eleanor Sheffield hears about this." Georgia ended her connection with Marjorie at the Eden Point Café and rang up Eleanor Sheffield, the wife of the pastor of the Eden Point First Methodist Church with the news.

Soon all twenty-six customers on the Eden Point Telephone Exchange had heard about Miss Lydia's romance.

Thomas greeted the curious shopkeepers as he escorted Lydia up Front Street toward the drugstore. "We seem to be attracting a great deal of attention," he said as he nodded to a man standing, broom in hand, on the sidewalk in front of Carl's Barbershop and Shoeshine Emporium. "Either that or everyone in town sweeps the sidewalk this time of day."

Lydia glanced over her shoulder to find a string of men and women diligently wielding brooms along their stretch of walkway. Ahead of them, other employees, manning brooms, stepped out of their stores to sweep. "I don't think this has ever happened before."

"The synchronized sweeping or Lydia Turner strolling up the street with a gentleman by her side?" Thomas asked.

"The sweeping." Lydia looked up at him as he squinted against the bright afternoon sun. She could see the permanent lines crinkling the corner of his eyes and the flecks of gray at his temple.

"And the other?" His tone of voice was light and teasing.

Lydia answered him in kind. "What about it?"

"Are you spoken for?" Thomas asked.

The expression on Lydia's face took on a dreamlike quality. She smiled as she studied the cracks in the sidewalk.

Thomas exhaled slowly and shifted Robert from one shoulder to the other. "So there is someone."

She shook her head. "There was."

"How long has it been?"

"Nine years." Lydia met his gaze. "I was seventeen. He clerked in the store. We used to walk out together at night on warm evenings, up and down Front Street—well, within sight of the neighbors and my parents."

"You strolled along the main street in town when there's a beach just across the dunes?" Thomas didn't find the idea of sidewalk strolling in full view of curious onlookers nearly as romantic as walking along the beach at dusk. "Didn't you ever go to the beach?"

"Of course we did." Lydia laughed. "Every Sunday after church we all packed a picnic and headed for the water."

"All?"

"The whole town," she explained. "In the summertime, all of Eden Point picnics on the beach after church on Sunday. It's a town tradition."

"Nice tradition," Thomas agreed. But not what he had in mind. "What happened? Why aren't you Mrs. Store Clerk?"

Lydia shrugged her shoulders. "It didn't mean anything. It was just one of those summer flirtations."

"That you remember in vivid detail after nine years? No, Lydia, it won't wash. It might have been a summer flirtation for him, but it meant more to you. I think you fell in love with Mr. Store Clerk."

"How did you know?" Lydia couldn't believe Thomas Sullivan was prying the secret out of her so easily when she'd never told anyone else how devastated she'd been when her summer romance ended.

"You're not the flirtatious type."

"I might be." She sounded hurt.

Thomas smiled down at her. "I didn't say you couldn't flirt and be successful at it," he explained. "Just that you don't make a habit of it."

"What makes you so sure?"

"If you made a habit of indulging in summer romances, you'd have more memories to look back on. There would be a host of store clerks for you to keep track of. Not just one."

"So there you have it," Lydia replied, a bittersweet edge to her voice, "the reason all the shopkeepers in Eden Point turn out en masse with their brooms in hand. Lydia Turner's strolling down the street with a man. The first man in nine years who actually offered to walk her home."

"I should be a very busy man soon, what with all the sick men in town. What's wrong with them? Surely they can't all be blind?"

"They aren't," Lydia assured him, "just particular. They don't have to settle for a set-in-her-ways spinster who's more than a bit long in the tooth, when there is a new crop of fresh young girls of marriageable age every year. And in a town where the single women outnumber the single men nearly three to one, the fellows can afford to be choosy."

"Long in the tooth, huh?" Thomas teased, "Now, there's an interesting concept." He did some quick arithmetic. "You're what? Twenty-six?"

She nodded.

"That's interesting, not ancient," Thomas told her. "It's an age when most woman are just beginning to realize their potential. The single young men in Eden Point must be fools."

"They wouldn't agree with you." Lydia giggled.

"Now that's a nice sound," Thomas said as he stopped at the front door of Turner's Drugstore. "You should do it more often."

She blushed, then opened her purse and removed the front-door key. "It'll be good to have the store open to customers again. The doors can stay open until closing time and I . . . you . . . won't have to keep locking and unlocking them." She put the key in the lock, then opened the door.

"*We,* Lydia." Thomas leaned over and whispered near her ear as he preceded her into the store and started toward the stairs to the apartment with Robert fast asleep in his arms. "*We* won't have to keep locking and unlocking them."

"Only for a month," Lydia called up to him as he topped the stairs and disappeared around the corner. "After that, you'll have to find yourself someone else."

"I don't know if there is anyone else for me." Thomas had turned around and was standing above her on the landing. The expression on his face and in his green eyes was serious.

Lydia's heart seemed to catch in her throat once again at the sight of Thomas cradling his son in his arms. She'd never seen any man handle a child so gently, so tenderly, not even her father.

"Let me tuck Robby into bed and I'll be right down. We need to talk about our arrangement a bit more and work out the details."

"We can do that at the lawyer's office," Lydia said. "Get some sleep. You look almost as tired as Robert. I'll lock up on my way out and see you in the morning."

"Lydia."

She ignored the pleading note in his voice. She needed to get away from him for a while to think about their arrangement—about what she was letting herself in for. And she desperately needed to be out of the building before she ran up the stairs and demanded that Dr. Thomas Sullivan let her tuck his precious little boy into bed. "Good-bye. I'll see you in the morning."

"Wait for me," he said, "please."

Lydia was tempted to do as he asked, but her feelings of self-preservation kicked into gear. "I'll be right next door above the carriage house if you need me."

"Lydia!"

She hurried outside, slamming the door behind her.

"Maman?" Robert stirred in Thomas's arms.

"No, son, it's Papa." Thomas sighed heavily, then kissed his son's sweaty brow. Thomas had just about given up hope that Robby would ever wake up and ask for him, but maybe Lydia was the answer. Robby had responded to her. Maybe Lydia could help heal the both of them. "Go back to sleep. Everything is going to be all right."

Lydia spent the rest of the afternoon cleaning the carriage-house apartment, scrubbing the floor and bathroom basins with a strong solution of carbolic acid, washing walls, and fumigating the horsehair furniture. The last tenant, a conductor for the railroad, had contracted influenza and died in the clinic shortly before her father succumbed to the disease. The apartment had remained empty and uncleaned until two days ago, and Lydia wasn't taking any chances. She had already aired out the one-room apartment and sprinkled the mattress in the mantel bed with insect powder to kill any lice or bedbugs, then took extra precautions by covering the mattress with a rubber sheet taken from the clinic, followed by two freshly laundered bottom sheets and a clean top sheet and blanket. It was late, long after ten o'clock in the evening, before she felt tired enough and safe enough to crawl into the foldaway bed.

She'd worked herself into a state of bone-numbing weariness, yet sleep eluded her. Her mind replayed the day spent in the company of Dr. Thomas Sullivan and son. Thomas was an interesting man, a unique man, an incredibly handsome man who seemed unaware of the magnitude of his attraction. Yet by his own admission, he was just a bit scandalous. And Robert . . . Lydia sighed. He was a beautiful child, but so sad and lonely, it made her heart ache. She wanted to help him, to teach him to smile again, to become the lively, loving little boy he was meant to be. He needed love and laughter and the companionship of other children. He needed to feel secure and know that someone waited at home for him, someone who could share his dreams and accomplishments and soothe away the disappointments and heartaches. Lydia punched her pillow and wriggled around on the lumpy mattress. A man like Thomas Sullivan needed a wife, and a boy like Robert needed a mother. If only she could help them find what they needed . . . Lydia lay back against her pillow and studied the plaster ceiling. There were plenty of single women in Eden Point. Even if Thomas had been a rake in the past, surely she could find a perfect wife for him—one willing to overlook his past. Someone who would love Thomas and Robert all the more because of it. She made a mental list of all the eligible women in town, then gritted her teeth as she compiled their good points. Mary Lynn Cooper was an accomplished hostess, a former debutante, and a veteran of innumerable dances and teas. She'd make a perfect doctor's wife except that she'd once confided to Lydia that she despised the pawing that went along with courtship and had no use for runny-nosed children. Well, there was Eva Simmons or Janet Godby. . . .

By the time the clock on the side table chimed midnight, Lydia had dismissed every marriageable woman in town as an unsuitable mate for Dr. Thomas Sullivan—every marriageable woman in town except one.

Hadn't he said twenty-six was an exciting age for a woman? Hadn't he kissed her . . . not once, but twice? Hadn't Robert spoken to her when he refused to speak to anyone else? Lydia smiled up at the ceiling as she recalled the wonderful feel of Thomas's lips on hers, then pulled her extra pillow close against her body and settled down to sleep.

SIX

Lydia didn't hear the gossip until later the next afternoon when she accompanied Thomas and Robert to the lawyer's office.

"Hello, Miss Turner." Pete Garvey stood up from behind his desk and greeted Lydia as soon as she entered his office. "I've been expecting you."

Lydia returned the greeting. "Hello, Mr. Garvey. May I present Dr. Thomas Sullivan and his son, Robert?"

Garvey stepped around his desk to shake Thomas's hand. "It's a pleasure to make your acquaintance, Dr. Sullivan." The attorney released Thomas's hand and clapped him on the back. "I've had the contracts for the sale of the late Dr. Turner's estate drawn up for a week or so," he explained. "Of course, I left the amount blank." He turned his wide-toothed grin on Lydia. "We've all been real upset at the prospect of losing Miss Turner, so you can imagine how relieved we are to know she's staying in Eden Point. May I be the first to congratulate you on your upcoming nuptials?"

"What?" Thomas and Lydia blurted in unison.

"Well, it's no big secret," the lawyer said. "At least it isn't anymore. Marjorie Eddings at the café told Georgia Murphy at the telephone exchange and"—he shrugged his beefy shoulders—"Georgia told nearly everybody in town about the two of you."

"What about us?" Thomas asked.

"That you were staying with Miss Turner in her parents' house. Amos at the depot confirmed it. I don't know about where you come from, Dr. Sullivan, but around here, that can mean only one thing." Pete turned to Lydia. "Do we need to fill out the paperwork so the business belongs to Dr. Sullivan, or are you planning on keeping the property in your name?"

"No." Lydia turned a bright shade of red. "You don't understand—" she began.

But Thomas interrupted. "None of this affects the sale of her late father's property. I intend to purchase the business. She's to be paid the full asking price."

Pete Garvey grinned. "Now, that's what I like to see. A man who believes in paying his way." He walked back around to his desk and pulled out a stack of papers. In less than an hour the transfer of ownership was complete. Turner's Drugstore, the medical practice, and clinic had been bought by Thomas Sullivan, M.D.

Lydia was quiet as they left her attorney's office. She had felt a tremendous sense of relief as Thomas signed his name to the papers. Her responsibility to the people of Eden Point had come to an end. She had fulfilled her obligation to the town and to her father's memory. She had sold the practice and the drugstore, and ensured the future of the town. Eden Point would continue to be the only town for miles around with a doctor, a clinic, and a pharmacy. Lydia Turner had done her duty, and in one month's time, she'd be free to move on to another town and another way of life. But now that the deed was done, she didn't quite know what to say to the new doctor in town—especially since his connection to her—Doc Turner's spinster daughter—had made him the topic of gossip. She excused herself as soon as they reached the drugstore and hurried next door to the carriage-house apartment.

Thomas knew that the gossip about them going around town upset Lydia. And she had every right to be upset. She'd done her best to find a physician to fill her father's shoes in Eden Point, and the town had repaid her with gossip and innuendo. The idea that his association with Lydia Turner, on a purely professional level, had made her the topic of curious eyes and wagging tongues angered him. He'd never meant to damage Lydia's good name. He'd damaged enough.

When she failed to appear at the drugstore by nine o'clock the following morning, Thomas was worried. He decided to pay a visit to her apartment. And he took Robert with him.

Lydia had finished dressing but hadn't unbraided or brushed her waist-length rope of light brown hair when she answered the knock on her door.

"Good morning." Thomas stood on her threshold. He stared at her, and his sharp green-eyed gaze didn't miss a thing about her appearance. "I apologize for interrupting your toilette, but we"—he glanced down at Robby—"were concerned about you."

"Thank you," Lydia said. "But you needn't worry about me." She started to close the door.

"We brought coffee." Thomas held out the cup. "With cream and sugar."

Lydia relented. She stepped back and invited them into the tiny apartment. *"Bonjour, Robert."*

The little boy stared up at her, and his big brown eyes seemed too large for his face. *"Mademoiselle, tes cheveux ressemblant à ceux de maman."* He moved closer and reached out to touch Lydia's braid. He fingered the silky strands at the end, then smiled up at her. *"Tu as une brosse?"*

Lydia turned to Thomas for translation.

"He says you have hair like his mother's," Thomas said.

"Do I?"

"I remember Françoise's hair as being a darker shade of brown without so many golden-blond streaks. After Robert was born, she loved to sit on the chaise and have it brushed."

Lydia leaned toward Robert. "Would you like to brush my hair while I drink my coffee?"

Robert nodded eagerly.

"My hairbrush is on the basin in the bathroom." She pointed to the door on her right.

Robert hurried toward the bathroom to collect Lydia's brush.

While he was gone Thomas took the opportunity to look around Lydia's new living quarters. Though clean, the apartment was a definite step down from the home she'd grown up in. It wasn't really one room, Thomas realized, but two. Added on at a later date, the bathroom was separate from the main room. Other than that, the carriage-house apartment was just as Lydia had described. He glanced down at the rumpled covers on the unmade mantel bed on the opposite side of the room and experienced a twinge of guilt. "You slept on that?"

"Why not?" she asked, a bit defensively. "You spent years sleeping on an army cot."

"I didn't have a choice," Thomas said. "You do."

"Not any longer," Lydia reminded him. "The living quarters above the drugstore belong to you now. Or have you changed your mind about buying the business?" She took a sip of her coffee. "Shall we cancel the deal before the paperwork is recorded?"

Thomas took a deep breath. "Well—" He broke off as Robert returned from the bathroom with Lydia's tortoiseshell hairbrush clutched in his fist. She smiled at him, then sat down on the edge of the bed. She patted the mattress and Robert climbed up onto the bed beside her. Lydia unplaited her long, light brown hair and fanned it out behind her. He balanced on his knees in the center of the bed and began to brush. Thomas watched with something akin to envy as his son worked the hairbrush through Lydia's long mane.

"Les cheveux de mademoiselle sont jolis," Robert murmured as he ran his hand over the section of hair he'd just brushed.

"He says your hair is nice," Thomas translated.

Lydia glanced over her shoulder and smiled at the little boy. *"Merci beaucoup, Robert."*

Robert grinned in reply and continued brushing.

Thomas swallowed the lump in his throat. Robby had hardly paid attention to anyone since they'd left Paris. But within minutes of meeting Lydia, he'd begun to respond to her. While it was true that Robby hadn't yet spoken in English, he had spoken to Lydia. Only to Lydia. And that confirmed Thomas's feelings about Lydia Turner. She was special. It made what he was about to do so much easier. "Lydia," he began, "I've been doing a lot of thinking since yesterday."

"I was afraid you'd change your mind after hearing the gossip," Lydia said. "I can't blame you."

"The gossip going around town has nothing to do with my decision to buy your father's business," Thomas told her. "I've bought it. That's final."

"Then what is it?" Lydia turned to look at him and a worried frown creased her forehead. "What's wrong?"

"I don't think it's right for you to move in here while we— Robert and I—live in your home."

"It's the only practical solution," Lydia explained. "This place is much too small for you and Robert. And you need to be close to the office and the clinic in case someone needs you. Besides," she said brightly, "it's not so bad and it's only for a few weeks." She took another sip from her coffee cup, then set it aside.

"I wanted to talk about that, too," Thomas said. "I was hoping I could talk you into staying in Eden Point longer than four weeks."

"How much longer?" Lydia winced as Robert caught the brush in a snarl.

Thomas leaned over, wrapped his arms around Robby's slight form, placed his right hand over his son's, and gently worked the hairbrush through the tangle in Lydia's hair. "Indefinitely."

"I don't understand."

"I'd like you to move in with us."

Lydia couldn't believe her ears. She got up from the bed. Her hair slipped through the bristles of the brush and fanned out behind her as her rapid strides measured the room. "That's impossible."

Thomas followed her. "Not if you agreed to look after Robert as well as the drugstore." He held out her hairbrush.

"You mean like a nanny?" Lydia grabbed the tortoiseshell handle.

"No." Thomas's green eyes darkened with emotion. "I mean be my wife."

Lydia gasped. "You're joking."

"I'm very serious," Thomas replied. He reached out and caught several locks of her hair. He rubbed the strands between his fingers. Robert was right. Her hair was nice. It felt like silk. Thomas reluctantly allowed the silky strands to fall from his fingers as he turned to his son. "Would you return mademoiselle's brush to the bathroom?"

Robert climbed off the bed, walked over to Lydia. He stood perfectly still as she offered him the hairbrush.

"You're not making any sense." She waited until Robert left the room, then gathered her mass of soft brown hair, twisted it into a knot on top of her head, grabbed a handful of pins from the top of the mantel bed, and pinned the topknot into place.

Thomas reached over and pulled the hairpins loose. Lydia's thick mane tumbled down past her shoulders. "I'm making perfect sense. You don't really want to leave the drugstore or Eden Point."

"That's beside the point—"

"Don't give me an answer yet. Take some time. Think about it." He toyed with another lock of her hair.

"But, Dr. Sullivan . . ." she began.

"Thomas," he whispered, gently using the silky strands to pull Lydia closer.

"Thomas," she answered, staring up at him as his handsome face moved ever closer to hers. "Why me?"

"Because you're good and kind. Because I think it's criminal to deprive you of your home and livelihood when I can do something about it. Because I need you to help me, and Robert needs you," Thomas answered honestly.

Lydia couldn't hide her disappointment. This was her first marriage proposal and it wasn't exactly the stuff girlhood dreams were made of. She shook her head. "We don't really know each other, and other than the business, we have nothing in common."

Giving in to the urge, Thomas lightly touched her lips with his own.

Lydia felt his kiss all the way to her toes.

"Wrong," he reminded her. "We have this."

She looked up at him and Thomas kissed her again.

"Just think about it."

She knew she should refuse, knew that nothing good could come of a marriage based on convenience instead of love, but she couldn't bring herself to refuse him. There were worse things in life than being married to a handsome doctor, worse things than having a beautiful five-year-old boy to mother, and moving away from Eden Point was one of them.

SEVEN

"One sixty-seven, one sixty-eight, one sixty-nine, one seventy." Lydia sat on the high stool at the counter of the pharmacy counting quinine pills. She was interrupted by the loud ring of the telephone box in the hall between the pharmacy and the office.

"Lydia, can you get that?" Thomas shouted. "We're up to our elbows in antiseptic."

With the doctor's office due to open on Monday morning, Thomas and Nurse Ida Jenkins were busy scrubbing and sterilizing equipment while Lydia conducted an inventory of supplies and prescription medicines on hand in the pharmacy.

The place was a madhouse and the phone hadn't stopped ringing all morning and Lydia already had a whole page full of messages to relay to Thomas. She scooped up the quinine pills, poured them into the big brown bottle, and placed the container on the top shelf, out of Robert's reach; then she climbed down from her seat. She grabbed the writing tablet from the counter and took great care to step around Robert and his toys. Lydia had spent the morning clearing a space for his building blocks and toy soldiers on the two bottom shelves of the counter beside her chair and kept an eye on him while he played.

"Telephone." Robert looked up from his German battlements as Lydia walked by.

"That's right, Robert. Telephone." Robert's accent was French, but Lydia, far from being discouraged by the child's continued refusal to speak English, complimented him on his English anyway. "Wait here," she instructed, "I'll be right back."

She lifted the telephone receiver on the sixth ring. "Turner's Drugstore. Yes, hello, Mrs. Sheffield. No, the store won't be open until Monday. Dr. Sullivan is busy at the moment. I'll tell him Reverend Sheffield is keeping the the second Sunday of next month open. Yes, ma'am. Thank you. 'Bye." She jotted down Eleanor Sheffield's message, looked at the previous messages, and decided that she might as well take advantage of the break and deliver them all in person.

Lydia hung the receiver on its hook and walked down the hall to Thomas's office. "That was Mrs. Sheffield."

Thomas looked up from the sinkful of surgical instruments. "Who's Mrs. Sheffield?"

"Eleanor Sheffield," Lydia told him. "She's the wife of Raymond Sheffield. Reverend Raymond Sheffield, the pastor of the First Methodist Church."

"Check the book." Thomas nodded toward the daily diary lying open on his desk. "If she needs an appointment, give her whatever is available for Monday."

Lydia read his list of patients. As far as she could tell, Thomas's first day of practice was booked solid. He'd be lucky to get a lunch break.

"I don't think she needs an appointment," Lydia glanced down at the message she'd written. "In fact, I think she called to remind you of one. She said to tell you that she's the best organist in town and that Reverend Sheffield is keeping the second Sunday of next month open."

"For what?"

"She didn't say."

"Then call her back and find out." Thomas's patience had worn thin. He'd been working since seven unpacking the boxes of medical books and supplies he'd ordered. The telephone hadn't stopped ringing, Lydia had interrupted him a dozen times, and each time he'd felt sure she was going to give him her answer. And each time he'd been disappointed. Lydia gave no sign that she was even considering his marriage proposal.

"Don't snap at me, Dr. Sullivan." Lydia had put up with his surely disposition this morning as long as she intended to. Thomas Sullivan, M.D., hadn't so much as smiled at her today after kissing her breathless and proposing marriage yesterday. And if his surliness was caused by his having second thoughts about asking her to be his wife, he should come right out and say so. "I've been working just as hard as you have trying to take inventory before we open on Monday, and what with answering the phone and jotting down messages to give to the doctor, I've counted the same one hundred seventy quinine pills three times!"

For a moment Thomas was afraid Lydia would burst into tears. "Rough morning?"

Lydia nodded. "Who would have thought that everyone in town would decide they just had to talk to the new doctor? My tablet is full of messages." She waved the writing tablet under his nose.

"Who called?"

Lydia consulted her list. "Harold Thompson, editor of the *Eden Point Gazette,* called to say he had reserved space for a write-up about you on the society page, and the printing department called offering two cents a page on layout and design of advertisements, stationery, and engraved invitations."

Thomas frowned.

"Christine Damon from Damon's Jewelers called to tell you they're having a sale on gold and can make you a good deal on diamonds."

"I haven't met any of these people. If they don't need my services, why are they calling?"

"Everyone in town knows who you are and what you do. You've come to town and purchased a business. Times are tough in small towns. Maybe this is the Eden Point Merchant Association's way of introducing themselves," Lydia suggested, "and the services they sell to you."

Thomas agreed with Lydia. Her answer made perfect sense. He smiled. "Is that it? The reverend, the newspaper, the jewelers?"

"No," she continued, "Davisson's Department Store said they have a sale on men's and ladies' dress wear." Lydia glanced over at Thomas's new nurse. Fondly called Nurse by just about everyone in town, Ida Jenkins had worked for Doc Turner for as long as Lydia could remember and knew every single sale Davisson's had planned weeks, even months, in advance. "Nurse, did you know about the sale at Davisson's?"

Ida shook her head. The tight, iron-gray pin curls bobbed beneath her starched white cap. "Haven't heard a thing about this one, but I've been out of circulation since your father's passing. I wonder if they have that sky-blue serge I wanted on sale?" She winked at Lydia. "Now that I'm employed again, I might be able to afford it." There was no doubt that she'd be able to afford the blue serge suit. After telling her that experienced, registered nurses, especially nurses who'd graduated from New Haven Connecticut's School of Nursing, were worth their weight in gold, Thomas Sullivan had offered Nurse Ida Jenkins a handsome salary, double what she'd earned working for Doc Turner. Nurse now earned more money per week than any other woman in Eden Point. "We'll have to run down there after work and see," she suggested to Lydia.

Thomas cleared his throat. "After work is after we get everything done. Lydia, are there any other messages?"

"Carmichael's Florist has a special on roses, daisies, chrysanthemums, and forget-me-nots. Clyde Prescott at Prescott Motors wants to know if you'd like to look at his new touring sedans, Casey at the boardinghouse said to tell you he had a case of champagne, and Fred Gunter from Gunter's Bakery wanted to know if you prefer white, yellow, or chocolate cake beneath white frosting."

"Chocolate," Thomas answered automatically.

Lydia put a check mark above the specified flavor. "I'll call him back and tell him."

Nurse Ida turned her back on Lydia and Thomas. She leaned over the sink, bracing her considerable bulk against the white-enameled counter as her shoulders began to shake.

"What is it?" Lydia demanded when she realized Nurse was doubled over with laughter. "I don't get it. What's so funny?"

Nurse waved her hand toward Lydia's writing tablet and gasped out the word, "Messages."

"What about them?" Thomas was beginning to suspect something was amiss.

"Any more?" Nurse struggled to control her laughing.

"One," Lydia answered. "And it's the strangest one of all. Dottie Farmer called."

Nurse laughed harder.

"Who's Dottie Farmer?" Thomas demanded to know.

Lydia's brow furrowed. "The high-school French teacher."

"Let me guess." Thomas chuckled. "She wants me to speak to her class. Tell them all about Paris in the springtime."

Lydia shook her head. "That's what I thought, too. But she called and offered to watch Robert whenever you need someone. She said Marjorie Eddings told her your little boy didn't know any English, that he only spoke French."

Nurse snorted.

"What is it?" Lydia and Thomas simultaneously demanded an explanation for the town merchants' baffling behavior.

Nurse straightened and turned to face them. "Well . . ." She began ticking the messages off on her fingers. "You've got the reverend of the First Methodist Church, Lydia's church, and his missus calling to tell Dr. Sullivan she plays the organ and he has a Sunday open. The editor of the *Eden Point Gazette* says he's holding space for a newspaper article on the doctor, then happens to mention the going rate for printing advertisements, stationery, and engraved invitations. Christine Damon's put her gold jewelry on sale. Davisson's Department Store calls to relay the news that they're putting men's and ladies' wear on sale at the same time when Lydia and I both know they've never done anything like that before. Carmichael's Florist has a good price on roses, daisies, chrysanthemums, and forget-me-nots." She held up another finger. "You've got Clyde Prescott offering you a car, a known bootlegger offering you a case of champagne, Fred Gunter asking your preference before he bakes your cake, and Dottie Farmer—who has raised four kids of her own—offering to take care of a five-year-old boy who only speaks French." Nurse gave them a minute to digest the information she presented. "It sounds to me like—"

"The town's planning a party for Thomas," Lydia guessed. "We've got two new citizens in Eden Point." She danced down the hall and behind the pharmacy counter, then lifted Robert off the floor. Robert looped his arms around Lydia's neck and held on tightly as she waltzed him down the hall. "We've got a highly trained physician and his beautiful brown-eyed son here to take care of us. That's reason for the whole town to celebrate."

"Close," Nurse said.

"But no cigar," Thomas completed Ida's thought. The telephone calls sounded innocent when taken one by one, but when lumped together they had a much deeper meaning. Thomas had the sinking feeling that he and Lydia were being set up. "There's more going on here than a simple welcoming party." He smiled at the sight of Lydia dancing Robby around the office. "I can understand the need for cake, music, and flowers, maybe even new clothes and transportation, but I can't for the life of me understand why I'd need to visit Damon's Jewelers for gold and diamonds." He paused. "Unless . . ."

"Exactly!" Nurse exclaimed.

Thomas grinned. "It looks as if we're a done deal, Lydia, my dear."

Lydia stopped dancing. "Of course we are," she agreed. "We've signed the papers, the money's in the bank, and any day now, the *Gazette* will print the legal notice."

Nurse snorted again, louder this time, nearly choking on her strangled laughter. "Lydia, honey, forget about business. The doctor is trying to tell you—"

"Lydia," Thomas began, "the people in town aren't giving me a party. They're doing their utmost to give *us* a wedding."

"A wedding?" Lydia squeaked. "Us?"

"Why not?" Thomas asked. "You heard the rumors. You know what they're saying about us. Your attorney even congratulated me in his office the other day. You remember."

"Pete Garvey congratulated you?" Nurse interrupted.

"He did," Thomas confirmed.

"Well"—Nurse sniffed—"he's not known for his tact."

"It doesn't matter what the town wants," Lydia said. "Regardless of what everyone thinks, you haven't besmirched my reputation. You've been a perfect gentleman."

"I should think so!" Nurse exclaimed.

"There's no reason for you to feel that the town can coerce you into marrying me," Lydia concluded.

"Coerce?" Thomas repeated. "No one can coerce me into what I want to do. But since you haven't said anything, I guess the answer is no."

"I haven't said anything yet," Lydia murmured, "because you told me to take some time and think about it. I didn't want you to think that I'd enter into something as serious as marriage without giving it proper consideration. I thought I'd wait a few days before I told you of my decision."

"A few days?" Thomas said. "I couldn't stand a few more days of this." He looked over at Lydia and his dark green eyes sparkled. "I can't get any work done with all this calling."

Lydia smiled, a shy tentative smile that said more than words. "I'd be honored to be your wife, Thomas. I'd like the opportunity to try to be the kind of mother Robert needs."

"Hallelujah!" Nurse exclaimed, lifting Robert from the counter and hugging him closely. "We're having a wedding after all!" She carried the little boy out of the room and into the hallway.

"Nurse?" Thomas stopped her. "Where do you think you're going?"

"I'm going to call Fred Gunter and place the order for chocolate cake beneath the white frosting."

"*Chocolat!*" Robert shouted.

Nurse laughed and squeezed the child a bit tighter. "Then Robby and I are going to make four of the biggest chocolate malts Turner's Drugstore has ever seen. Take your time," she urged the two of them, "and get to know one another a little bit. Engaged couples have more leeway than other folks, so don't spend all your time talking."

"Nurse, wait." Lydia hurried to the doorway.

"What is it?" Ida paused.

"Be sure and put two extra cherries on Robert's malt," she instructed. "I promised him a treat every time he says something in English and he really likes maraschino cherries."

"Okay," Nurse replied, nodding her approval as she carried Robert down the hall and into the drugstore.

Thomas walked up behind Lydia and whispered in her ear, "What did Robby say in English?"

"Telephone and chocolate," Lydia answered proudly.

"Are you sure it was English?" Thomas had heard Robby give the word "chocolate" a definite French pronunciation.

Lydia turned and smiled up at him; her big hazel eyes sparkled with delight. "I understood him perfectly, so he must have been speaking English." She conveniently ignored the fact that the two words were basically the same in either language.

And Lydia tried to ignore any other doubts she had as well.

EIGHT

It was amazing how things changed once Lydia and Thomas became officially engaged. The gossip about them sharing the upstairs living quarters ended abruptly once word got out that Lydia was occupying the carriage house. Thomas and Robert accompanied Lydia to church on Sunday and stood proudly by her side as Reverend Sheffield announced Miss Lydia's engagement to Dr. Thomas Sullivan to the congregation. On Monday morning, when the doctor's office and Turner's Drugstore reopened, the town of Eden Point turned out in record numbers, and by Monday afternoon, nearly everyone referred to the new doctor and his son as "Miss Lydia's new family."

And though they'd only been engaged for a little over a week, Lydia and Thomas had begun to think the same way. Following the routine she established with her father over the years, Lydia resumed her habit of making breakfast in the morning before work. She let herself into the drugstore with her key and quietly made her way up the stairs to the kitchen.

Thomas came out of the bathroom to find coffee heating on the stove and Lydia frying bacon. "What are you doing?"

"Cooking breakfast." Lydia cracked a half-dozen eggs into a china bowl. She hummed as she worked, incredibly happy just to be home again. And not home alone, as she'd been for the past few weeks, but sharing her home with Thomas and Robert. She looked up. Thomas's shirt was undone. She could see the thick curly hair covering his chest. She whisked the fork around the bowl a bit faster. "The coffee's ready."

Thomas followed Lydia's gaze to the center of his chest. He hurriedly buttoned his shirt, then moved toward the stove, closer to Lydia.

Lydia grabbed a cup and saucer from the cupboard and handed it to him, then quickly poured the steaming coffee. "Cream and sugar?"

"Black." He took the coffee, then leaned against the wall, watching as she removed the bacon from the frying pan, allowing it to drain on a plate lined with brown paper.

She emptied the excess grease from the frying pan, then poured the eggs into the skillet. "How do you like your eggs?"

Thomas leaned over her shoulder. He caught a whiff of her tantalizing perfume as he glanced at the eggs in the frying pan. Seeing that she'd already whipped the eggs into a yellow froth, Thomas teasingly replied, "Scrambled?"

"Hard or soft?"

Lydia's fragrance surrounded him. She smelled of soap and morning air and scrambled eggs and an enticing blend of rosewater and vanilla. Thomas couldn't get enough of the scent of her. Her innocent question took him by surprise and several moments went by before the words penetrated his brain. His mind suddenly filled with images of making love to Lydia. Hard and soft, fast and slow, body to body.

Lydia stirred the eggs. "Thomas?"

He shook his head. "Whichever you prefer," he said. "As long as the eggs are fresh, I'm not particular."

Lydia smiled. "You're very easy to please. Daddy always liked them just so." She looked up at him.

There was nothing "just so" about Thomas. There seemed to be a certain carelessness to the way he did almost everything. The spontaneity he'd shown in becoming engaged. Could he change his mind again just as easily? Control, she thought to herself. She had to control her fearful thoughts.

"How about Robert?" she asked finally.

"Fluffy."

"Then we're all in accord." Lydia expertly scrambled the eggs, then opened the oven to check the progress of her pan of biscuits. She closed the oven door, then turned to the cupboard and took down three plates. She handed them to Thomas along with the silverware and napkins. "Do you mind setting the table?"

Thomas stared at her for a moment, dumbfounded. When he was in the army, he'd always thought of himself as handy around the cook fire or a kitchen—able to heat up tins of beans and meat, or fry an egg with the best of them, but, he realized, he'd never helped a woman with domestic chores, not even Françoise. He'd never had an opportunity. There were always other people around to take care of the domestic chores. In fact, he couldn't remember a single instance in the time he shared with her when Françoise had cooked a meal for him. He set a place on the table for each chair.

"No, not there." Lydia pointed to the chair that had several thick volumes of medical books stacked on the seat. "Over there." She indicated an empty chair.

Thomas removed the place setting and put it where Lydia directed. "What about Robby?" he asked. "Isn't he going to join us?"

"Of course he is," Lydia answered, "but I have a special plate for him." She took Thomas by the elbow and led him to the cupboard. "On the far right side of the top shelf. I can't reach it."

Thomas took down a child's plate, hand-painted with fanciful scenes of baby woodland creatures cavorting around the rim.

"And here." Lydia opened a kitchen drawer and removed a children's set of silver—the knife, spoon, and fork—made for smaller hands. Taking the silver and the plate to the sink, she carefully washed and dried them. "My mother bought them for me as soon as I could eat properly, and I used this plate and these utensils at every meal until I turned ten and asked to use the grown-up plates. They've been stored away since then. And I've been waiting for the opportunity to take them down and give them to my oldest child."

Thomas smiled at her. "You might want to save them a bit longer."

Lydia stared at him. "But Robert will be my little boy,

too, as soon as we're married." She searched Thomas's face. "Won't he?"

"Of course he will, sweetheart. I just thought you might want to wait until we have a child together."

"But that wouldn't be fair to Robert," Lydia said. "He's your firstborn son and the first child I'll ever call my own. He's already lost his real mother. I would never allow him to lose his birthright."

Thomas studied the young woman standing before him, the woman he'd pledged to marry. Though they'd only been engaged a week, and their engagement had been based more on practical than romantic notions, Lydia had already reserved a space for Robby within her heart. He recognized the depth of her love for his son. He'd seen the spark of anger flash in her hazel eyes when he suggested she wait to give her gifts to another child, a different child, a child of her own body. And in that moment Thomas knew he loved her.

"Lydia," he asked in a humble, almost reverent tone of voice, "may I kiss you?"

She nearly dazzled him with the brightness of her smile as she raised her chin and offered him her lips. "Be my guest."

The kiss was sweet and tender and chaste in the beginning, but then Thomas moved his mouth over hers in a way that could never be described as chaste. He nibbled at her lips, flicking the seam of her mouth with the tip of his tongue.

And Lydia responded with a depth of passion she didn't know she possessed. She opened her mouth and kissed him back, copying his movements, imitating the way his tongue caressed hers.

Lydia and Thomas were so engrossed in their kissing, they didn't hear the front door open or smell the smoke.

"What's burning?" Nurse Ida walked into the kitchen.

Thomas let go of Lydia and stepped back.

"Besides the two of you?" Nurse added.

"My biscuits!" Lydia grabbed a hot pad, opened the oven door, pulled out the pan of biscuits, and dropped it on the range top. "They're ruined."

Ida looked at the pan of biscuits. "I think they're salvageable. The tops look okay. Probably only the bottoms are burned and you can cut them off. My Eddie, God rest his soul, did love to get romantic in the morning. My family ate many a bottomless biscuit over the years."

Lydia blushed. "I've never burned a batch of biscuits in my life."

Nurse Ida laughed. "You've never had a good-looking man in your kitchen before." She opened a kitchen drawer, pulled out two paring knives, and handed one to Lydia. "We might as well get busy." Nurse Ida turned the biscuits out of the baking pan and began to demonstrate the proper procedure for salvaging burned bread. She picked up a light fluffy piece of bread, sawed off the charred crust, then turned to Thomas. "You go and wake Robert and tell him breakfast is ready. And you"—she turned to Lydia—"get the milk, butter, and jam out of the icebox. I'll finish this." Ida cut the blackened bottom off the last biscuit.

Thomas left the kitchen.

"Well," Ida said, as soon as Lydia set the bottle of milk, crock of butter, and the jar of jam on the table, "I have to admit I was worried about the suddenness of your engagement to Dr. Sullivan, but I think the two of you are going to be fine." She leaned over and hugged Lydia. "I'm happy for you, Lyddy, my girl."

"Thank you, Nurse." Lydia embraced the older woman. "I'm happy for me, too." She glanced at the doorway. "He's a fine man."

"Yes, he is," Nurse agreed, "and an excellent doctor."

"I think Daddy would approve of my choice for Eden Point and for myself." Lydia couldn't seem to stop smiling. She put the plate of bacon on the table along with the bowl of fluffy eggs and the bottomless biscuits. "Would you hand me that place setting on the counter, please?"

Ida lifted the child's plate and silver and smiled. "I remember when your mother ordered this plate for you. You were just a tiny thing, but you were determined to sit at the table and eat with your parents. I remember your mother saying that a girl big enough to eat real food ought to have her own special dinner plate and utensils."

Lydia nodded. "Mama was like that."

"Yes, she was a fine southern lady. And I remember the day you asked your mama to put your plate up. She cried like a baby after you left for school. She cried all day long. Your daddy had to come up here and comfort her. Her little girl had become a young woman."

"I didn't know."

Nurse Ida brushed her hand across her watery eyes. "What I'm trying to say, Lydia, is that you've grown into a woman your mother would be very proud of."

"Thank you, Ida," Lydia said. "Thank you for telling me."

"I thought you ought to know," Nurse said. "I've watched Dr. Sullivan work for over a week now. He's good, and what's more, he's dedicated. I'm proud to be associated with him. And that little boy of his"—Ida paused—"will steal your heart."

"He's already stolen it," Lydia admitted. "I love him as if he were my own flesh and blood. I only wish I could get him to talk to me."

"You've worked wonders with the boy, Lydia."

"It wasn't me," Lydia replied modestly. "It was the chocolate malts with the extra whipped cream and the cherries on top."

"Don't sell yourself short, Lyddy girl," Nurse Ida scolded. "You're the only one in town who believes that soda fountain has magical healing powers."

Lydia pretended to look shocked.

"The rest of us know the magic comes from you." Ida picked up the coffeepot and poured coffee into the cups Lydia handed her, then seated herself at the round oak kitchen table. "Doc Sullivan, breakfast is ready," she called, before settling her bulk onto the chair to enjoy her first cup of morning coffee.

Thomas appeared in the doorway with Robert by his side. Robert's face was still pink from the soap and water, and his baby-fine hair had been combed, parted, and slicked into place.

"Good morning, Robert," Lydia said.

"Bonjour, mademoiselle." Robert looked up at Lydia, then frowned. *"Il faut que tu te brosses les cheveux."* He pointed to her hair.

"Oh, Robert, I'm sorry. I was in a hurry this morning and I pinned it up without thinking." Lydia felt a pinprick of guilt. Robert had enjoyed brushing her hair the other morning. And now he seemed to be disappointed. She leaned closer to the child. "I'll tell you what. Tonight, after supper, I'll take down my hair so you can brush it. Okay?"

Robert nodded.

"Good." Lydia smiled at him. "Now, how about breakfast? I made scrambled eggs, bacon, and biscuits. And I have a surprise for you." She spooned a portion of the fluffy eggs onto his plate, took a moment to arrange them to her liking, then added two strips of bacon and a biscuit. She set the plate on the counter, then walked to the kitchen window and broke a tiny sprig of parsely from the pot of herbs growing in the window and used it to garnish Robert's breakfast. Thomas lifted the boy onto the chair stacked with medical books and pushed him close to the table.

Lydia waited until Robert was settled, then placed her special plate in front of him.

"Merci, mademoiselle." Robert thanked her automatically, then glanced down at his plate and shrieked in delight.

Lydia had created a work of art. The scrambled eggs were arranged in the shape of a rabbit, the bacon became the fence row, the biscuit the moon, and the sprig of parsley represented the lettuce growing in the garden.

"Regarde, Papa." Robert pointed to his plate. *"Le lapin est dans le jardin!"*

Lydia took a deep breath. She knew it was probably hopeless, but she had to try. "English, please, Robert. I don't understand."

Robert looked at Lydia, let out an exasperated sigh, then repeated what he'd said to his father—in English—very slowly, so Lydia could understand. "I say, 'Look, Papa.' "

Thomas held his breath as Robby spoke.

Robert glanced up at his father. *"Lapin?"*

"Rabbit," Thomas answered.

"Rabbit," Robert repeated. "The rabbit is in the garden." He pointed to his plate to let Lydia know he recognized her artwork, then picked up a slice of bacon and bit into it. *"Bon."*

Lydia's heart seemed to catch in her throat. She wanted to jump up and down and shout and cheer her success. Looking up at Thomas, she knew he felt the same way, but she didn't make a fuss over Robert's decision to speak English. Lydia simply treated it as an everyday occurrence. "I forgot to pour your milk." She picked up the bottle of milk and held it out for Robert to see. "Would you like plain or chocolate?"

Robert grinned.

"Chocolate," Thomas, Nurse Ida, and Lydia replied in unison as Lydia reached into the cupboard for the can of chocolate syrup.

NINE

Over the course of the week, mealtimes quickly became Lydia's favorite part of the day because it was the one time they were able to have together. She outdid herself at breakfast, finding ways to make it special. When she served boiled eggs, she drew funny faces on the shells. When she fried eggs, she used egg rings to shape the egg whites into hearts. Her pancakes arrived on the table in a variety of flavors and forms, and her omelets were fluffy and light and stuffed with ham and cheese, which, she learned, brought sighs of pleasure from both Robert and Thomas.

Robert. In a week's time, he'd blossomed into a lively little boy. He chattered nonstop now, satisfying his unending curiosity about his surroundings by asking a variety of questions in his mix of French and English. Lydia did her best to answer all of them—sometimes using her best schoolgirl French. She dried the last of the breakfast dishes, then glanced over at Robert, who sat at the kitchen table drawing another picture for Lydia to display. She rolled down her sleeves and buttoned her cuffs, then looked down at the watch pinned on her blouse. "It's time for us to go down and open up the store."

Robert nodded. *"As-tu lavé mon assiette aussi, Lydia?"* Ever since Lydia had explained the significance of the special plate with the animals painted around the rim, Robert took great pains to make certain nothing happened to it. The animal plate had become his most cherished possession.

"Oui," she answered patiently. Thomas had translated Robert's questions after their first breakfast together and Lydia learned that Robert was asking if she'd washed his plate along with the others. She no longer had a problem

understanding what he meant because the little boy asked the same question after every meal. "And your cup and knife and spoon and fork as well."

"As-tu mis mon assiette tout en haut?"

Lydia smiled. She'd explained that she put the plate on the top shelf to keep it from getting broken, and now Robert felt compelled make sure she continued the practice.

"You can bring the picture you're working on," Lydia reminded him, "and your crayons." She'd purchased a school desk, a schoolbag, a slate, and some chalk as well as drawing paper and crayons to help Robert occupy his time while she worked in the drugstore. And Lydia made it a point to pack lunches of cold meat sandwiches and fruit during the noon break so she and Robert could walk across Beach Street, behind Eden Point School, to the playground. Lydia knew how important it was for a child to get out in the sunshine, to run and jump and play—especially after being cooped up in the store most of the morning. Lunch at the playground was a Turner-family tradition. When she was a child, Lydia's mother had packed lunches for the two of them to take to the playground. Some days, when business was slow, Doc Turner and Nurse Ida ate with them, but most of the time Lydia had her mother all to herself. In the week since she and Thomas had become engaged, Lydia had made lunch at the Eden Point School playground a Sullivan-family tradition. And she hoped that one day soon she and Robert would be sharing their lunches with Thomas.

Thomas. Lydia was worried about Thomas. He had been working so many long hours since the practice reopened. He left immediately after breakfast each morning and worked throughout the day, often skipping lunch and rarely going to bed until the wee hours of the morning. Though the towns-people probably wouldn't say much about it if she didn't leave at a proper hour, now that she and Thomas were officially engaged, Lydia always left the apartment after she finished the supper dishes, helped Robert get ready for bed, and allowed him to brush her hair. She waited until Thomas made his clinic rounds and came upstairs, then retired to the carriage house. She had heard several whispered comments from the ladies who frequented the store that she and Thomas weren't walking out the way young couples ought to do when they were courting, but it was hard to carry on a courtship with a thriving drugstore, medical practice, and a lively five-year-old boy to take care of.

Lydia didn't voice her feelings about her engagement or the niggling belief that for some reason, Thomas was purposely avoiding her. She had never been one to dwell on things she couldn't change. She tried to look to the future, to the life she would build with Thomas and Robert. At night, she lay awake, in the single mantel bed, watching the lights go on and off in the different parts of the store. She knew when Thomas tucked Robert into bed, and when he left Robert's room to go into the kitchen to work on his patient charts. For some reason, she couldn't seem to fall asleep at night until she knew Thomas had finished work. When the lights went out in Thomas's bedroom, Lydia allowed herself to lie in bed and remember his kisses. She dreamed of the nights when he would hold her in his arms and make love to her.

Thomas's kisses were magical. He made her feel things she had never felt before or ever thought she'd feel. He made her long for things she couldn't explain, emotions she couldn't name. Lydia brushed her cheek with the back of her hand. Her cheeks were hot, her face flushed. Just thinking of Thomas kissing her or touching her made her react that way. She wondered if Françoise had felt the same way.

"Mademoiselle?" Robert took hold of Lydia's hand. "Miss Lydia?"

"Yes?" Lydia felt a warm, fuzzy feeling each time Robert said her name in his halting English.

"Il faut aller à la pharmacie," Robert reminded her, pointing to her watch. "It's time to go to the pharmacy."

She looked at her watch. "Oh, my goodness, Robert, we're late. Get your things and we'll go downstairs and open up."

Robert gathered his drawing supplies and tucked them into his new waterproof schoolbag. Lydia picked her handbag up off the kitchen table, then she and Robert hurried down the stairs to unlock the drugstore.

As soon as they entered the store, Lydia placed her purse on the shelf under the cash register, took her work smock off the peg, and buttoned it over her dress. Robert settled into his school desk, removed his pictures and crayons from his schoolbag, and resumed his coloring, occasionally glancing up to watch Lydia go about her morning routine. She opened the safe and removed the cash-register drawer. She put the drawer full of money into the register, polished the marble countertop and steel fixtures of the soda fountain, flipped the closed sign to OPEN, and unlocked the front doors.

"Good morning, Lydia."

Lydia glanced up from her work. "Good morning, Mrs. Sheffield." The pastor's wife stood at the pharmacy counter. "What can I do for you?"

Mrs. Sheffield held up a prescription. "Dr. Sullivan asked me to give this to you."

Lydia read the prescription, then reached over and took a big bottle off the shelf. She retrieved a funnel from the drawer and a small brown bottle from the stock on the bottom shelf. She poured medicine from the large bottle into the smaller one and screwed on the cap. Lydia wrote out the label and glued it onto the bottle. "Aren't you feeling well?"

"Oh, it's just a little cough and sore throat," Mrs. Sheffield told her. "But don't worry, I'll be well enough to sing at your wedding."

Lydia nodded.

"We're still on for the second Sunday in May, aren't we?" Eleanor Sheffield asked.

"Yes, of course." Lydia met Mrs. Sheffield's gaze. "Why?"

"Well, Christine Damon at Damon's Jewelers mentioned yesterday at the Methodist Ladies' Union meeting, that Dr. Sullivan hadn't come in to look at her stock of engagement rings or wedding bands."

"Dr. Sullivan has been very busy," Lydia replied in Thomas's defense. "He hasn't had a free moment to himself since the practice reopened."

"Surely he's not too busy to buy a ring for his intended? Or has he already given you one?" She stood on tiptoe, trying to catch a glimpse of Lydia's left hand.

Lydia set Mrs. Sheffield's medicine on the counter. "That will be ten cents."

Eleanor Sheffield frowned. "Lydia, dear, please put it on our account. Oh, and add a couple of those fine Key West cigars." She pointed to a display of tobacco products. "The reverend does so like to relax with a good cigar."

Lydia placed two of the cigars on the counter next to the bottle. "That's ten cents for the cigars and ten cents for the cough medicine. I'll add it to your account," she told Mrs. Sheffield as she opened her ledger and found the page with the Sheffields' account on it.

"And, Lydia dear, I'm not criticizing, but you haven't been to Davisson's Department Store to select your wedding dress or to Carmichael's to talk about floral arrangements."

"I already have a wedding dress, Mrs. Sheffield," Lydia said. "I plan to wear my mother's."

"Oh, but, my dear, it's old . . . fashioned," Eleanor amended quickly.

"It was my mother's," Lydia said simply. "That's all that matters to me."

"Yes, dear, but what about the other details of the wedding?"

"Vivian Carmichael has excellent taste. I'm leaving the floral arrangements up to her. She knows what I like."

"But the music, the decorations, the invitations . . ." Eleanor couldn't believe her ears.

"Mrs. Sheffield, I'm sure I'll love any song you select. And the Methodist Ladies' Union has agreed to decorate the church, Fred Gunter is baking the cake, Marjorie Eddings at the Eden Point Café is catering the reception, Harold Thompson of the *Eden Point Gazette* and Georgia Murray have agreed to send out invitations."

"It sounds as if you intend to let the town of Eden Point plan your wedding ceremony," Eleanor commented.

"Why not?" Lydia fastened her intense hazel gaze on the pastor's wife. "The townspeople helped plan my engagement."

"Well, you seem to have thought of everyone except

Davisson's, Damon's, and your escort and attendants."

"Nurse Ida is going to be my matron of honor," Lydia said. "And you can tell Julia Davisson that Ida plans to buy her wedding ensemble at Davisson's. Pete Garvey's going to escort me down the aisle, and Robert is going to act as his father's best man."

"Surely not," Eleanor whispered. "I mean Marjorie Eddings hinted that Dr. Sullivan's little boy is . . ."

Lydia sucked in a breath and waited for Eleanor to continue. What did she know about Robert? What did the town know about the facts surrounding his birth? And who was repeating the gossip? Her patience stretched to the limit, Lydia concentrated on her breathing in order to control her rising temper. "Is what?"

Eleanor searched for the right words. "Tetched in the head."

"Tetched?" Lydia's voice rose. "Robert is one of the smartest children I've ever met. How many children in Eden Point do you know who speak two languages?"

"According to Marjorie, he doesn't speak two languages," Eleanor pointed out. "He only speaks one—French."

"Marjorie Eddings doesn't know what she's talking about," Lydia said. "Robert speaks English when he chooses to, and he does it beautifully."

Eleanor smiled. "Why, Lydia, you've developed some rather fierce maternal instincts already. I'm glad to see it." She picked up her medicine and the Key West cigars for the reverend and placed them in her shopping bag.

"Thank you, Mrs. Sheffield." Lydia gritted her teeth as she managed a semblance of a smile. "And you may tell Christine Damon not to worry about Dr. Sullivan coming in to buy a ring from her. I plan to shop for his and Robert's gift at Damon's Jewelers."

"She'll be glad to hear it." Eleanor waved. "Good day, Lydia."

"Good day, Mrs. Sheffield."

"Au revoir, madame," Robert piped up from his desk behind the pharmacy counter. "Good-bye."

Lydia waited until the bell on the front door announced

Mrs. Sheffield's departure, then walked behind the counter, leaned over Robert, and kissed him on top of his head. "You're one of the smartest and sweetest little boys in the whole world, Robert Sullivan, and I'm very, very proud of you." She kissed him again, then ruffled his soft brown curls.

"Lydia, don't go yet." Thomas glanced up from his seat in the living room as Lydia closed the door to Robby's room. She wore her work smock over her dress and her long brown hair hung down past her shoulders. Thomas watched as she slipped her hairbrush into her pocket. He envied his son the hairbrushing ritual he and Lydia had established and wished he'd been included. He wanted to touch her soft brown hair, to tangle his fingers in the long, silky strands and smell the soap and rosewater and vanilla fragrance that was uniquely Lydia. Thomas thought she grew lovelier every day.

She paused, squinting in the direction of Thomas's voice. He sat on the sofa in the living room. "Thomas? Why are you sitting alone in the dark?"

"Waiting for you."

Lydia walked into the living room and sat down beside him. Though she couldn't see his face clearly in the dark, she recognized the weariness in his voice. "Why didn't you come in and say good night to Robert?"

"I didn't want to intrude. Robby looks forward to brushing this"—unable to resist the urge, Thomas reached over and fingered several strands of Lydia's soft hair—"so much." He breathed in her scent as he let the silky threads slip through his fingers.

Lydia's breath caught in her throat at his touch.

"But I wanted to talk to you."

"I'm surprised." She couldn't believe she'd spoken her thoughts aloud.

"Oh?" Thomas raised one eyebrow. "Why is that?"

"From the hours you've been keeping lately, I would've sworn you've been avoiding me." Lydia sounded as if she were teasing, but she wasn't.

Thomas leaned his head back against the sofa, closed his

eyes, then stretched his long legs out in front of him. "I have been."

"What?"

"It's the truth, Lydia," Thomas said. "I've been avoiding you."

"Why?" she asked. "Have I done something wrong?"

"No."

"Have you changed your mind about our engagement?"

"Of course not." Thomas opened his eyes and looked at her. "You're the best thing that's happened to me in a very long time. I couldn't have bought this"—he waved his arm to encompass the room—"if you hadn't agreed to stay and help. And, Lydia, you've done more than help. You've—" His voice broke. "You've brought my son back from the edge of darkness."

Lydia placed her hand over his. "I haven't done anything special, Thomas."

Thomas turned to look at her and studied her lovely features in the dim glow of the light in the hallway. "You're what's special, Lydia." He couldn't seem to get his fill of the sight of her.

"If you feel that way, Thomas, why have you been avoiding me?" Lydia held her breath as she waited for his answer.

"Lydia, I've been avoiding you because I feel that way— this way," Thomas told her.

"I don't understand."

"God, Lydia, you're driving me crazy." Thomas raked his fingers through his short-cropped hair. He inhaled, then slowly expelled the air in a rush. "I can't be in the same room without wanting you. Every time we get within a few feet of each other, I want to take you in my arms and kiss you."

"Do you?" Lydia breathed, leaning closer to him.

Her shoulder brushed his and Thomas shot up from the sofa like a rocket and began to pace the length of the living room. "Yes."

"Then kiss me." Lydia stood up.

Thomas stopped in his tracks. "I can't." He didn't turn around.

Lydia walked up behind him. "Why not?"

He let out a sigh of pure male frustration. "Because I don't want to stop with just a kiss." Thomas managed a shaky laugh. "My control isn't what it should be when I'm around you. If I kiss you now, I'm afraid I won't be able to stop. I want to make love with you. I don't want a chaste good-night kiss and nothing more."

Lydia smiled at him. "Thomas, please kiss me." She reached out and put her hand on his shoulder.

Thomas jumped as if she'd burned him, stepped back, then turned to face her. "If I do," he said, "I won't be able to stop. Not tonight. It's been a long time for me."

"How long?" She couldn't contain her curiosity.

"Too long." He winced as he answered. Lydia deserved to know the score.

Lydia didn't show her surprise; instead she did what she could to ease Thomas's discomfort. "I'll bet it's been even longer for me. Much, much longer."

Thomas pulled her into his embrace. "Lydia, Lydia," he scolded, smiling in spite of himself, "don't you realize the danger you're in?"

"Show me." She challenged as she leaned into his chest, pressing her body close to his, feeling his burgeoning length against her stomach, hoping to assuage the ache he awakened deep inside her.

"Sweetheart." Thomas drew in another shaky breath. "I'm trying very hard not to compromise you before the wedding."

"Don't," Lydia ordered.

"Don't what?" he asked.

"Don't try so hard." Lydia wrapped her arms around Thomas's neck, stood on tiptoe, and pulled his face down to hers. "Compromise me."

That was all the prompting Thomas needed. He leaned down and kissed her, then bent at the knees and lifted Lydia into his arms. Cradling her against his chest like a child, he carried her out of the living room, down the hall, and into his bedroom.

TEN

Thomas placed her on the bed, then took off her shoes. He undressed her carefully, gently, as if she were a package wrapped in precious paper he couldn't afford to tear. He removed her work smock and her blue-and-white-striped shirtwaist, peeling the smock and the blouse off her shoulders and down her arms until Lydia was left with nothing above her waist except her corset. His hands shaking from the effort of holding himself in check, Thomas fumbled with the tiny buttons of her whalebone corset and cover.

Lydia slipped her hands beneath his and slowly unbuttoned the white cotton undergarment, revealing herself to him. She couldn't quite meet his intense green-eyed gaze, so she turned her face to the pillow and lay there, half-clothed, her breasts peeking out from the white cotton, waiting for Thomas's reaction.

Kneeling on the bed beside her, Thomas stared at her. He had never expected . . . never dreamed . . . "God, Lydia," he breathed, "you're too lovely for words." He touched the soft pearly-white skin of her breast with the tip of his finger. Her pink nipples puckered in response and Thomas leaned forward to kiss first one and then the other. A gold oval-shaped locket rested in the valley between her breasts, and he felt the warmth of it against his face as he nuzzled her there, breathing in the heady rose-and-vanilla scent of her.

"Thomas?" His name was soft, slurred.

"Hmm?"

Lydia buried her face against his wide shoulder and nervously toyed with a loose thread on his jacket button.

Thomas raised his head and recognized the desire in Lydia's

69

hazel eyes. He removed his jacket and tossed it aside. He took his gold watch out of his vest pocket and put it on the nightstand, then shrugged out of his vest and shirt.

Unable to stop herself, Lydia watched him undress. Shy and unsure, she was nevertheless fascinated by the process. Her fingers ached to bury themselves in the thick furry pelt covering his chest. He stood up to take off his trousers and she scrambled off the bed.

"Where are you going?" Thomas unbuckled his belt.

"To take off my skirts." Lydia blushed bright red as he unbuttoned his trousers, then pushed them along with his underwear off his lean hips and down his long legs. Lydia stared at her first sight of a young, healthy, handsome, undeniably virile man.

"Lydia?" Thomas stood naked and proud before her. "It's all right. If you don't want to continue this, we can stop."

Lydia found her voice. "I don't think I want to stop."

"Are you sure?" There was something about the look on her face that made Thomas ask the question. He wanted Lydia to know she had an option. And though Thomas offered her a graceful way out, he prayed she wouldn't take it.

"Yes." A second later, before her courage could fail her, Lydia unhooked her skirt and petticoat and let them fall to the floor in a puddle at her feet, then quickly shimmied out of her drawers and stockings.

Thomas grinned, a lopsided grin meant to put her at ease. "There. That wasn't so bad, now, was it?"

Lydia shook her head.

"See." He held out his arms. "I'm just like the illustrations in the anatomy books."

"No, you're not," Lydia blurted.

Thomas chuckled. "Aha, so you have peeked at the pictures in *Gray's Anatomy*."

She glanced down at her feet.

"I wondered," he teased. "I knew there was more to Miss Lydia Turner than just prim and proper."

Lydia squeezed her eyes shut in an attack of embarrassment.

"So you looked at the illustrations of naked men, huh?" Thomas moved closer and lifted Lydia's chin with the tip of his finger. "Ever play doctor?"

She blushed.

"Lydia," he said softly, "look at me."

She opened her eyes. His green eyes were darker than she remembered.

"I want to make this good for you, but you have to help me."

"I don't know how."

"Yes, you do," Thomas said. "I know you're feeling awkward and uncertain. So tell me what I can do to make it better."

Lydia stared at him for a moment, then whispered shyly, "Kiss me."

He did. And then Thomas did something even better. He led her back to the bed and taught her the ways of love. He taught her with his hands and his lips and his body, with a passion and an urgency that long years of celibacy made all the sweeter. And when Lydia cried out her pleasure as he spent himself inside her, he knew his long years of emptiness were over.

"Five and a half years," Thomas said as they lay together on the big bed in the room that had previously belonged to Lydia's mother and father.

"Mmm?" Lydia snuggled up close to Thomas's side, resting her head on his shoulder. Completely sated and blissfully happy, she rubbed her nose in the thick furry mat covering his chest and pressed a kiss on his bare nipple.

"It's been five and a half years since I've made love to a woman." Thomas tightened his hold on Lydia.

"But you were with . . ." She propped herself up on one elbow so she could look at Thomas.

"Françoise was ill. No, actually, Françoise was fine until . . ." Thomas paused.

"You don't have to tell me, Thomas. Your life with Françoise and your feelings for her are separate and apart from me. I understand that. There's no reason for you to share those intimate memories."

"I want to tell you. I want you to understand. I don't want secrets between us." Thomas took a deep breath. "I met Françoise in Panama. She and her mother were visiting her father, who was an engineer on the canal. She was young, pretty, vivacious, very French. I was attracted to her immediately." He punctuated his sentence by placing a reassuring kiss on Lydia's soft, silky brown hair.

"I'd been in Panama over a year, working in the hospital, treating malaria, dysentery, and a hundred other jungle maladies. Françoise came into my life like a breath of fresh air. In less than a month's time, we were lovers. Several weeks later Françoise accompanied her mother back to France. We exchanged a few letters. When I got leave, I went to Paris. Françoise was nearly four months pregnant with Robby and already bedridden. And she'd never mentioned it."

Lydia gasped. "Thomas, I'm so sorry."

He kissed her hair once again, inhaling the fresh clean scent. "She had had rheumatic fever as a child. Her heart couldn't take the additional burden of pregnancy. Françoise grew weaker and weaker and there wasn't anything I could do. I didn't know about her heart condition until it was too late. She never told me. If I had known, I wouldn't have . . ."

"Loved her?" Lydia asked gently. "Wanted her?" She smiled at Thomas. "I don't think so."

"I wouldn't have taken chances. There are ways to prevent conception," Thomas said. "I'm a physician, I know how."

"But if you'd done that," Lydia replied logically, "you wouldn't have your son."

"We never had intimate relations after Robby came. His birth damaged her already weakened heart. And I couldn't . . ." Thomas rolled to his side. Lydia lay facing him. Bare inches separated them. "She refused to marry me. Refused to tie me to an invalid." He paused. "Sometimes I can barely remember her face. And as for the rest . . . It seems like a lifetime ago since I held anyone in my arms, or made love to them."

"And you feel guilty for making love to me." Lydia moved back, away from him.

"No, Lydia." He said her name with such tenderness. "I don't feel guilty because we made love. It was wonderful . . . incredible. Making love with you was better than anything I've ever experienced. I'm happy. You make me feel that way—complete and happy." Thomas moved closer and closed the gap between them. "I think maybe you are the other half of me. The part that was always missing, and I wonder if—" He stopped.

"If what?" Lydia hated to make him continue if his admission was going to cause him pain, but she knew in her heart it was better to lance the wound than to let it fester.

"If I failed Françoise."

"Oh, Thomas . . ." Lydia kissed him. "How did you fail her? You loved her. You didn't know about her illness until Robert was born and afterward . . . well, you stayed by her side as much as you could. You stayed until the end and you remained true to her. You didn't take anyone else into your bed. I don't think a woman can ask for a greater sign of devotion than that." She sighed. "I only hope one day you'll love me half as much."

"I love you more."

"Thomas." Lydia breathed his name, stunned by his confession, unable to comprehend the realization of her dreams.

"I do." Thomas trailed a line a kisses from her mouth down her neck and back up again. "I tried to deny it. I tried to talk myself out of it. And I tried to avoid it. I hate to sound disloyal to Françoise's memory, but I don't want to feel guilty anymore for falling in love with you. She's dead. I can't change that. I want to put away the pain and the grief and the heartbreak. I've suffered enough. Robby's suffered enough."

"Are you sure what you feel for me is love?" Lydia asked. "I mean, maybe it's . . ."

"It's love, Lydia. Except for Robby, I love you more than I've ever loved anyone in my life."

Lydia flung her arms around his neck and covered his face

with kisses. "If that's the case, then there's only one thing for you to do," she whispered in his ear when she stopped kissing him long enough to speak.

"What's that?" He recognized the teasing, flirtatious note in her voice and wondered what she planned to recommend.

"Physician," she quoted, "heal thyself."

"Any suggestions?"

"Ever play doctor?" Lydia blushed as she hid her face against Thomas's warm neck.

They made love again. Thomas took his time as he caressed her. The urgency that had permeated their first lovemaking was tempered by the desire to prolong the ecstasy for as long as possible. Lydia proved that she'd learned her lessons well. She gave of herself freely and openly, with a passion that took Thomas's breath away. She tempted and teased and demanded until he thought he had nothing left to give. But she showed him there was more. She coaxed him on to greater heights of passion. When it was over, when they had reached the soul-shattering crescendo, Lydia and Thomas fell into a deep, dreamless sleep, wrapped in each other's arms.

Thomas opened his eyes, several hours later, to find Lydia, propped on one elbow, looking at him. The bedside lamp gave off a dim glow, but the rest of room was dark. "Good evening, Dr. Sullivan," she whispered as she leaned down to kiss him.

"What time is it?"

"I don't know. I just woke up myself."

Thomas reached over onto the nightstand and groped for his pocket watch. He flipped open the lid and Lydia found herself staring at the miniature of a beautiful, black-haired woman. "One-ten."

But Lydia wasn't interested in the time any longer; she wanted to know about the woman in his watch. "Is that Françoise?" She felt the first swift stab of jealousy rush through her. She held her breath waiting for Thomas's answer.

"No." Thomas followed her gaze to the miniature painted

inside the watch case. "It's my mother, Janet Claire Cheshire."
He smiled. "The miniature was painted shortly before she
married my father. She died when I was in college. My
father followed her soon after. This watch belonged to him.
My mother gave it to him on their wedding day." He closed
the lid and showed Lydia the inscription. "See."

Lydia read the fanciful gold script. " 'All my love, forever
and always, Janet. Eighteen December 1886.' What a wonderful idea."

"Does this mean I'm getting a new watch for a wedding
gift?"

"You're getting a plain gold band," Lydia said. "I thought
I'd get Robert a pocket watch."

"Don't you think he's a bit young?" Thomas asked. "He's
only five and he doesn't even know how to tell time."

"He'll learn to tell time once he starts school and it will be
something he can keep for always."

Thomas held up his hands. "All right, all right. You convinced me."

"Do you have a picture of Françoise I can use?" Lydia
asked.

"Françoise." Thomas looked surprised. "What a nice idea.
Lydia Turner, you're a very special woman and you're going
to make a wonderful mother." He kissed the tip of her nose,
then sat up. His stomach rumbled loudly. "And I'm pretty sure
that in a week or so, you're going to make some doctor a
marvelous wife—if you can learn how to cook," he teased.

"If I learn how to cook?" Lydia punched him lightly in
the arm. "I've been cooking for you for over a week. And
I haven't heard any complaints."

His stomach growled again.

"Up until now." She smiled at Thomas. "If I remember
correctly, you worked through supper this evening."

"And I've worked up quite an appetite since supper, too."

Lydia grinned at the innuendo. "So have I."

"I know." Thomas stood up and reached for his robe.

She wrapped the sheet around her and swung her legs over
the edge of the bed.

"No," Thomas said. "You stay there."

"Where are you going?"

"Don't worry, I'll be back in a few minutes." He pulled on his robe and left the bedroom.

But Thomas was as good as his word. He returned in a few minutes with a basin of warm water and a washcloth. He set the basin on the nightstand, then walked over and pulled the folding screen from the corner of the room to the side of the bed. "I thought you might appreciate a little privacy."

Lydia blushed. "Thank you." Thomas understood that even after all they'd shared in bed, she still felt a bit awkward and shy out of it.

Thomas removed his bathrobe and draped it over the top of the screen. He sat on the bedroom chair and pulled on his trousers. He was still buttoning his shirt when Lydia stepped out from behind the screen wearing his dark green robe.

"Ready for supper?" Thomas stood up.

"There should be some chicken and dumplings left over," Lydia said. "I can reheat it in few minutes."

"Chicken and dumplings sounds good," Thomas said, "but it also sounds so . . . so . . . ordinary." Lydia might have been offended if she hadn't seen the teasing light in his eyes and heard the mischievous tone in his voice. "After the extraordinary lovemaking we just shared, I don't think I can settle for ordinary food."

"What did you have in mind?"

"Nectar of the gods."

"Which is?" Lydia prompted.

"Chocolate malts." Thomas took her by the hand. "C'mon, let's go."

Hand in hand, they tiptoed down the stairs to the soda fountain and feasted on chocolate malts.

ELEVEN

Lydia heard Robert crying in the night. She eased out of bed, pulled on Thomas's green robe, and hurried down the hall to Robert's bedroom.

"Maman." Caught in the throes of a bad dream, Robert cried out for his mother over and over again.

The sight of him tore at Lydia's heart. She sat down on the edge of the bed. She lifted Robert out of bed and carried him to the rocking chair. She sat down on the big wooden rocker and cradled him close to her body. "Shh, shh, it's all right, baby. Everything is all right. Lydia's here." She rocked back and forth in a slow, steady motion as she hummed remembered bits of lullabies from her own childhood.

After a while Robert opened his eyes and recognized her. "Lydia?"

"Uh-huh?"

"I had a bad dream."

"I know. I heard you crying." She smoothed his damp brown curls off his forehead. "Can I do anything for you? Get you a glass of water? Or something to eat?"

Robert shook his head.

"Do you need me to walk you to the *toilette*?"

"Non." He tightened his hold around Lydia's waist.

"Would you like me to tuck you in?"

"Lydia?" His brown eyes seemed too big for his face as he looked up at her.

"Yes, sweetheart?" She stopped rocking.

"Will you stay with me?" Robert yawned widely and rubbed at his eyes.

"Of course." Lydia settled Robert more comfortably in her lap, then resumed her rocking. The child laid his head against her breast, wrapped his arm around her waist, and closed his eyes. Lydia continued rocking until long after he'd fallen asleep.

Down the hall, in the big bed, Thomas reached for Lydia and encountered cool sheets where her warm body had been. He rolled out of bed, pulled on his trousers, and began a search for her. He ended the search in Robby's room. Lydia was fast asleep in the rocking chair with his son curled up in her lap. Thomas winced as he eased his son out of her arms. He carried Robby to the bed, tucked the covers up close around him, then placed a gentle kiss on his forehead. When Robby was settled, Thomas turned his attention to Lydia. "Lydia," he whispered.

"Hmm?" She barely opened her eyes.

"Come back to bed, love." Thomas put his hands on her waist and pulled her to the edge of the rocking chair. "C'mon, Lyddy, put your arms around my neck."

She did as he instructed.

"That's my girl," Thomas praised as he lifted her up into his arms.

"What?" Lydia awoke momentarily as he picked her up.

"It's all right. I'm just taking you back to our room."

"Robert?" she asked.

"He's asleep in his bed."

"But—"

"He's fine, Lyddy," Thomas soothed. "Go back to sleep. Everything is fine."

And everything was fine as long as the night lasted, but the morning brought disaster. Thomas and Lydia had overslept.

Nurse Ida arrived at the apartment promptly at seven and knocked on the backdoor. Robert answered her knock. The kitchen was empty. "Where's Lydia this morning?"

Robert didn't answer.

"How about your father?"

The little boy stared at her.

Ida took off her cardigan sweater and hung it on a peg near the backdoor. "Well, I know he didn't go off and leave you alone. He must be making rounds. I'll call down and check." Nurse walked to the wall phone, cranked the dial and reached Georgia Murray at the switchboard. "Georgia, this is Ida. Can you connect me with the clinic? Yes, I know it's downstairs, but I'm upstairs and I'm too old to make unnecessary trips up and down the stairs. That's why we have these dad-gummed telephones—so I won't have to."

Georgia made the connection, and in a few seconds Nurse Ida was talking to Lizzie Carmichael, the night nurse at the clinic. "Has Doc been in to make his rounds?" she asked. "Is he in his office? No? Well, I'll have Georgia ring the phone in the drugstore. Good-bye." Knowing Georgia Murray made a habit of listening in on telephone conversations, Ida depressed the receiver, released it, then asked, "Did you hear that, Georgia? What are you waiting for? Ring it."

Ida let the handpiece hang by its cord while she walked to the front door of the apartment so she could hear the telephone in the hallway between the doc's office and the drugstore. She counted ten rings, then went back to the phone and picked up the handpiece. She clicked the receiver. "You can quit ringing, Georgia, he's not answering. No, there's no emergency that I know of. I just got here for breakfast and found the doc's little boy sitting at the table by himself. Lydia doesn't have a telephone in the carriage house. And I just got here. I haven't had time to walk over to her apartment and check. No, there's no reason to worry. I'm sure she's just running a little late this morning. I'll call you when I find them."

Nurse Ida hung up the phone muttering something about Georgia Murray being the nosiest dad-gummed woman in Eden Point, maybe in all of Florida. She turned to Robert, sitting at the kitchen table. "Would you like to run next door to the carriage house and see if Lydia's there?"

Robert shook his head.

"She's not at the drugstore," Ida said. "She didn't answer the telephone." She stood in the middle of the kitchen and thought for a moment. Lydia hadn't shown up for breakfast and neither had Doc Sullivan. No, it couldn't be. . . . Surely, they hadn't . . . Ida thought, but they were young, healthy, engaged to be married, and obviously head over heels for one another. She turned to Robert once again. "Do you know where Lydia and your father are?"

Robert nodded.

She smiled at him. "Well"—Nurse Ida held out her hand— "don't just sit there. Let's go find them."

Finding them didn't take long. Robert put his small hand in Ida's larger one, then led her down the hall, away from the kitchen, to the big bedroom.

Before Ida could knock, Robert flung open the door, then let go of her hand and ran down the hallway to his own bedroom, slamming the door behind him.

Lydia opened her eyes, saw the white uniform, white stockings, and white shoes, and recognized the woman standing in her bedroom. "Morning, Ida."

"Morning, Lydia." Ida stared down at her. Lydia lay curled on her side; her shoulders were bare and the covers were caught at an angle across her breasts. The only part of Doc Sullivan that was visible was the strong, tanned arm wrapped possessively around Lydia's hips. "Sleep well?"

"Uh-huh." Lydia stretched luxuriously and bumped into Thomas's warm furry chest.

He kissed Lydia's shoulder, then levered himself up on one elbow so he could kiss her properly. "Morning, sweetheart." He caught a glimpse of white uniform out of the corner of his eye and responded automatically, "Good morning, Nurse."

Lydia's hazel eyes opened wide as she came fully awake with a start. Her heart seemed to leap into her throat, and for once, it wasn't caused by Thomas's warm lips. "Thomas."

He chuckled. "Yes, Thomas. Who else were you expecting?" His attention was completely focused on Lydia.

"Nurse Ida."

Thomas sat up and met his nurse's amused gaze. He jerked at the blankets, making sure that he and Lydia were covered.

"Good morning, Doc," Ida said, "I came for breakfast, but I guess you overslept this morning, and from the looks of this room. . . ." She let her gaze sweep meaningfully over the bedroom, to the clothes strewn all about, the mussed bed, and the two lovers in it. "I'd say you and Miss Lydia certainly had reason to."

Normally, a nurse's presence in his bedroom wouldn't have disturbed Thomas. Like most doctors, he'd trained himself to fall into a deep sleep almost anytime or anywhere. During his years of medical training and his stint in the army, sleep had been a rare and precious thing. Thomas had often slept on cots, in tents, on the ground, in empty hospital beds, on operating tables, in wagons, in ambulances, and once or twice in the morgue. He was accustomed to waking and finding a woman in a white nurse's uniform standing over him. But he had never had a nurse catch him in bed with a woman. Stammering like a schoolboy, Thomas began, "Nurse, I can explain. . . . It isn't what you think—"

Ida cut him off. "We're all over twenty-one and know the facts of life. There's no need to explain this to me, but you've got a mighty confused little boy down the hall."

"Robert." Lydia breathed his name. "Oh, my goodness." She turned to Thomas. "What am I doing in here? He was frightened last night. I promised Robert I'd stay with him." She reached for Thomas's robe, then scrambled out of bed.

"I woke up and you were gone," Thomas explained. "I found you holding Robby on your lap, sound asleep, in the rocking chair in his room."

"You should have left me where you found me." Lydia rounded on Thomas as she yanked her skirt and petticoats off the arm of the chair and began pulling them on.

"Lydia, you were asleep in a chair! A damned uncomfortable wooden one, I might add. With forty pounds of little boy on your lap."

"But he was frightened and I promised him I'd stay with him."

"He was fine, Lydia. He was fast asleep. I thought you'd be more comfortable in bed."

"In your bed," she accused. She picked up her blouse and put it on.

Thomas's green eyes shimmered angrily. "Was I wrong, Lydia? Did I misread the situation? Didn't you want to be here?"

She couldn't lie to him. She wouldn't pretend she didn't enjoy waking up in his arms. She couldn't look Thomas in the eyes and say she wasn't thrilled to know he had missed her in the night and gone looking for her. "But I gave Robert my word, and now I've broken it. I need to talk to him. Explain the situation." Lydia was afraid that talking to Robert wasn't going to do any good, afraid that she'd done permanent damage to the fragile trust she'd been working so hard to earn, but she didn't want to worry Thomas. He'd been so proud of what she had managed to accomplish in a few short weeks.

"I think that's a good idea." Thomas nodded. Privately, he doubted that Robby would say much until he got over his anger and disappointment at Lydia. Thomas understood his son's feelings. He knew Robby felt Lydia had abandoned him. He knew Robby needed the security of Lydia's love and the comfort of her arms to chase away the bad dreams, but Robby had to learn to share her with him. Lydia loved both of them. And Thomas needed her arms around him just as much as Robby did. Thomas sighed. He hated to see Lydia disappointed. He knew firsthand how formidable Robby's anger could be. But he didn't want Lydia's hopes crushed. In the past few weeks, she had succeeded with Robby where he had failed. Maybe she could succeed again.

Ida looked at Doc Sullivan, then at Lydia. "I think the doc's right, Lyddy girl. Robert's a child and children have a way of forgiving and forgetting." She put her arm around Lydia's shoulder. "Go talk to him while I make us a pot of coffee."

"Make it strong, Ida," Thomas said. "I could use a cup."

As Ida steered Lydia out of the bedroom her gaze met Thomas's. Though she didn't say anything out loud, the expression on her face told him not to worry. They could all use a cup of the strong caffeine-laden brew.

"What about breakfast?" Lydia asked.

"Don't worry," Ida said, "I still remember how to scramble eggs. Go on."

Lydia tapped on Robert's door. There was no answer, but she could hear him crying. She carefully turned the doorknob. Thank goodness, he hadn't locked himself in. "Robert?" she called as she eased the bedroom door open and stepped inside. She waited for him to acknowledge her presence, and when he didn't, she walked over to his bed and sat down on the edge of it. "Robert, I'm sorry."

"Go away." Robert's voice was muffled by his pillows. "I want my *maman*."

"I know you do," Lydia told him. "But she's not here. I'm here and I'll listen if you want to talk." She reached out and gently touched his back.

Robert shrugged her off. "You're not my *maman*."

Though this was the truth, his words cut at Lydia's heart. "I know," she said softly, "but one day soon, I'll be your step-*maman* and I'd like very much to be your friend."

"I don't like you anymore."

"Why not?"

"You like Papa better than me." Robert rolled over and faced her defiantly.

"Oh no, Robert." Lydia hurried to reassure him that his assumption wasn't correct. "I love you both very much."

"You slept in Papa's bed." The look in Robert's brown eyes was one of betrayal.

"Yes, I did," Lydia agreed. "And once your papa and I are married, I'll be sleeping in his bed every night."

"I used to sleep in *maman*'s bed," Robert confided, "until Papa came home. Then she let him sleep in her bed with her."

That revelation was another stab to Lydia's heart. But she put aside her hurt feelings and tried to explain. "Married people sleep together, Robert. When I marry your papa, my place will be beside him."

"When you marry my papa, will you be my *maman*?"

"No one can ever take the place of your mother, Robert. But we'll all be living together as a family. I'll do for you the things mothers do for their children and I'll love you as much as if you were my own little boy."

Robert shook his head. "I don't want you to marry my papa. I don't want to be your little boy. Go away. I want my *maman*!" Burying his face in his pillow, he turned away from Lydia.

She stared at him for a minute, then left the room. She hurried down the hallway, through the kitchen. She walked past Nurse Ida and Thomas without so much as a backward glance and out the backdoor. When she reached the ground, she sprinted across the sand and gravel to the safety of the carriage house.

"Control," she warned herself, "don't lose control."

TWELVE

"Lydia!" Thomas came out of his chair like a shot and followed her down the steps and across the yard to the carriage house. "Wait!"

She ran faster. She had to make it to the safety of her little apartment before the tears started to fall. She had to be alone when her world fell apart.

Thomas caught up with her. He reached out and gently grabbed hold of her arm. "What is it? What did he do to upset you so?"

"He doesn't want me." The tears she had been holding back began to flow. "Robert said he'd didn't want me to marry you. He didn't want me for his stepmother."

"Well, that's too bad," Thomas told her, "because I intend to marry you and make you my wife."

"You can't," Lydia said, "not if Robert doesn't want me."

"Lydia," Thomas said gently, "Robby isn't doing the choosing. I am." He leaned forward and tried to kiss away her tears, but Lydia wouldn't let him. "Robby hasn't stopped liking you. He's just angry and lashing out."

Thomas fumbled in his jacket pocket. He'd meant to give her his gift this morning when she woke up, but they had overslept and disaster struck. He pulled out the ring box and placed it in her hand. "I thought about this last night when we were celebrating our engagement over chocolate malts. I planned to give it to you this morning." He smiled a lopsided, self-deprecating smile. "I had a lot of fine plans for this morning, and most of them involved making slow, sweet love to you."

Lydia stood very still. She looked down at the box in her hand.

Thomas saw the look of bewilderment on her face and realized that she hadn't been completely sure of him. "Lydia," he said softly, gently, "did you think I would change my mind about marrying you once I had you in my bed?"

"I didn't know," she admitted, stumbling over the words. "You didn't . . ." She let the words hang in the air between them.

"Marry Françoise?" Thomas shook his head. "No, I didn't. But only because she wouldn't agree to marry me." He smiled down at Lydia. "Don't turn me down. Please say yes."

"Yes, but—" she began.

"No buts." Thomas leaned down and brushed his lips against her hair. "Go ahead. Open it."

She lifted the lid. "Oh, Thomas, it's exquisite." Lydia had never seen anything like it. A perfectly round, lustrous pearl, mounted in a gold-prong setting, rose above a circle of tiny seed pearls and diamonds.

Thomas watched the expression on her face. "I think it's perfect for you."

"Why?"

He smiled down at her. "Because perfect pearls, like perfect soul mates, are very, very rare. You're my soul mate, Lydia. And it took me years to find you, almost as long as it took the oyster to form this pearl." Thomas read the question in her eyes. "This ring belonged to my mother. She was the last person to wear it. It's been in safekeeping since she died. My father had it made especially for her. When Mother died, my father gave me this ring to give to my bride." He paused. "If you don't like it, if you'd rather have something more modern, a diamond or something, tell me."

"No." Lydia shook her head. "This is more precious to me than something new." She looked up at him and frowned. "But are you sure you want to give it to me now? Robert isn't going to be happy about it."

"I'm not as concerned about Robby right now as I am about us. Lydia, what about you? Are you happy? I know our engagement was sudden and not entirely of our own making. I know you lost your home and your job when I bought the drugstore and the medical practice. I know you think I offered to marry you out of a sense of guilt. And, in a way, that's true. But it's only part of the truth. I think I began falling in love with you the first time I saw you unraveling the fastener on your jacket, but I knew for sure when you insisted Robby should have your special plate."

Thomas took the ring out of the box and slipped it onto the third finger of Lydia's left hand. "Sweetheart, I love my son. I want what's best for him. And I believe with all my heart that loving you, marrying you, providing him with a mother like you is the best thing I will ever be able to do for Robby."

"Oh, Thomas." Lydia flung her arms around his neck. "I love you so much."

"Do you?" He hugged her tightly, then set her back away from him so he could see her face.

"Of course I do," she said. "How could you doubt it after last night?"

"You never told me."

"I thought you knew," Lydia explained simply. "Everyone else in town could see it. I fell in love with you the moment I saw you come out of the depot and onto the platform. It was like being struck by lightning."

"Then I'm afraid you're just going to have to make an honest man out of me," Thomas teased. "After last night, it wouldn't be fair to do otherwise."

"What about Robert?" Lydia asked. "I love you, Thomas, and I want us to live together and be a family, but I won't let you choose between Robert and me. If Robert still doesn't want me to be his stepmother by the time of the wedding, we'll have to postpone it. And if he decides never to accept me, then . . ." She let her words trail off, unable to voice her most horrible fear.

"Lydia, the wedding is next week, and the townspeople are looking forward to it almost as much as we are," Thomas protested. "Robby's a child. He's an angry and a jealous little boy, but he loves you. There's no doubt about that. He'll come around eventually, but it may take longer than a week."

"I'm sorry, Thomas, I want to marry you and I want to be a mother to Robert. But I'm not going to be the cause of more heartbreak for Robert or for you. I love you both too much. If he doesn't change his mind, then . . ."

Thomas didn't like Lydia's decision, but there didn't seem to be much he could do about it. She had made up her mind and all he could do was try to change it. Thomas glanced down at the ring on her finger. His ring. "What do we do in the meantime?" he asked.

"The best we can," Lydia replied.

But their best didn't seem to be good enough for Robert. No amount of apologizing on Lydia's part and no amount of explaining from Thomas would budge the stubborn five-year-old boy. Robby was angry and disappointed in his father and Lydia and he wanted to make sure they understood that. He emerged from his bedroom for breakfast when Ida called him, then refused to eat off the plate Lydia had given him. Thomas insisted that he eat the food put before him on the plate set before him, and the battle of wills began. Robby stubbornly clamped his mouth shut and shook his head. Thomas excused himself from the table, took Robby by the hand, and led him down the hall to his bedroom.

"You didn't spank him, did you?" Lydia asked as soon as Thomas returned to the kitchen alone.

"No, I simply explained the terms. Robby will stay in his room until he apologizes for his behavior. Here." He shoved Robert's schoolbag full of drawing supplies at Lydia. "No coloring, no drawing, no soldiers, no toys at all until he apologizes. And"—he glanced at Lydia and Ida—"I don't want you to bribe him with chocolate malts. He's behaved badly and he should face the consequences of his action."

"What about work?" Lydia asked. "I have to open the store in an hour."

Thomas looked at Ida. "I suppose we can hire someone to stay up here with him."

"Up here? But, Thomas, he loves to spend time in the store," Lydia protested.

"I know," Thomas said. "Sweetheart, I don't enjoy this any more than you do, but I'm not going to let Robby think he can pitch a temper tantrum whenever he's unhappy with our decisions. He's the child, we're the adults. We make the rules." He turned to his nurse. "Ida, do you know anyone who would be willing to spend the day with a stubborn little boy."

"Maude Brown," she replied, "Amos's wife. But she doesn't speak a word of French."

"That's okay." Thomas managed a smile. "Because Robby's not speaking."

"I'll call her," Ida volunteered, then stopped dead in her tracks and slapped herself on the forehead. "Oh, dear, I forgot to call Georgia back."

"When did Georgia call?" Lydia asked.

"I called her when I got here this morning," Nurse Ida explained, "when I couldn't find you or Doc Sullivan." She glanced down at the watch pinned to the front of her uniform. "There's no telling how many rumors she might have started by now." She started toward the telephone, but Thomas stopped her.

"Nurse, about this morning . . ."

Ida stared down at him, using her most intimidating nurse's glare. "As far as I'm concerned, what happened between you and Lydia is your business. I don't make it a habit to spy on a husband and wife in the privacy of their bedroom. And since I consider you two"—she fixed her gaze on Lydia—"all but married, I won't be barging in again."

"Thank you, Nurse." Thomas breathed a silent sigh of relief.

But Ida wasn't finished. "I do suggest, however, if you intend to continue your sleeping arrangement, that you lock your bedroom door, and that you"—she turned her icy stare back on Thomas—"consider some means of contraception, Doctor. Until you're married, we have Miss Lydia's reputation to consider and—"

Thomas's face reddened. "I get the point, Nurse, and with the wedding a week away, I don't think we have to worry, but the matter of contraception is entirely up to Lydia. But I'd certainly welcome another child into the family." He glanced at Lydia.

Lydia turned several shades of red, then glanced down at the floor, too embarrassed to face Ida or Thomas.

"Well, I've said my piece," Ida said flatly. "Do I still have a job?"

Thomas laughed. "Of course you do. And, Nurse . . ."

"Yes, Doctor?"

"I appreciate your concern and your advice."

Nurse Ida grinned. "Well, I'm off to call Maude. Shall I ask her to be here by nine?"

Lydia nodded.

"And ask if she can spend the day and fix lunch," Thomas added.

"Robert and I always go to the park for lunch," Lydia said.

"Unless Robby apologizes, he'll be eating all his meals alone in his room. And besides," Thomas said, "I thought we might have lunch at the café and do a bit of shopping at Damon's Jewelers on the way home." He held up his left hand. "I need to be measured for my ring." Silently he prayed he'd have the opportunity to wear it. His emotions were raw, and he was very much afraid Lydia was going to refuse his offer of marriage. And Thomas wasn't sure he could accept a life without Lydia.

Lydia went about her normal routine as she opened the drugstore, but it was different without Robert. She missed him terribly and she wanted to go back to the apartment to check on him. But she respected Thomas's wishes and prayed that Robert would find it in his heart to forgive her for disappointing him and to give her another chance.

Thomas entered the drugstore a little before noon. "Any word from Robby?" He had instructed Mrs. Brown to call if his obstinate son expressed a desire to apologize.

Lydia shook her head. "No, and I've been waiting for the telephone to ring all morning."

Thomas was philosophical. "Maybe he'll come around by suppertime." He patted his jacket pocket. "I brought the picture of Françoise you wanted. She had a photograph of them made and tinted shortly after Robert was born. I used to keep it in my quarters."

"And now you keep it in your office," Lydia said.

"Yes. And I want a framed wedding portrait of you to go beside it." He took the photograph out of his pocket and offered it to Lydia.

"No, I . . ."

"Open it, Lyddy, look at that picture of Françoise."

Torn between feelings of curiosity and dread, Lydia accepted the photograph.

The image in her hand showed a young woman of eighteen or nineteen, dressed in white lace, holding an infant on her lap. Lydia couldn't see much of the baby, for he was swathed in yards of delicate white fabric and wearing a white lace cap that covered most of his face, but she knew it was Robert. She turned her attention away from the baby and stared at his mother. Françoise had been beautiful. Her face was a perfect oval and her features finely sculpted. In the photograph, she looked fragile and delicate, almost ethereal. There was no evidence of the sparkling vitality Thomas remembered, except perhaps in her eyes. Lydia recognized those eyes. She'd seen an almost identical pair every day for the past few weeks. Robert had inherited his mother's features. His was a childish representation of Françoise's face.

"Now you know," Thomas said. "Robby is the spitting image of his mother. And this"—he took the photograph away from Lydia and put it back in his jacket pocket—"was his christening picture. It was the only photo I had of his mother, and also the only one of him as a baby. I've kept it with me all these years to remind me of the thing I wanted most." He looked at Lydia. "A family. A wife and children. And another chance."

Lydia reached inside her blouse and pulled up the chain holding the gold locket. She opened the fastening of the locket and spread the two halves open for Thomas to see. In one circle was a picture of a man and a woman on their wedding day, and the other image showed the same woman posing with a little girl. "I know," she whispered. "I've always had the same dream. I wanted another family. Only this time I want to be the mother." She stepped closer to Thomas and tilted her face up at just the right angle to receive his kiss.

Thomas murmured as he bent to kiss her, "I don't think I can stand a postponement of the wedding."

"I don't think I could stand it, either," Lydia told him. "I just pray he'll change his mind about me."

THIRTEEN

So did Thomas. But praying didn't seem to be doing much good. Robby proved to be much angrier than either one of them expected. It had been two days since he'd told Lydia he didn't want her as a mother, two days of lying in his room staring at the walls, of eating the meals Maude Brown fixed for him, two days without paper or crayons, or toy soldiers, or the drugstore, or chocolate malts, or Lydia.

On the surface, everything seemed fine. But beneath the surface, everyone was stretched to the breaking point. Lydia had already mentioned calling off the wedding, and though she went through with the plans, even going so far as to have her gown cleaned and to pick up Thomas's ring and Robert's gift from Damon's Jewelers, her heart wasn't in it.

She hated the silence and she missed Robert terribly. This was worse than when he first arrived. Then he had spoken only to her. Now he didn't speak to anyone. She didn't think she could go on pretending everything was going to be fine much longer.

Robert had spent two days punishing them, and when he finally emerged from his room, later that second night, to apologize for his behavior, he did it in rapid French.

Lydia couldn't understand a word.

After supper, Lydia continued their normal routine as if nothing had happened, but Robert refused her help in getting ready for bed and went so far as to shove her hairbrush back into her hands when she offered it to her. But not even that rejection could make Lydia give up. She tucked him into bed, drew the covers up around him, and tried to kiss him good night.

"All right, I understand," she said. "I know you don't want me around. I'll go, but I wanted you to have something special." Lydia stared down at the little boy, but she couldn't tell if he was listening to her. "A wedding present from me. I didn't realize it until a few days ago, but Sunday is Mother's Day." Robert continued to look away, but this time Lydia thought he might be listening. "It's a holiday we have here in America to remind us of how dear to our hearts our mothers are, how much we love them and appreciate them. I want to be a part of your family, but now—" Her voice broke and Lydia struggled to keep her tears from falling. "I know what it's like to lose a mother, Robert. Mine died, too. I always wished my father would marry Ida, but then those things can't always be arranged to suit us. Anyway"—she brushed back a tear and took the gift box from Damon's Jewelers out of her skirt pocket—"this is for you." She offered the gift to Robby, and when he didn't take it, she balanced the box on the side of the bed, turned off the light, and left the room.

If Robert heard her crying as she closed the door, he gave no indication of it.

"Come here," Thomas said when she came out of Robert's room.

She walked into his outstretched arms.

He hugged her tightly. "You've had a rough day."

She nodded against his shirt.

"Don't cry, Lyddy."

"I can't help it. I wanted this so much. I wanted us to be a family. I wanted to marry you and be a mother to Robert, but now . . ."

Warning bells went off in Thomas's brain. He could see their future together slipping away, and all because his son had decided to throw a jealous tantrum and make Lydia's life a living hell. "Now?" He sounded calm as he asked the question, but inside, Thomas was quaking with fear.

"Now I don't see how we can make it work."

"You promised you'd give it a week," Thomas reminded her.

"I know, but it isn't fair to the people of Eden Point for me to continue to let them think there's going to be a wedding right up until the last minute. They've gone to so much trouble, done so much work."

"Hang the people of Eden Point!" Thomas yelled. "What about me? What about you? It's not fair to us for you to give up now. Don't throw what we have away!"

"Do you think I want to? I just don't know what else to do," Lydia confessed, crying even harder. "I've done everything I could think of. He won't talk to me and he wouldn't even look at me when I tried to give him his wedding gift."

Thomas couldn't think of what to say to comfort her, so he offered her another form of solace. "Would you like me to brush your hair for you?"

Lydia managed a smile. "Thanks, but I'd rather you didn't. It wouldn't seem right." They'd come to an agreement the night they made love. Robert would have the privilege of brushing her hair at night before she went to bed and Thomas could enjoy the opportunity in the morning before she got dressed.

Thomas nuzzled her neck. "Am I going to get the chance?"

Lydia didn't pretend not to understand what he was asking. "I don't think so. Not tomorrow morning."

"The day after?"

"I don't know."

Thomas released her, then raked his fingers through his hair in a sign of frustration. "Maybe I shouldn't have accepted his apology. After all, he did it in French."

"You never stipulated that it must be in English," Lydia reminded him.

Thomas quirked an eyebrow at her. "I know. And I'd be very proud of him for being so clever if I weren't angry with him for being so stubborn."

"Don't be angry with him, Thomas. Try to understand."

"I do understand. The world and the life Robby knew back in France are gone. He's confused and upset and uncertain. How do you explain to a five-year-old boy that change is always upsetting, and that you and I are making just as many adjustments as he is? How do you explain that compromising and learning to live with each other's good sides and bad sides is all a part of loving other people and being part of a family?"

"I don't know, Thomas. I've never been a parent before."

Thomas shrugged his shoulders. "Neither have I." He looked at Lydia and saw the sadness in her eyes and knew he couldn't give up. "But lack of experience has never stopped me before now. I'll go talk to him again."

"Thank you."

Thomas smiled at her. "You'll have to do better than that if you want me to step into the ring with Robert Thomas Sullivan."

She looped her arms around his neck and pressed her body close to his.

Thomas leaned down to kiss her and caught a whiff of the irresistible fragrance that was uniquely Lydia. "God, Lydia, what is that fragrance you wear?"

"Rosewater with a touch of vanilla extract added in."

"Rosewater, vanilla, and Lydia. Enough to drive a man crazy with wanting you." He kissed her lightly on the lips. "You'd better go home now. I can't kiss you without wanting to make love to you." Reaching up, Thomas loosened her hold on his neck. His hands shook with the effort of holding his emotions in check. "What did you do with your gift?"

"I left it on his bed."

"Okay." Unable to resist, he gave in to his impulse and kissed her again. "I'll do my best. Don't worry. Just go home and dream of me."

"You're all I ever dream of," she whispered.

Thomas groaned and leaned his forehead against hers. "Don't give up on me, Lydia. Don't give up on us. Please."

"Good night, my love," Lydia said softly. "Don't fail me," she added silently.

"Good night, sweetheart." He walked her to the backdoor, then stood watching as she crossed the yard and went up the stairs of the carriage house. He waited until the lights came on in the window, then closed the door. Taking a deep breath,

Thomas went down the hall and knocked on Robby's door.

"Robby? I know you're in there. May I come in?"

There was no answer.

Thomas opened the door anyway. His son sat in the middle of the bed with a ragged German-made Stieff teddy bear clasped against his chest. The tissue-paper-wrapped package from Damon's lay unopened beside him.

Thomas walked over to the narrow bed and sat down on the edge. He reached over and removed the brown plush bear from Robby's arms. "Did you know I bought this bear for your mother before you were born?"

Robby shook his head.

"I did," Thomas told him. "I gave this little fellow to your mother to help keep her company while I was away, but only until you got here, because then she'd have you to keep her company. Once you were born, Teddy was supposed to keep you company." He smiled at the grimy teddy bear. "And it looks as though he's done a pretty good job."

Robby nodded.

"I guess you've been able to talk to him when you haven't wanted to talk to me. And I suppose he kept you safe and made you feel loved when *maman* died and I wasn't there?"

Again Robby nodded.

"I'm very glad Teddy was able to help you." Thomas looked up and met his little boy's solemn brown-eyed gaze. "But you know, Robby, sometimes old friends like Teddy aren't enough. Sometimes we need to love real people who can talk and walk and share things with us. The kind of things that toys can't share. I loved your mother very much. And I wanted to make her well again, but I couldn't."

"You could!" Robert burst out. "*Grandmaman* said you were a great doctor, but you were too busy with the American soldiers to take care of *maman*."

"Your grandmother said that about me?"

"*Oui.*"

"And did you ask your mother?"

"*Oui.*"

"And what did she say?"

"She say no one could help." Robert stared at his father, challenging him to say otherwise.

"Your grandmother is a very wise woman, Robby, but she was wrong. Your mother was very sick. I tried to help her. I wanted very much to make her well, but I couldn't."

"But you're a great American doctor." Robert lunged into his father's arms, buried his face in Thomas's shirt, and began to cry.

Thomas choked back his own tears. "Even great American doctors can't change God's will. I'm sorry, Robert, I'm very, very sorry." He held his son cradled against his chest. "I know you're angry and hurt. You have every right to be. A terrible disease snatched your mother away from you. And then I took you away from Paris and your grandparents—everything you've known and loved. But what I want you to understand is that it's all right to be angry, even bitter, for a while, but not too long. Because life offers you other opportunities, other chances, if only you get over your hurt and take them.

"When we came here, I just wanted to get away from the bad things we'd been through—the war, the illness, and your mother's death. I didn't expect to find Lydia. And I never expected to fall in love with her."

"You love Lydia more than me, more than *maman*," Robert sobbed.

"No, I don't," Thomas explained gently. "I love Lydia as much as I love you and I love her in a different way than I loved your mother. I know you probably don't understand, but there's a difference in the way you love people. You love your grandmother as much as you loved your *maman*, but in a different way, just as your love for your mother is different from the way you love me."

Robert took a moment to try to understand and accept what Thomas was telling him. "What about Lydia?"

"You can love Lydia without being disloyal to the memory of your mother." Thomas thought for a moment, trying to figure out a simple way to explain these complex emotions. He glanced down at Teddy and mentally begged Lydia's pardon for comparing her to a stuffed toy. "Lydia is kind of like Teddy. She's someone to talk to when you're sad and lonely, and someone to take care of you and protect you from harm, someone to laugh with and have fun with and tell your secrets to, because you know she'll love you without question. She's the special lady in your life who wants to do the things for you that your mother would have done, to give you all the love and joy you deserve to have. What I'm trying to say, Robby, is that if you let her, Lydia can be your very best friend in the whole world."

"Would *maman* want me to have a friend like Lydia?"

Thomas smiled, then ruffled his son's dark curls. "*Maman* would want it very much."

Robert glanced up at his father. "Would *maman* like for Lydia to sleep in your bed with you?"

Thomas answered the blunt question as best he could. "Having Lydia sleep in my bed makes me happy."

"Would *maman* like for you to be happy?"

Thomas paused—he wasn't quite sure how to answer honestly. Then he thought about the sadness he'd seen in Françoise's eyes over the years, the pain and the guilt she endured in silence because she thought she'd become a burden to him. And he remembered the love she'd had for him. "Yes, Robby, I think *maman* would want me to be happy. I think she wants both of us to be happy." He hugged Robert, kissed him on the forehead, then picked up the present Lydia had left and handed it to Robert. "And if you'll open this box and see what Lydia bought you, I think you'll understand just how much she cares about you and just how lucky you are to have her."

Robert held the box for a second, then ripped open the paper and lifted the lid. Inside, on a bed of velvet fabric, lay a gold watch. A child-size gold watch. Robert picked it up by the chain and held it in his hand, then ran his fingers over the words engraved on the lid. "Read it, Papa."

Thomas complied. " 'A mother's love is with you always.' " He flipped the watch over. On the back, it was dated and signed simply "Lydia." Thomas swallowed the lump in his throat as he handed the watch back to his son. "Open it," he urged.

Robert did. And inside, he found a copy of the picture he'd seen all his life: his mother in her white lace dress holding him on her lap.

Robert hugged his father, then holding the precious watch tightly in his hand, he climbed off the bed and ran out the door and down the hall, yelling "Lydia!" at the top of his lungs.

Thomas stood on the back steps watching as Lydia, answering Robby's call, hurried barefoot out of the carriage house, wearing only her nightgown.

Robby didn't pause, but ran straight for her, and he was halfway across the backyard before she reached him. "Robert, what is it? What's wrong?"

Robby flung his arms around her waist and buried his face in the folds of her nightgown.

"What is it? Are you hurt?"

The words seemed to pour out of Robby's heart. "I love you, Lydia. I love you. I'm sorry I was bad." He held up the watch for her to see. "I want you to be my *maman,* too. Please, Lydia, I love you."

Lydia bent down and lifted Robert off the ground, and hugged him to her breast. "I love you, too, Robert, very much. And there's nothing I want more in the world than to be your second *maman.*"

EPILOGUE

The wedding of Miss Lydia Turner to Dr. Thomas Sullivan occurred right on schedule at two o'clock in the afternoon on Sunday, the eleventh of May, 1919. And Thomas and Lydia breathed sighs of relief. He had married her. She hadn't turned him down.

The Merchants' Association of Eden Point, Florida, had outdone themselves for this wedding. And the whole town turned out to see it.

Vivian Carmichael's floral arrangements were the most spectacular she'd ever done, and nearly everyone agreed that Eleanor Sheffield's selection of wedding songs brought tears to the eyes.

Julia Davisson prided herself on Nurse Ida's choice of a blue silk instead of a blue serge dress, and Christine Damon congratulated herself on having the good sense to sell two wedding bands, a child's gold pocket watch, a ladies' gold charm bracelet with a nurse's charm, a string of beautifully matched pearls, and a pair of engraved gold cuff links to the bride and groom.

The wedding was a huge success for the people of Eden Point, for Miss Lydia, Dr. Sullivan, and little Robert.

The only problem had been getting Miss Lydia to dress at the church instead of at home. Because the doc and Robert didn't want her anywhere near Turner's Drugstore until they were ready to present her with their surprise.

Georgia Murray, Dottie Farmer, and Maude Brown had worked all morning to get things ready. Fred Gunter had baked the biggest and prettiest wedding cake the town had ever seen, and Marjorie Eddings spent most of the night cooking up the

101

fanciest French hors d'oeuvres this side of Paris. And with Doc Sullivan's permission, Harold Thompson, editor of the *Eden Point Gazette,* agreed to take pictures for the Merchants' Association Catalog.

Miss Lydia's wedding was a town event, and when the vows were done, the rings and kisses exchanged, and the rice thrown, Thomas invited the entire population of Eden Point to Turner's Drugstore for the celebration.

Robert opened the front door as Thomas swung Lydia up into his arms and carried her over the threshold.

She looked up at the huge banner hanging over the soda fountain and burst into happy tears. Marjorie Eddings hadn't been the only one working late. Unbeknownst to Lydia, Thomas and Robert had created a work of art full of rainbows and hearts and trees and houses and stick people—three to be exact—all of it framed between gigantic letters that read: HAPPY MOTHER'S DAY! LOVE, YOUR NEW SON, ROBERT SULLIVAN.

Then Thomas carried Lydia to the soda fountain and whispered something in her ear. She laughed in delight, nodded her head in agreement, then got down to work.

And while the rest of Eden Point celebrated her wedding by helping themselves to the free food and drink provided by the Merchants' Association, Lydia Turner Sullivan, her husband, Dr. Thomas Sullivan, and son, Robert Sullivan, draped an old sheet over her wedding dress, tied aprons around their necks, and proceeded to make and serve chocolate malts with extra whipped cream and cherries to everyone in town.

EMMA'S DAY

by

Jill Metcalf

❧

ONE

Zanesville, Ohio
1878

Beams of sunlight shone through narrow cracks in the barn's ceiling boards, hitting his face, waking him. If that weren't enough, a cock crowed annoyingly and his horse shuffled through clean straw in the stall beside him. Ward Hamilton groaned and wearily turned his stiff body, stretching his long frame as he moved onto his back. When he managed to open his eyes and look around, he saw a small boy standing just beyond his booted feet at the end of the stall.

Ward waited for the child's reaction.

None came.

The boy continued to stand there with an index finger in his mouth. He just stood and stared.

"Boy," Ward croaked.

The child turned and fled.

Ward closed his eyes briefly before reluctantly getting to his feet. He could use another hour or two of sleep, but now that he was discovered, he supposed he'd best move on. The boy's father would probably be out to the barn with a shotgun soon.

Timmy Franklin ran smack into his grandmother's legs as he charged through the open barn door.

"Timmy," Emma scolded softly, even as she gripped his slender shoulder to steady him.

"Man," Timmy said, pointing.

Emma looked into the dark cavern of the barn, narrowing

105

her eyes suspiciously as she searched beyond the beams of sunlight that crisscrossed the blackness. She saw nothing. "A man?" she questioned the child. "Where, Tim?"

The boy continued to point.

Emma stepped beyond her grandson and snatched up one of the weathered two by fours that was used to prop open the wide double barn doors. So armed, she entered the stillness. "Stay back, Tim," she said over her shoulder.

The man was standing, stretching, when she found him in a vacant horse stall.

Emma raised her weapon.

"I mean no harm," Ward Hamilton said quickly. He raised a hand, palm out.

Emma hesitated, knowing she might be acting foolishly. Still . . . "What do you want?" she asked.

"I'm sorry I startled your boy," he said. "I took shelter from the rain last night. That's all. I'm sorry if I've frightened you."

His voice was deep, his intonation cultured sounding, but he looked thoroughly disreputable. He was a big man, tall and muscular and fit. His hair appeared black in the meager light, graying at the sides. It was the black stubble of a heavy beard that gave him an unsavory appearance. But the look in his eyes was not the hardened one she might have expected from a criminal or a degenerate. No, the look in his eyes was honest . . . yes, honest.

He appraised her in return. He wondered if she would first club him or throw the bucket she held instead. The woman was tense, ready to defend herself—that was for certain. Fair-haired and amber-eyed, she was also quite lovely, quite fragile. "I thought I could make it to town before the storm hit," he said conversationally. And then with a slow smile, he explained, "But the skies opened up and I took shelter here. It was dark and pretty wet out there so I settled in," he added by way of apology. When the woman failed to respond, Ward said the only thing he really could say, "I'll just saddle my horse and be on my way." But he didn't move, not wanting to startle her.

Emma stared at him for the space of a long, relieved breath. And then she lowered her weapon and nodded, taking a step back. "Fine," she said softly.

A cow bawled and Ward glanced at the animal tethered in a narrow stall across the way. Her udders were full to bursting. He looked at the bucket in the woman's hand and then raised candid, brown eyes, smiling. "Could I milk her for you?" he asked. "Seems the least I can do in return for the use of your barn."

The wise thing to do would have been to ask him to leave the property and quickly. She and Timmy were alone and, except for her own determination, defenseless. But she wasn't feeling particularly wise. He was a stranger and yet she felt she had known him before. She was drawn to him in a curious way. That shouldn't be, but there it was. "Yes. All right," she said, extending the bucket toward him.

"Name is Hamilton," he said conversationally as he walked around her. "Ward Hamilton."

"Emma Parker," she returned softly.

He liked her voice. It reminded him of satin.

He walked right up to old bossy.

"Talk to her. Let her know you're there."

Talk to a cow? He frowned and said, "Ho, cow." He stepped to the side of the bony hips and the cow turned her head his way, raising her nose in the air as she bawled again in her discomfort.

Emma watched his awkward, cautious movements. He stood beside the animal, looking extremely doubtful as he bent and examined the full milk sacks. Quickly, she moved toward a square supporting beam, snatched up the three-legged milking stool that hung there, and walked to his side. "Have you done this before?"

Ward straightened to his full height and grinned down at her. "No."

She laughed lightly. "Then why on earth would you volunteer?"

"Seemed the thing to do," he explained. "And I'd like to give it a try."

Emma shook her head and positioned the stool, motioning that he should sit. "Where are you from?" she asked and there were a hundred other questions behind that one.

"New York."

Her head tipped to the side a fraction and she frowned down at him. "What on earth are you doing out here?"

"Starting over," he said quietly, and without missing a beat, "What do I do?"

Emma watched him clamp a large yet gentle hand around a swollen teat and ducked her head in an attempt to hide her telltale blush. She dropped down on her heels beside him and her skirts billowed out around her bent knees. "Just pull down and squeeze," she said.

He tried it. It worked and he laughed proudly as a stream of warm milk shot into the bucket. Feeling confident, Ward wrapped the fingers of his other hand around another teat; he wasn't as coordinated with his left hand, but he eventually had two streams of milk shooting rhythmically into the bucket.

Emma watched the steady movements of his hands, remaining crouched beside him until she became conscious of his body heat, so close was she. Feeling a stranger had invaded her personal space, she stood and stepped away a pace. "Are you hungry?" she asked quietly.

Ward's head turned, his cheek very close to the cow's belly as he smiled at her. "I am."

His smile was devastating. Emma nodded, frowning as she turned away. "Come up to the house when you've finished," she said in a defensive tone.

When she walked outside, Timmy was running around the spacious yard, harassing the rooster.

"Come along, Timmy!" Emma called as she lengthened her stride and walked to the house in a no-nonsense fashion.

Reluctantly, the boy gave up the chase and followed his grandmother.

The rooster, feeling cocky and triumphant, crowed a scolding.

Inside the house, Emma removed four pans of baked bread from her oven before heading to the root cellar to fetch yesterday's crock of milk. Once she had positioned Timmy at the table with a cup of cool milk and a heel of warm, buttered bread, she sliced thick strips of bacon and cracked open eight eggs, dropping the contents into a bowl. She whipped the things to a froth, stopped suddenly, frowning at the eggs before, with a feminine shrug, cracking two more. "He said he was hungry," she murmured.

Timmy, seated on a booster board, beat a steady tattoo on the chair with a booted foot.

Emma turned and frowned at the three year old.

He stopped. "Who that man, Gram?" he asked.

"A hungry man, darling," she said as she added milk and butter to her eggs. "We're going to give him some breakfast."

Ward walked with a long, steady gait toward the backdoor, careful not to spill the milk that filled the container. The house was white and neat, with black trim and gingerbread fascia below the porch roof. The wide porch seemed to run completely around the house and the floorboards had been painted gray. The windows from the kitchen had been pushed high and the inner door stood open to catch any morning breeze that might flow by. It was a pretty house, a comfortable looking house.

Ward's boot hit the bottom of four steps with a thud.

Emma Parker whirled from her stove toward the sound. She hurried across the room, pushed open the screen door, and reached for the bucket of milk. "If you'll wait here," she said nervously, "I'll bring some breakfast out to you."

So he wasn't to be allowed in the house.

For a fleeting moment he resented the fact that Emma Parker could not recognize an honorable man when she saw one.

Turning his back to the door, Ward lowered his buttocks to the top step and stretched his long legs, resting his feet two steps below. He shouldn't blame her for being cautious. And he should be grateful that she had offered a hot meal. But somehow that wasn't enough.

The screen door banged lightly and bounced against the door frame a time or two when she came out onto the porch. The boy had followed her but was staying close to her skirts, staring up at him with curiosity.

The plate was heaped with crisp bacon and a mound of scrambled eggs. Two thick slices of bread rested off to the side, and Ward could tell the stuff was still warm by the way the butter had melted into it. He reached for the plate. "Thank you, Mrs. Parker," he said respectfully. "This looks good and smells even better."

"There's more if you wish," she said, looking into his eyes and then silently extended a mug of steaming coffee. "I wasn't sure . . . would you like milk?"

Ward shook his head. "Thanks."

Timmy moved from her side, but Emma gently pulled him back, pushing him before her into the kitchen.

Ward stared at her through the dark screening, shrugged his shoulders in resignation, and returned to his place on the steps.

The food was wonderful. Hot. He hadn't taken well to trail food; he was accustomed to finer fare, and beek jerky just didn't cut it.

He was savoring his coffee, the empty plate resting on the floorboards next to his hip, when a single-horse buggy came up the lane and drew to a halt near the house.

The lone occupant and driver was a young woman, blond and pretty and innocent looking. He grinned wryly at that last thought as she stood to descend and he noticed her swollen belly.

Reacting quickly, he set his cup aside and hurried toward her. "Let me help," he said.

The woman smiled curiously, but remained where she was. She did not move until he reached the side of her rig and extended his hand.

"Thank you," she said as she cautiously stepped over the side.

Once she was on solid ground, Ward let go of her hand and smiled winningly. "You're entirely welcome," he said easily.

The woman's head tipped to one side as she looked up at him. A familiar movement somehow . . . And then he remembered; Emma Parker had executed a similar motion just a short time ago in the cool darkness of the barn.

"I'm Katie Franklin. Who are you?" she asked directly.

"My name is—"

The screen door banged loudly and Timmy called, "Mama! Mama!" as he made his way hurriedly, awkwardly on his short legs, down the steps. The boy ran to the young woman and threw his arms around her legs.

"Hello, sweetheart," she said happily.

Ward watched, smiling and confused. He had thought . . .

Emma Parker stepped out onto the porch and waited, drying her hands on an apron. The mother and child were still talking and giggling.

After a moment Katie faced the stranger with her son balanced on her hip. "I'm sorry. We've been separated for a few days," she explained. "You were about to tell me your name."

"Ward Hamilton," he said, moving closer. "I, uh, thought the boy belonged to Mrs. Parker."

Katie laughed lightly. "He does, after a fashion. Timmy is Emma's grandson."

He stopped in his tracks. "What?" His eyes darted to the woman on the porch before he frowned at Katie, who was enjoying a good laugh.

"What a wonderful reaction!" she said.

Now Ward felt truly foolish. "Well, she looks . . ."

"Terrific," Katie supplied. "And young enough to still have babies of her own," she added without hesitation. "I continually tell Mother that, but now that she's a grandmother, she has this idea that she's become quite antiquated."

The woman was forthright, he had to give her that. As a matter of fact, he liked her *because* of that. " 'Antiquated' is not a term anyone could apply to Mrs. Parker," he said.

Katie laughed again. "It appears we might have some opinions in common, Mr. Hamilton," she said slyly.

He watched her walk up the porch steps, view his plate and

then buss her mother's cheek. The two women and the boy disappeared from view and Ward stood staring, dazedly, in their wake.

"Who is he?" Katie asked as she lowered Timmy to his feet.

Emma reached for a cup and poured her daughter some coffee. "He took shelter from the storm last night. We found him in the barn this morning."

Katie eased herself onto a chair, smiling as her mother joined her at the table. "He's exceptionally good-looking, Mother."

"He's a wanderer, Katie. I don't think he's eaten in days. He probably doesn't have a penny."

Katie almost choked on her coffee. "Mother, he may be trail worn but his clothes are quality. And those dusty boots are new and expensive. I'm surprised you didn't notice."

"I'm surprised that you did," Emma countered. "How was your trip?"

"I was homesick," Katie said bluntly. "And don't try to change the subject."

"There is no *subject*, Katie," Emma said firmly.

"You've left a guest standing in the yard, Emma. That's not like you."

"He's been fed," she said, taking shelter behind a cool manner. Emma knew from experience not to signify the slightest curiosity about a member of the opposite sex; Katie would latch onto the possibility of a romance and run with it. "I should imagine he is now saddling his horse."

Katie got to her feet and walked toward the screen door. Ward Hamilton was tending to *her* animal. She stepped outside, retrieved his empty plate and cup, and said, "Would you like more coffee, Mr. Hamilton?"

Ward had led the little mare close to the hitching rail and was snapping a lead onto the bit ring. He looked up and nodded. "Thank you."

Emma glanced out the window, surprised that she was not thoroughly vexed with her daughter. Katie always had been a schemer. When Katie returned to the kitchen, Emma displayed an appropriate amount of disapproval. "I'm not interested," she said firmly.

Katie grinned over her shoulder as she returned the coffee-pot to the back of the stove. "Yes, you are. You wouldn't have given him a meal otherwise."

"Katie." Emma sighed. "Don't start with those dreams of yours again."

"I'm not, Mother. I'm just curious about him. By his accent he's from the east and—"

"New York," Emma supplied. "That's all we need to know about him."

"That might be all *you* need to know," her daughter returned.

Emma sighed as she watched Timmy follow his mother outside.

Katie joined Ward and sat on the top step, handing him his cup as Timmy plopped down between them.

Ward grinned at the child. "Handsome boy," he said.

Katie smiled and caressed the back of her son's head. "Thank you."

"When is his brother expected?"

Katie smoothed her dress over her swollen belly. "Late September, I should think." She stared at him. "Do you think it's a boy?"

Ward threw back his head and laughed. "I have no idea about such things. Perhaps I should have phrased the question differently."

"Do you have children, Mr. Hamilton?"

"The name is Ward and the answer is no," he said flatly. His eyes moved away from her then, and his smile disappeared as he gazed around the yard. "This is a pretty place your parents have here, Mrs. Franklin."

"The name is Katie," she said wryly, "and the place belongs to Emma. She bought out here after Daddy died several years ago."

Ward looked at her again. "You call her *Emma*?"

"That's her name."

He nodded and shrugged; somehow it seemed disrespectful.

But then, Emma appeared more like Katie's sister than her mother. Perhaps that was the reason. "What did you mean by 'out here'?"

"Out from town," she explained. "It was quite a surprise that Emma would move here, really. But I suppose she didn't want to rumble around alone in the big house in Zanesville."

Ward seemed suddenly alert. "I was headed for Zanesville when the storm broke last night. I take it I'm not far from the town?"

Katie's head tipped toward the north. "Just over the rise and around the bend," she said. "About thirty minutes' ride."

"Is that where you live?" he asked quietly. "In town?"

"On the edge of town, yes. My husband, David, and his brother, John, own a general store in town. David and I have been over to Columbus to purchase stock for the store the past two days."

Ward's gaze dropped to the boy, who had slipped away and was creeping up on the harried rooster. "And the lad stayed with his grandmother," he said thoughtfully. Then he was smiling at Katie. "Perhaps I could escort you back when you're ready to go," he said. "I've purchased the Jessup place. Do you know it?"

Katie was stunned and looked it. "The Jessup place? We're about to become neighbors, Ward Hamilton!" She laughed.

TWO

Katie proved to be a good neighbor to the new arrival over the following weeks. She didn't insist, but she made it clear that a hot meal was his anytime Ward had a mind to join them for supper. He gladly took her up on her offer a time or two.

Ward had landed in Zanesville, Ohio, two weeks before his belongings arrived from the east. Consequently, his living conditions were slightly rustic. He purchased a number of kitchen items from David Franklin's store and, with Katie's help, eventually had that room functional. Now, if she could only teach him to cook. He tried, but dinner with the Franklins was definitely more palatable than his own efforts and certainly less lonely.

His first task was to make himself a bed. A large bed, long enough that his feet would not hang over the end.

The huge shed at the rear of his property was perfect for his purposes; just as his agent had described. It was there he felt most at home, most content. And his workshop was in operation within two days of his arrival.

"David told me you purchased a number of tools," Katie said.

He looked up from his work and smiled. She was standing in the wide, open doorway and Timmy was clinging to her hand. "Hello. Come in."

She stepped inside, glancing at a variety of wood stacked neatly off to the side. He certainly had a large supply. "Perhaps David and John should have added lumber to their inventory," she teased. "We could be rich!"

He had spent a good deal of money about town in a very

115

short time. He didn't doubt that she knew that. It was, after all, a small town.

"We've come to invite you for Sunday supper," she said.

Ward picked up a rag from the workbench and wiped sawdust from his hands. "That's very kind. Thank you."

Timmy wandered a few steps away, squatted, and picked up a wood shaving to examine.

"You don't look like the type of man who would build furniture," she said as she examined the piece on which he had been working.

Ward smiled crookedly. "What type of man do I look like?" he asked quietly.

Katie turned her attention back to him. "Actually, you look more like a banker. Something along that line."

He laughed shortly, although what she had said wasn't particularly funny. "*Actually*, I used to work at 'something along that line'."

"Really?"

He nodded his head, twisted at the waist, and threw the rag onto the cluttered bench. "I tried my hand at a number of things." He had owned several successful businesses outright and had sold them all.

"Carpentry was obviously one of them," she said, examining the quality of his work.

"It was a hobby," he explained. "One I had little time to enjoy until now."

"Until now?" she questioned.

"Let's just say I've changed my life to accommodate new interests."

"All right," she said lightly. "We can say that."

He grinned. He liked her. She seemed like his daughter somehow. He liked her a lot.

"You're also welcome to join us if you're planning on attending church," she said.

Church? He hadn't thought about church in years. Perhaps now was the time. Perhaps returning to basics included returning to religion. "I think I would like to join you," he said.

"Good. If the weather is fine, we like to walk. I'll send

Timmy over to fetch you when we're ready to leave."

That was fine. That was good. And the day turned out to be even better than he had expected, because Emma Parker joined them.

Clearly, she had not been told that Ward was to be part of the family Sunday, however, and he felt a little bad for that. Emma turned instantly skittish.

He stepped up beside her as the others walked on the side of the road in front of them. "I'm sorry," he said.

Emma looked at him askance. "Sorry about what, Mr. Hamilton?" He was garbed in black, a complete suit of well-tailored clothes, and he looked as if he could give a crown prince a run for his money.

"Ward," he said. "You hadn't expected me to be a part of your day."

Emma's attention seemed focused on Timmy as he grasped his parents' hands and was swung off his feet between them. "I was simply surprised. Katie neglected to mention that you would be joining us. No need to feel sorry." That sounded cold, even to her own ears and, in spite of the baffling girllike jitters and apprehension that seemed to accost her whenever he was around, she tried to soften her manner. "It's very nice to see you again," she added graciously.

They walked on in silence for several moments, she with her hands straight down at her sides, he with his clasped behind his back.

"I just cannot get over the fact that Katie is your daughter," he said after a time.

Emma's head turned toward him. "What's so unusual about that?"

He shook his head. "Not *unusual*. That isn't what I meant. You just seem so . . . well . . . you must have practically birthed her from your own cradle."

Emma laughed, a bit shocked by his choice of phrase. "I shall take that as a compliment."

"It was meant as one, I assure you." A moment later he was laughing at his own ineptitude. "It's been many, many years since I've tried to flatter a pretty woman," he murmured.

"Obviously, I've lost my touch."

Emma's complexion pinkened as she studied the backs of her family. "You haven't done so badly, Mr. Hamilton. I assure *you*."

He smiled at her then, examining her youthful beauty. He determined there and then, however, if he ever got to know her well, he would advise her against wearing gray; the color was too matronly and somber for her.

When they had all settled quietly in the Franklin pew and had bowed their heads for the first prayer, Emma Parker opened her eyes slightly and stared at the strong, muscular thigh beside her. There was something about him that made her afraid, and yet there was something that drew her to him also. He was a virile man, she told herself as her thoughts strayed from the droning tones of the minister. He was in his early forties, she suspected, but he had the firm, fit body of a much younger man. Phillip had never been virile. Phillip had always been old. At least to her. She decided that was it; she had never received the attentions of a young man, and Ward Hamilton had a way of seeming attentive. Witness the way he had lightly touched her elbow to escort her in polite fashion down the aisle of the church. And he had stood aside with her, his hand gently riding the back of her waist as they waited until the Franklins had taken up their places in the pew before Ward could urge her along the bench before him. She still felt the warmth of those fingers on her back.

She also decided she would stop these foolish mental meanderings and pay attention to the Lord's word.

And then Ward Hamilton turned his bowed head and smiled at her.

He watched Emma surreptitiously all afternoon, her comings and goings from inside the Franklin house and back to the porch. The men made themselves comfortable on chairs under the protective shade of the porch roof. A cooling breeze drifted up from the Muskingum River, a pleasant relief from the late-June heat.

David had outdone himself with his latest batch of ale, and

the women took no exception to the men sipping slowly, but steadily, of the cold brew throughout the afternoon.

Emma had prepared a light lunch of bread, cheese, and fruit to tide the men over, including little Timmy, until Katie's huge ham could be cooked to well-done. Emma was always nervous of pork in the heat of summer, but Katie was certainly well experienced in the curing of the meat.

"Boiled potatoes?" Emma asked as she selected several from the wooden bin.

Katie turned from scraping carrots and nodded. When she saw the small number of potatoes Emma had chosen to clean, however, she frowned. "Mother, one thing I've learned about Ward Hamilton in the short time I've known him—you cannot throw just one extra potato in the pot when you ask him to dinner. Ward likes his food."

Emma picked out two more large potatoes, but one comical look from Katie sent her back to the bin for more. "You can't be serious?" She laughed as she stared at the mounds of vegetables that covered the work counter.

"He seems to burn it off quickly," Katie pointed out.

"Doing what?" Emma asked.

Her daughter grinned, slanting Emma a teasing look. "Why don't you ask him?"

Emma sighed and shook her head in mock disgust.

"I'm serious, Emma," Katie said. "You talk to him. You said you need new beds for the boys' dormitory."

Emma was surprised by what Katie was apparently trying to tell her. "You mean he makes furniture?"

She nodded, slicing cleaned carrots on a cutting board. "I was over there two days ago. He's turned the big shed at the back of his property into a workshop. You should see the beautiful bed he's making for himself, Mother. I think it's going to be big enough to be a playground," she added, laughing.

"Katie!" Emma breathed.

"What?" she returned, laughing in the face of her mother's obvious disgust. "Don't be so stodgy, Emma," she scolded lightly.

"I am a *lady*," she said pointedly.

"You're a *woman*, Mother," Katie returned in a soft, quiet tone. "Or have you forgotten that?"

It was Katie who asked Ward about the beds at supper that evening.

"Single beds?" he asked, before raising his fork from his plate.

Katie nodded. "Three. For the shelter. We could come to an agreement of the price, I'm sure."

He shrugged off her comment. "What kind of *shelter* is this?"

"We get a lot of transients coming off the river," Emma explained. "Young men, usually. They're all on their way to finding a better life. Trying to prove themselves, I suppose. Most of them don't have the price of a cup of coffee let alone the price of a bed."

"And you put them up for the night?" he asked in wonder. "Where?"

"The house where Katie was born."

"And you feed hungry strangers," he added softly. He was growing more in awe of her by the moment.

"Don't recommend me for sainthood, Mr. Hamilton. The house is very large. Only a small portion of it is used to shelter the needy. The remainder is a profit-making inn. Those who can afford to pay, do. Those who can't, don't," she added.

He watched her cut a small wedge of ham, following the movement of her fork to her delicate lips. "You started and manage this . . . inn?" he asked curiously.

"That's correct. I oversee the running now, as I'm not in town all that frequently," she explained. "Others manage the place day to day on my behalf."

Wonder of wonders; she was a businesswoman and an employer. And she looked so damned fragile. He was also of the impression that Emma Parker did not *care* to come to town too frequently. Intriguing. "I'll make your beds, Emma," he said easily.

"Your estimate of the cost, Mr. Hamilton?" she asked.

"I'm certain we can come to an amicable agreement," he said evasively.

Katie sensed something happening and grinned at David.

"I like to be aware of my expenses beforehand," Emma prodded.

"Very well," he said, resting his fork on the side of his plate. "The beds will be gratis."

Emma was thoughtfully surprised; three beds were the equivalent of a great deal of time and effort. The materials were surely costly as well. She became suspicious as she stared across the table at him and weighed his offer. Such a costly gift would leave her indebted to him.

He knew that she understood.

"What is it you want, Mr. Hamilton?"

"I want you to call me Ward," he said quietly.

Katie moved her hand beneath the table and squeezed her husband's thigh. She suspected that Emma and Ward had forgotten there was anyone else in the room. The entire scene was wonderful!

Emma remained suspicious.

"And I thought you might indulge me in a small favor," Ward added.

This was it. She knew something else had been on his mind. "A small favor?"

"Well"—he grinned—"from my perspective, it's an enormous favor. But I'm hoping not so enormous that you will turn me down."

"Speak your mind, *Ward*," she said.

He laughed. "I was hoping you would agree to attend the Fourth of July celebrations with me."

That didn't seem like such a terrible sacrifice.

Refusing to look at her daughter, Emma agreed.

An hour later she was lamenting her decision. "I don't know what got into me," she said. "I can't go anywhere with Ward Hamilton."

Katie placed another clean dish to drain. "Why ever not?"

"I'm a *grandmother*, darling," Emma wailed.

Katie dropped a soapy cloth into the pan of water and turned on her mother. "What a ridiculous thing to say! You're a young woman, Emma. A *beautiful* young woman. Of course you're going with him."

"I am not."

"Then have the beds made by someone else," Katie said in frustration. "You can afford to pay."

Suddenly weary, Emma walked to the nearest chair and plopped down on it—an action so lacking in grace, Katie was stunned.

"This has nothing to do with beds," Emma sighed.

It might have more to do with *beds* than her mother could imagine at this point in time. Katie smiled at the thought. "I know," she said gently. She walked across the room and joined her mother at the table, sitting on the near chair. "You're attracted to him, aren't you, Mother?" she asked kindly.

"Now who's ridiculous?" she asked scornfully.

"You *are*."

Emma was silent for a long time, refusing to look at Katie. Finally, head bowed, she said softly, "There's just something about him."

"I have the feeling he's someone special," Katie said warmly. "I've watched him with you, Emma. I think you owe it to yourself to learn more about him."

She did look up then. "I had twenty good years with your father. I can't just pretend those years didn't happen."

"I notice you said 'good'. You didn't say 'wonderful'."

"Of course they were wonderful," Emma said forcefully.

Katie went to the stove and poured two cups of coffee. "Daddy has been gone for more than two years, Mother," she said as she placed the cups on the table and returned to her seat. "I don't believe he would expect you to live a life of loneliness."

That comment just proves you didn't know your father well, Emma thought. But then Katie surprised her.

"Or would he?"

Emma's startled amber gaze met Katie's earnest expression.

The reflection in the younger woman's eyes mirrored a thousand thoughts.

"You deserve to be happy, Emma," Katie said.

"I have everything I need. Your father left me well—"

"Material things and wealth," Katie ridiculed. "Mother, tell me something. When was the last time my father kissed you before he died?"

Emma started to leave the table, but Katie reached out and clamped onto her hand, keeping her there.

"I loved him," she added quietly. "He was a good father. But I don't believe he was a good husband."

"Don't talk of your father this way," Emma beseeched.

"I'm not being disrespectful. I know he gave you a good life. You were young and he gave you all you didn't have. But, Mother, I don't remember him ever reaching out to touch you with affection. I don't remember him ever kissing you. Not so much as a friendly peck in greeting. I know he loved us, but he wasn't demonstrative. I don't believe we women are equipped to live that way. We give affection and caring and love and we need that in return. Even just a little. I know I couldn't stand it if David didn't show signs of warmth toward me."

Emma was moved by her daughter's impassioned speech, but she steeled herself against it. "I'm beyond that now, darling. And we don't miss what we've never had."

"What a sad statement that is," Katie murmured. "*Both* those statements are very, very sad, Emma."

Emma rose, touched her daughter's cheek affectionately, smiling. "Don't feel sad, Katie. I'm not suffering. Believe me."

Katie watched her beautiful, gracious mother glide across the room toward the door. "Mother, why did you never have more children after you birthed me?"

The question halted Emma before she disappeared beyond the door. It was a question she could not bear to answer.

And it was an old question. One that never received a reply. "You give shelter to the young!" Katie called. "As if you could be mother to them all. Why?"

She looked briefly at her beautiful daughter, her only child. "Katie," she said softly, "Ward Hamilton makes me afraid."

Katie Franklin believed Emma Parker was more afraid of *herself*!

THREE

The entire town of Zanesville was a-flurry this Fourth of July 1878. Actually, had Ward but known it, any celebration could bring the townsfolk eagerly together. They had much to celebrate. The Civil War had touched them little, and their financial growth was strong. Ohio was generally a very prosperous state, and the people of Zanesville enjoyed a number of the riches.

"It's a fine day for a party," Ward said as he guided the single horse-drawn rig through the crowded streets.

Emma sat quietly beside him.

Ward ducked his head, attempting to gauge her feelings. "Are you sorry you joined me?" he asked softly, in that deep, nerve-shattering voice of his.

Emma's eyes darted to his and looked away. "Of course not."

"Katie and David and Timmy will be joining us for supper, you know. Will that improve your spirits any?" he teased.

Emma dared to look up at him apologetically. "I'm sorry. I'm not very comfortable."

"I can see that," he said bluntly, but not unkindly. "Why?"

"I'm not entirely certain," she told him. She had a number of thoughts on the matter, but none she could confess to him. He was somehow overwhelming and she had never encountered the things she felt when she was around him. She suspected her nervous stomach would not allow her to enjoy the picnic supper, however.

"Am I the first man you've stepped out with since your husband's passing?"

Emma stiffened her spine, determined not to give him too

125

much to read into her response. The bare truth was, she had *never* stepped out with a man. This was a whole new world to her and she wasn't quite certain what to expect. Emma had not "stepped out" with Phillip before their marriage. There had been no courtship. "Yes," she said firmly.

He nodded, looking at passersby, smiling and tipping his hat in greeting as they moved across town.

She noticed that many of the women seemed to *reach*, in a manner of speaking, to capture his attention.

After several long moments of silence between them, he asked, "How old were you when you married him, Emma?"

"That's a very personal question," she said quietly.

"Yes, it is," he returned, keeping his eyes straight ahead.

"Sixteen," she said after a moment. She heard him draw in a deep, disapproving breath.

Katie had hinted to him that her father had been much, much older. "Why? Why would you marry at such an age?"

She laughed sorrowfully and stared off toward the horizon. "My parents gave me to Phillip and he brought me here from England. It isn't such a terrible thing as you might think," she added defensively. "He took me out of poverty and gave me everything. Including my beloved Katie."

He caught the hint of pain that underlay her words and became alert, staring at her even though she refused to look his way. "He must have loved you very much," he said, although it was more a question than a statement; he was fishing.

"You are entirely too personal," she scolded ineffectively.

"Did he?"

"Yes," she said succinctly.

He knew that she was lying.

Emma and Katie had outdone themselves with the celebration feast. They shared their collective offerings of chicken, ham, salads, bread, cheese, and pie. Apple pie that Emma had made for the occasion.

Ward had brought along two bottles of fine wine and he poured the four adults an ample sampling as Timmy wandered around on his short legs and sampled food from everyone's plate; no one was spared.

"What would you like, sport?" Ward asked as Timmy squatted, surveying the contents of the stranger's plate where it rested on the man's lap. Ward picked up a piece of cheese and broke off a small bit. "How about this?" he asked.

Timmy tipped his head forward and Ward pressed the cheese between the child's lips.

Emma laughed when he quickly drew back sopping fingers. "He gets a little overzealous when it comes to food."

Reaching for a linen napkin, Ward smiled. "Nothing wrong with his appetite," he said wryly.

Emma laughed again. The wine had done much to settle her jangled nerves and her riotous stomach. And she suspected Ward's warm and witty personality might have gone a long way toward making her feel more comfortable. He treated her as if she were a queen. Not as royalty, that would have been false. More like an *earthy* regal. No matter that she couldn't put words to it, she liked his own distinctive brand of attention. He made her feel special.

Several glasses of wine had passed their lips, in addition to a good quantity of food, before dessert was served.

Apple pie that had Ward watering at the mouth and groaning unhappily because he couldn't eat more. "That was, by far, the best pie I have ever eaten," he said as he flopped back on his elbows and stretched out his long legs.

Katie was in much the same position except she had the benefit of David's lap for a pillow. "Mother is the best cook in the county!" she said expansively.

David grinned across the devastated remains of their meal. "I think we're going to have a drunken baby," he said lightly to Ward.

Katie could not take offense. She'd had less than a glass of wine and no one could fault her. She was merely content next to her husband, and Timmy had curled up against her with his head in the crook of her arm.

The day was drawing, softly, to a close.

Suddenly, energetically, Ward got to his feet and reached

a hand down to Emma. "Will you walk with me?" he asked softly.

"Do you guarantee I will feel better, walking off this supper?" she said lightly.

He nodded and smiled, relieved that she had relaxed over the course of the afternoon. "Guaranteed," he said.

She reached up, took his hand, and was pulled easily to her feet.

Once she was standing, Ward gently tucked her slender hand into the crook of his arm.

Katie grinned happily at them as they passed her by.

"We'll be back," Ward said with a smile for her.

"You'd better," Katie informed him, and broke into a giggle that she tried to hide against David's shirtfront.

"She's tipsy," Emma said worriedly.

"She's happy," Ward returned. "Don't worry."

"How can I not worry?" she questioned seriously. "She's my only child."

"Why is that?"

Emma blinked stupidly. "Pardon?"

Or not so stupidly, since he was certain she was trying to deflect the conversation. "Why is it you have only one child, Emma? You appear to be a warm, caring woman who should have many."

"It isn't something I can discuss," was all she would say.

He sensed her pain and assumed that something had gone physically wrong either during or after Katie's birth. He had blundered royally into this one; perhaps the woman could not have any children after Katie. "I'm sorry," he said softly.

Emma merely shook her head.

The silence became awkward as they strolled together through the diminishing daylight. He had ruined the easy camaraderie between them and Ward was silently cursing. He understood now, however, that questions about *her* past were taboo. "I'm forty-three," he said at last.

Emma's head rotated in his direction and she frowned. "I beg your pardon?"

"Forty-three and young at heart," he teased.

She laughed, startled by his confession. "I don't recall asking," she said.

"You were wondering."

"I was not," she returned defensively.

"Well, I feel better for having told you," he said. "I didn't want you thinking that I'm truly an *old* man."

She laughed again. "Hardly! Why, you're only five . . ."

Now he laughed, throwing back his head before bending over her hand and bringing it to his lips. "I'm sorry. I took advantage at the end of a long day."

"And after two glasses of wine," she said with feigned distress. In fact, she never worried about her age; she felt young most of the time; except when she remembered she was a *grandmother*. But, she realized, it didn't matter to her that he knew she was thirty-eight.

He stopped walking on the edge of the clearing and turned to face her, staring into her lovely, oval, amber eyes. "Thirty-eight," he murmured. "And widowed for how many years?"

"The better part of three," she said.

"Too young."

"It happens to many—"

"He didn't love you well, I think," he said, interrupting her.

"You can't know."

"I can, Emma," he said earnestly, softly. "Anyone who cares to look closely will know."

She tried to turn from him, to walk away. He pulled her back.

"I have this nagging feeling that we should have met long, long ago," he said.

Emma frowned up at him. "How much wine did you imbibe?"

He ignored her question as he looked at her lovely face. "Before your marriage. Certainly before mine."

"You neglected to mention that you were married," she said stiffly.

"I'm not. Now." He raised his hand, intending to touch her shining, fair hair, but Emma started and pulled her head back. "I just wanted to touch. It looks so soft," he said quietly. "And pretty."

She stood stone still, indecision reflected in her features as she looked up at him.

"I would never touch you to cause you harm," he said quietly as his fingers moved slowly toward her temple.

The deep reverberations of his voice caused a shiver to ripple through her body.

Ward detected her reaction and smiled as he lightly stroked her hair. "I imagine this is lovely when it's free," he said.

It had taken her the better part of a half hour to perfect the tight coil. "Don't you dare," she muttered.

He laughed, knowing her threat was justified. This was neither the time nor the place. His hand fell away as he resolved to make a time and a place. Soon. "Come along," he said, tucking her hand in the crook of his elbow again. "I'd best take you back."

They strolled past groups of happy people, some of whom were in the process of packing up to return home as the day's festivities were nearing a close. Sleepy children rode in adult arms, small heads bobbing against adult shoulders. The carriages and buckboards had been grouped at the edge of the clearing, and throngs of the weary, but content, made their way to their own conveyance.

A man walked ahead of them, carrying a small girl whose head rested on his wide shoulder. The child's eyes continually drifted closed, then she would fight her weariness and they would open again. At least partially. Both Ward and Emma were caught by the beauty of the girl.

"Pretty little thing," Ward said.

Emma raised her hand and waved to the girl. The girl waved back halfheartedly and Emma laughed. "She's very sleepy."

Ward looked down and silently studied his companion as Emma continued to smile at the child ahead of them. He was right in his thoughts, he knew it. She was a woman who should have birthed several children. But she hadn't, and the *why* of it puzzled him.

Suddenly he was caught openly staring when she looked up at him.

"Do you have children?" she asked.

He shook his head. "Regrettably, no."

There was genuine disappointment in his voice as he spoke, and Emma could feel his sorrow. "I'm sorry."

He looked off to the distant horizon. The sun was heading for bed. "My wife had a child," he said tightly. "A boy. He's not mine, however."

Emma did not want to think what she was thinking, but his pain could leave her with little else to believe. "Oh, my God," she breathed.

His head bobbed a time or two. "There was fault on both sides, Emma," he explained. "She was lonely and I was working." He shook his head in self-derision. "I was too busy to even suspect that she was having an affair." He heard her scandalized intake of breath and smiled sadly. "Yes, I know it's shocking," he said flatly.

"Do you still love her?" she dared to ask, wondering how deep his suffering must be.

"I think we both fell out of love a lot of years ago," he said. "We'd become caught in the *routine* of our relationship, you see. I loved my work and she loved what I could give her. The one thing I neglected to provide, I suppose, was affection. Amazing how clear everything becomes after the fact, isn't it?"

"That doesn't excuse her behavior," Emma said sternly.

He looked down at her, stopping to face her. "Doesn't it?"

She shook her head. "No. She was your wife."

"Every living creature needs love and affection, Emma," he said.

"There is also honor and commitment," she pointed out.

In his eyes she saw puzzlement, and his dark brows arched high on his forehead, questioning.

"You're speaking from experience, aren't you?" he asked.

She refused to answer and damned herself with her silence.

"I asked you earlier today if your husband had loved you very much," he said softly. "You lied," he added bluntly.

Emma removed her hand from his arm and turned to walk away.

Ward's hand snaked out and he caught her upper arm, gently pulling her back to face him. "You lied," he said again with conviction.

"I didn't," she said firmly. "He loved me in his way."

He let her go then, frowning as he slowly followed in her wake. He was puzzled by her and he wanted to know more. But his was not idle curiosity. Ward Hamilton was also emotionally moved by this woman, and he was a little surprised by that. It had been a lot of years since a woman had captured more than a fleeting interest from him. An evening of companionship, a night of passion, these were things in which he had occasionally indulged. No ties, no bonds, no promises. And Julia hadn't wanted anything to do with him during the final two years of their dying marriage. He had been at the point where her rejection hadn't even hurt anymore. He suspected, strongly, that a relationship with Emma Parker would be very different from any he had heretofore experienced.

There were two things Ward knew he wanted. The first was to see Emma again, and the second was to determine whether she suffered as much internal turmoil as he when they were together.

Emma's arm burned where he had touched her and her stomach had taken flight again. She lamented the fact that she could not seem to control her emotions, this warring of wanting to be with him and this fear that she should not.

She remembered Katie's headlong plummet into trauma and torture when the poor girl had fallen in love with David. From Emma's perspective, and in her recollections, her daughter had suffered pure, unadulterated hell combined with uncontrollable bliss. Love was a wayward thing, a fickle thing. She had watched Katie suffer through the early stages of the disease, and Emma knew she herself was experiencing some of the symptoms. And she chided herself for that absolutely asinine thought. She barely knew Ward Hamilton. And yet he was having a potent influence on her emotions. Something told her . . . some inner voice, some perverse sense told her he might have the same effect on her very existence.

FOUR

Emma avoided town for the next several days. Oh, she knew in her heart she was avoiding the possibility of meeting up with Ward. It was all too confusing and she felt a little silly, actually. Her mind would drift off in unheard of directions at times. Ever since that Fourth of July. Spending the entire day with him had been pleasant, to say the least. He was a gentleman and he made her feel like a woman. She confessed to herself that she had not felt that way in a very long time. Since Phillip's death, Emma had moved through the days, functioning but not really feeling too much. Other than when she was with Katie and Timmy and David. They made her feel warm. And she knew she was loved by them. But it was a different sort of love from what she thought a woman might experience with a man like Ward Hamilton.

Phillip's love had been constant and she had always felt secure, but his kind of love had been distant. There had been no *passion* in him. Emma had not thought that a vast fault in Phillip; it was more a minor shortcoming. Something he lacked and something she had learned to live with over the years. In retrospect, she realized she might have thought differently.

She had satisfied her need to be *needed* with Katie, back then. And with any cause that would help her retain her image of herself as a female, a role she had carefully conceived over the years. But while she had felt fulfilled as a female, Emma had never felt fulfilled as a woman. Ward Hamilton seemed to make her want to know what that *role* would be like, but, strangely, she feared finding out at this stage of her life. She was thirty-eight years of age and yet she felt like a young,

133

inexperienced girl whenever she thought of him. She should
know all there was to know about being a woman. And the
fact that she didn't made her feel foolish and inept.

"Where have you been?" Katie asked as she placed a second cup of coffee beside her mother's hand. They were in
Katie's kitchen and had just finished lunch.

Emma came back to reality with a start. "I'm here," she
said with a guilty smile.

"You were miles away," her daughter commented as she
eased her burdened body onto a wooden chair. "Thinking
about Ward?" she teased.

Emma shot her a disgusted, mocking frown. "Don't be
silly."

"What's so silly?" Katie asked reasonably. "I think he's
a lovely man. I stress the word 'man'," she added with an
impish wink.

"Katie, let's change the subject, shall we?" Emma suggested wearily.

Katie shook her head. "I don't think so, Mother. I think we
should talk."

Emma laughed briefly over her daughter's tone. "Who's the
parent here?"

"Over this particular subject, the subject of your sharing
in a relationship, I sometimes think I am," Katie told her
seriously.

"Katie, I will never have another relationship like the one
I shared with your father," Emma said patiently.

"I sincerely hope you don't have another relationship like
that, Emma," Katie said softly, and quickly held up a hand to
silence the protest she knew would follow. "I know. We've
had this conversation before. Daddy was good to us and I
agree. But I also want to see you happy." Katie's throat
suddenly constricted with emotion, causing her to hesitate.
"You deserve so much and you ask for so little," she said
brokenly. "You were always *doing* for him and for me and
you never asked for anything in return."

Emma was shocked to see that tears were actually gathering
in her daughter's eyes. "Darling . . ."

"Please let me finish," Katie said, drawing on firm determination. "I don't know that Ward Hamilton is the man who can give you all that you deserve, but I suspect he could be if you let him. I would love to see you wildly in love, Emma. It would be wonderful to see you laughing and happy and . . . passionate. I don't think Daddy could do that for you. Or with you. I don't ever recall seeing any hint of passion between you two and that makes me very sad. It makes me think you have missed a great deal."

"I don't really appreciate your pity," Emma said defensively.

Katie recognized the remark for what it was; a cover-up to her true feelings. "You don't have to marry the man, you know. Just share some pleasant times with him, get to know each other a little. You may find you enjoy his attentions, Mother," she said firmly. "And there is no reason to feel shame over enjoying a man's attentions. That's a rule according to Katie," she added with a warm smile.

"Butterfly dreams," Emma muttered, looking away. "Airy, misty fantasies."

"They are not *dreams*, Mother. I think he has some feelings toward you," Katie threw in quietly. It was a much needed enticement. "And I think you have feelings toward him."

Emma thought about everything Katie had said. She'd had many of the same thoughts during recent days. "What makes you think he has 'feelings' toward me?" she asked after a long silence.

Katie wanted to laugh for joy, convinced she had got Emma to thinking. But she didn't laugh. She reached out and touched her mother's hand. "Oh, Emma, I've seen it in him. I see the way he looks at you. If you'd let yourself go, you would see it, too."

Emma shook her head and smiled with chagrin. "I have to admit I like being with him."

"There you go!" Katie said triumphantly.

"Now I'll never be able to face him," she added ruefully.

"Well, you'd best screw up your courage, Emma," Katie said dryly. "Ward asked me to have you come to his house the next time you were in town. The new beds are ready and he wants to arrange with you for the delivery."

Emma felt suddenly panic stricken and looked it. "Katie, you could have made that arrangement."

"Not me," she said quickly. "The inn is your territory."

Emma's eyes narrowed suspiciously. "You're a devious daughter."

Katie merely laughed.

There was a path being worn in the grass between the Franklin and the Hamilton homes and the cedar hedge was showing a distinctive archway where branches had been cut away to allow the residents of each home to take a shortcut to visit their neighbor. Katie had pointed out to Emma that she needn't walk down the length of the hedge to get to Ward's two-story house.

"I had no idea you and David saw so much of him," Emma had commented.

"I've gotten in the habit of throwing several extra potatoes in the pot," Katie replied lightly. "The man can't cook, Emma. I've seen his efforts."

"You're feeding him regularly?" Emma thought that an imposition; Katie was huge with this baby and tired easily.

"I don't mind," she said. "He's convinced David that they should do the cleaning up after suppers." She laughed. "I sit back and supervise their efforts. And Ward buys food, generously, and just delivers it here."

Emma frowned. "And you don't object?"

"I've never had it so good," Katie said happily. "And David looks really cute in an apron," she added gaily.

Emma, too, had laughed.

She stooped down and moved cautiously through the hole in the hedge while she mentally assessed the conversations she and Katie had shared during the afternoon.

It was strange how one man could come to town and so quickly affect their lives. But, clearly, Ward Hamilton was doing just that. He had won David's and Katie's friendship with no effort at all. And he was enough of an influence in her life to cause Emma to doubt the degree of contentment she felt with her current existence.

As she walked around the side of his house, following the steady sound of a hammer meeting wood, Emma realized that her life had been only an *existence* for many years. She had not been living, not really. She had been going through the motions. Perhaps a little companionship was needed and if she happened to find some fun along the way, all the better! Where was it written that a grandmother should not have fun? But, being truthful with herself at last, Emma knew she wanted . . . needed . . . something far warmer than mere companionship. And Ward Hamilton seemed to be the catalyst driving her toward this need.

The double doors to his workshop had been thrown open and Ward was working at a sawhorse in front of the shed. He had removed his shirt against the heat of the day, giving her pause. She stopped, staring across the distance that separated them, and watched the sun turn the sweat on his shoulders and arms into glistening beads that reminded her of tiny, sprinkled diamond chips.

He sensed her presence, of course, and she started walking toward him again the moment he looked up.

Ward smiled, setting his tools aside before reaching for a rag to wipe his damp skin. "Hello, Emma," he said as she approached.

"Hello," she returned.

"It's hot," he added as he ran the cloth across the front of his chest.

Emma laughed, not so much because his comment was a definite understatement as because the sight of his broad, hair-covered chest was unsettling, and laughter masked her unease.

Ward noticed that her eyes followed the movement of his hand and was surprised to realize that she was uncomfortable with the sight of his partial nakedness. The woman had been married, for heaven sake! "I'm sorry," he said, in response to her distress. "Let me just get my shirt."

Emma shook her head. "That's not necessary. Really." She was embarrassed, *confounded* actually. But only because she could not seem to take her eyes off him. "Katie gave me your message. That's why I'm here," she said, and was pleased that her voice grew stronger and increasingly steady as she spoke. "I understand you've completed the beds?"

He nodded his head. "I'll assemble them once I move everything to the inn. You just tell me when, Emma."

Emma looked up at the sky, trying to judge the time. "I suppose it's a bit late in the day," she said. She looked at him and smiled. "You'll need a few hours to work there, I assume?"

"Three or four hours, at least."

"Tomorrow morning at eight?" she suggested. "I'll meet you there." Oh but that was businesslike! Too *much* like business. "On second thought, I'll come here. We can go to the inn together."

Ward grinned at her change in strategy; not that he was reluctant to go anywhere with her. He was just puzzled. Somehow she seemed different today—an odd mixture of bashful and bold.

"That will be fine," he said easily. "I'll have my wagon loaded before eight."

Emma nodded and turned away, swirling back to face him almost as suddenly. "Will you need any help?"

It did not take Ward long to make up his mind to test the waters a little. "All I'll need is your company," he said.

She seemed pleased by that.

Blushed just like a schoolgirl.

"I'll see you tomorrow at eight, Emma," he said softly.

FIVE

The day they spent together at the inn had been more fun than any other day Emma could remember. She had never known a man who could be as open and witty as Ward. They did not waste one moment of the day talking about things that were not happy or funny. Past lives were forgotten for just those few hours.

He taught her the names of the tools he used and the uses for each. Then he told her she could be a carpenter's assistant if she ever needed a career to fall back on. She liked that about him; he could say silly things with a straight face and get away with it.

"I feel as if I've found a new friend," she'd said with a shy smile at the end of the day.

"You have, Emma," he'd told her. "You have."

And so she asked him to Sunday supper at her country home.

And, daringly, she told Katie and David they were not invited.

Emma had suggested that he arrive any time he chose. He could rock away the afternoon in the shade of the porch, if that was what he wanted to do. Ward thought that might be a good start to the day. He arrived at one.

"Hello!" she called from the porch.

Ward waved in greeting. "I'll stable my horse, if that's all right?"

Emma nodded and disappeared back inside the house.

She pivoted nervously in a few circles in the center of the kitchen, trying to decide what she should do first. "Get the beer," she whispered, and darted toward the trapdoor to the cellar. "The man will be thirsty."

Moments later the screen door opened and he was standing there, occupying a good portion of her kitchen!

"I'm glad you came early," she said hurriedly. "I stole some beer from David for you."

He laughed. "You *stole* it?" He reached out and took the corked bottle she offered.

"I'll get you a glass," she said, turning away.

Ward took hold of her wrist and pulled her back. "Emma? Relax."

She looked up at him and frowned. "I am relaxed," she said.

He shook his head and set the bottle on the round table. When he turned back to her, the look in his eyes was understanding and intense. "I think I'm going to do what I've been wanting to do for weeks," he said.

Emma smiled nervously as he moved closer. "What might that be?" she asked anxiously.

"I'm going to kiss you," he whispered as he wrapped his arms around her and gently pulled her close.

"I don't think this is a very good idea, Ward," she said worriedly.

"You're wrong, Emma," he murmured, lowering his head. "Wrong."

His face drew nearer and Emma blinked, her eyes almost crossing as she continued to watch. She could feel the warmth of his breath on her mouth before his smile disappeared. And then his lips touched hers ever so softly, warmly, moving across her mouth to the left and then the right in sweet caressing nibbles. But then the testing seemed to be over and Emma raised her arms to his shoulders as Ward pressed his lips firmly against hers.

His arm pulled gently against her waist, moving her close enough to his body that they could share their respective heat, bringing her breasts against his chest. She had full, high breasts and he knew the feel of those firm globes was something he should not think about. Not now. Not with their first kiss. He wanted to go slowly with her. From the day she had come to his shop and been so unsettled by seeing him without his shirt, he had suspected something was wrong. She'd been married, true. But something about her past was not right. About that marriage to Phillip, the older man.

Emma felt her breath catch in her throat as he appeared to pay some sort of homage to her. He was gentle and tender with this kiss, taking it slowly, giving her time to be aware of every sensation she had never felt before. Her breasts began to ache, much like they would a few days before her monthly, her nipples drawn into tight buds, and she found herself pressing against his chest in the hope that he could somehow relieve the discomfort she was experiencing.

Ward raised his head, knowing that much more of this would lead to other things. He smiled at her and gently cupped the side of her face. "I believe we have much to think about, Emma," he said softly. "Much to talk about and share. I want to get to know you better. Will you agree?"

Still dazed by the way he had made her feel, Emma nodded her head slowly, her expression sweetly inane.

He laughed lightly. "It isn't that dire, sweetheart. Don't frown so."

She realized then that he must be aware of the tautness of her nipples and drew back, pressing her arms over her breasts for protection. "I didn't mean to frown," she said quietly as she looked into those dark brown eyes of his; he had the longest, most beautiful eyelashes she had ever seen on a man.

He knew her breasts were hurting her, knew also that he could provide her some relief. But the fact that she was obviously so responsive to him made him keep his distance. "Let's take our drinks outside," he said. "I want to talk with you."

At his encouragement, Emma added a second beer to the tray she prepared and then followed him to the west end of the porch.

She had carefully arranged comfortable woven rocking chairs in the best place to catch a summer breeze and had set a small table between the two.

Ward quickly destroyed all of that.

He moved the table forward and placed the two chairs closer together before he turned to relieve her of the tray. "Sit," he said softly. "I'll pour." He did just that and left the two glasses filled with cool brew on the table.

He sat beside her, resting an ankle on his opposite knee as he reached for her hand and stared off at the horizon. "It's so very peaceful here," he said.

Emma had been staring at their joined hands that rested on the arm of her chair, staring in wonder and feeling on the verge of some miraculous, forbidden discovery.

When she failed to respond, Ward turned his head to look at her and saw her staring down at their hands as if they belonged to someone else, as if no man had ever held her hand. That clinched it. "Emma, I'm only going to ask you this once and I hope you will reply," he said softly. When she raised a curious gaze to his eyes, he smiled supportively. "What you tell me will be known by only me. But I have to know."

She waited for the question, nervous but trusting that what he had just said was fact.

"I want you to tell me about your marriage to Phillip," he said firmly.

Whatever she had been expecting, it had certainly not been that. "Isn't talking about old affairs a little gauche, Ward?" she teased.

He didn't smile. "I'm not asking about an *affair*. I'm asking about your marriage and how it was for you."

Emma looked away, disengaging her hand from his before she leaned forward, taking the glasses from the table and giving one to him. "I'm not certain what you're asking," she said softly.

"I've asked you if he loved you," he said patiently, "and you said he had, 'in his own way,' or words to that effect. I've asked why you did not have children after Katie and you replied that was something you could not talk about." He stared at her profile, refusing to take his full attention from her. "I have no mean intentions, Emma. I had expected us to share a simple kiss of affection, but you responded to me in that kitchen as if you were a girl newly awakened. And yet you've been married. I simply want to understand."

"I couldn't help what happened in there," she said unhappily.

Ward reached for her hand again and squeezed gently. "Don't ever apologize for *that*," he said. "Now or in the future. I think I know how you felt. I felt the same and I'll be damned if I'll apologize," he added in a lighter tone.

"Ask me the questions," she said softly as she took in his tender smile. "I'll answer."

"All right," he said, shifting in his chair until he could see her more easily. "Katie has hinted that her father was a good deal older than you. Is that true?"

Emma nodded. She had made up her mind that she would answer his questions as truthfully and as completely as possible. "Phillip was forty-seven and I was sixteen at the time we married."

More than thirty years between them! "Why, Emma? Why would your parents give you to a man thirty years your senior? Or to any man at that tender age, for that matter?"

She could only respond with what she knew for certain. "My parents had too many children and Phillip wanted me. At least I assume he must have wanted me." Feeling unsettled by his concentrated stare, his narrowed eyes, and deepening frown, Emma used the act of drinking as a means of escape.

"That's all you know?" he asked quietly.

"Yes."

"You '*assume*' he wanted you? Didn't you feel love from him, Emma?"

With a weary sigh, she returned her glass to the table and looked out at the fields of ripening wheat. "He did love me, but Phillip was not a demonstrative man. He had difficulty showing affection. But he cared well for Katie and me. We wanted for nothing. He had concern for us and we learned to accept that as his form of love. He was a good man, Ward. There is nothing I can find fault with in him. I could have desired to be loved to distraction, I suppose, but I got over that wish once I matured."

"But you missed so much," he said softly. He looked down at the amber liquid in his glass, thoughtfully sorting through his own thoughts, choosing carefully among all the things he needed to know, wanted to know about her. He took a long drink after a time and set his glass aside before facing her again. "And what about the babies, Emma? Can you talk about that? Did something happen when you had Katie?"

Frowning in confusion, Emma said, "I don't understand."

"I mean . . . after Katie, were you unable to have more children?"

A painful, purple blush stained her face and neck. But Emma was determined to speak. If she was ever to share her secret in her lifetime, she knew it must be with this man. "It wasn't that I was unable," she said achingly. "Phillip never came to me after I birthed Katie."

Ward visibly started with shock. "What?"

Thinking he had not heard, she clarified. "He never once made love to me after Katie was born," she said unhappily.

But he had heard and understood the first time. "Oh, my God, Emma. Why?"

"I think it was because of Katie. Rather, because I labored so hard to get her here. It took more than two days, Ward, and even the doctor was amazed that I survived. Phillip apparently vowed I would never go through that again. He didn't tell me, mind you. The doctor overheard and told me years later when I cried because I thought I was no longer appealing to my husband." She smiled, ducking her head and trying to hide her mortification. "By the time Katie was two, I was confused and miserable. Not knowing what to do to get my husband back. Blaming myself for being less than desirable. Except I wasn't wise enough or experienced enough to even understand the meaning of desire. I simply knew I was unhappy and I cried constantly, it seems to me now. It was silly really, because I wasn't all that enamored of what Phillip did to me for us to get Katie."

"Oh, Emma." He sighed. The more he heard, the angrier Ward was getting. "Did he never give you a little pleasure? Release, at least?"

That baffled her, quite clearly. "Release?" she asked stupidly.

Ward leaned forward in his chair, moving closer to her, taking her hand between his own. "Pleasure. Release. In bed, sweetheart. When he made love to you, did it never feel good?"

She blushed heatedly again. "I think we're getting a little too personal," she murmured stiffly.

"Oh, Emma. He cheated you in so many ways."

Emma suddenly felt as if she had to come to Phillip's defense. "He was a good man," she said firmly.

Ward realized he had pushed too far and sought to salvage the remainder of their afternoon together. "I'm certain he was in many ways, but, Emma, you must realize that the man was ignorant of your needs. That doesn't mean he was bad. That means he was ill-fated. Unfortunately, you both suffered."

"I don't feel as if I suffered," she pointed out.

"That's because, sweet Emma, you don't know what you've missed."

Emma was beginning to feel miffed.

Ward could see he was verging on trouble. "All I'm saying, is that you've missed the wonders of loving, of being cherished and wanted and of needing in return. That something special between a man and a woman. I'm hoping I can help correct that deficiency."

Now she was confused. "But you said you didn't have a loving relationship with your own wife," she said as gently as she could.

Ward felt the bite, however. "We had it in the beginning," he said unhappily. "Somehow it fell away."

"Well then, you can hardly pity me," she said. "You've suffered the same condition as I for many years."

Ward shook his head. "What you fail to understand is that I could find some of it in other places."

When she continued to look blank, he smiled and rubbed her wrist affectionately with his fingertips. "I found affection and release for my baser needs with a mistress, Em."

He knew he had shocked her with that, could tell by her deep intake of breath. "We all have our needs, desires, hopes, and dreams," he said. He raised his eyes to her, smiling warmly. "We share a facade of well-being, Emma," he said. "Let's do something toward shoring up that facade. Let's seek more and all there is."

She listened to him intently, daring to conjure up visions of Katie's butterfly dreams.

"Have you ever been courted, Emma Parker?" he asked.

SIX

It was the best summer, ever, for them both. They were comfortable together. He made her laugh.

Initially, Emma had tried to keep Katie from dreaming bigger dreams than the relationship warranted. She countered Katie's high hopes with arguments that pointed out the advantages of living her current, comfortable and uncomplicated life.

Katie would not give up hope, however. In her mind, and in her heart, she believed that Emma deserved more than a solitary life. She wanted to see her mother with someone wonderful, and the more Katie learned about Ward Hamilton, the more she came to know him, the more she believed he was worthy.

And as the hazy days of summer rolled on and the promise of autumn seemed a distant possibility, Emma became caught up in her daughter's dreams for her.

Ward was an ideal companion. They had a great deal in common and yet they differed enough in their own thoughts to engage in stimulating debates on occasion. They talked easily and teased each other incessantly. But underneath all the teasing, there was a growing tension that Emma was not certain she understood. It was not an unpleasant thing between them. On the contrary, she felt it was somehow healthy and natural. So she did not fear it; rather she was confused. Ward treated her in a way she had never been treated in the past and he made her feel so very feminine, so very special. With maturity, Emma had gained a hard-learned poise, grace, and sophistication. But she had never acquired any degree of confidence or pride in herself as a woman.

With Ward, it was different. With Ward she held her head a little higher and there was a lightness to her step that had never been there before.

Ward adapted well, and happily, to his new life, and he knew Emma was more than a little responsible for that. There was an easiness between them that he had never experienced with Julia, even in the beginning. Emma was genuine and warm and giving. She demanded nothing and he found himself wanting to give her everything.

His love of woodworking could easily have mushroomed into a profitable business as word of his quality workmanship began to spread. He did not want that, however. He had built and sold more profitable businesses than he cared to think about, and did not want to be caught up again in unending demands and routine. He had broken away from the habit of constant work because, fortunately, he had recognized there were other things in life to enjoy.

Life was good when one had the time to be fully conscious of each moment of every day.

Life was rich when one had the time to fully appreciate every nuance of a gracious, caring, and beautiful woman.

Life was sweet when rushes of emotion and pulses of passion were created from a shared, simple glance.

"Have you always noticed the seasons?" he asked.

It was a strange question, and the look Emma sent him told him so.

He shrugged and reached for her hand, resting his head on the back of his chair as he smiled at her. "I haven't," he said. "At least not that I recall. I don't remember noting whether it was winter or summer or anything in between at any given time."

"Obviously the weather isn't important to you," she observed.

"It is this year," he said quietly. "I find myself wishing this season would never end." They had spent every summer Sunday together sitting on her porch or Katie's, often holding hands, relaxing and sharing their lives. "I want to be able to sit on the porch like this with you all year round."

"We could," she suggested with a grin, "if we dress for the occasion."

"Or cuddle up and share our body warmth," he teased, raising his dark brows to underscore the suggestion.

He had not made love to her. Not yet. But holding her and kissing her had not been enough for a very long time now and Ward wanted them to do something about that. He respected her enough not to push the issue until she was ready. But his desire to love her completely had been strong from early in their relationship and over the past weeks he found himself almost constantly in a state of arousal. He cared for Emma, he loved her and he *wanted* her in a way he had never experienced before. He knew that making love with her would be the crowning touch to the bond that had formed quickly between them—a bond that had substance and strength and durability.

And, lately, he had noticed a subtle change in her, small signs that suggested to him that she wanted him. He wasn't certain, however, whether she was afraid to make her desires known or whether she was just afraid.

He thought it high time that he found out.

He was mulling over the most appropriate manner in which to broach the subject to her when Emma surprised him by taking the matter into her own hands.

Emma was feeling an unusual strain in this sudden silence between them. She had experienced a shift in her feelings toward him weeks ago, and suspected she was feeling what Katie had hinted at in conversations that only women share. It was mortifying for Emma to realize that her own daughter was more experienced and knowledgeable about matters of the heart and physical loving than she. And it was more than a little embarrassing being thirty-eight years old and in possession of so little knowledge of seduction.

The one thing in her favor, however, was that she felt she could discuss anything with Ward.

Still, she was blushing with humiliation before she even began to speak. "I was very young when I married Phillip," she said softly. "Very young and very ignorant."

Ward had turned his full attention upon her the moment she had begun to speak. And he was dismayed to witness her obvious discomfort. "Emma?" he said softly.

"I know I told you I didn't like what we had to do to get Katie," she said painfully. "I regret that I told you that."

"Do you, Em?" he said softly. He smiled, tugging on her hand until she moved from her chair and stood in front of him. "Sit, love," he said softly, pulling her down onto his lap. He wrapped his arms around her and pressed her head onto his shoulder. "I've been wondering if you were ready to talk about this," he said quietly.

"I didn't know if you were," she whispered uneasily.

He grinned, looking down at the top of her golden head. "Aren't we a pair?"

Her head bobbed a time or two.

"Perhaps we're too old," she offered.

He laughed. "We're not, sweetheart. Believe me."

"I've been feeling confused," she said. "And nervous."

"I'm sorry, Em. I wish you had told me. I've been trying to be so damned noble and not rush you."

She tipped her head back until she could see his face.

He smiled and traced her frown with the tip of his finger. "I've wanted to make love to you but you had to want me, too."

"I want to make you happy," she said.

He kissed the tip of her nose affectionately. Clearly, she was acting on past experience. As if giving herself to him was something she *must* do for his benefit alone. He hated that and he was going to teach her differently. And yet she had admitted to feeling confused and nervous, and that made him realize just how innocent this woman really was. A great deal of her education had been neglected. Phillip, if he were alive, should be shot.

"Tell me what you feel when I touch you," he said softly.

That was something she had thought about quite frequently of late. "I feel so many things," she said without hesitation. "I feel that I don't want you to stop."

His smile grew warm and tender. "That is what I needed to hear," he said.

He got to his feet then, holding her securely in his arms as he turned the corner of the house and walked toward the backdoor.

"Are you taking me to my bedroom?" she asked worried-ly.

"Unless there is somewhere else you would rather go," he teased. He dipped his knees so that she could pull open the screen door. He caught the thing with the heel of his boot and slipped inside. "I want to love you, Emma," he said softly as he walked down the narrow hall toward the stairs. "I swear I will not hurt you."

"I know you won't," she said.

He stopped at the top of the stairs and looked down at her. "You're not afraid?"

Emma shook her head, knowing it was true. There was a gentleness in him, despite his size and strength. It would be different with him.

"Which way?" he asked.

Emma pointed to the room at the front of the house.

It was a pretty room, a feminine room, appointed with cost-ly, cherrywood furnishings. The coverlet was white, which caused him only brief dismay as he requested that she reach down and sweep it back before he lowered her to the center of her bed.

He sat near her feet and began to unlace her high boots. "I love you, Emma," he said quietly. "I don't think I've told you that in proper fashion. Such small words and yet they can be so difficult to say. I suppose that's because their meaning carries such impact." He smiled at her then, dropping one shoe to the floor. "We're strange animals, we humans. We hold things inside, hold love in our hearts, and yet we have difficulty saying the words." He turned his attention to her other shoe.

"I suppose it's fear that makes us reluctant to express our feelings, too," he added. "Some niggling doubt that makes us hold back in self-preservation. Protection against rejection, in case love isn't a mutual thing." He flashed her another confident smile as the second boot joined its mate. "Before this day is over, Emma Parker," he whispered, "you'll have no fear, no doubts, no need to protectively hold anything inside." He leaned over her then and dropped a sweet, tender, lingering kiss on her lips before he got to his feet and surveyed the room.

Emma frowned in confusion as she watched him look around. Her frown deepened when he bent to light the small lamp on the table beside the bed; it was midafternoon, the sun was high and the room was bright with daylight. "What are you doing?" she asked when he walked toward the windows.

Ward reached up and pulled the heavy draperies together, darkening the room. "I'm creating a mood, my love," he said as he turned toward the bed.

Emma was trying not to think back on her previous experience; she wanted this to be different. But she realized that Phillip had always come to her in the darkness and she was thinking it did not bode well that Ward had created a similar condition. Only the soft, shadowy glow from the lamp offset total blackness.

Ward sat down on the side of the bed and removed his boots before stretching out on his side beside her. He smiled, propping his head on one hand while he let his free arm rest lightly across her waist. "Do you have any idea how very beautiful you are?" he asked softly.

"Is that why you want me?" she asked.

He laughed lightly. "Yes," he said firmly. "Because you are beautiful on the inside as well as the outside."

"I think you're beautiful, too," she returned.

He leaned forward and pressed a gentle kiss on her forehead. "Men are not *beautiful*, my love."

Emma's gaze did not sway, nor did her thinking. "You are," she said easily.

"I shall take that as a compliment," he said. He took her hand then, caressing the backs of her fingers before easing their hands beneath his shirt and pressing her palm against his chest. "Feel that, Em?" he asked softly. "My heart races like that every time I'm near you. It's telling you how very much I want you."

She smiled softly and nodded her head. "I'm ready, darling," she whispered.

Ward blinked in surprise. "I beg your pardon?"

Emma felt certain he had heard, but his thoughtful frown and the extending silence confused her. "I'm sorry, I thought . . . if you're not ready, Ward, well . . ."

"Ready?" Ward murmured, rolling onto his back. Suddenly Phillip Burgess Parker was in that bed between them. "Jesus," he hissed softly.

Emma did not know what she had done, other than ruin their first encounter before it had begun. Mortified, she turned away to leave the bed.

Ward's arm shot out and gently pulled her back. "Where are you going?"

Emma shook her head, refusing to look at him as tears threatened to spill over her lashes.

"Oh, Emma," he whispered as he rolled onto his side and pulled her into the security of his arms. "I love you, Em," he said. He began to kiss her, sweet stolen kisses that glanced warmly across her eyes and nose and lips. "You are *not* ready, my sweet innocent," he said between caresses. "Let me teach you. Let me love you."

In the moments that followed, he banished Phillip Parker from their midst, did away with all his angry thoughts of the man and all Emma's memories of what had occurred before. This was a new world, *their* world, and he was going to open it up to her and serve a platter of love that would leave her dazed and sated.

Emma's heart began to pound in anticipation of his next touch, his next kiss. He made her feel things she had not known her body was capable of feeling. He made her a glutton, greedy for more when he bared one breast and took her painfully taut nipple between his lips. He suckled her until a hot tension flowed through her, an exquisite pain that forced her to half turn toward him, drawing her legs tightly together as she sought relief from an ache she had never felt before.

"I know," he whispered before pressing her onto her back. He towered over her, smiling his understanding. His need was great, his aching, throbbing erection demanding. But he would not cheat her or himself.

He concentrated on making them naked then. Slowing the pace by teasing her with caresses that maintained a level of tautness in their bodies that heightened their anticipation of what was to follow.

When he had removed the last of their garments, he pulled her full length against his body and held her there while his hand roamed slowly down her back, caressed her buttocks, and then pulled her leg over his. "Feel?" he breathed close to her ear. "Emma," he murmured tenderly.

Each breath became increasingly difficult as he pressed her onto her back once again. Emma watched the passion grow in him, felt it growing within her own body as his hands and lips moved over her. Her breasts were not soothed by his attentions, but ached all the more. She closed her eyes and pressed her head back into the pillow, gasping her need, calling his name, pleading for his help.

Ward moved his hand downward from her belly, his fingers moving slowly over her soft mound until he reached her center.

That first touch brought her half off the bed.

"Oh!" she gasped.

"It's all right," he murmured before his lips moved over hers.

He played with her only briefly, knowing they were both dangerously close to the heights he had wanted to reach with her. And when it happened, he wanted to be with her.

He moved over her, positioning himself between her legs, tucking his hands beneath her hips, tipping her upward to receive him. He pressed forward slowly, watching her, seeing her eyes half close in passion as she felt him slip inside her.

She felt the exquisite pressure extend deep inside her body and gripped his shoulders, pulling him upward, against her.

And then he was withdrawing. "No," she whispered frantically.

He smiled and pressed his face into her silken hair as he began to move within her. He rocked her gently in his love, until he felt her body tightening around him.

"Ward," she cried frantically.

He raised his head and looked at her then, stared at her through eyes that were drugged with need. Watched her face contort with passion and saw her eyes open large and wide, a brief moment of surprise that was fleeting and yet so intense he knew he would never forget. He pressed deeply into her, rotating his hips against her as he pulled her into his arms just as she exploded.

She arched against him, her body wrenching spasmodically beneath his and tightening around him, releasing and tightening again until he, too, erupted into a jarring climax that held him, that pulled him, that compelled him to pour himself into her. "Uhhh!" he breathed close to her ear.

His shoulder muscles tightened beneath her hands, his body hot and rock hard on hers. The perspiration on their strained bodies blended between them. With eyes closed, Emma concentrated on the feel of him. The moment was draining away, slowly, slowly, leaving her flushed and exhausted. Leaving her dreading that moment when he would remove himself from her, regretting that she no longer felt filled by him, anticipating with loathing the loss of his body heat and the comfort of his weight. It was all so new and it was all so wonderful.

"Oh, Em," he whispered on a lingering, labored breath.

Ward became conscious of his weight on her then and pressed his lips against her warm, flushed neck before he attempted to pull away.

The moment his shoulders moved upward, Emma tightened her hold. "Don't," she said brokenly.

He raised his head, moving just enough that he could see her face; tears were silently slipping down her cheeks. "Emma?"

"I didn't know," she whispered. "I didn't know."

His concern turned to understanding and his expression softened as he wrapped his arms completely around her. "I know, love," he said softly. "I know." He kissed away a tear and then another, feeling her laboring for breath, feeling a force building inside her that he knew would have to be released. "Let it go," he whispered lovingly. "Just hold on to me."

It was the culmination of all that had happened between them just now, and the liberation of all that had not in her past.

He rolled with her onto his side and then to his back, pressing the back of her head with the palm of his hand as she buried her face against his chest.

"I'm sorry," she cried brokenly.

"Don't be," he said easily. "Not with me."

She clung to him, moving up on his chest until she could put her arms around his neck and press her cheek against his. "I don't . . . know why . . . I'm . . . doing this," she choked.

He smiled and tightened his arms around her back. "That's all right, sweetheart, I think I do."

"I never cry," she said angrily.

"Obviously it's past time you did, Em."

Moments later she sighed wearily and Ward turned his head closer to hers. "All right, love?" he asked as his hand circled slowly on her back.

She nodded, bumping his shoulder with her chin. And then, to her chagrin, she hiccuped and he laughed.

"Lord," she muttered, hiding her face against his neck. "I'm thirty-eight, a grandmother, and I'm behaving like a child."

"I don't mind the way you're behaving," he said softly. "It makes me feel needed." And it went a long way in convincing him he had made a difference; she had reached, surpassed, a turning point in her life.

Emma dared to raise her head and look at him. "I think I needed you a long time ago," she said earnestly.

Ward nodded his head, smiled softly, and wiped at the moisture on her cheeks with the pad of his thumb. "We've shared your coming out, so to speak. That's very special, Em."

Her head dropped onto his shoulder. "I'm feeling drained," she said as her eyes drifted closed in spite of her wishes. "I'm sorry, darling," she whispered.

"Sleep," he said.

Emma shook her head. "I have to see to supper."

He laughed, knowing she didn't have the strength to walk beyond the bedroom door. "We'll sleep," he said firmly. "And after we've slept," he whispered, gently settling her against his side, "I'm going to make love to you again. Better?" he asked when she was comfortable and he had drawn a light cotton sheet over them. "And then, perhaps, we'll raid the pantry."

Ward had no idea how long he lay awake beside her, holding her in the crook of his arm. He listened to the soft hint of her breathing and knew each time her lungs filled with air when her breast moved caressingly against his side. He closed his eyes, enjoying the soft feel of her, the warmth of her, and knew again a need for her, as evidenced by the rigid erection that lay tight against his belly.

Emma was the first to awaken, drifting reluctantly to consciousness until she realized that Ward still lay beside her. It was a wonderful way to awaken, with a warm, loving body next to hers and a strong arm holding her protectively. It was a security she had never felt before and she knew, if she were never to lie with him again, she would never forget this moment. She took it into her heart, to shelter and protect it there, and then she opened her eyes, smiling, as she tipped her head back and realized that he slept.

His hair was thick and wavy where it wasn't gray; the silver seemed to be much straighter than the rest. She wanted to reach up and finger-comb it off his forehead, but she feared waking him. His dark lashes rested well below his eyes and curled upward at the ends. Those beautiful lashes were one of the first things about him that had caught her attention, she remembered. Well, one of many things, she recalled fondly. Her gaze drifted downward and caught at the spot where her hand rested on his chest. Her fingers were buried in the thick, dark mat that covered him, and she noticed that the soft hair lay in whorls around his flat nipples. It was a revelation that male nipples were not so markedly different from her own. His body contoured to a narrow waist, but what caught her attention then was the lengthy protuberance beneath the sheet that lay flat against his belly. She was immediately in awe, not only of him, but of herself for having adjusted to take him. The nature of their bodies was astonishing in their differences and in their ability to accommodate to each other.

Emma found herself abashed by her continuing curiosity about him. Phillip had only come to her in the dark of night, performed his business and just as quickly left her alone to sleep. And Emma felt she had diminished herself enough with her ignorance. She would be damned if she would admit never to having seen a naked man at her age. It would be easier to look at him now, she decided, rather than gape foolishly in surprise at first sight of him, with Ward looking on.

His left arm was around her, his right thrown out across the mattress, and the cotton sheet was draped lightly across his waist. She had only to lift the white material and peek.

Ward remained perfectly still, as he had the past several moments, occasionally feeling small, almost indistinct movements from the woman at his side as she carried out her inspection of him. He wanted her to look her fill and satisfy her curiosity while she felt she could do so unobserved. He suspected she would get over this shyness once she had completed her excursion of discovery.

The warm air of the room felt cool against his skin when she lifted the sheet a fraction. He couldn't prevent a small grin when she released a startled gasp upon seeing him for the first time. Emma dropped the sheet immediately and tucked her offending hand tight against her chest.

Ward was sadly disappointed.

He waited a decent interval, but her appraisal had not left him unaffected and his erection was becoming increasing uncomfortable.

He needed her.

He wanted her.

Now.

He stirred, moving slowly as if from sleep, and then turned on his side to face her.

Emma raised her eyes to his, warmed by his narrowed look of passion, still heated from her thoughts about him. He had stirred her blood and he had yet to raise a finger toward her; it was inconceivable, but it was true. She understood *need* now, and she wanted him to do something about it. "I peeked at you," she said boldly.

Ward didn't say anything; he simply continued to stare heatedly.

But there was a hint of invitation in his eyes that Emma quickly interpreted. Still, she hesitated, fearing she might do or say the wrong thing.

"What do you want, Em?" he said softly.

That made her heart pound and the blood thunder in her head. "I want to touch you," she said, with little hint of hesitation; she was growing bolder as she realized he was subtly encouraging.

Ward hooked his foot in the sheet and pulled the thing down below his hips. "I want to be touched by you, love. I need to be touched, too." He took her hand and laid the flat of her palm over that part of him that so fascinated her. "I like to be touched everywhere," he said huskily, and then he lay down on his back.

He watched her, his hand circling lightly across her back as he felt her slowly caress the length of him, testing his reaction and getting one. Her startled gaze fell on his eyes when she heard his harsh intake of breath.

He smiled, his hand stilled on hers. "I'm very sensitive to your touch, Emma," he said softly. "If you play with that too much, I may not have time to love you again before it will be over."

Emma blushed lightly, but she giggled. "Really?"

Ward nodded his head.

Emma got to her knees at his side and his hand rested on her thigh as she slowly inspected his body from his toes to the top of his head.

It was the most arousing thing, just watching her, her intensity.

She reached out and placed her fingertips on his ribs. The muscles beneath his skin rippled in reaction.

He touched her breast and felt her nipple harden against his palm. He pressed against it.

Emma's head dropped back and her eyes closed as she reached for that elusive feeling. "I don't think I can explore anymore right now," she whispered frantically.

And suddenly she was on her back and Ward was leaning over her. They had teased each other into an aroused state with a few heated looks and barely a touch. He kissed her demandingly as he entered her, pushing home. He rotated his hips, moving against her in slow time, small circles. "Move with me," he urged.

Emma easily caught on to the movement as his hand on her hip guided her. Quickly, a small flutter where his body joined hers caught her attention. "Oh, God," she gasped. "It's happening."

He quickened his pace, locking his elbows to keep his weight from her, allowing her the freedom to move with him in tempo.

And then she stopped, her body tense, pressing back into the pillows. "Huhhh!" she breathed.

He reached for her, holding her, pressing his erection against her as her body rocked beneath him. She had barely stilled before he was moving, pressing and withdrawing as he whispered harshly, "Now, Em!" A few short, quick strokes and he grew frighteningly rigid. And then he dropped his head down beside hers, moaning as his lower body jerked and snapped until he pressed himself deep within her. A few moments later he had barely recaptured his breath before he started laughing, a deep, throaty, awe-inspired laugh.

"Ward?" she questioned, tightening her arms around his back.

"I must think I'm a boy again," he said against her ear. "I'm reacting to you as if I were a boy."

Emma smiled. "*Boys* don't do this," she said.

"You're wrong," he said softly, before rolling to his side.

Emma frowned, raising her head as he pulled her against his side. "You weren't a *boy*, surely, when you first made love to a woman?"

"I wouldn't call it 'making love,'" he said lightly as he brushed a soft curl from her cheek. "It was more like a brief athletic experience."

Emma laughed, momentarily dropping her forehead onto his shoulder.

"Actually," he drawled, enjoying her laughter, "I lost control before I'd even removed my trousers."

She laughed again. "How old were you then?"

Ward raised his eyes and smiled at her. "I was fifteen, I suppose. My father decided it was time I became a man and took me to a very exclusive . . . *house*."

"I know what that means," she said with a hint of disgust. "I'm not totally innocent."

"You certainly aren't," he teased.

Her expression softened and her fingers played lightly in the hair on his chest. "I think that was very cruel of your father," she said. "You must have been embarrassed."

"Not at all," he told her. "We had a long talk, Father and I. I agreed to go quite readily."

"Oh."

He nodded his head. "He had caught me eyeing a neighbor's girl. I understood quickly that he would rather pay for me to visit a professional than have a scandal break out in the neighborhood."

"Ward!" she breathed.

"Well," he said defensively, "young men don't always have the control to react with foresight, Em. As I recall, I was pretty much preoccupied by the urges of my body. My *mind* was almost completely numb."

She giggled again.

He eyed her severely. "You're enjoying yourself, aren't you?"

Emma nodded.

He smiled lovingly and gently stroked her cheek. "I'm glad," he said softly.

Emma shifted on the bed, turning until she was facing him. Her breast pressed against his side as she placed her elbow on his chest and propped her head up with her hand. "And now you're feeling like that boy again?" she asked.

"A little wiser, a little more experienced, perhaps. But the jury is still out on the matter of *control*," he added ruefully.

Emma nodded, giggled softly, and kissed his cheek affectionately.

She was happy, looking like a young girl, smiling and giggling. He was glad he was seeing her this way. He somehow doubted anyone else ever had.

She looked into his eyes for a long time, the laughter slipping away as she summoned the courage to say what she wanted to say. He had been so right about people's reluctance to say those little words. And yet how could she not say them when she felt so strongly. And besides, she no longer felt uncertain about him loving her in return. "I love you, Ward," she said softly.

His smile vanished. Tipping his head forward, he cupped his hand behind his ear. "I beg your pardon?"

"I love you," she said firmly.

He continued to stare, as if his wits were dim. "Again?" he said.

"I love you!" she hollered, laughing.

"That's better," he said, dragging her into his embrace.

SEVEN

August slipped by on the wings of stolen embraces and secret nights of loving. They shared precious hopes and dreams and reveled in this newfound love that seemed stronger than either had dared to hope. They swam naked in the river during the heat of many afternoons and made love on the grassy banks, under the shade of a sheltering willow. They grew comfortable in their love and each other; no longer did they hide feelings protectively from each other. Ward spent most nights at the house in the country, slipping back to his own home in the predawn hours.

But they hadn't fooled Katie for a moment.

Actually, it was approximately a week after Ward and Emma's first intimate experience that Katie approached him.

"I want to know what your intentions are toward my mother."

Ward looked up from the chest he was making to see Katie standing in the open doors of his workshop. He thought she looked terribly burdened by her pregnancy. He set aside his chisel and hammer and reached for a rag. Wiping his hands, he walked slowly toward her. "My intentions are honorable, Katie. I promise you that."

"You're making love with her," she said.

Her assurance momentarily stymied him. And then he reached for her hand. "Come and sit down," he said, leading her to the bench outside against the wall. "You're sounding angry," he said as he sat beside her. "I don't think that's good for you right now."

"I won't be if you tell me you love her and plan to do the honorable thing," she said heatedly. "And don't try to deny it, Ward. There's never a light shining from any window of your house at night anymore."

Ward frowned. "And that has led you to the conclusion that I'm making love to your mother?" he asked in wonder.

Katie snorted angrily. "That and the fact that Emma is positively *glowing*."

That sounded to him more like the clue that would have given them away. Katie was a very perceptive young woman, and it was true what she said about her mother.

Ward gripped her hand between both of his. "I do love her, Katie," he said softly.

"If you hurt her, I'll . . ." Her head snapped around, and she frowned at him then. "What did you say?"

He smiled. "I love your mother."

Her eyes searched his, looking for the truth. When she found it, Katie wasn't certain what to say. "You mean it?" she asked stupidly.

Ward nodded his head. "We had decided to tell you soon, Katie. We've hardly had time to formulate our plans."

"Plans?" she questioned dully.

He laughed and squeezed her hand. "For a wedding. We thought we should wait until—" He cut his sentance short when Katie pressed the fingers of her free hand against her lips and tears welled up in her eyes. "Ah, don't do that," he pleaded—not in her condition.

Ward was feeling miles out of his element.

"You're going to be married?" she choked.

He could see she was fighting to regain control. "Your mother wanted to tell you," he said. "Now I suppose we've ruined that for her."

Katie shook her head. "She'll never know that I know," she said softly. "I could lie to the devil while I was sitting at God's right hand, if it would make her happy."

Ward was so deeply moved by the strength of this young woman's love and conviction, he wasn't certain how to safely respond. "Could I hug you?" he asked quietly.

Katie smiled a watery smile and moved closer, into his arms.

"She's lucky to have you," he said, squeezing her gently, affectionately.

"I'm lucky to have Emma," she returned. "She's a wonderful mother. And, she's my best friend."

He let her go and they stared at each other, smiling.

"You're not angry now?" he asked, even though he felt strongly that she was not.

"How could I be angry now that I know how you feel?" she said. "You're exactly what I've prayed for. Emma called those prayers my 'butterfly dreams' because she thought my hopes for someone wonderful to love her were totally elusive." She stared at him thoughtfully for a moment, wondering if she should give voice to the reasons behind those dreams. And looking at his kind face, those dark, intelligent, and understanding eyes, she decided. "Has Emma talked about my father?" she asked.

Ward became cautious. Emma's secrets were hers to reveal. "Some," he said.

"He was good to us, but I never saw any signs of affection from him like I see from you when you're with her. Ever since I've been old enough to understand how wonderful love can be, I wanted the best of it for Mother."

"As you receive the 'best of it' from David?" he asked lightly.

She grinned and nodded. "He's a terrific man," she said. She stared thoughtfully toward the back of his house. "I think there should be one day set aside every year to honor very special mothers like Emma," Katie said.

He smiled and gripped her hand between them. "I think you honor your mother *every* day, Katie," he said softly.

"She hasn't had much fun during her life," Katie said thoughtfully. She looked at him askance. "I think with you it might be different."

Ward stared at her and said earnestly, "It will be."

She grinned, lightening the mood. "We could make an Emma's Day," she said. "We could surprise her with a dinner just for her. Just because we love her."

"All right," he agreed. "We'll make an Emma's Day."

"When?" she asked excitedly.

He laughed. "Not until after you birth this child!" he said. "You make me nervous when you get excited."

Katie laughed, too.

That night Emma groaned in despair and acute embarrassment. "How am I ever going to face her?" she mumbled against his neck.

Ward had not kept Katie's knowledge a secret from her, of course; he wouldn't lie and he would not place Katie in the position of lying to her mother.

"Katie is a grown woman, Em. She has one child and is expecting a second. Don't you think she's aware of what lovers do?"

"But not her *mother*!" she wailed.

He laughed. "I suspect all mothers hope their children never stop to think about what parents do behind closed doors."

"Katie *thinks* too much," she said, looking up at him, frowning.

He smiled and stroked her arm slowly from shoulder to wrist. "She told me about her 'butterfly dreams,'" he said. "She's sensitive and caring, sweetheart. She wants to see you happy."

Emma nodded as she watched her fingers raking slowly across his chest. "I'm lucky to have her," she said softly.

Ward captured that hand and held it still. Emma had the ability to arouse him with a mere look, and her touch could drive him to distraction. But there was one thing more he wished to discuss with her.

"Emma, there's something we've avoided discussing this past week and I think we should talk about it now."

His tone was soft but serious, and Emma understood this was a matter that deserved her undivided attention.

She propped herself on his chest, her hand supporting her chin, facing him the way he had already come to enjoy; her slight weight felt good on him.

"I'm ready," she said simply.

He smiled, wrapping her free hand in his against her hip, remembering the shock he had felt the first time she had said those words to him. But that was another time and things were different now. "Emma, you're a young woman still and I think we have to think about the possibility that you could conceive."

She smiled. "I've thought about that, darling," she said quietly. "But"—she hesitated, not wanting to hurt him— "there were no children from your previous marriage, Ward, and . . ."

He was shaking his head. "I don't know that that was because of me, Em. Julia did not particularly desire children. At least by me. And, there are ways a woman can look after that sort of thing." And there were others means as well, although he hesitated to tell her. "But preventative measures are not always successful, and I strongly suspect Julia resorted to other things at least on one occasion," he said flatly. "After the fact, Em."

Emma thought about that for a moment, frowning, her eyes growing large and round with disbelief as his meaning took hold. "You mean she rid herself of your child? Oh, my God, Ward."

He squeezed her hand. "I only *suspect*, Emma. When I confronted her with my suspicions, Julia denied my suggestion. I have no proof. I've only told you this because of us. Because I want you to be prepared, in the event."

"Well, you can rest assured *I* would never do such a thing," she said hotly. The very idea made her ill. "I would be happy if we made a child," she said sincerely.

He looked into her eyes, searching. "Would you, love?"

She nodded her head insistently. "Very happy."

"You wouldn't be afraid? You had such a hard time with Katie."

"I was very young," she said. "I think perhaps too young."

"Your doctor thinks the same," he said quietly.

Emma's brows arched upward in surprise. "I beg your pardon?"

"Don't be angry, love," he said quickly. "I had to know."

"You spoke to Dr. Trimble about me? Ward, how could you?"

She was flushed, but he wasn't certain whether her reaction was from anger or chagrin.

"Katie mentioned in passing that the doctor who brought her into the world was the same doctor who would deliver her child. I wanted you, Em," he said tenderly. "But I would not take the chance of losing you. I had to know if there was any possibility of risk to you or your health."

"If there had been some risk, you wouldn't have made love to me?" she asked in wonder.

Ward shook his head, his dark-eyed stare locked with hers.

How could she remain angry in the face of such devotion? "Then I would have been forced to seduce you," she said baldly. "The risk is mine to take, Ward."

He grinned. "You would have *seduced* me?" he teased.

Emma laughed. "I would have worked up the courage eventually," she said. "I'm not certain whether I possess the needed skills, however."

"You do," he said assuredly. "Don't ever doubt it, my love."

Emma leaned forward and dropped a sweet kiss on his lips by way of thanks. Then she just stared at him, smiling foolishly.

He returned the smile. "What are you thinking?" he asked lightly.

"How would you feel about a baby?" she asked softly. "We haven't discussed your feelings in all of this."

"If it happens, Emma, I will be delighted."

And knowing him, loving him, hearing the conviction in his voice, Emma knew it would be so. How could Julia have *not* given this man his child? But she would not think about that now. She would not think about that ever again. From this point onward, she would think only of the present, and the future, with him.

The look in her eyes suddenly became full of merriment. "How many grandmothers do you know who are hoping to become mothers again?" She laughed. "I can already hear a few disgusted voices in this town if I should ever grow a big belly."

"Will that bother you?" he asked, smiling at her laughter.

Emma shook her head. "Not at all."

"Then we're agreed, Em?" he asked cautiously. "We won't worry?"

"I won't," she said easily. "You should."

Suddenly a frown dropped across his face. "Why?"

"Because I will get fat and ugly!"

He breathed away again. "You will never be ugly, Emma," he said softly as he rearranged her position in the bed. When they were lying on their sides, facing each other, he grinned. "I think you would be a very lovely pregnant lady," he said.

She rolled toward him and whispered, "If you give me your baby, darling, I'll prove you wrong."

Ward propped his head on his hand, his eyes lowering to admire her breast as he caressed her there. "I thought grandmothers were supposed to be a staid lot," he teased softly. "Sedate, prim, proper. All of that."

"You've been meeting up with the wrong type of grandmothers, dear," she said on an indrawn breath.

"I think you must be right," he mummured as he lowered his head toward her breast. "Lord, Emma," he breathed.

EIGHT

Their conversation about babies had taken place over a month ago now, and Emma had not seen her monthly since. In fact, she had cheerfully told Ward she had hopes of not seeing it for more than nine months. His heart rate had quickened when she told him that. He had long ago given up hope of ever becoming a father. They weren't certain of anything yet, of course. It was far too early.

Now they were waiting.

In the meantime, their wedding day was upon them. Their courtship had been brief but intense, and neither Ward nor Emma doubted the rightness of what they were about to do. Tomorrow would be their day, his and Emma's. They would share a few hours with Katie, David, and Timmy, of course, but Ward had already laid plans for his evening alone with his wife.

They would appear before the justice late morning, with Katie and David standing with them. Then an early celebration dinner, which would include a large roast specially ordered by Ward, before he took Emma home to the country house. He had purchased the best bottle of champagne in all of Zanesville, along with a selection of cheeses for a light, late-night supper.

Ward had no advance bridegroom jitters as he bounced up the side steps to Katie's home. He was a happy man. He held the paper-wrapped roast in the palm of his hand and held it high for presentation to his almost stepdaughter, as he knocked on the door.

He stood there for what seemed like a long interval, receiving no response. He knew Katie was home; she seldom ven-

tured far alone these days. And then he heard her call out
softly and he breathed a sigh of relief as he opened the door
and stepped inside.

His relief was short-lived, however.

Katie's look of stunned surprise was nothing compared with
the utter disbelief that flashed across his face when he saw her
holding her wet skirts away from her body.

"It just happened," she said. Her water had broken and was
still forming a puddle at her feet.

"Oh, Lord," he muttered, leaving his package on a nearby
counter before moving to her side. "Katie, it's only the first
of September," he said stupidly.

She smiled apologetically, shaking her head. "I can't help
that, Ward," she said.

Timmy wandered near his mother, but Katie placed her
hand on his shoulder and held him away. "Just a moment,
sweetheart," she said, before looking up at Ward again. "Would
you get me some toweling from the bottom cupboard in the
pantry, please?"

Timmy sensed something was amiss and did not take well
to being held off. He began to cry.

"Oh, Timmy, not now," she whispered.

Ward reversed direction and picked the boy up in his arms.
"Come on, sport, you can help me," he said as he continued
on into the pantry.

Katie reached out for the towels as he returned.

Ward held back, towels in one hand and Timmy settled on
his forearm. "What are you going to do?"

Katie smiled patiently. Men! "I have to wipe the floor."

"No," he said firmly. "I'll do that after we get you upstairs
and in bed."

"Ward . . ."

"And you need to change into something dry."

"Ward," she said again, more firmly. "Nothing is going to
happen right away. I don't have any pain."

He blinked. "Oh," he said, making her laugh. "Don't laugh,"
he pleaded.

She laughed all the more. "It might be a good thing," she

howled. "The baby could just pop out!"

The blood drained from Ward's face. "I'll get David," he muttered.

Katie regained control and sobered enough to stop him before he could take two steps. "I don't think we need pull David away from the store just yet," she said.

Timmy was clinging to Ward's neck with one hand, two fingers of his other hand were stuck in his mouth for comfort.

Ward smiled with chagrin. "Better David here than me," he said.

"Coward," she said affectionately. "What are you going to do when it's Emma standing here in the same predicament as me?"

"Panic," he said bluntly.

Katie laughed again.

"I really wish you wouldn't do that," he muttered.

"Perhaps you would be good enough to fetch my mother while I clean up here," she said, smiling. "But don't flail the horse, Ward. There is plenty of time. In fact," she added apologetically, "I'm afraid I might ruin your wedding day."

"*Delay*, Katie," he said. "Not *ruin*."

Ward sat Timmy on the counter, with a caution to the boy not to move, before he walked to the center of the kitchen and fanned the towels out over the puddle on the floor. "Don't you dare bend to pick those up," he warned. Clearly, he had set aside his original anxiety. "I'll look after this."

Katie looked down at her extended belly. "Truthfully, I think I would have difficulty."

Now he laughed, but briefly. He stood beside her and bent to kiss her cheek. He cared a great deal for this young woman, this child of Emma. "Will you be all right?" he asked. "Should I fetch some dry clothing from your room before I go?" He just could not imagine how she managed the stairs, so burdened was she.

She smiled, briefly touching his arm. "I'll be fine," she said softly.

"I'll take Timmy with me, then," he said. "You just care

for yourself," he added as he scooped the child up and walked toward the door.

"Ward!" Katie called, before he could leave. When he turned his head, his expression questioning, she smiled. "I'm very happy that Emma has found you."

Ward had occasionally felt fatherly toward Katie, but never more so than now. "I'm exceptionally happy that I've found her, too, dear," he said warmly. "For a number of reasons."

Emma had been busy all morning making and decorating her very special carrot cake, and it was taking forever to form the small sugar roses for the center. She was placing the second of five roses on her masterpiece when she heard a wagon pull into the yard. Darting a look beyond the screen door, she recognized Ward's bay horse immediately. "Dash it," she muttered, looking around for a clean towel, "he's not supposed to be here today." And the cake was to be a surprise. She scurried to a cupboard, snatched two clean, white cotton towels, and flung them lightly over the cake before rushing to the door.

Timmy made a beeline for his grandmother the moment his feet hit the ground. He liked Ward, but Emma was better; she gave him treats. "Gram!" he called.

"What are you two up to?" she asked, frowning in confusion.

Ward helped Timmy up the steps as he spoke. "Everything is fine, Em," he said, "but Katie asked me to come and get you."

She frowned at him, her eyes almost crossing as she continued to stare even while he bent to press a quick kiss on her lips. "The baby?" she asked.

He nodded.

"It's only the first of September," she said stupidly.

Ward now realized how inane that sounded. "That's my line," he muttered.

"She's in labor?" she questioned. Clearly, Emma just could not believe what was happening.

"Not labor," Ward said as they followed Timmy into the

kitchen. "Her, uh . . ." He motioned with his hand, below his waist and toward the floor.

Emma managed, somehow, to interpret his sign language. "Her water broke?"

He nodded his head.

She laughed lightly at his discomfort. "Oh, Ward," she teased.

"Well," he said defensively, "this is all new to me."

Timmy could smell warm cookies and was trying to scale the front of a cupboard in a vain attempt to reach the platter on the countertop.

Emma picked him up with an arm around his waist and held him while he made his selection. "Only two," she said as he made a grab for a third. "I'll take him upstairs with me while I pack a few things for overnight."

"Overnight at my house?" he asked hopefully. "Depending on Katie's schedule, of course," he added.

She laughed. "Of course," she returned.

Left to his own devices, Ward wandered around the kitchen with his hands in his pockets and his mind switched to off. He spied the mound in the center of the kitchen table and lifted the edge of a towel to peek. "Bet I wasn't to see that," he muttered ruefully as he dropped the cloth back in place.

Moments later they were on the return trip to Zanesville, with Timmy riding the high wagon seat between Emma and Ward.

"Did Katie send Timmy to fetch you?" Emma asked.

Ward shook his head and snapped the reins lightly over the bay's rump. "I picked up the roast from the butcher and was delivering it to Katie." He smiled wryly at her. "*It* happened as I walked into her house."

"Poor Ward." She giggled.

"I did not panic, however."

"No?"

"Hardly at all," he admitted.

She smiled at him fondly. "This will be a whole new experience for you, darling," she said softly.

"I'll observe from the sidelines."

"Perferably from across town?" She laughed again.

He shook his head and grinned. "Not at all, Em. I've never had the opportunity to be so close to a birthing before now. I'm looking at this as a learning experience," he said. "So I'll know what to expect and what help I can be to you when it's our turn."

Emma reached above her grandson's head and touched Ward's arm. "I do love you," she whispered.

"Ditto!" he said with a happy smile.

Ward almost dropped in his tracks when they found Katie washing the kitchen windows. "*What* is she doing?" he whispered frantically to Emma.

Emma handed him her small valise. "I went on a cleaning spree just before Katie came along," she explained quietly. "We women have some strange compulsions at times."

Ward wouldn't disagree with that. He stared at Katie as if she were about to commit murder.

"It will be all right, darling," Emma whispered. "Would you take my things up to the guest room."

He wasn't that far gone. "No," he whispered in return. "You may not be staying in the guest room."

Emma would not argue with that; she did not think she could sleep alone anymore, in any case, and had not been looking forward to trying.

Ward returned her valise to the bed of his wagon.

No one in the Franklin house slept that night, however. With the exception of Timmy. Ward and Emma made up a small cot for the child in the front room of the house, where Timmy would less likely be disturbed by all the comings and goings.

Katie's labor started at ten o'clock that evening. But this second child was in more of a hurry than Timmy had been, and shortly after midnight, Ward was sent dashing across town for Dr. Trimble.

David was pulled from Katie's side and ousted from the room the moment the doctor arrived.

Ward was standing in front of the iron stove, watching

three large kettles of water that would not offer up one single bubble.

David looked grim when he joined his friend.

"With *two* of us watching, there will be no boiling water, for certain this night," Ward suggested.

David smiled at the man's attempt at humor. "We could pace the floor," he said.

"Is that to be our lot for the duration?"

David shook his head and reached for the coffeepot from the back of the stove. "I'll go back to Katie when the doctor has had some time with her."

"Really?" Ward asked. He was in awe of the man now. "Will you stay to see the baby born?"

David poured coffee into two mugs, nodding his head as he carried them to the round, wooden table at the far end of the room. "Won't you stay with Emma?" he asked.

Ward blinked, feeling incredibly stupid. "I hadn't thought that far, I suppose."

The younger man smiled. "To hell with convention, I say. Katie wants me there most near the end and whatever Katie wants at that time, believe me, I'll do my damnedest to see that she gets it," he volunteered.

Ward walked across the room and sat facing the handsome, fair-haired man.

"Do you want to know about it?" David asked.

"I think I may have a need to know," Ward admitted.

David grinned knowingly and crossed his arms, leaning his elbows heavily on the table. "It isn't easy watching the woman you love suffer, Ward. I'll be honest with you about that." He went on to explain the ways in which he could help his young wife by supporting her back when the need to push was greatest, letting her squeeze his hands until he feared his fingers would snap, wiping her brow, and encouraging her with softly spoken words, even when she turned on him and snapped a reply. "They can get testy when they're in that much pain," he said. "Ignore it. I don't think women even remember the things they say during a time like that."

"Obviously you feel it worth the abuse," Ward said wryly.

David looked directly into the older man's eyes. "It is the most incredible thing you will ever experience."

Emma hurried into the kitchen then, wiping her hands on a crisp, full-length apron. "David, Katie wants you," she said, moving quickly to the stove. "She's crowning already," she added in a tone of disbelief.

David dashed from the room and Ward felt a surge of excitement pump through his veins.

"I'll take those up," Ward said, running across the room to her side.

Emma carefully wrapped the metal handles of the kettles in toweling before he touched them.

"Is everything all right, Em?" he asked as he followed her up the stairs.

"It's happening very quickly," she said. She stopped outside the door of Katie and David's bedroom and turned, relieving him of one of the kettles. "I'll be out in a moment for the other," she said, and disappeared inside.

When she returned a moment later, Ward had not moved a muscle. He did when he heard an animalistic growl issue from the other side of the partially open door, however. He flinched.

Emma took a moment to reassure him, knowing how much he cared for her daughter. "Everything is going well, darling," she said softly, briefly touching his cheek. "Katie will be able to rest soon."

"That's good," he said.

Ward felt strangely lost and at loose ends when Emma disappeared this time. He was the only one who couldn't be of use and he wasn't certain exactly what to do with himself. So, he backed up to the banister, rested on his buttocks and crossed his arms over his chest to wait.

He thought about going through this with Emma and decided David was wise; it would be much better to be on the other side of the door, knowing exactly what was going on, rather than waiting outside in ignorance.

Ward wasn't certain how long he remained there, but certainly no more than twenty minutes passed before he heard

a long-drawn-out scream followed, shortly thereafter, by the
wail of a newborn.

He stood tall and grinned.

And waited.

When the door opened, he was there to greet Emma as she
walked toward him holding a small bundle of white. "A boy,"
she said.

"Oh, Em," he whispered. She looked beautiful, natural,
celestial, and he knew in his heart that there would be only
one thing that would increase her present state of happiness—
if that child were her own. And he also knew he would never
forget the sight of her standing there like this.

"He's absolutely beautiful," she said with pride.

Ward looked down as she raised a corner of the blanket,
and lied. "He truly is, love."

"We won't be much longer," she said, accepting a devoted
kiss on the cheek from him. "I'll fix you some breakfast."

But Ward was shaking his head. "I've put your valise in
the guest room, Emma. I think you need some sleep." She
opened her mouth to protest, but he placed a finger over her
lips. "And Katie will need you close by tonight."

Emma did not have to feign her pout. "I'll miss you," she
whispered.

"Me, too, love," he said.

The following afternoon Ward looked through the open
doors of his workshop to see Emma standing there.

"Katie doesn't need me for a least a few hours," she said.

"Are you certain?" he asked, not daring to believe. With
Emma absent from his bed, he had slept only fitfully. And
seeing her standing there, looking slightly shy, he felt as if
he hadn't made love to her in a thousand years.

"She told me."

Ward grinned, lowering his tools onto the cabinet he was
making. "I do love Katie," he said softly.

Emma tried not to giggle with excitement as they dashed
across the grass to the backdoor of his house.

NINE

They delayed their wedding by only one week.

David and Katie were there as witnesses, as planned. But a friend of Katie's had been brought in to sit with the two children for an hour. Timmy was suffering bouts of jealousy over the new arrival who was taking so much of his mother's time. The three-year-old wasn't in fit form for public appearances.

Emma looked like a goddess, dressed in pale gold silk damask that draped softly to show a white satin underdress. Pale, soft curls peeked from beneath her white cap and veil and she carried white tea roses that Ward had shipped in from Columbus—it was the second shipment of the costly, tiny buds, but the florist was happy and Ward did not care. An exquisite woman deserved an exquisite bouquet. That was how he thought of the matter.

Ward looked taller and more broad-shouldered than ever in his black cutaway coat and suit. He stood head and shoulders taller than Emma, and Katie thought they made a beautiful, *youthful* pair. The shining silver blended in Ward's dark hair gave him a touch of elegance and refinement, not age.

Katie's friend Regina—bless her heart—had prepared most of the supper during the short time the foursome had been gone, and they stepped into the house to be greeted by the inviting odor of roasting beef. Ward had made the local butcher a happy and more prosperous man as well.

Emma smiled at Katie's friend the moment she realized all the young woman had done. "Thank you, Regina. This was all very thoughtful."

"You're more than welcome, Mrs. Parker." Regina frowned

up at Ward, a man she had met for the first time less than two hours ago. "Oh, dear," she muttered.

Ward smiled. "Hamilton. Mrs. *Hamilton* now."

Embarrassed, Regina fled their midst with a few mumbled good wishes.

The moment the door closed behind the woman, the men shed their coats. Ward fetched a bottle of champagne from the depths of the well, where it had been cooling, and David set out Katie's best wineglasses.

Emma lavished considerable attention on Timmy these days; the poor lad was like a little lost soul. "Come and sit on Gram's knee," she coaxed, and lifted the boy when he backed up to her. "Do you think a cuddle would chase those blues away?" she crooned.

Ward watched her while he tackled the wire and cork on the bottle. He smiled, as everyone smiled when they watched Emma soothe a child. She was a natural, to his way of thinking. He also continued to suffer bolts of astonishment each and every time he was somehow reminded that she was a grandmother. Emma simply did not look the part.

And then it hit him. "Oh, my God," he said.

Three pairs of adult eyes turned on him.

"What is it, Ward?" Emma asked in alarm.

"I'm a *grandfather*!" he groaned.

There was a moment of stunned silence before Emma rocked backward with laughter. And then everyone laughed. Except Timmy, who was confused.

In the next moment a champagne cork popped and hit the ceiling.

The celebration had begun.

They gathered round the kitchen table, laughing, teasing, and telling old tales.

Katie would sip only enough to toast her mother and Ward's happiness. "I'll have a drunken baby," she said.

Ward moved close to Emma and rested his arm on the back of her chair. "Happy?" he asked softly, when she turned to smile at him.

Emma nodded her head and tipped toward him for a kiss.

Katie had turned her back, half-sheltered by her husband, as she nursed baby Jeffrey, and missed the exchange.

But David saw. "Oh, Lord," he drawled teasingly. "Katie, these two are worse than we were. And we were young and more eager to—"

Ward held up his glass to halt the flow of words. "Don't say it and don't count on it," he said. "An abundance of years does not diminish—"

"Ward," Emma warned.

" . . . the other," he finished with a grin.

Katie smiled over her shoulder. Her mother's complexion was glowing softly on the pink side. *Pink* with happiness. And the sight of such happiness was long overdue.

Emma and Katie spoke quietly on the porch late that afternoon as Ward and David shook hands at the backdoor.

"By the way," Ward said. "When you have a spare hour or two, perhaps you could come out to Emma's and give me a hand digging up a monstrous tree trunk."

David frowned. "A stump?"

"A big one. That old oak at the far end of the yard, near the barn, went down in the last storm. It's going to take at least two men and a team to get rid of the thing. But, the sight of that stump is driving Emma mad."

David laughed, knowing his mother-in-law fairly well. "I know. I know. It's making the yard look untidy. I'll be glad to come out and give you a hand," he added.

Ward clapped the younger man on the shoulder. "Thank you, my friend," he said as they joined the women on the porch.

"Thank him for what?" Emma asked curiously.

"David and I are going to 'de-stumpify' your yard," Ward said as he casually dropped an arm across her shoulders.

"De-stumpify?" Katie asked, frowning. "Is that a word?" she asked her husband.

"It must be, darling," he said, taking her elbow. "Say good night to your *parents*."

Katie grinned, tempted to say something suggestive, but she did not want to embarrass her mother. In fact, Katie wondered if Emma knew about the conversation she and Ward had shared in his shed a few weeks ago. "Good night, Emma," she said softly, kissing her mother's cheek. She faced Ward and reached up on her toes to kiss his cheek. "Good night, Ward."

Ward had never appreciated the benefits of being part of a family unit until he had met this young woman. Katie was at least partially responsible for a number of good things that had recently happened in his life, and for that he would be eternally grateful. He smiled and touched her cheek affectionately. "Good night, my dear," he said quietly.

And then he was taking Emma's hand and leading her away.

"They're staying in town tonight?" David asked as they watched the couple approach the breach in the hedge.

Katie laughed. "Ward said he didn't want Emma's damned rooster waking him at dawn the first morning of his honeymoon."

As they approached his house Ward veered off to the left. Emma stopped in her tracks. "Where are you going?"

"To the well!" he called quietly. "I'll meet you inside."

"More champagne," Emma murmured as she picked up her skirts and walked on. "Sweet man." She giggled. Actually, she thought she might have drunk quite enough of the stuff; she was feeling very bold and in need of her husband. And it had seemed to take an eternity to get away from Katie's house. "How shocking!" she scolded, laughing lightheartedly as she climbed the stairs.

Emma was draping her veil over the back of a chair when she looked up to see Ward standing in the open doorway holding a large tray.

"A snack for milady," he said, walking toward her. "You have to keep your strength up, Em," he teased.

Emma laughed as she examined his gift. Cold chicken, cheeses, bread, and champagne. "This looks lovely, darling. I only wish I were hungry."

"You will be after a little exercise," he said lightly.

She laughed again. "Ward, you have a way of making me feel young."

"You are young," he said, taking up the challenge of the bottle for the second time that day. "You do the same for me," he added.

Emma just stood there. Watching him. Loving him.

"It's amazing that I can feel mature and fatherlike one moment," he observed. "And feel like a young buck the next," he added with a wink.

"Is that how you feel," she whispered, "like a 'young buck'?"

"That's what you do for me, Em," he said softly as he popped the cork. He looked at her briefly between pouring glasses of wine. "Have I told you how lovely you are in that gown?"

"At least three times," she said. "But I could stand to be told again."

"You make me a proud and happy man when I see you in that gown," he said. He pressed a delicate glass into her hand and raised his glass in a toast. "There is only one thing that would make me prouder and happier," he told her. "Seeing you without it."

Emma shot him a bold smile. "I might say the same about that handsome suit of yours."

"Really, madam?" he drawled. He took her glass and set both on the table that stood between two high windows. "We *are* bold this evening," he whispered as he advanced on her.

"Could we stop talking, Ward?" she pleaded softly. "I think the champagne has gone to more than my head."

He threw back his head and laughed, even as he picked her up in his arms. "I think the good Lord has blessed me with the perfect mate, Em," he teased.

"You shouldn't say things like that," she scolded.

"Why not? Everyone deserves recognition for a job well done. He made you perfect, Emma Hamilton."

He stopped beside the large, high bed and set her on her feet. "Turn around, love," he said softly. "Let me help you."

Emma presented her back, staring at the wide bed while

he attended to the small buttons at the back of her gown. She wasn't surprised by the size of the thing; Ward had made and installed one just like it in her bedroom at the country house. He hated not being able to stretch out in bed.

A moment later she felt the coolness of the September evening air hit her skin when Ward pushed the gown from her shoulders.

"Cold?" he whispered against her ear.

"It isn't the cold that makes me shiver," she whispered in return.

His hands moved more quickly then, spurred by their mutual need. "Don't wear the corsets anymore, Em," he said softly. "You don't need them."

She turned to face him, stepping out of her petticoats as he removed his shirt. "I can't go about half-dressed," she pointed out.

"When I hug you, I want to feel *you*, not whalebone. And besides, the damned things will squash our child."

Emma's eyes followed the course of his hands as he shucked his trousers. "I'm convinced," she said.

They stood there, facing each other for a moment, naked and unashamed. He, proudly erect, and she, warmly flushed.

"Don't play with me tonight, darling," she whispered. "I need you now."

There were no more words. Ward picked her up and lowered her gently to the center of the bed, where he joined her and joined *with* her.

Afterward, candlelight danced softly, in yellow hues, across their skin as Ward lay propped up beside her, studying her body. His hand stroked her slowly while she lay on her back with eyes closed, basking in the afterglow of his loving.

"What do you think, Em?" he asked quietly.

She knew exactly what he was asking; his hand was circling slowly over her belly. "I'm hopeful, darling," she whispered.

Ward lowered his head, just long enough to gently kiss her ear. "There will be finger counting if you're carrying now," he said.

"I don't care."

He stared down at her until she opened her eyes. "You *don't* care, do you?"

Emma shook her head. "I've done nothing for which I'm ashamed," she said. "I love you and there's certainly no shame in that."

"I wish I'd met you twenty years ago," he said. "I feel as if I've been cheated of all those years with you."

"You haven't," she said, smiling. "We'll make up for those twenty years."

He stared at her, long and hard, and eventually raised his hand to stroke her cheek tenderly. "Yes, you make me believe we will," he whispered.

TEN

Indian summer was glorious, warm summerlike days in which Ward could work outside and cool nights that tinted the leaves of the trees from a pallet of bright colors.

Ward had moved to the country house with Emma, adapting easily to country life. The damned rooster continued to irritate him each morning, but with that exception, he had made the transition from fast-paced city slicker very easily. He liked his life now. And he loved Emma to distraction. There was nothing he would not do for her, and he knew she felt the same. They were wonderfully content and very much in love.

It was the latter part of October and Katie was feeling strong again. She had adjusted well to having two young children to care for, so much so that she had carefully planned the special day she and Ward had talked about so many weeks ago.

When the Franklins arrived at the country house, Emma greeted them with frowning curiosity. "What a nice surprise," she called as she moved down the steps from the house.

David jumped down from the carriage and hurried around to Katie's side. He took his infant son from him wife's arms and turned to place Jeffrey into Emma's waiting arms. Timmy was whimpering for his grandmother's attention before his father could reach to help him down. Once the child was on his feet and clasping a handful of Emma's skirts, David grinned at his mother-in-law wryly. "You're *certain* this is a *nice* surprise?" he muttered.

Emma laughed lightly, finger-combing Timmy's fine hair. "Of course it is," she said happily.

Katie received assistance descending from the carriage from

her husband then. "Let me take Jeffrey," she said, moving to her mother's side.

Emma would not give the infant over. "No," she said, shaking her head, "I don't have him nearly enough."

Katie shrugged, kissed her mother's cheek, and reached for a large basket that David had retrieved from the backseat of the rig.

Frowning in curiosity again, Emma stretched her neck to see what else David had back there. "What's all this?" she murmured. "And why is David away from the store on a Saturday?"

"It's a special day," Katie told her, her smile growing in greeting as Ward stepped up behind his wife. "Hello," she said. She took a step toward him and Ward bent to receive a kiss on the cheek from her. "Have we pulled you away from your work?"

Ward had set up a new workshop in a little used shed near the barn. He smiled, relieving her of the basket. "I was more than ready to be pulled away," he told her.

"*What* special day?" Emma questioned softly.

Katie winked at Ward and he nodded, giving the young woman license to reveal the surprise. "It's Emma's Day!" she said happily.

Timmy caught his mother's excitement and jumped up and down, clapping his hands. "Emma's Day!" he parroted.

Emma stared at her daughter, clearly not understanding.

Ward placed his hand on Emma's shoulder and bent, speaking softly. "Katie wanted to honor you in a special way, Em."

"Me?" she asked stupidly. "Why?"

Katie laughed. "Because you are *special*!" she said. "Because we love you. Because you do so much for all of us."

Tears rose instantly to Emma's eyes. "I don't do anything," she whispered, suddenly shy and overwhelmed by all the attention.

"You devote every moment of every day of your entire life to us, Emma," Katie told her. "Today is *your* day. We're going to devote this day to you."

"Let the celebration begin," David said, before moving toward the steps. He was carrying a second basket in one hand and had tucked a small keg of ale under his arm.

Katie lifted Timmy, balancing him on her hip as she walked beside her mother, following the two men.

"This is a wonderful thing you're doing, darling," Emma said softly, emotionally. "I'm very moved."

"Good," Katie said grinning. "I was extolling your qualities and virtues to Ward when I came up with the idea."

"When was this?"

"When you first began sleeping with him," she said lightly. "*Long* before the wedding, Mother," she teased.

Emma stopped, staring in horror as a blush crept over her cheeks. "Katie!" she breathed.

"Well, what is wrong in saying it?" she pointed out. "I knew you were. I would have thought something seriously wrong if you hadn't."

Emma shook her head, a slow smile turning her delicate lips as she came to accept that this, too, would be an open and shared topic between them. Knowing Katie had been aware of the depth of her relationship with Ward in its early days of their relationship had been one thing. Having Katie say the words had been another. Still, the two women had long ago moved comfortably into a close friendship as Katie had matured, and there had been little they had not shared over the years. Emma knew she should not have been surprised by Katie's frankness.

Katie touched her mother's hand. "All I care about is seeing you happy, Emma," she said. "And I see that in you now. Particularly when you look at him."

Emma bussed her daughter's cheek. "Thank you, darling," she said softly.

David was unpacking food and wine from the largest of the baskets when the women entered the kitchen.

"Where's Ward?" Emma asked.

David shrugged his shoulders as he removed a large bowl of bread pudding from the depths of the basket. "I don't think he's far away," he said with a mysterious grin.

Katie opened the top of the smaller basket and tipped Timmy sideways over the thing. "You take that and give it to Gram," she said.

Seconds later the child was holding a beribboned package.

"What's this?" Emma asked, teasing her grandson. "Is this for me?"

Timmy nodded as Katie set him down and immediately retrieved Jeffrey from her mother's arms.

Ward returned to his wife's side then and quietly slipped a second package onto the countertop beside her. "Presents?" he teased, affectionately kissing her cheek.

Emma shook her head, admonishing them for having squandered good money. But Ward could see how pleased she was.

Timmy was clamoring to "See!" as Emma removed the pink ribbon and paper packaging from the gift he had given her.

"Up!" Ward groaned, making a show of lifting the boy and settling him on his forearm.

"Oh," she whispered, removing the delicately woven shawl.

"From me!" Timmy proclaimed, and everyone laughed.

"Well, thank you, darling," Emma murmured as she kissed his cheek. She wrapped the gift around her shoulders then, admiring the softness. "It's beautiful."

"Winter is coming on and you need to keep warm," Katie said, with a wry smile. "That's for those rare moments when Ward isn't around."

Timmy did not understand why all the adults were laughing.

Ward pushed the second parcel along the counter. "And this is from me," he said. "Happy Emma's Day, love."

Emma felt like a girl and continued to blush like one as well. "I've said you shouldn't have done this, but it's wonderful!" she chirped happily.

Ward's gift stunned her not so much because of its beauty, but because she simply could not believe he had remembered a casual comment she had made months ago. "You remembered this?" she asked in wonder. It was a rosewood music box and the top was inlaid with delicate squares of mother-of-pearl. She had mentioned to him that she had once seen a music box in David's store and the thing had fascinated her.

"Turn the key on the bottom," he told her.

She turned it several times, and when she released the key, a sweet tune began to play. A delighted smile instantly wreathed her lips as Emma continued to stare. "What is it?" she asked in wonder.

"It was written by Tchaikovsky," he told her. "An excerpt from *Romeo and Juliet*."

"It's wonderful," she breathed, and turned her beautiful smile on him. "It would be wonderful to hear the entire piece."

Ward nodded his head, already thinking that they should take a trip to Columbus and attend the theater there. Emma would like that.

Emma was afraid to express her wish to see such a thing; he might purchase the entire production! "This is beautiful, Ward," she said as she fingered the smooth, cool top of the box. "Thank you," she whispered as she stood on her toes and pressed a tender kiss on his lips.

The tune wound down and Timmy bent and stretched, reaching for the music box, interrupting the concentrated gaze of love they shared.

"Wow!" Ward said lightly, turning away with the boy. "Let's find something that's safe for you to play with." Anticipating this visit, Ward had fashioned a number of wooden animals for the child. He picked up a small open box that he had left on a low shelf. "These little fellows have just been waiting for a new owner," he said as he set the box and the boy on the floor in a safe corner of the room.

Both of Timmy's small hands dived into the box and he squealed in delight as he removed a cow and a sheep.

Katie stood beside her mother, watching the scene with a gentle smile. "There's a man who loves children," she observed softly.

Ward heard and turned his head, grinning. "That's just as well."

David returned to the kitchen with a blanket-lined basket in which his youngest son would sleep. "Timmy!" he asked in feigned excitement. "What do you have there?"

Timmy held up both hands, an animal in each.

Katie had turned a suspicious look toward her mother. "What does he mean by that?"

David took Jeffrey from Katie's arms and stared curiously at each of the women. "What's going on?" he asked.

"I'm waiting to find out as well," Katie said softly.

Ward walked to his wife and tucked her beneath his arm.

Emma's complexion glowed with happiness, but obviously she was uncertain of how her news would affect her daughter and her son-in-law. "Now, Katie . . ."

"Oh, my God," Katie breathed, realizing the truth without the words being spoken.

"What?" David asked witlessly.

Katie squealed with delight and somehow managed to float upward, wrapping her arms around the couple's necks.

David stood back and watched the happy scene of hugs and laughter and shared kisses. As understanding dawned he, too, began to smile. "Well, well," he drawled, winking smartly at Ward. "Katie, don't strangle them," he said as he laid Jeffrey onto the soft padding of the baby's basket.

Katie backed off then, grinning madly as she smoothed the sleeve of Emma's day dress. "I'm finally going to have that brother and sister I've always wanted."

"Hold on," Ward growled affectionately. "We're expecting *one* child here."

"One never knows what will follow," Katie told him cheekily.

Chaos seemed to reign in the kitchen for the next hour as excited adult chatter filled the cozy room. The bottle of wine was opened to toast a far happier occasion than Katie had anticipated this day. The younger woman moved around the kitchen with an efficiency born of familiarity with the room as she continued to repeat the same words of wonder and happiness.

"It isn't all that remarkable," Emma said dryly at one point. "We aren't *that* old."

Katie shook her head. "I wasn't referring to your age, Emma." she explained as she grinned at Ward. "The odds of this ever happening were pretty grim until a few months ago."

Katie had their supper warming before Jeffrey began to wail with hunger. She picked the baby up and cooed to him as Ward offered his wife a few murmured words. The women retired to the comfort of the front parlor as the men left the house.

Timmy followed the two men, toddling across the yard in search of that pesky rooster.

Emma and Katie sat at opposite ends of the settee, smiling at each other as sweet sounds of a baby's contented suckling reached their ears.

Suddenly Katie's head dropped back briefly and she laughed. "It's wonderful!" she crowed.

Emma smiled softly. "Thank you, darling."

Something in her tone caused Katie's laughter to disappear. "There isn't anything wrong, is there, Emma?" she asked slowly.

Emma shook her head, still smiling. "You realize this baby will come early, don't you, Katie? There could be some talk. I hope you won't be embarrassed by that."

Katie flashed a severe look. "I won't be embarrassed," she said. "Will you?"

"No."

"Good," she said succinctly. "And what's a month or two? Babies come *early* all the time," she added cheerily.

"That's true," Emma returned softly. She calculated that she and Ward would be parents sooner than eight months after their marriage.

Katie stared down thoughtfully at her son, her mind returning to old wonderings for a moment. "Mother," she said quietly. "Is the reason you didn't have more children because of what Daddy *didn't* do?"

A long silence followed as Emma wondered what she should tell her daughter. Katie's suspicions were strong and not unfounded, but admitting the truth seemed of little purpose now. "Your father loved me, Katie. I believe that," she said softly.

Katie nodded her head, agreeing to leave the question be. "There won't be any concerns about you carrying this baby?" she asked awkwardly.

Emma smiled. "Because I'm no longer a strong young woman of twenty?" she teased. "Is that what you're asking?"

Katie grinned. "I suppose that's it. I simply did not know how to word it delicately."

Emma laughed. "No concerns, darling. I've seen Dr. Trimble and he agrees that I'm fit. Actually, I've felt exceptionally well lately."

Katie looked down at her son and moved him to her other breast. "It's hard to believe you'll be doing this soon," she said lightly.

"I'm looking forward to holding and nursing a baby again," Emma said with quiet reflection. "It's been a long time. I'm looking forward to the baby and me curling up in Ward's arms on a cold winter night."

Katie wondered if her mother had forgotten she was not alone, so intent was Emma in studying Jeffrey. She also knew instinctively that Emma had never curled up in Phillip's arms while holding *their* baby. Somehow that made her feel very sad.

"David likes to hold me at night when I feed Jeffrey," she said quietly.

Emma nodded. "I think Ward will, too," she said. "It makes everyone feel closer, doesn't it, sweetheart?"

Katie told her mother it would.

And she grieved silently because Emma was only going to discover that after her *second* child was born.

At the age of thirty-nine.

"Don't think of the past, Katie," Emma whispered with certain insight. "Be happy for me. It's very special to be my age and experience new things."

Katie laughed. "You make it sound as if you're ancient!"

Emma smiled and smoothed her skirt over her still-flat belly.

*   *   *

Ward and David circled the oak stump, frowning. Both men
had removed their shirts against the heat of the midday sun.
They had dug a trench around the base of the stump, but were
quickly getting nowhere.

"I suspected this might happen," David muttered. "We could
dig for a month and this thing would not move."

Ward agreed. "Maybe we could hollow it out and plant
flowers in the center," he said dryly. "Think Emma would
like that?"

David shook his head and laughed. "Not our Emma!" he
said emphatically. He dropped his shovel and walked toward
the rig he had left beside the barn. "I'll be right back!" he
called over his shoulder.

Ward stared glumly at the stubborn stump for a moment,
trying to reason out another method of attack. When Timmy
flashed by, chasing poor old Soloman, Ward called, "Your
gram's going to give you a scolding for chasing that rooster!"

Timmy stopped.

Soloman stopped.

The two stared at each other for a moment.

When Timmy turned away, the rooster crowed.

"He don't play," Timmy told Ward. "He's mean."

"He's a lot more than that," the man muttered, reaching
down and scooping the boy up in his arms. "Let's get a drink
of cool water," he said as his long, easy strides carried them
in the direction of the pump.

Emma came down the back steps and met them there.

Ward spied the wooden bucket she carried and reached for
it. "You're not carrying water," he said firmly.

Emma stood beside Ward, holding Timmy against her skirts
as she watched her husband fill the bucket with water before
reaching for the dipper that hung from the pump.

Ward raised his arm, drinking deeply of the cool water as
Emma watched.

"You are magnificent," she murmured, openly admiring
him.

Stunned, Ward tipped forward, brushing at the water that escaped the dipper and dribbled down his chest. He grinned at his wife, looked askance at Timmy, and then raised his eyes to hers again. "I'm glad you approve, madam," he said softly.

"Oh, I do," she returned proudly.

"Might I say the same of you?"

"You might," she said cheekily.

But David approached, spoiling their moment of play.

Emma frowned at the three sticks held by her son-in-law. "What is that?"

"This is dynamite, Emma," David said. "This will succeed where Ward and I have failed."

Ward frowned. "You're going to blast that stump?"

David nodded. "*We* are, yes."

Emma did not think she liked having dynamite set off near her house or her husband. "It's too dangerous," she said.

But David was set to conquer. "We'll have that thing out of there in minutes," he said. "Would you keep Timmy up at the house though, Emma, please? I don't want him running around here."

Emma flashed Ward a worried frown. "Leave the stump," she pleaded.

Ward raised his hands in resignation. As long as David knew what he was doing, blasting the stump out of the ground was at least a solution.

After several moments of discussion, Emma herded Timmy toward the house, believing that men were far more stubborn than any stump of wood would ever be.

"I sincerely hope you know what you're doing with that stuff," Ward muttered as they approached the object of their attention.

David grinned. "What can be so difficult?" the younger man asked. "All we have to do is shove the sticks under the damned stump and stand back."

Ward's eyes rolled heavenward. "That's the extent of your knowledge, David? You told Emma—"

"Do you want to continue trying to dig this thing out?" David countered.

Ward admitted he did not.

David shoved the three sticks of dynamite far apart, under the base of the stump.

"You're certain that isn't too much?" Ward asked doubtfully. "We don't want to blow the barn."

How much was too much? It was a big stump.

David took a good look around the immediate area and shrugged. "We might damage the edge of these shrubs," he said, pointing, "but that's all. Stop worrying."

David removed a small box of matches from his pocket and brandished the package at the offending stump. "This is going to end all of our problems," he said. "And then we can go up to the house and have a long, cool drink of ale."

That part sounded all right to Ward.

Suddenly three fuses were hissing and both men were running toward the far corner of the barn.

"There will be toothpicks flying through the air!" David laughed. "Thousands of 'em!"

There was a thunderous roar that caused pain even though both men had pressed their hands over their ears. Wood splintered and shot up in the air along with chunks of roots and earth. Ward dared to peek at the scene and narrowed his eyes as he inspected the flying debris.

"Oh, Lord," he breathed as he pulled on David's shirt sleeve to get the younger man's attention.

The forceful yank did the trick and David looked at his companion. "What?"

"Look!" Ward whispered harshly.

David looked, just as the last of the feathers were drifting back toward the ground.

"Oh—oh."

"Well said," Ward drawled wryly.

David closed his eyes against the scene. "We got the stump," he muttered.

"Yep."

"And the damned rooster?" he hissed.

"Yep."

"Emma set a lotta store by that rooster," David added, pained.

"Yep."

Both men looked at each other for a long, long, silent moment.

"I think we should go get ourselves an ale," David suggested at last. "And let the womenfolk know that the stump removal went well."

By silent agreement, they knew they would not be telling Emma about the demise of poor old Soloman. Not today. This was Emma's Day, and neither man wanted to ruin Emma's supper.

And as much as that rooster had been the bane of his quiet, country existence, Ward dreaded the moment when he would be forced to tell her.

Sunrise would never be the same.

Ward finished banking the fire and climbed the stairs toward their bedroom. It had been a fine meal that Katie had prepared. It had been a fine day, with the exception of Soloman's misadventure. Ward was feeling mighty guilty about that. He had debated whether to explain the accident to Emma tonight or in the morning and made up his mind to speak to her tonight.

Until he saw her sitting up in their bed.

Waiting for him.

"What took you so long?" she asked, smiling. "Are you becoming reluctant in your old age?"

He laughed. "Reluctant? To come to your bed?" he asked in feigned wonder as he quickly removed his clothing. "Hardly, madam," he murmured as he stretched out beside her. "I lose twenty years every time I climb those stairs to you."

Emma smiled warmly. "We both do, darling," she said. She reached out and smoothed the silvery hair at his temples. "It was a marvelous day, Ward," she said. "You spoil me with all the wonderful things you do."

Like killing your rooster? he thought, flinching. "It was Katie's idea," was all he said.

Emma snuggled down against him, resting her head on his shoulder. "I believe Katie took rather well to the idea of having a sibling," she said.

Ward laughed shortly, surprised. "How did you expect her to react?"

"Well, it must be just a little disconcerting for a grown woman to watch her own mother grow fat with child," she said.

"Perhaps some pious, prudish, straitlaced little miss would respond that way," he said as he rested the palm of his hand on her belly. "That is not our Katie, however."

"No," she said quietly. "That isn't our Katie."

Ward was concentrating on following the path of his hand. "Em, I think you're getting a little rounder," he said.

Emma rolled fully onto her back to give him access to her body.

She stared intently at his dark eyes as he concentrated on inspecting her for signs of change. How she loved him. How gentle he was, how loving and devoted. She trusted him completely with every fiber of her being, every moment of her existence. Emma did not know what she had ever done to deserve him, but she would be forever grateful that she had.

"You are rounder," he said softly, convinced that she was. Ward lowered his head, and his lips replaced his hand on her belly. He kissed her worshipfully before rising up to smile at her. "You're feeling well, aren't you, Em?" he asked.

"You know I am," she said, smiling warmly. "As close as we are, you would know if it were otherwise." She frowned at him then. "You're not going to worry about me for the next six months, Ward?"

"I simply want you both well and healthy," he said.

"We will be, I promise."

"You have no doubts, starting a family at our age?"

She laughed. "No! But it would appear you do!"

"No," he said firmly. "I'm living in eager anticipation," he added sincerely.

"I could do with a little anticipation," she murmured suggestively. "Right this very moment."

He grinned as his hand fondled her breast. "Obviously, pregnancy hasn't turned you away from me," he said softly.

"I think it's made me want you more," she admitted. "I hadn't thought that possible."

A passionate light sparked in his eyes. "Do you want me, Em?" he breathed as his head lowered toward her.

The sun had not yet risen high enough to assault the bedroom with a single ray of light when he heard it.

Ward bolted up in their bed and waited.

The sound came again and he frowned in concentration as he waited for a third occurrence to confirm the matter for him.

When it came, he sighed, frowning in resignation as he fell back against his pillows.

"What's wrong, darling?" Emma asked sleepily.

"Was that Soloman?" he muttered.

"Of course it was Soloman," she said, confused.

Silent laughter welled up inside him, causing Ward's chest to heave and convulse.

Emma caught the motion and turned to see him fully. "What are you doing?"

"I'm forever to be tormented by that damned rooster!" he said through his laughter. "This shall be my reward!" he added dryly.

Emma propped herself up, truly concerned about his mental condition. "Ward, have you been drinking ale while I slept?"

He shook his head, wiping tears of merriment from his eyes with the back of his hand. He looked up at her then, grinning in the face of her worried frown. Hooking his hand in her hair, he pulled her down on top of his wide chest. "Good morning, my love," he murmured.

ELEVEN

April showers had flooded the land for three days, and Emma was determined to have chicken for supper.

Ward was normally not averse to going out to the henhouse to get their supper. It was a far cry from the bold men of old who ventured out to the bush against unbeatable perils to bring home wild game for their ladyloves. But as Ward saw it, he was still half–city slicker, and beheading a chicken was hazardous enough for him. Particularly this day; he had left the door to the henhouse half-open when he entered, with the result that several of the ladies were running around the pen, squawking and screeching in the rain as Ward pursued first one then another.

He was trying to herd the birds back into the safety of the henhouse, but the wily hens seemed to know what he was about and wanted nothing to do with him. Soloman settled himself on the fence and crowed.

Drenched through to his skin, Ward straightened and frowned at the male bird. "Well, you get them inside," he grumbled and headed to the smokehouse to fetch one of the curing hams that hung there.

He slapped the rain from his hat before he entered the kitchen.

Emma took one look at him, the condition of him, and the ham in his hand, and said, "Oh, dear."

"Those hens don't like me, Em," he said wearily as he dropped the ham on the counter.

Emma grinned as she lowered her bulk slowly to a straight-backed wooden chair. "Soloman doesn't think much of you, either," she said lightly. Ward had eventually told her of his guilt the night he thought he and David had blown the bird into something smaller than chicken croquettes. "Don't worry, darling," she soothed as she pressed her hand into the small of her back. "The cow and I still love you."

Ward frowned at her attempt to gain ease and knelt beside her chair. "Let me do that," he said, replacing her hand with his own, massaging deeply into her aching muscles with his fingers. "I'll be glad when this baby comes, Em," he said worriedly.

Emma smiled tiredly. "Me, too," she confessed. "I don't think it will be much longer," she added.

He had noticed that the baby had dropped lower in her belly, and Emma told him that was a good sign. Ward was growing impatient, but not for his own sake. There was little about Emma he did not notice and he had noticed that she was becoming very tired.

"Actually, Ward," Emma said quietly, "I hate to send you out in the rain again, but I was wondering if you might ride for the doctor."

It took a moment for her meaning to register, but the minute Ward caught her message, his head snapped up. "It's time?"

She nodded, smiling as she wiped rain from his forehead with her fingertips. "I've been in labor for a few hours now."

Ward jumped to his feet. "What? Why didn't you tell me? How could I not see?"

"You've been chasing chickens for hours," she exaggerated teasingly as she reached for his hand. "I'm sorry about the chickens, Ward."

"I don't care about the damned chickens," he said. "Let me get you up to bed, Em. Then I'll go for Katie and the doctor."

"I don't need to go to bed. You've been through this before, darling. Remember, Katie?"

He remembered. He remembered he had been scared to death and Katie had not been his *wife* birthing his *child*.

"I am not going to panic, Em," he told her severely. "I've been over this a hundred times in my mind and I know exactly what needs to be done and how I can help you."

Emma smiled at him tenderly. "You just have to be with
me, Ward. That's all the help, all the strength I'll need."

He nodded. "You'll be all right while I'm gone?"

"Go, darling," she said fondly.

Ward slapped his sodden hat back on his head. Turning
back, he issued one last command. "No cleaning windows
while I'm gone."

She laughed.

He did not take time to saddle his horse, but slipped the
bridle into place and mounted the big bay. The afternoon light
was more akin to evening time as the heavy rains persisted.

Ward rode first to the home of Dr. Trimble and set that
man on his way before stopping to request that Katie come
out to the house.

Katie flew into action.

"I think it's easier for me to actually *birth* a child than to
worry about what my mother will go through," she told David
as she threw a few belongings for herself and Jeffrey into a
valise.

David and Timmy could return to the house at any time.
But if Katie stayed on in the country, Jeffrey would need to
be with her.

Emma remained calm and tried to calm her worried family,
too. "For heaven's sake," she told them firmly. "I've done this
before."

And then a severe pain struck her and she was forced to
brace herself against the back of a chair.

Dr. Trimble nodded to Ward and the message was fairly clear.

"Come on, my love," he said softly as he picked her up
in his arms. "If you want to walk, I'll walk with you. But
upstairs, Em. In our bedroom."

When he entered the room with her, Emma was once again
gripped by pain. "Hold on," he told her, and her arms tightened around his neck. When she breathed again, Ward laid her
carefully on the bed. "Is this where you want to be?" he asked.

Emma smiled up at him and nodded. Moments later she
suddenly reached for his hand, arching her body upward.

Ward sat beside her, living through hell, living through the next moments of contractions that seemed to go on for hours. There were moments when he actually hated himself for doing this to her.

Actually, Emma had a short labor, as compared to her first child, and as Soloman crowed and heralded the dawn she pushed to relieve herself of her child.

"That's it, Em!" Ward breathed. "She's here!" He had been supporting her back, and now he eased back against the head-board, letting her rest against his chest. "Oh, Emma," he whispered as the child was laid on his wife's belly.

Emma was laughing and crying at once. "A girl," she whispered as she took stock of fingers and toes. "A perfect little girl."

Like her mother, Ward thought. He watched Katie take his daughter from the hands of Dr. Trimble, his dark eyes following the younger woman as she moved toward a corner of the room that had been prepared in advance.

"She's just going to wash her," Emma said perceptively.

"I knew that," he returned. Still, it was difficult to have the child taken that far away.

Dr. Trimble suggested then that Ward might want to leave.

"Why?" he asked the doctor.

"Well . . ."

Emma gripped Ward's hand then, distracting both men as she moaned softly.

Ward took exception to the good doctor suggesting he might be faint of heart. "I know about the afterbirth, Doctor," he said. "I'm staying with her."

Somehow, that process seemed worse for Emma than the actual birth. Ward's heart did not stop thumping painfully in his chest until she was relieved and lying back, exhausted.

"She's all right?" he questioned the doctor as he frowned down at the pale face of his lovely wife.

"Fine," Trimble said, smiling.

Katie approached then, holding his daughter. "Do you want to take her and show her off to David?" she said with a broad smile. "I've left her little basket on a chair near the stove. It's warm there for her."

Katie had expected Ward to look horrified at the very thought of holding an infant so tiny. She had been grossly mistaken.

His eyes dropped to the red, wizened face of his child as Katie carefully laid the baby in his arms. "She's pretty ugly," he said dryly. "Until tomorrow, right?" he asked hopefully.

Katie laughed. "She's going to be beautiful."

Ward looked at Emma then, his eyes mirroring his wonder of her. "If she becomes half the woman her mother is," he said softly, "she'll be remarkable." He turned his gaze on Katie then, smiling fondly. "Like you."

Katie blushed at the compliment. "Go on with you!" she said softly.

Ward shook his head. "I don't want to leave her."

"We're going to make Emma more comfortable, Ward," Katie explained. "And then she'll sleep for a bit. Go have a drink of brandy or something with David and come back later."

As soon as Katie and Dr. Trimble left Emma, Ward returned to their room and sat in a chair he pulled up to the bed.

She was sleeping, but he would wait.

He had something he had forgotten to tell her.

Hours later Emma's eyes fluttered a time or two before she fully awakened and stared into the smiling eyes of her husband.

"Hello," she whispered.

"Hello, my love," he said softly.

"Where is she?"

Ward grinned and got up from his chair, moving beyond the foot of the bed to a chair near the fire. "I put her here so she would be warm," he explained, bending over the basket he had left on the chair. Seconds later he turned with their daughter securely tucked against his chest.

Emma smiled as he walked toward her. "You look as if you've done that a hundred times before."

Ward smiled, too. "I haven't, but it's strange—with her I feel very confident."

Emma turned slowly onto her side, bending her arm to create a warm nest as Ward placed the baby there.

"Are you in pain, Em?" he asked, frowning. He had noticed how cautiously she had moved.

Emma smiled up at him briefly, shaking her head as her gaze lowered to the infant in her arms. "I'm feeling nothing but proud," she said.

He knelt beside the bed and watched as Emma unfastened the tiny row of buttons on the yoke of her nightdress and stroked the baby's cheek until she turned her tiny head toward the breast that was awaiting her. The infant took firm hold, startling Emma.

Ward grinned. "She's strong," he said proudly.

Emma smiled up at him. "We're a *pair*," she said, remembering.

Ward took her hand in his and they savored several moments of silent intimacy with their daughter between them.

"How long have you been sitting here waiting for me to awaken?" Emma asked eventually.

"Hours," he said bluntly.

"You should have gotten some sleep, Ward. You look tired."

He shook his head. "I had something to tell you."

She smiled. "What did you have to tell me, darling?"

"Two things, really," he said, raising his free hand to cup his daughter's head gently with his palm. "Firstly, that I love you."

"I know," she said softly. "I love you, too."

"Second," he whispered, staring into her eyes. "I wanted to thank you. For everything. For being you. For loving me. For *her*," he added with such intense emotion that happy tears welled up in Emma's eyes.

"You are very welcome," she managed.

"And we are not going to do this again," he added.

Emma looked confused. "Do what?"

"Have more children," he told her. "My heart has been in my throat for weeks, Em," he said. "I don't want to see you go through this again."

Emma smiled mysteriously.

She was older now. Wiser now.

And she suspected fate had placed this man in her barn, and her life, for a reason. Possibly a *number* of reasons.

Reaching up to touch the fine, silver hair at his temple, Emma murmured, "We'll talk about *children*, darling. We'll talk."

AUTHOR'S NOTE

Dear Reader,

I hope you enjoyed reading Emma and Ward's story as much as I enjoyed writing it for you.

Emma's Day is meant to be a salute to all the women in the world who give so lovingly, caringly, and selflessly of themselves.

This story is for you!
Happy Mothers Day!

COMING HOME

by

Teresa Warfield

❧

ONE

Taney County, Missouri
Spring 1911

A lover's kiss is coming soon.

Eighteen-year-old Rachel Cameron withdrew from the earthenware mug sitting on the oak table before her, then gathered courage, eased forward again, and tipped the dish to have another look inside of it.

Her eyes widened. Sure as Moses, the coffee grounds had formed a perfect circle in the bottom of the cup.

Rachel jerked back, nearly toppling the mug, and gripped the edges of her white apron. Blame it all! She didn't believe the nonsense Gramma Cameron was always rattling about, things like "When your left ear burns, someone is saying something mean about you," and "When a spoon drops and the handle points in a certain direction, that means visitors will come soon from that way. . . ." Gramma's sayings were nothing but silly Ozark Mountain superstitions—that's what the teachers at the St. Louis girls' school had told Rachel, and she was smart enough to believe them.

She gathered and stacked the family's four dirtied plates from breakfast, casting a scowl or two at the mug. She hadn't really seen that ring. No, she surely hadn't.

Or had she?

She eased toward the cup, tipped it again, and glanced down.

Certain-sure, the ring was still there. And a ring like that was something. A ring like that, formed from grounds settled in just the right places, was a pretty unusual occurrence.

211

Her friends and teachers at school would laugh at her for
even thinking what she was thinking: that maybe they were
wrong and her grandmother was right after all. That maybe
there *was* something to all the beliefs and lore Gramma had
told her most of her life—before Gramma had convinced Pap
to send her to the school, "where Rachel can learn the way
she wants to." That had been four years ago, but Rachel had
spent every summer at home—her father's only condition.
Until recently.

The cabin door creaked open and in walked her little brother, Ben, suspenders holding up his trousers. Lydia Cameron
followed the eight-year-old boy, her silvery hair pinned in a
knot to the top of her head. Her yellow dress was made from
homespun rather than material bought from the store in Brush
Lane, a nearby hamlet. She looked fresh, like spring, her face
bright, her green eyes sparkling as she lifted a bucket of milk
and placed it on the table. Little Ben did the same with the
bucket he toted, then Gramma fastened a disbelieving gaze on
Rachel.

"I hate to forever peck at you, Rachel," she said, sighing. "But
you don't seem altogether here this mornin'. Daydreaming, so
we almost didn't have biscuits made for your pap when he came
in from tendin' the hogs. And now . . . me'n Ben have been out
milking for a good hour, an' you don't even have the dishes
warshed." She eyed the book Rachel had placed facedown in
one of the four chairs surrounding the table.

Rachel had meant to hide the book—*Lost Face* by Jack
London—before Gramma and Ben returned from milking so
Gramma wouldn't know she'd been reading while she was
supposed to be tending to the morning dishes. But there the
book lay, condemning Rachel.

"There's a time for this an' a time for that," Lydia said
gently. "I know it's been hard for you since you came home
from St. Louis for good. If I'd my way, you'da stayed right
where you wanted to stay an' kept on with what you were
learnin'. But your pap . . . he's protective of his own, y'see.
He allowed he was losing touch with you while you were in
the city, an' that you might be real different if the city folks

had hold of you too long. I know it's been a spell since you helped us tend the place, Rachel, but you don't want your pa settin' after you. Do your chores, then your reading."

"Yes, Gramma," Rachel said, hanging her head in embarrassment. Her grandmother had recognized early on, when Rachel was perhaps a year older than Ben, that Rachel loved to read, and she had taken down from the loft her collection of old dime novels, ones involving Wild Bill Hickok, the James brothers, Floyd Edings, Belle Starr, and a number of other illustrious figures. She had read them all to Rachel, who loved getting caught up in the adventures. But when Rachel had learned to read well, she read the dime novels to herself over and over.

Now, of course, Rachel had gone on to bigger, more respectable "literature," as Mrs. Steele at the school called the writings of Mr. London and many others—O. Henry, Edwin Robinson, Harold Wright, Mark Twain . . . Still, Gramma Cameron had taught her to read, then encouraged her love of it. She had talked Pap into sending her to the big St. Louis school when Rachel had thought such a thing couldn't possibly be accomplished. She knew her father felt that once she completed the primers at the Brush Lane school, she was finished with her learning—a girl didn't need any more than that, after all. And reading instead of tending to her chores was the way Rachel was thanking Gramma for all she had done to make sure Rachel continued school long after being let out of Brush Lane.

Nodding at Rachel's response, Lydia Cameron turned back to the buckets of milk, never one to give too long a going-over. She ruffled Ben's strawberry-blond hair just as Rachel put the coffee cup she'd been staring into on top of the stacked plates. Then she carried the pile of dishes to the small tub sitting atop a cabinet her father had built and placed against one wall years ago. She had managed to fill the tub with water before she'd picked up Jack London's book, thinking that reading was more entertaining than washing dishes. She had even managed to clean the spoons and forks.

She set the plates beside the tub and pushed them back and to the right so they wouldn't be accidently knocked off. The damp rag she'd left beside the tub before picking up her book hit the floor with a soft plop, and Rachel groaned inwardly, hoping Gramma hadn't noticed it.

"Reckon we'll have visitors soon," Lydia said. "Usually by evening when someone drops a dishrag."

"Rachel says she don't put no stock in your s-sup'shitions," Little Ben chimed, his tongue stumbling over the *s* sounds. In the week Rachel had been home, he'd lost both upper front teeth.

Rachel felt her face grow hot. She hadn't meant for Ben to repeat that, but she should have known that he would. "I didn't say nothing of the sort."

"Did too!"

"Oh, just you never mind. Go on'n help Pap down at Mr. Stephens's lumber mill."

"Ain't old 'nough. Pap says so."

Rachel twisted around. Ben had stepped around Gramma and now stood between her and Rachel. "I've never heard him say that," Rachel countered.

"You ain't been home long 'nough to've heard him say it." Ben propped his fists on his hips. " 'Sides, you did too say that 'bout Gramma's sup'shitions. Don't tell no shretcher!"

Rachel took a deep breath. "I'm not *lying*."

"It's called a shretcher, Pap says so! He says you got too much city in you up thar in St. Louie."

"It's *there*, not 'thar,' and I don't care what Pap says!"

"That's enough," Gramma said sternly, taking Ben by the shoulders. "Ben, go hoe the garden. I'll be 'long directly."

Ben reluctantly shuffled away. There were times when he was cute, when he was precious, when he looked a lot like Mama had. But there were times, too, when he could be a downright irritation.

He went, giving the front door a harder shove than needed to shut it.

Lydia tipped her head and regarded her granddaughter through narrowed eyes. "Ben don't mean no harm, Rachel. He just repeats things like any youngun'll do."

"He shouldn't repeat things like that."

"Was what he said the truth? That you don't put stock in the things I say?"

Rachel glanced down at the puncheons and twisted her lips. "Some of the things . . . they're hard to believe, is all."

"You never had any trouble believin' 'em before."

Before I went to school in the city, she means.

"No matter how much book learnin' a body gets, Rachel, there're still things—signs—that only the good Lord can show us. You might 'llow I'm just a silly old woman, but I've watched the comin's an' goin's in these mountains for years. I ain't always right, but then neither is anybody. One thing's for sure. When you waggle your tongue, people find out, an' sometimes without tryin'."

Oh, but wasn't that the truth? Rachel thought, ashamed that she'd hurt Gramma Cameron's feelings. She wanted to crawl beneath the table, go hide in the cellar . . . She wanted to take back what she'd said about not putting stock in Gramma's superstitions.

But she still wasn't sure she believed in them anymore. Some things could simply be *explained*. The number of days between the new moon and the first snow wasn't always the same as the number of snows that came that winter. For three years, Rachel had kept track—had kept a record—and it just wasn't always so. Like a lot of other things just weren't so.

"I'm going to help Ben," Lydia said. "After you warsh the dishes, clean the milk with the cloth an' store it in the springhouse. Sweep up an' make the ticks, then you can read all your book you want till we set about fixing supper."

"Yes, Gramma," Rachel said, not even thinking of objecting. She fetched the rag from the floor just as Gramma walked back out the same door she'd come in. Rachel could have predicted that—Lydia Cameron believed that bad luck would come if a person didn't walk out the same door through which she had entered.

There was no denying the thrill one got while reading Gramma's dime novels. Rachel always became the hero or heroine, racing along on a fine steed, sometimes outrunning

the lawman, sometimes *being* the lawman who was chasing
the bandit. . . . Belle Starr, filled with courage and daring,
was Rachel's favorite. Of course, Rachel would never mount
a horse and rob a bank and she'd surely never condone anyone
doing such a thing, but Belle Starr was no less exciting just
because she robbed and wreaked havoc throughout the Ozarks
and Indian Territory.

At some point during the day, after the morning dishes had
been washed, the milk strained, the floors swept, and the
ticks made, Jack London's picturesque tale began to drag,
and Gramma's dime novels started calling to Rachel. She
succeeded in ignoring the urge to climb up into the loft where
she and Little Ben slept, go to the one far corner, and find the
box where the books were kept.

The next morning she walked with Pap and Ben upriver
to the lumber mill where her father worked most every day,
and Pap roused Ben with the story of Belle Starr's famous horse
race in which the Bandit Queen lost five hundred dollars,
then promptly won five thousand. Ben's eyes were aglow
with excitement, and Rachel suspected hers were, too. She
hid her enthusiasm by walking with her head bowed, not
wanting anyone who came along to think she actually felt
moved while listening to the outrageous story. There was no
truth to it, and she had learned at school that if there was no
truth to something, it shouldn't be repeated.

But despite what she'd been taught, she climbed up to the
loft later—after she and Ben had left Pap at the mill and
returned home, and after Gramma had taken Ben and a few
pies and gone visiting in the wagon—and found the box of
dime novels.

Now here she sat overlooking the White River, cradled
in the arms of an oak, partially hidden by newly dressed
branches. In the house she had risked being discovered with
the silly novel in hand or close by if Gramma and Ben, or Pap,
returned earlier than she expected. She became too caught up
in the heroes' and heroines' adventures to sit in the house
and read—any family member could walk right in. She had
decided she needed a hiding place, and so she had chosen

the old but sturdy oak. From a small branch, she'd even hung the leather pouch in which she hid the novels just in case any of her family should come home early and she was forced to climb down.

She had just read the first line of a Bandit Queen adventure when a dove cooed from somewhere nearby.

Rachel tensed, knowing what Gramma Cameron would say: "When an unmarried girl hears a dove coo, the first man to ride by will be her future husband."

"Silly superstitions," Mrs. Steele had called a few of Gramma's beliefs when Rachel had repeated some of them shortly after arriving in St. Louis for her first session at school. They were unrealistic and shouldn't be given much mind, if any.

Rachel settled back against the oak limbs and began reading again.

She whizzed through the first book, climbing rocky mountain ledges and hiding in caves with Belle. Then she picked up a second novel, in which the Bandit Queen decided to steal into a camp and take some horses in the middle of the night. That was Belle, daring and outrageous, exciting and—

Rachel heard the unmistakable whicker of a horse, then a strong breeze swayed the lighter branches and almost made off with her pouch; the poke twisted near the end of the small limb. Rachel put a hand out to steady it.

She glanced down, trying to see between the branches. Had Gramma and Ben returned already? Surely not. They would have arrived at the Stewarts' only a short time ago, and after leaving there, Gramma planned to go on upriver to see the Howitts. Besides, if Gramma were returning, Rachel would hear the noisy creak of the wagon.

She heard whistling instead and suddenly knew the whicker hadn't come from the Cameron horses. Pap whistled sometimes, but the mill was a mile to the west, and she and Ben had *walked* with Pap to the mill this morning because the early-spring days were nice and cool and pretty. Unless Pap had borrowed a horse . . .

Rachel finally glimpsed the rider, coming from the east, and the man she saw darn sure wasn't her father. She twisted on the branches and craned to have a better look at the foreigner.

His honey-colored hair glowed softly beneath the afternoon sunlight, made all the brighter by its glittering reflection on the river. He was lean and clean-shaven, his hair tumbling slightly over his brow; in the back, it just touched the collar of his dark blue shirt. Something about the way he rode, easy but erect, his shoulders and head held straight and proud, made Rachel think he wasn't a hillsman. No . . . no native rode that way, with an air of stirring self-assurance. The man resembled more of a city gentleman come to the country for a spell. Rachel wasn't sure whether to climb down from the tree and make his acquaintance or just sit and peer down at him.

He must have felt her stare; as he drew nigh to the tree he manipulated the reins he held, making the horse skitter in a circle while he glanced about, first off to the purple slopes and grayish-blue ledges set back some distance from the riverbank, then around in general, then up.

Rachel shrank back into the inviting curve formed by the two branches against which she'd been lying. But surely her calico dress, decorated with tiny red flowers, did little to help hide her.

She wanted another look at the stranger. She surely did. She liked the way he sat atop that horse, the way he seemed to be in such command of it.

His horse quieted; there was not one little whicker or even a thud from a hoof on the ground. Rachel couldn't help herself—she rose and strained to see if he'd disappeared. She'd be horribly disappointed if he had.

He had.

She shifted in the branches, steadying herself on one, thinking she would climb down and get a drink from the well on the other side of the hill. In these last few moments her mouth had suddenly gone dry. She propped the novel she'd been reading on the juncture of the branches and moved an inch or two, starting down around the book.

"There you are. Hiding in the tree," a rich masculine voice said.

Rachel switched positions so fast this time, she lost hold of the branch and slipped. She and the novel went tumbling. Other branches snagged at her dress, tore one sleeve, then she landed on her stomach on the soft new grass, having eased the fall with her outstretched hands.

For a moment she couldn't move; she'd had the breath knocked out of her. Then the foreigner was at her side, turning her, asking if she was all right.

Rachel managed to sit up and have a look at her sleeve. Torn beyond repair, she thought grimly. Her arm beneath had been so scratched and cut, it smarted something fierce. She moved her back and neck around, then shifted her legs. Everything but her arm seemed fine. She reckoned she'd be sore all over for nigh to a week, but at least she wasn't twisted and broken.

"Timothy Benton's the name," the man offered. "Lord, but why were you camped up yonder in that tree?"

"Wasn't 'camped' up there," Rachel snapped, surprised that he talked a little like a hillsman. There was some polish on his speech—he said "Lord" instead of "Lawd"—but she couldn't imagine a city gentleman saying "up yonder." One would say "up there," without even turning it over in one's mind.

"I didn't mean to frighten you into falling," he said.

She gained her feet and stood glaring, pulling the torn sleeve away from the wounds on her arm so it wouldn't stick to them as they scabbed over. "Well, what did you mean to do?"

A grin pulled at one corner of his mouth. His eyes were a vivid turquoise blue. "Catch whoever was spying." His gaze shifted to the novel that lay facedown in a tangle of newsprint pages.

Rachel's eyes flared at the sight. The pages were old and yellowed and slightly curled around the edges. She was always real careful whenever she read the books *because* they were so old—and because Gramma treasured them. She hoped the pages hadn't been ripped on the way down from that tree.

"Belle Starr," Timothy Benton mumbled, stepping forth to scoop up the book.

"No, don't!" Rachel cringed. It wouldn't do for this polished man to know she'd been reading a dime novel. It just wouldn't do.

He gave her a curious look.

"It's Gram—I mean, it belongs to my grandmother. She's had it for years an' years, and I don't—*wouldn't* want anything to happen to it. She don't—*doesn't* know I have it right now."

She said the last rather sheepishly, and she was thankful when he glanced down at the book, breaking their eye contact.

He brushed a blade of grass from the novel's cover—from the sketch of Belle—then looked up at her again. "I see. . . . You're something of a bandit yourself." Amusement coated his words and sparkled in his eyes.

"I ain't, I . . ." Rachel set her teeth hard, then grabbed for the novel.

He held it up, just beyond her reach.

"What're you doing?" she demanded.

"I want to look at it, is all."

"Don't pretend interest in that there book!"

"It's 'thar' not 'there,' " he teased, correcting her in the opposite way she'd corrected Ben yesterday morning. "And I'm not pretending. I was raised in the hills around Springfield, and I grew up listening to legends about the Bandit Queen. But I never thought to discover her hiding contraband in a tree."

Rachel's faced heated. "There ain't nothing illegal about dime novels. Stop funnin' and give it to me! And don't make like I'm Belle Starr." She made another grab for the book, but he held it out of reach again.

"When you're reading, don't you fancy yourself to be her?" he asked.

"No!"

"We all—"

She stomped on his foot. Her boots were just as heavy and thick as his, she reckoned, and she found that to be true when he grimaced, dropped the novel, and danced around in a circle, holding his foot. She picked up the book, dusted it off, then stood watching him. She wasn't too satisfied with what she'd done, but it had seemed the only way. . . . Pap would tan her backside, certain-sure, if he ever learned of this. But for now, nobody but she and the foreigner knew what she'd done, and the truth was she enjoyed the sight of him holding his smarting foot and doing a jig. Tease her, would he? Refuse to hand over the book? Correct her English when she was hard enough on herself about it?

"That'll learn you," she muttered under her breath. At times she was self-conscious about her speech and ways, but right now she felt proud to be a mountain native. . . . *Don't you fancy yourself to be her?* That was city talk, coming from a city person, if she'd ever heard one. And while she normally wouldn't mind, his teasing made her mad.

On the other side of the hill just ahead lay the Cameron orchard and farm. Rachel started for the slope, thinking she'd put some salve on the cuts on her arm and hope they wouldn't turn red.

"I *did* grow up hearing about Belle Starr, from an uncle who had a collection of dime novels," Timothy Benton called. "You didn't need to stomp on me."

She spun around. "Teasing's a mean practice, don't you think?"

He lowered his booted foot. "Perhaps. You may have convinced me."

"Well, I surely hope so."

He watched her for a moment, staring at her with his stunning eyes. Then he shook hair from his forehead as a grin stole across his lips. "Could we start over?"

"Don't reckon that'll help."

"It might."

"Maybe it will, maybe it won't," she said smartly. He had a way of looking at her with his head tipped and a fresh smile on his face that made her nervous and excited all at the same time. Her heart sped up just a bit, and she didn't think it did so just because she was angry.

He inclined his head the way she'd seen a few gentlemen do with their ladies in St. Louis. Then he began talking, with nary a hint of the Ozark dialect in his speech. "Timothy Benton, at your service, miss. I'm originally from near Springfield, Missouri, though I've spent the last nine years in Chicago pursuing my interest in journalism and in novel writing. I'm now setting a novel here in my home state—in the mountains—and so I've come home to view the scenery. Which, I might add, is just as captivating as I remember it, and growing more captivating with each second."

He said the last in a soft tone, and Rachel strained to hear. She stared at him for a spell, him with his bright eyes and smile, him with his smooth way that could surely make a girl forget that when he didn't need or enjoy the scenery here no more, he'd pack up and be on his way back to Chicago. It was that way with most foreigners. They took what they wanted, then left. And most didn't give a hoot about any consequences they might be leaving behind.

"I've seen upward of a thousand slick men come tomcattin' through the hills, Mr. Benton," she said quietly, "especially during spring and summer. I've seen enough to know I don't care to see another one or get involved with one. Maybe you are from near Springfield. Just maybe you are. But somewhere along the way your roots got planted somewheres else."

She started off again, unable to walk fast enough.

"Wait," he called.

She stopped walking. Why, she didn't know. She'd seen at least three friends—including Susie Howitt, who lived just upriver—be left with a growing belly and no husband. Sometimes a stranger came through, stopped for a spell, won a girl's heart, then left her high and dry—and pregnant. The native men did their share of tomcattin' around, sure enough, but they didn't just leave a girl like that. The babies born from relations between hill girls and foreigners were always accepted by their Ozark kin, and the mothers were never made to feel terrible about themselves and what they'd done. But they still had broken hearts, and Rachel had vowed after seeing that happen to Susie last summer that it would never happen to her. Never. She wouldn't allow it.

Yet here she stood, despite her vow, letting the smooth Timothy Benton walk right up to her, lean over one of her shoulders, and say softly, "All right . . . Howdy, gal. I 'llowed how the city talk might hep impress you, but durn it all—it ain't working. Don't go peckin' at me 'bout it now, it's jes' somethin' I learned 'long the way. Some city folk don't take you serious if'n you come to town talkin' this way. But I'll use this here hill talk if you want when speakin' with you. An' don't go 'llowing I'm teasing agin, neither. Jes' tryin' to catch yer eye somehow. I'd go an' tow in a big one off a trotline if tha'd do it, or commence to distillin' 'shine. . . . You say it, pretty gal, an' I reckon I got no choice but to oblige. Even if one full night of distillin' only got me yer name."

Rachel closed her eyes. Never in her wildest dreams had she ever thought to feel such a thrill go through her for one man, especially one who was clearly a hillsman—no foreigner could ever learn to talk like the mountain natives.

She pressed the novel to her fluttering stomach, not knowing exactly what to think. He could be *either* a city gentleman *or* an Ozarker. And because there were two sides to him, he confused and frightened her all the more.

So did the superstitions, because she was turning them over in her mind, thinking they just might have something to do with him. The ring of coffee grounds in the cup yesterday morning had suggested that a lover's kiss would come soon, and the dove cooing this afternoon had suggested that the next man who came riding by would be her future husband. That was *him*. *He* had come riding by not an hour after she'd heard the dove coo!

She couldn't let the foolish beliefs cloud her mind. She simply *couldn't*. They weren't assurance that if she accepted Timothy Benton's obvious advance, he wouldn't leave her in the end as Susie had been left. He's only come for a spell, she told herself, and just don't you go getting caught up with him. No matter who he is or where he's from, he's still tomcattin'.

"My name is . . ." She swallowed. "It's Rachel Cameron, an' I'll thank you to mount your horse'n go on about your business. It ain't here, Mr. Benton."

She heard him inhale deeply, felt him withdraw the warmth of his body. She stood stock-still, waiting, until she heard his horse's hooves thudding on the soft riverbank grass.

Then she turned and watched him ride off.

TWO

A few days passed during which Rachel found herself wondering about Timothy Benton from time to time—if he'd turn up near the Cameron place again, how he could be a hillsman but also pass for a city gentleman if he prettied up the right way and affected the smooth speech he had used on her. She had never met anyone like him; people were usually one way or the other. Even with all the learning she'd done, her roots still showed whenever she was angry or frustrated or irritated. She thought they even showed some whenever her emotions were just fine.

She spotted him at the mill one morning when she and Ben walked there with Pap. He was standing near the sluice with some other men, and at first she didn't pick him out because he wore duckin's—overalls—like his companions. Her father kissed her good-bye on the cheek, then walked off to join the men. Seconds later she realized she was still holding the leather poke containing Pap's dinner, and she and Ben walked over to give it to him.

All the men standing with Pap, except Timothy Benton, said, "Howdy, Rachel." Timothy stood leaning against the sluice, watching her, soft sunlight enhancing the color of his eyes.

"Mornin', Mr. Benton," she said, not liking the fact that he didn't speak to her.

He dipped his head in that way of his, but didn't open his mouth. She lifted her chin and waited. . . . The other men shifted a bit, obviously growing uncomfortable, and Little Ben tugged on her hand, telling her that they had to get back—Gramma was waiting for him to help clean the barn and for her to make butter. But she was determined at least to get a "howdy" out of Timothy Benton. She was determined not to let him be so rude.

Finally he stepped forward and gave a bow the likes of which she'd never seen, sweeping one hand across his waist in front, bending low, then slowly—lazily—straightening. "And a very good morning to you, too, *Miss Rachel*," he said, as if she thought of herself as the queen of the Ozarks.

The other men laughed, even Pap, surprisingly enough. Rachel inhaled deeply, fighting the urge to stomp Timothy's foot again—and all the men's. She had tried to be sociable, but he seemed bent on getting revenge for the way she'd put him off the other day.

"I've got butter to make," she mumbled, gathering her skirt and turning away.

"Some perty fine butter it'll be, too," Lloyd Somers called as she walked off. "Law, yes! Riled as you are, *Miss Rachel*, it'll be some perty fine butter!"

"Stirred an' whipped jes right!" Frank Ladd agreed, laughing. "Don't you be forgettin' the frolic up th' Howitts 'morrow night, *Miss Rachel*."

"You promised me a dance," Jed Lemmens called.

"Oh, you're a bothersome lot, all of you!" Rachel shot heatedly over one shoulder.

They laughed.

"You sure are a perty thing," Lloyd called. "Hair the color ah corn silk."

"Sure enough!" Jed agreed. Frank made some comment about how her eyes glowed like a wildcat's when she was angry.

She wished she could just forget the "frolic." But Gramma had already reminded her of it twice, and Susie Howitt was her best friend, so she couldn't very well stay home and pout—and avoid seeing Susie and her new baby. Both Lloyd and Frank would want to dance with her, too, and maybe, just maybe, she would turn them away as she'd turned Timothy away the other day. After all, they were helping him make fun of her.

"C'mon, Ben," she said, taking her brother's hand and urging him along. What hurt her the most was that Pap didn't defend her. He let those men go on and on! Why, even now they were talking about how she'd been on the "up" side since coming home, and Pap wasn't arguing against that.

"Believe we've got some splittin' to do," Timothy said. The men grumbled that he was right, then they dispersed to go about their business.

The frolic—or "play party"—was just getting under way when the Camerons arrived at the Howitts' shortly after dark the following evening. The women and girls had gathered in the house to lay out food—cracklin' bread, sliced ham, johnnycakes, hominy, and biscuit bread made from wheat flour—and the men and boys had gathered out near the horses to share a jug of whiskey. Rachel's father—Paul—and Little Ben joined the men and boys while Lydia and Rachel went inside the house to help the women.

A covered gallery or "dog run" connected the Howitts' two cabins. The cabins were built of closely fitted logs, and heavy, rough boards hung on wooden hinges formed the doors. The roof was clapboard, and the floors were logs split in two and laid with the flat side up. Medicinal "yarbs"—herbs collected and strung together—hung from the rafters, giving the place an earthy, spicy smell above the scent of all the food. A number of women sat in straight-backed chairs with split hickory bottoms, and some gathered near the large fireplace in one cabin where a set of deer antlers hung above the mantelpiece, or "fire-board." A long table had been pushed against one wall, and dishes of food covered it. At both ends of the table and on the fire-board sat tin bowls filled with grease. Twisted rags were stuck in the grease; when lit, they provided a nice amount of soft light.

Rachel's grandmother remained with the older women in the first cabin they entered while Rachel walked through the dog run to gather with the girls in the other cabin. Toting a wide-eyed baby boy on one hip, Susie grabbed and hugged Rachel soon after the girls spotted each other.

Rachel squeezed Susie tight, then drew back, smiling, to have a look at her friend. Susie's coppery hair glowed in the oil light. Her blue eyes danced.

Rachel released a long breath she hadn't been aware of holding. "You look real good, Susie."

Susie returned the smile. "What didja expect, Rachel? That I'd lay down an' die jes' 'cause that feller didn't stick around?"

"I never thought that so much. I just . . . well, I didn't think you'd be happy, that's all."

"Lookit you," Susie said, stepping back. "You look perty. An' talking so . . . like you've been learning an awful lot. You're going to make us all real proud. S'pose you got college plans now?"

Rachel shook her head. "Pap won't hear of it. I had it all arranged to go to the St. Louis school another year, but he said no, he wanted me home—that I'm past the age to marry an' have *babies*."

Susie rolled her eyes. "These men up here . . . land sakes! They think cookin', cleanin', an' spreadin' our legs is all we're good fer!"

"Susie," Rachel admonished softly, blushing.

"Well, it's true! That painter man of mine . . . he might've left me to care for John here myself," Susie said, jerking her head toward her babe, "but he was never on me all the time 'bout cookin' an' cleanin'." She grinned. "He liked the other an awful lot, though."

What she said might have been funny if Rachel didn't feel so bad for her that her "painter man" had run off. Susie had really loved him. She had wept on Rachel's shoulder most of last summer, her belly swollen with child, her heart shattered.

Rachel glanced down at her feet and shuffled them a bit, not knowing what more to say.

Susie smoothed back a strand of Rachel's hair. "Now, don't go mopin' on 'count of me. I'm all right now—see? Me'n John here took a likin' to each other right when he was born. Mam'n Pap, brothers an' sister . . . they've all takin' a liking to him, too. There ain't nothin' to feel sad 'bout no more, Rachel. 'Specially not tonight. We're gonna have a fine time. I hear Lloyd 'n Jed have their eyes on you."

Rachel glanced up, frowning. "Frank, too, unfortunately."

Susie laughed. "You're smoother'n sweet milk, talkin' so good." She hugged her again. "I'm proud of you. You'll go back to school, wait'n see."

Rachel wished she were as optimistic. As long as Pap said no, that was the end of furthering her learning. Paul Cameron was traditional in many ways, and when he made up his mind about something, he was as strong as a team of belligerent oxen.

The baby waved one arm and laughed all of a sudden at nothing in particular. Rachel laughed, too. He had Susie's big blue eyes and brown hair, and he had four teeth, two on the bottom and two on the top, making him all the cuter. Rachel couldn't help herself—she reached for him, then pulled her arms back, quicklike. "Guess I ought to *ask* if I can hold him," she said sheepishly.

"Shucks, Rachel, you ain't got to ask," Susie scolded, handing him to her friend. "But you wanna be careful now. Those boys who're sweet on you might jes' like the way you look with a youngun on your hip."

Rachel laughed, though nervously this time.

"Why, look, it's Rachel Cam'ron!" someone said from across the room—from near the ladder leading up to the loft, Rachel thought.

"Surely is! I heard she was home. Lloyd talks 'bout her most all the time!" someone else exclaimed, and Rachel knew almost immediately that the speaker was Maggie, Lloyd's sister.

Other girls began gathering around Rachel, welcoming her home. But others stood back a piece, gazing skeptically, whispering among themselves.

Still, the atmosphere was a nice one overall, and as Rachel became involved in numerous conversations, answering questions about her school and the teachers and St. Louis, she was truly glad she hadn't begged off coming to the frolic

tonight. She realized that the reason she hadn't called on
Susie since coming home, and hadn't wanted to attend the
frolic, was because she feared Susie was miserable, and she
hadn't known what to say to or do for her friend. She was
relieved to know Susie was fine.

By and by, the gathering began to disperse, and Susie, who
had disappeared for a while, reached for John and announced,
"Ma says the food's all set. Pap's rosinin' up his bow, an' you
know the boys're waiting to choose girls for "Skip to My Lou."
Go on'n have fun now!"

Shouts of excitement went up, but beneath them were low
murmurs, whispers about who would choose whom—and even
who would end up back in the bushes before the night was
through. Rachel heard talk about that new fellow, Timothy
Benton, how he was sweet on Irma Wallace and would surely
pick her. Rachel bristled a little, though she wasn't sure why.
She didn't care a fig about his business or who he'd taken a
liking to.

As she joined the crowd filing out the front door, she
thought she saw him sitting with Gramma in chairs arranged
near one of the many torches lodged in the ground around the
clearing. And sure enough, when the crowd thinned, she saw
that it *was* him talking with Gramma. He glanced up, met her
gaze, and dipped his head. At nearly the same moment Frank
appeared and asked if she'd be his partner.

Despite the many times she had told herself yesterday and
today that she wouldn't dance with Lloyd, Jed, or Frank tonight,
even if they *begged* her to, she took Frank's arm and let him
lead her to the circle forming in the center of the clearing. She
thought she saw a flash of something in Timothy Benton's eyes,
then he turned his gaze back to Gramma, who was apparently
in one of her talkative moods.

Moments before, Timothy had met Lydia when she walked
up to him and offered a plate of cracklin' bread—corn bread
seasoned with bits of crisp brown pork. Her gray hair was
brushed back and pinned in a chignon at her nape, and she
was just thin enough, just bent at the shoulders enough, and

just kindly enough that he immediately thought of her as a grandmother. Part of his heart had gone soft for grandmas long ago. Both of his had been doting women who always had room on their laps for all three of the Benton children—him, his brother, and his sister. His grandmothers had died of different ailments long before he thought they should have, one the summer he'd turned sixteen, and the other soon after he had arrived in Chicago and found a job as a newsboy.

"Don't know you from these parts," Lydia had said after introducing herself in the customary way, with a howdy, her first name, and a handshake.

"Ain't from these parts," Timothy had responded, accepting the plate of food. Weeks ago, upon returning to the Missouri mountains, he had found slipping back into the hills dialect easy, and that had surprised him. He'd thought he had been away too long, thought he had lost touch with his roots. Not so.

He provided his name over the plate and told Lydia he was from near Springfield, but that he'd been in Chicago a number of years, working for a newspaper and writing novels, and that he had returned to the Missouri hills because the setting for his new book was the Ozark Mountains. It was the same information he'd given the rather saucy Rachel Cameron after she had tumbled from that tree and flashed her tawny eyes at him.

"Where're you staying?" Lydia asked.

"The old Newton place. I've been there for nigh to three weeks, and this is the first bit of cracklin' bread I've had since coming home." He bit into a chunk of bread, wondering briefly if she might say, "But this ain't yer home. Yer some forty miles from Springfield." The thought shamed him now because if you were a mountain native, you were a mountain native, no matter which part of the mountains you were from, and no one made you feel like a foreigner. At least that wasn't the common practice, he thought wryly, thinking of Rachel again.

"Well, I'll be," Lydia had said, settling on a chair. He'd taken the one next to her. "That's not a mile gone from our place. Go 'round that bend in the river an' thar we are."

He had begun to get suspicious then. Around the bend in the river . . . That would be the orchard that sat back from the river about a quarter of a mile. That would be Paul Cameron's . . . Rachel Cameron's place.

He had glanced up and met Rachel's gaze then as she stepped outside the cabin, and he'd thought not for the first time that she was the prettiest girl he had seen in these parts. There was something about her. . . . She was saucy, but she didn't give him the eager, coy glances some of the unmarried hills gals did. She held herself aloof for some reason, and he sensed that she did so because she was determined to be a little different than the others. She interested him a great deal—and not because he was looking to "tomcat" around. He'd done his share of that in Chicago—no use lying to himself or anyone about the matter.

The only problem was, he didn't think she'd let him get near her except to say good morning in a crowd, or in what had seemed like a crowd as he'd stood near the mill sluice yesterday morning, admiring the haughty tilt to her chin and the golden braid that tumbled over her shoulder. The wispy end of it had caressed the underside of one nicely curved breast, and he had fought to keep his gaze on her face. He'd had fun irritating her, and Lloyd, Jed, and Frank had eagerly joined in. Timothy had been surprised that Paul Cameron had grinned a bit himself during the teasing. But later, while Timothy and Lloyd were stripping logs, Lloyd had explained that Paul didn't approve of Rachel getting citified up there in St. Louie, where she'd gone to school, that he thought it was high time she settled down—most gals in the hills were married and settled at least by the time they were sixteen. Timothy had commented that he was a bit "citified" himself. Lloyd had given him a hard look, then muttered, "Reckon so, but Rachel's a gal, and things ain't the same up here for women as they are for men."

"Women up here know their place" was what Lloyd had really been saying, and Timothy had suddenly wanted to defend Rachel's desire to go to school and increase her knowledge.

But his biggest fear was not being accepted here anymore. He had changed—he knew he had changed—but the Ozarks and a certain way of life were still in his blood, and he very much wanted to be a part of it all again, at least while researching his current novel. So when Lloyd had turned and started off, Timothy hadn't stepped into his path and argued the point of women knowing their places.

Cowardly . . . that was damn cowardly, he thought now.

"Would that be the Cameron place?" he asked Lydia as he watched Rachel tip her head and accept Frank's arm. He was glad the couple walked into the clearing to join the circle instead of going off into the shadows as a few couples had already.

"It surely is," Lydia responded. "Paul Cam'ron's my son."

Timothy ate more bread, still watching Rachel and Frank. Then he glanced at Lydia. "And Rachel?"

"Why, Rachel's my granddaughter." Lydia followed his gaze, then slowly turned her head back his way. "But that ain't what you're wantin' to know necessar'ly. She's eighteen, just home from school in St. Louie. Has a need for book knowledge that ain't gonna get met fully s'long as she's living under my son's roof, I ain't proud to say. Her ma felt the same way—that schoolin' for a girl was a waste of time. For a boy to some extent, too. I tried to raise Paul to think diff'rent, but some of his pap's thinkin' got into him, I'm afraid. She ain't married. . . ."

Timothy battled a grin and lost. "I'm that obvious, am I?"

"Obvious as the bull after the cow."

He coughed, choking on the bread. It took a lot to embarrass or startle him, but damn if Lydia Cameron's directness didn't. He managed to clear his throat as she chuckled. "Not that obvious!" he objected.

"Durn near. It's the look in your eye."

Keith Howitt strummed his fiddle, and the dancers for the play-party tune formed their circle. A minute or so later Keith launched into the lively "Skip to My Lou," and people began singing the lyrics. Lydia Cameron's booted foot tapped, keeping time with the tune.

"You're a learned man, Mr. Benton," she remarked presently. "Bet you brought an interestin' book or two from Chicago."

He smiled. "One or two? Hell, I brought a wagon load of books. I'm still tryin' to find a waterproof place in the cabin to store them. I keep thinkin' I'll have to build one."

"Maybe so. No one's lived up in that place fer a coupla years, maybe three. Tar paper's probably blown off the roof by now."

"There was no roof when I got there," he said with a laugh. "I saw the place advertised for rent in a Springfield paper. Didn't think to ask what condition it was in. I was excited to have found a house so easily."

"Paul could help fix it up."

"Paul's, uh, been rather cool to me at the mill. I don't know that I'd ask him to help me with the house."

"He's always cool to newcomers. He'll warm up."

They watched the dancers skip and shuffle. Rachel and Frank soon joined Jed, who had been left in the center of the circle. Jed and Rachel formed an arch with their hands, and Frank danced under it, then the new couple returned to the circle and Frank called in another one. It was exactly the way Timothy remembered the dance being performed, and not only did he enjoy watching it, as he had many times during his childhood, but also he enjoyed watching Rachel.

She was dressed in a pretty calico dress, decorated with golden flowers that enhanced her glowing hair. There was no braid tonight; she had pulled her hair back and secured it with a ribbon at her nape. It waved to the middle of her back. She smiled and laughed as the song went on and the new couple joined Frank. Even her skin seemed to glow. Her eyes shimmered with excitement.

"Pretty little thing, ain't she?" Lydia asked.

Timothy turned a smile on her. "She surely is, Mrs. Cameron."

Her hand began tapping out the rhythm, same as her foot. "What kind of books do you got up thar?"

"Literature mostly."

She looked confused.

"Novels, short stories, poems, written by famous or soon-to-be-famous authors. Some of my own books," he said, his smile widening.

"Ya don't say. . . ."

He nodded. "I've had two published. They've done well. I'm no Sam Clemens—Mark Twain—but I'm workin' on it."

"I'm a bit appreciative of writers m'self."

"I wouldn't mind sharin' my books," he said. "That is, if you and Rachel would be interested."

"We surely would be! We could come callin' soon?"

"If you don't mind the leaky roof."

She chuckled. "That's a natural happenin' in these parts, Mr. Benton. For now, I'm 'llowing you ought to grab one of these gals an' join the dancing."

"What about *you*?" he queried, placing the plate on the ground near the right side of his chair.

She raised both brows. "Me? Dancin'?"

"Certain-sure. I bet you're the best dancer in Taney County."

She tried waving him away. "Pshaw! Get on with you!"

"Now," he said, taking her hand, "if you can run a farm, I know you can dance."

She put a hand to her mouth and giggled behind it like a schoolgirl.

But soon she joined him in a break in the circle.

THREE

Gramma and Timothy Benton were called into the center of the circle almost as soon as they joined the dancing. Rachel watched Gramma and Harold Simpson form the arch for Timothy to dance under, then Timothy turned and scanned the circle for the couple he wanted to call in. Rachel found herself hoping . . . and she silently scolded herself for a fool. Timothy Benton was trouble where she was concerned. Nothing but trouble. She somehow knew that in her heart.

He called her and Frank's name.

Rachel wanted to back out, beg off, quit the dance. But Frank grabbed her hand and pulled her inside the circle, and her mouth seemed frozen shut all of a sudden. Under Timothy's warm gaze, her legs felt weak, her heart leaped, and she wanted to duck her head shyly. But there was nothing shy about Rachel Sue Cameron, not really, and there surely wouldn't be just because Timothy Benton had a way of looking at her that made her feel nervous and fluttery inside.

So she danced with Frank, then lifted her hands high to form an arch with Timothy.

She wasn't sure of the precise instant she realized that that ring in the bottom of Pap's coffee cup that morning *had* been trying to tell her something. One second she was looking straight into Timothy's eyes because she didn't want him thinking she was afraid of him. The next, she was caught in his spell.

His gaze held hers, then shifted to her lips and lingered. His hands were large and warm, his eyes caressing. Then Frank danced under the arch, and Rachel broke away, pushed her way out of the circle, and ran. She'd never much liked the forests at night—Gramma had told her a tale or two about ha'nts—so she ran into the house instead, hoping that most everyone was outside, involved in the dance and other things.

They were. The cabin where her friends had met earlier was empty of people. Rachel sank down on a stool near the hearth, bent, and placed her head in her hands. Timothy Benton might be from near Springfield originally, but he was a drifter, and she couldn't let his eyes urge her into his arms. He'd sure as Moses take her to the bushes or some such place, do his business, then he'd be gone, either right away or soon afterward. People would feel sorry for her, and she'd be raising a child without a father. Her heart would be broken, and she'd sit and cry all the time the way Susie had last summer.

Why did some men run off and leave the woman and the baby? Wasn't there any sense of pride, any sense of compassion, any worry about what would become of the mother and the child? Was there a man alive who felt that women were good for more than cooking and cleaning and spreading their legs, as Susie had so crudely stated?

"I, uh . . . I hear you went to school in St. Louis," Timothy Benton said from nearby.

Rachel jerked her head up. She hadn't even heard him come inside! And here she was, alone with him while he stood leaning against one corner of the fire-board, looking as confident as he had that morning at the mill.

"Why'd you follow me?" she demanded, standing.

"Well, it sure wasn't to hurt you," he answered. "Would you sit back down and stop lookin' like you're about to bolt again?"

"What d'you want?"

"To have a conversation with you, if possible."

"Why?"

He ran a hand through his hair. "Because you interest me, that's why. *Why* do you interest me? Because you're pretty and you have smarts about you. *Why* do I think you have smarts about you? Because you have a way of talkin' and carrying yourself and not involvin' yourself with just anybody. *Why* did I choose you and Frank? Because I wanted to dance with you, an' that doesn't mean I'm tomcattin'." He shook his head. "Honestly, Rachel, simmer down."

"Then what are you doing, Mr. Benton?" she asked cautiously. "No true hillsman likes a woman with a mind of her own. So what *are* you doin'?"

He glared. "You're determined to make me feel like an outsider, aren't you?"

"Most people who come driftin' through are exactly that."

"I was born and raised—"

"I know. Then you went to the big city."

"So did you."

"If I was a man, I wouldn't snatch a girl's heart then leave her pregnant."

Timothy opened his mouth to say something more about her having gone to the city for an education, too, but shock snapped his lips together. He shifted his gaze to a dark vein in the heavy fire-board, then turned it back to Rachel. "Did I leave a girl pregnant somewhere?"

She blushed. "I didn't mean that exactly."

"Then what exactly did you mean?"

"That . . . well . . ." She clenched the fingers of one hand around the fingers of the other and twisted. "You know. Men come through sometimes, win a girl's heart, then just move on. My friend Susie Howitt . . . She took up with an easterner, a painter fellow from Connecticut. He left last spring, just up an' left. Susie's got a baby now. In my mind it shouldn't ought to work that way." She sank back down in the chair, placed her hands in her lap, and stared at them.

Timothy watched her for what seemed a long time while the crowd outside went through an entire verse and chorus of "Old Dan Tucker." He certainly wasn't ignorant of the fact that some men came through, took what many mountain girls were all too eager to give, then moved on and never looked back. But he wouldn't do that; he had too much appreciation running through his veins for family, instilled in him by his parents and grandparents.

He nudged his shoulder from the fire-board, shoved his hands into his duckin's bib, and mumbled, "Twenty-nine eighteen East Second Street."

Rachel looked up. "What?"

"Just so anyone ever suspects me of doin' such a thing— which I wouldn't—it's my Chicago address."

A few moments of awkward silence ensued. He watched her brows shoot up, then settle. Finally she went back to twisting her hands in her lap.

"You don't know me, Rachel," he said softly. "I'm sorry about Susie, but blaming me for what her artist beau did is not right."

"I don't blame you," she responded without looking up.

"You just don't trust me. You're determined to make me feel as if I don't belong. You went off to school. . . . How would you have felt if you'd been made to feel like a foreigner after you returned?"

"I have been, a bit."

"Because you want to do something more than what most hill women do?"

Glancing up, she nodded. Sparkles lit her eyes.

He nodded, too. "That's right—I understand. My family and friends laughed at me when I talked about writing. An industrious Ozark man farms and hunts, maybe works at the local mill or in the mines. To do anything other than that . . . people think you're strange."

She looked back down. "I only want to learn more, to read more an' . . . What does it matter if the breakfast dishes don't get done right after breakfast? If the butter gets made a little later than it shoulda been?"

"I was late many a morning milking the cows," he said, agreeing. He gave a little laugh. "And I can't count the number of days I cleaned the barn out of habit, all the while pretending I was Jesse James off on another train-robbin' adventure."

That drew a weak smile from her. It was the first time he'd seen her smile, and he tipped and dipped his head to have a better look.

"Did you really read dime novels?" she queried, glancing up again, still smiling.

"Did I!"

She laughed.

"Now, don't you be laughing at me, Miss Rachel," he said, feigning indignation. "I take my readin' a mite serious."

"They're not true."

"No. But at the time you're reading them, they're true in your mind."

The oil light flickered red in her tawny eyes and danced orange on her otherwise golden hair. Sobering, Timothy held her gaze.

Her eyes returned to her hands. "Susie ain't the only girl I ever saw get pregnant and be left alone. She just . . . We talked about it a lot, so I just never thought she'd take up with a drifter and let him do *that* to her. You know—rolling in the bushes."

Timothy resisted a smile. "There's something called passion, Rachel, and *that*—making love—shouldn't be regarded with distaste. Don't make it sound like a dirty thing."

"Seems like a dirty thing," she mumbled.

He shook his head. "You just don't know, do you?"

"What?"

"You've never been with a man."

Her jaw dropped open. A second later she jumped up and headed for the door. "You've no call to say such a thing!"

"Don't run again, Rachel. I didn't mean to offend you. I wasn't askin' you to go to the bushes, or anywhere else, with me."

Her hand was on the door latch. She paused, went very still, then glanced at him over her shoulder, her eyes wide and shimmering.

"C'mere," he urged gently.

She stared a moment longer, then her feet moved her in his direction.

Timothy stepped forward and lifted his hands to cup her jaw. She gasped, but he eased her fear somewhat with a soft "Shh. I won't hurt you." He dipped his head to touch his lips to hers.

"There now, was that so frightening?" he asked, withdrawing.

"You're sweet on Irma Wallace," she accused, "so why'd you kiss me?"

"I'm sweet on . . . ?" He frowned. "I called at the Wallaces' farm a time or two to ask for work and I spoke to Irma. We spent some time sitting by the river talking, but that doesn't mean I'm sweet on her."

"Irma says you are."

"Irma is dreaming."

"You're conceited."

He groaned. "There's no satisfying you, Rachel Cameron!"

"Why don't you stop trying?"

"Maybe I will."

She tossed her head in her uppity way, then spun around again and exited the cabin, pulling the door shut hard behind her.

Saucy gal, he thought, rubbing his jaw. But he quickly decided she was worth going after, and he left the cabin only a few minutes behind her.

Outside, Lloyd and Frank stood talking to her beneath a tree in the shadows cast by overhanging branches. Timothy resisted the urge to walk up, take her by the arm, and lead her away from the two bloodhounds. She probably wouldn't let him anyway. He ended up joining Lydia and a few other older women, answering their questions about Chicago.

But a little later he approached Keith Howitt and requested "Weevily Wheat." Rachel was still talking to Lloyd and Frank beneath the tree, but sneaking glances at *him* now and then. He approached her from behind and took her hand, not loosening his hold when she opened her mouth to object.

"Don't 'llow Rachel wants to dance right now," Lloyd said, gazing at Timothy with narrowed eyes.

Frank stepped forward. "C'mon, Rachel. We was jes' going fer a walk."

"Talk about tomcattin'," Timothy muttered under his breath, pulling Rachel back against him. "And just what do you think their motive is for asking you to walk with them?" he whispered in her ear.

She inhaled deeply. "Well . . . truth is, I'd rather dance than walk, Frank," she told the men loudly.

"City feller got some sort of hold on you, Rachel?" Lloyd asked. "Yep, I can see he sure does. Right thar on yer hand."

Timothy released her and was surprised when she slid her hand back into his. She didn't want him to leave. She wanted to show Frank and Lloyd that she wanted to go dance with him, that he wasn't coercing her.

"No," she said. "I really want to dance with him, Lloyd. And he's from near Springfield. . . ."

Lloyd spit at the base of the tree. "Nope. He's from Chicago."

"Springfield," she countered.

"You're gonna end up like Susie," Lloyd warned in a low tone. "Takin' up with a stranger."

Timothy felt Rachel wince. The first lively notes of "Weevily Wheat" began, and Rachel pulled on Timothy's hand in an attempt to lead him away.

"Don't take kindly to strangers who come in'n take what rightly belongs to us," Lloyd growled—and the words were aimed at Timothy. "Might be you meet with an accident someday down at the mill."

A chill went through Timothy. He wanted to turn, walk up to the man, and tell him to watch who he threatened. But Rachel tugged at his hand again, and her wide-eyed look of apprehension made him decide to keep walking with her toward the dancing area. She wanted a brawl about as much as he did.

He and Rachel took places opposite each other in the two parallel rows that had formed, one of women, one of men, and watched the couple now swinging in the area between the rows. The man and the woman returned to their lines, then the next couple drew forth to swing. . . . When it came time for Timothy and Rachel to take the area, loop their arms, and swing about, she smiled, stepped forward, and he met her in the middle, never taking his eyes from her as they turned.

Once they were back in their places, she dipped her head and smiled again. Timothy couldn't resist smiling back.

Six verses of the song later, Keith Howitt's violin struck the last note, and the two rows bowed to each other. Then Timothy and Rachel met in the center again, but this time she looped her arm through his and walked off with him, laughing when he complained that his feet hurt, that he wasn't in condition anymore to attend too many frolics.

People wandered in and out of the cabin where the older women had gathered earlier to lay out food, and Timothy led Rachel into the house with the intent of getting johnnycakes.

"Sorry 'bout that business with Lloyd and Frank under the tree," she said as they stood near one far end of the table. "They ain't gonna be too nice at the mill from now on."

"Why did you do it?" he had to ask.

"Go off and talk with them, you mean?"

He nodded.

"Sometimes I think I can still be just friends with them. I've known the two of 'em all my life. Used to climb trees with Lloyd. But he's so different now. He looks at me different than he did when we climbed trees." She bit into a cake and chewed slowly.

"How old were the two of you then?"

"Last tree we climbed . . . Lloyd and Frank were thirteen an' I was nine. Then they got interested in other things—older girls mostly."

"Boys grow into men, girls grow into women, and the men and women naturally look at each other differently than the boys and girls did, Rachel."

She took another bite of the cake she held. "I like you, Mr. Benton, as much as I tell myself not to. But you scare me, an' I'd be lying if I said you didn't."

"Why don't you give me a chance, Rachel? You defended me to Lloyd, so you obviously see some good in me. A chance is all I want."

She swallowed the bite and glanced off at the table and the people gathering near it, then back to him. "Don't know that I'm ready for anything serious."

What she probably meant was that she liked him but didn't quite trust him. Timothy wasn't quite sure he trusted himself: his plan was to stay home for as long as it took him to write descriptions of the people and the mountains. He had felt he could best capture the essence of both by coming here. But he doubted that he would remain much longer than to the end of summer. Journalism was in his blood, and he was guaranteed a position on the staff of the *Chicago Star* when he returned.

He nodded slowly. "Well . . . we could spend some time readin' your grandmother's dime novels, if nothing else."

She laughed. He laughed with her. He heard Keith start into "Miller Boy" and he urged Rachel to finish that johnnycake real quick—he wanted to dance again.

"I thought you said your feet hurt," she teased.

"They do, but it's been years since I've enjoyed myself so much."

She finished the cake, and they went outside.

FOUR

Several afternoons later Rachel and Little Ben sat atop the crooked wooden fence their pap had built so no one would have to chase the hogs and goats from the garden and fields of corn. The animals got along pretty well for the most part. Now and then a sow littered and didn't take kindly to the goats or even other hogs coming around, but that only happened about once every year or two.

Dressed in boys' duckin's, Ben tossed dried corn from the wooden bucket he held and swung his legs back and forth, hitting his calves lightly against the rails. His bare feet were smudged with dirt. He wore a large straw hat that did a fine job of hiding his face from view. But he wasn't trying to hide his face. He just liked the hat Gramma had woven for him, no matter that it was too big.

"Why ain't you got your book?" he asked Rachel. "You ain't doing chores right now."

She swung her legs, too, and lowered her head a little so the sun wouldn't be in her eyes. "I finished it. Besides, sometimes I just like sitting with you and not doing much of anything."

"When're you gonna git you a man'n git married?"

She smiled. "Don't rightly know. When the right one comes along, I suppose."

He tossed more corn to the disinterested animals lying about. Later, when the sun cooled, the hogs and goats would eat. "Pap says ye ought to marry Lloyd. He done built himself a fine cabin down the river a ways. Ain't got to go far for his water, an' he's got a herd o' goats now'n chickens an' hogs. Took in a good crop lash year, too."

245

"And he's just waiting for a woman to put up this year's," Rachel remarked under her breath, not wanting to imagine herself cooking and storing the vegetables in jars on some high shelf. It wasn't the "putting up" and other work she'd mind so much if she married Lloyd. It was the suspicion that he'd never want her to bring a book into the house. It was the suspicion that he'd never want her to learn another thing outside of what she already knew—except how, exactly, to come by a baby. Or two, or three, or four, or five, or . . . Rachel sighed. She wished she, Lloyd, and Frank could just climb trees together still. But her childhood friendships with them were gone, as Timothy had pointed out. They didn't look at her as a playmate anymore, at least not as someone with whom to climb trees.

"I 'llowed we'd take Mr. Benton some eggs an' milk," Gramma said from behind them. "It ain't too rocky up that way, up 'round Brush Lane. We could git a horse or two up thar."

Ben swung his legs over the fence and hopped down, more than ready to leave right now. The leap unsettled the dried corn in the bucket, and kernels went flying. His hat flopped off. He reached down, grabbed it, and fixed it, a little askew, back on his head. "That's that new feller, Gramma? That one Pap don't like?"

Lydia Cameron nodded. "But you shouldn't not like someone just 'cause he's a little diff'rent, Ben."

"Mr. Benton's working at the mill right now," Rachel said.

"Only three days a week. Rest of the time he's readin' an' writin'." Gramma shifted a basket containing eggs and a bottle of milk from one arm to the other. "I talked to him quite a bit before an' after the frolic. He said we're welcome to come'n see his books anytime. Has a lot, he says."

Rachel's eyes widened. "Does he?"

Lydia smiled. "I figured that'd catch yer int'rest. Let's saddle the horses an' call on him. We'll trade the eggs and milk for a bit of time lookin' at his books."

Now Rachel swung her legs over the top rail and jumped down. Her skirt caught on a nail, but she quickly freed it and

followed Ben as he scampered away and Gramma as she lifted
her skirt and stepped over some stones.

Together the three of them readied the horses, Rachel and
Lydia tossing on and cinching the saddles while Ben stood on
a rickety stool to maneuver the bridles over the animals' heads.
Rachel mounted one horse, and Gramma Cameron handed Ben
up, settled him before Rachel, then handed up the basket of
goods for Timothy Benton.

"Careful of the eggs," Rachel warned Ben as he positioned
the basket in front of him. "And I'm sorry, but I can't see over
the hat. You'll have to take it off."

He grumbled but removed the hat. Gramma mounted her
horse and started out ahead of them, leading the way along a
beaten wagon trail that followed the river.

A breeze swept over the shimmering water, stirring Rachel's
hair. The air smelled of spring—sweet, like lilacs—and Rachel
inhaled deeply, hearing the trees rustle and the birds chirp. She
admired distant ledges and bluffs that grew hazy and grayish
blue in the distance. The horses whickered and shook their
heads, jingling the bridles. Ben held the basket up and steady
when their horse began climbing a rocky slope. On the other
side, they rounded the bend in the river and traveled another
two miles until the roughly shingled roof of the old Newton
place came into view above a cluster of trees on a hill set
back from the river about a quarter of a mile. They turned
their horses that way, and the animals climbed the slope.

"See, Rachel?" Ben said when she helped him down. "Not
one egg broke."

Smiling, she ruffled his hair. "I see. You did good."

She looped their horses' reins around a post lodged in
the ground just outside the fence, which was constructed of
eight-inch-wide pieces of wood nailed upright to boards. Three
or four inches separated each piece of wood, and the tops of
them had been sharpened.

The Newton cabin sat some ten feet back from this side of
the fence, and its history was well-known in these parts. The
cabin had been built in 1875 on the side of the hill. Then one
spring, after an uncommon amount of rain, the shifting of the

slope had caused the floors to buckle and the foundation to
cave in. But instead of building a new cabin on another part of
the family's land, Milas Newton had taken the original cabin
apart piece by piece and moved it to the top of the hill. The
cabin was sturdier the second time around, and it had stood
atop the hill some fifteen years now. The Newtons had moved
on—some of Milas's eight children had gone to Arkansas, one
had gone to Springfield to open a store there, some had passed
on, and Milas himself was buried near the far side of the base
of the hill. A chiseled stone marked his grave.

As Gramma hollered a greeting in the customary way,
Rachel followed her and Ben up to the covered porch that
spanned the length of the cabin. The overhang of roof cast
in shadow two buckets, a washtub, a small table, and three
chairs that most probably had been made by Milas or one
of his kin some years back; they appeared worn, and the
cane seats had been mended in spots with newer cane that
was of a lighter color and unfrayed. Railing surrounded the
porch and extended halfway up to each corner and middle
post. A swing held in place with strong pieces of twine sat
against the northernmost rail. Weathered logs formed the
house.

The door creaked open, and there stood Timothy Benton,
smiling at Gramma Cameron, then shifting his eyes to Rachel.

"I wondered if you'd take me up on that invitation," he said,
looking at Lydia again.

"Can't afford to be unfrien'ly to neighbors." She stepped
aside. "I brought Little Ben—don't know if you met him. An'
of course here's Rachel."

He smiled. "I'm glad you've come, Mrs. Cameron. . . . Ben.
Rachel."

Rachel smiled back, then looked off at one of the chairs.

"Gathered some eggs for ya," Ben said, marching forth and
holding out the basket. "Even milked one of the cows special,
just for you."

Timothy hunched to his level and peered into the basket.
"You don't say. . . ."

"Yep. I told ya so."

Rachel laughed, imagining her brother's nose wrinkled with confusion. "Ben, that means Mr. Benton's proud that we thought of him."

"That's right," Timothy said. Then he stood and withdrew from the door. "Why don't you folks come in? I just made some bacon, peas, and biscuits. There's not a lot, but we can share."

Aside from his somewhat polished speech, he certainly seemed like a hillsman now. An Ozarker's door was always open to neighbors, and all food in the house, no matter how little, was shared. Rachel even figured, with some humor, that he had a spare cornhusk tick that could be pulled out to accommodate someone who had traveled a spell and needed to rest.

Gramma entered the house first, then Ben pressed forth curiously. Rachel followed, smiling at Timothy. "You cook, Mr. Benton?"

"Surely do, Miss Cameron. Bein' a bachelor an' all."

Her smile widened.

"My, but you do have a lot of books!" Gramma exclaimed.

Rachel's attention was drawn to where her grandmother and Ben now stood near a wall of shelves that extended to the ceiling. One could hardly see the wall for all the books. Many stood in neat rows, others lay atop the rows, and still others were stacked on two small tables. The rich wood smell of logs filled the cabin, and a hint of fried bacon lingered in the air. But beneath those odors lay an unmistakable mustiness and the scents of paper, ink, and leather; they were smells Rachel recognized from the school and from the times she'd visited the St. Louis Library.

In her mind she saw images and could almost forget that she was in a mountain cabin. *Books.* Some worn. Some relatively new. Some cracked with age. Some with gold lettering that would glitter if the book were turned the right way. She saw smooth chairs and tables and heard—faintly—the soft voice of the librarian, Mrs. Kilgore, saying, "Don't forget to write your name and the date on the card." And Rachel had never once forgotten because she had wanted to be welcomed back to this place with its hundreds and thousands of books.

She drew close to Timothy's shelves, was drawn there by the number of books, by curiosity and amazement and fascination. She touched several bindings, then began reading titles. *Husl'ing, America, Songs That Never Die, Stories of American Heroism, Tom Sawyer, Huckleberry Finn, Roughing It, Reminiscences of the War, Uncle Tom's Cabin, Hot Stuff by Famous Funny Men, Every Man His Own Doctor, Advice to a Wife, Whirligigs and Strictly Business, The Finer Grain, The Town Down the River, Shepherd of the Hills* . . . The authors were wide and varied and the books weren't in alphabetical order according to author or title—or anything. But oh, they were *books*, and there were so *many* of them.

"I'm, uh, not always one for neatness and appearance, particularly where my home and books are concerned," Timothy said over her shoulder.

"It's . . . they're . . . you've got so many!" she half whispered. "An' there! What . . . ? Is it one of yours?" The gold lettering on the binding of one book in particular had caught her eye, and she read aloud, "*Glimpses of a Boyhood.* Benton."

He reached around her, pulled the book from the shelf, and placed it in her hands. She immediately opened it and paused on the title page to again read the title as well as his full name this time: Timothy Harold Benton.

"You can sit at my desk if you'd like," he offered, motioning to the other side of the cabin. There, three stacks of papers and an inkstand occupied a tabletop, and before the table sat a chair turned just enough to look inviting. Nearby, a typewriter and two more stacks of papers sat atop another table. A pottery mug had been placed on one of the stacks.

Rachel smiled at Timothy, issued a soft "thank you," then went to sit before his "desk." There, she reverently turned to Chapter One and began reading.

I was fifteen years old when I had my first real taste of Lake Michigan. Had always sat on her banks, tossed out lines, and brought in a bounty of pike, bass, and whitefish, all of which I took home and cleaned so my ma could fry 'em up. Those were some days, sitting on the grass, barefoot, feeling a tug on my line and watching and feeling it grow tighter and tighter, the summer sun burning up my back in a pleasant sort of way. Winter in Wisconsin can be mighty fierce, especially near the lake, and a body learns to thank the good Lord for the warm season.

    Don't get me wrong now. I'd seen some storms kick up on the lake. I'd seen twenty-foot waves drive in, swirling and growling and roaring finally when they hit shore. And in my fifty years since, I've seen bigger waves than that on Lake Michigan. I've seen whole houses and buildings blown straight away and even swallowed. But the summer I turned fifteen, when my ma passed on and my friend Captain Manning of the steamer Sheboygan *took me in as his own and I traveled with him, that was the year I came to know the lake. . . .*

Rachel glanced up from the book and met Timothy's gaze, though he now stood near the hearth with Gramma and Ben, spooning peas and potatoes onto a tin plate. She opened her mouth to say something, but she was too much in awe of him to utter a word, to utter an *intelligent* word, so she snapped her mouth shut and went back to reading.

Captain Manning saw that the boy's mother got a decent burial—a place in the town graveyard and a stone carved with her name and the words "She was a good ma." The boy figured he'd make do on his own. He still had their house and everything in it, and he'd seen his mother cook fish and make bread, so he thought he could do the same himself and just keep on as he'd been doing, except without her, of course. But Captain Manning pointed a long finger at him, nearly touching his nose, and said, "Now, Henry, you're not yet fifteen and you need somebody. You can't expect to get by on your own, though I've no doubt that you could. But it wouldn't be right. So you come along with me. I'll find you a job on the *Sheboygan,* and at night we'll eat together and visit, and you won't have to be all alone."

After a day or two of considering, Henry went to the ship and took Captain Manning up on the offer, and within months after the vessel set out, Captain Manning told him that if he was ever of the mind, he could call him Pa.

Timothy set a plate of food near Rachel's arm, then placed a tin cup filled with milk beside the plate. Rachel glanced up, and when he broke into a grin, she was certain the awe she felt for him showed on her face.

"You like it?" he asked, jerking his head down toward the book.

She nodded, a bit more eagerly than she'd meant to. "I want to read about Henry's adventures on the lake."

"Good. That's what I like to do—catch a person's interest and hold it. But I must admit, little effort went into doing that in *Glimpses of a Boyhood*. Henry took the story and raced off with it. I had no choice but to let him."

"It doesn't always happen that way?" she asked, hoping she didn't sound too simple.

He shook his head. "No. Oh, no. The second book is about the trials of an early Illinois family. The story didn't come as easily as Henry and his exploits did."

She glanced around and found that Gramma and Ben had settled on chairs near the hearth and were eating. "Where's your plate, Mr. Benton?"

He stuffed his hands into his trouser pockets and shrugged.

"You needn't have given us all your food. If you have another fork, we'll share," Rachel said, thinking he might be insulted if she told him to take the entire plate. He might consider that a refusal of hospitality. Most folks would.

He nodded at that and walked off to show Ben a wooden wagon and a team of horses he said he'd carved ten years ago before leaving Missouri. He'd kept the wood oiled, and the team could still pull the wagon as good as ever. Ben was welcome to have a try at it when he finished eating.

A minute or so later Timothy returned to the desk with an extra chair in one hand and a fork in the other. He situated himself to the right side of the table. Rachel pushed the book aside, though reluctantly, and they began sharing the food.

Ben soon slid from his chair, put his dirtied plate on the hearth, then turned his attention to the wagon and horses. Timothy had nailed the horses to a platform having small wheels so the toy could be pulled easily, and Ben had great fun pulling the team and the wagon in a wide circle around the cabin. Gramma took a book from the shelf, flipped it open, then smiled up at Timothy, saying how much she appreciated anything having to do with Buffalo Bill and his Wild West Show. "Imagine taking all those Indians to another continent, them all feathered up'n lookin' like they're ready for war. Had enough dealin's with Indians, coming here in the 1870s, to surely admire William Cody."

"He's quite a figure all right," Timothy remarked.

"You've seen his show?"

"A time or two. Not to take anything from Buffalo Bill, but Annie Oakley and her shooting held my interest more than anything else. She's a lady who knows how to handle rifles and guns. I doubt she's ever missed a target."

"Pshaw! Ever'body misses a time or two."

"Not Annie Oakley."

"Did Buffalo Bill really have all those adventures?" Rachel asked, unable to help herself.

Timothy leaned toward her and whispered, "You mean like in the dime novels?"

She felt her face warm. She took another bite of peas, refusing to meet his gaze.

"For the most part. Rumor is, some of his exploits are exaggerated."

"Well, that's a dime novel for you," she mumbled.

He tapped his book. "What do you think this is?"

"Not a dime novel."

"No—not a dime novel. But a novel, no less. A work of fiction, of make-believe. At least there's some truth to what dime novels contain. At least there really is a Buffalo Bill and an Annie Oakley. Just because my book has a leather binding and the title and my name in gold lettering, that doesn't necessarily make the book any more respectable than a dime novel. It just feels different in your hands."

"It doesn't have all that crazy adventure."

"Oh, Henry has adventure, and a lot of it. You haven't read very far."

"I'd like to read the whole book," she said, hoping he would offer to let her borrow it. She wouldn't ask. Having his own book . . . well, it must be a treasured possession. She'd take real good care of it if he offered to lend it to her, but she wouldn't ask to borrow it.

"Maybe you can come here some afternoons to read it, like now," Timothy responded. If he let her borrow the book, they might go long stretches without seeing each other. The job at the mill demanded long hours on the days he worked, and he wrote during the other days. He'd like to take his typewriter, put it on the table on the porch, and glance up now and then and be able to see Rachel either sitting in the swing on one end of the porch or lying on a quilt on the grass not far from the house. He liked having her near him.

She fidgeted, twisting her lower lip and twirling the fork in a little clump of potatoes. "I don't know. Chores an' all, you know."

"Maybe just a few afternoons a week, then."

"Maybe," she said, giving him a look from beneath her lashes. He didn't think she was aware of how incredibly charming a look it was, that it made his breath catch in his throat. The sunlight that managed to shine through the two cabin windows—one located not three feet away—made her eyes appear hazy, and it created a soft glow around her bonnet and the length of golden hair that flowed over one shoulder. The creamy peach color of her skin attested to the healthiness of the mountain air, and the pink-and-blue flowers decorating her dress suited her. Like her, they were an extraordinary breath of spring.

"I hope so," he heard himself say quietly.

"Only to read," she answered just as quietly.

He inclined his head. "Only to read, Rachel. You can do that while I type. There's a swing to one end of the porch."

"I saw it."

She took a bite of potatoes, and he wanted to wipe a little smear from one corner of her mouth. But the tip of her tongue darted out and collected the food before he could contemplate the matter further. He knew that loaning her the book would be the gentlemanly thing to do. But he just couldn't see doing that, not when he knew how it had captured her interest and that she'd definitely return to read the rest of it.

They finished eating, then he mentioned to everyone that he'd found a fairly decent boat stored in the barn. He'd repaired its hull and hauled it to the river, and there it sat now, waiting to be paddled about. He had rowed about in it one evening and was convinced it would hold up fine if they'd all like to go for an excursion in it. Lydia Cameron's eyes lit up with eagerness, and Ben couldn't get to the cabin door fast enough. Rachel grinned and teased that "excursion" sure enough sounded like a city word.

"Well, how 'bout if we jes' pole 'round the river a piece?" he drawled.

She laughed. He grabbed her hand, and they headed for the doorway through which Ben was just disappearing.

FIVE

"Do they find Mr. Brunner?" Rachel asked anxiously from where she sat on Timothy's porch swing days later. Days before, a simple mention of the fact to Gramma that she'd been invited to visit Timothy's place some afternoons to read had been all that was needed to secure her grandmother's permission; Gramma liked Mr. Benton an awful lot.

Shortly after Rachel's first visit to read two days ago, Timothy had moved his typewriter to the table situated on the opposite side of the porch, brought a chair out, put it before the table, and began working away while she read and turned pages. He'd done the same today, and now here they sat, him typing, her reading.

Smiling at her question, Timothy glanced up. "I can't tell you."

She twisted her mouth to one side and swung one leg. "Why not?"

"Because if I tell you, you won't need to read the book."

"I'll read it."

"I'm not telling," he said, and resumed typing.

She pouted for good measure, then went back to reading. Mr. Brunner was the *Sheboygan*'s first mate, a man Henry had quickly befriended after joining the crew aboard ship. Mr. Brunner had been blown clear off deck and into the water during a fierce storm outside a bay, and now some crew members of the *Sheboygan* were searching the area, hoping to find the first mate clinging to a piece of driftwood or something. Others had gone ashore about two miles away, hoping the man had somehow swum to safety. But two miles was a long way to swim in tumultuous seas. . . .

"I don't think they'll find Mr. Brunner alive," Rachel commented aloud.

"Why not?" Timothy asked between the clacking of typewriter keys.

"Well, he's old. 'A few years upwards of sixty,' Henry said. And he told Henry once that when his time came, he'd just sink down into the lake'n go to sleep, 'cause there was lake water, not blood, flowing through his veins. It seems like the right death for a man like Mr. Brunner. They might not even find him *dead*. They might not find him at all."

Timothy smiled again. "Read."

"You know an' you're not tellin'," she accused.

"Of course I know."

He typed more. She read more. Henry was with Captain Manning on deck, searching the surface of the water through spyglasses. The sun shone brightly, reddening Henry's arms, but he was worried about Mr. Brunner and refused to quit searching for long. Directly he lowered his spyglass and went for a drink of water. On the way to the water barrel across the main deck, he lifted a mop that had fallen rather than step over it—stepping over it would surely bring bad luck. They might not find Mr. Brunner alive if he did. . . .

"That's a superstition!" Rachel blurted, unable to help herself. "Stepping over a mop or a broom won't really bring bad luck." She'd heard the same foolishness from Gramma and she didn't believe it.

The clattering of the typewriter keys ceased. She looked up and found Timothy regarding her curiously. "Have you ever stepped over a mop or a broom and found out?"

"Well, no, but—"

"Try it."

His challenge made her pause. *Try it?* Intentionally step over a broom or mop just to see if bad luck would come? She didn't believe the superstition, but she couldn't see any point in stepping over one just to see if something bad would happen.

"Skeptical Rachel," Timothy teased. "A little part of you believes."

"No, it doesn't."

"Oh, yes it does."

"I thought you were more down-to-earth, Timothy Benton."

"An' you pride yourself on bein' jes' so, Rachel Cameron?"

"Don't make fun. I'm talking serious."

"So am I. I wouldn't butcher a pig when the moon's on the wane 'cause the pork just might shrink in the pot. And I've *seen* shriveled onions and beets that weren't planted durin' the dark of the moon. I've thrown cockleburs at a few gals' skirts to see if they were for me—some stuck, an' others fell away, and the cockleburs were usually right. I've even eaten pickles to cure myself of lovesickness, too."

"It surely didn't work."

"It surely did!" he objected, rising.

"You sound like my gramma."

He approached, pulling something from a pocket. Pausing before her, he held out his hand and opened it. A gray rabbit's foot and a slightly shriveled buckeye lay in his palm.

"They don't really bring good luck," she said, tilting her head and gazing up at him.

"Don't they? Why, Miss Cam'ron, I've been carryin' this here rabbit's paw for better'n ten years an' I've had a passel of good luck since I started."

"Don't be silly."

"Which would you like?" he asked.

She stared at the two items. "I don't. I—"

"Here now, take the rabbit's foot." He reached down for her hand, and she tried pulling it back. He slid a thumb under her folded fingers and forced them open, then he dropped the rabbit's paw on her palm.

"I don't need it. I have one!" she objected.

"*Have* one? Why, Rachel . . ." He smiled, his turquoise eyes sparkling with humor. "That must mean you believe. Why else would you have a rabbit's foot?"

She huffed. "That wasn't very nice, trickin' me like that!"

"One of my favorite things to do when I was a boy was looking for four-leaf clovers. Some beliefs might just be in our heads—there might be nothing to them at all. But the mind's a powerful thing. You wish for something, chances are you'll get it. 'Course, there's some work involved. You can't expect fortune to just come knocking at your door. And who are we to say . . . ? When a baby smiles in his sleep, maybe he *is* talking to angels. Don't be a pessimist, Rachel. Being pessimistic takes the fun out of life."

Rachel studied him in silence. He was right. She'd been a lot happier before the teachers at school had made her doubt some of the things she'd been taught by Gramma, before they'd made her feel ashamed.

"Have you ever pulled the petals from a daisy one by one?" Timothy asked softly, leaning toward her. His warm breath fanned her face. It smelled of rich coffee.

Her heart quickened. "Ain't never had no cause to."

Leaning closer, he lifted her chin with one finger. "You will someday. Someday you'll prove too much for a certain man to pass by. But he and you will both feel pulled by things that get in the way—fears, obligations, a life that's been established somewhere else. . . . You'll go and find yourself a daisy maybe, an' pluck the petals, saying, 'He loves me, he loves me not. . . . ' "

Rachel pushed his hand away. "You're a dreamer, Timothy Benton. I wouldn't waste a daisy for no man."

"Ah, but my dreams and hopes have taken me far. So do Henry's. The night after he picks up the mop instead of stepping over it, he sees a falling star and counts to three three times—real quick before the star fades—an' the next morning Mr. Brunner is found aboard a ship laid up in Sturgeon Bay. The ship's crew fished him from the water. Things might have gone differently if he'd stepped over that mop or if he hadn't counted when he saw the star."

"May have just been coincidence."

He shrugged.

"And daisy petals don't tell whether or not a person loves you."

"I hope you never have to 'waste' a daisy to find out, Rachel. I hope there's never any doubt."

Never any doubt . . . about *him*? She opened her mouth to say something more, wondering if he thought she was getting sweet on him. She'd set him straight. Tell him she knew better than to do that, since he wasn't here to stay. "I don't—"

Timothy pressed two fingertips against her lips and shook his head, murmuring, "Don't, Rachel. Don't." Straightening, he stepped back and buried his hands in his trouser pockets. Seconds later he pulled one hand out and rubbed it across his mouth. "I don't think you know how pretty you are," he said in a thick voice. "Read. I'll, uh—" He looked at his worktable. "I'll go back to writing."

Rachel watched him walk away, watched his shoulders move beneath his white shirt, his buttocks move with his trousers. Quicklike, she forced her gaze back to the book.

During the ensuing moments she and Timothy both managed to put their minds back on what they had been doing before the subject of superstitions had arisen. Rachel read at least seventy pages before he suggested she ought to be heading home.

He walked with her to the river, where they said soft good-byes. His eyes were narrowed and shaded by dark lashes and brows. He pulled both hands from his pockets, and for a long moment Rachel wondered if he might reach for her. She caught herself wishing he would . . . then he folded his arms across his chest.

She turned and walked away, silently calling herself a fool. Why in the world had she stood there like that, as if she expected a kiss good-bye? Her face burned with embarrassment. Even so, she glanced at him over her shoulder, smiled, and mouthed, " 'Bye."

She's getting under my skin, Timothy thought, watching her walk away. He wanted a photograph of her looking over her shoulder like that, the midafternoon sun highlighting her golden hair, her tawny eyes sparkling at him, her sweet pink lips curving up at the corners. He couldn't believe how incredibly refreshing he found her to look at. She wore boots, but earlier he'd watched from the corner of his eye as she unlaced them and pushed them off while reading, then pulled them back on shortly before walking outside with him. She'd removed

them in an unconscious manner, as if doing so were a perfectly natural thing, and he thought she'd only put them back
on because she felt self-conscious around him; she doubtless
ran barefoot around the Cameron orchard and farm most of
the time. Her blue-and-red serge dress trimmed with braid
around the high collar must be one she'd worn at school—the
mountain women dressed in homespun mostly with gingham
or calico thrown in here and there, purchased more than likely
during infrequent trips to the store in Brush Lane.

Timothy watched Rachel grow smaller and smaller until
she disappeared around the river bend, then he glanced off
at distant mountains where he'd been born and raised. Lately
he gave thought to not returning to Chicago, to staying on
somewhere in Missouri. He could write to the editors of the
Springfield Journal and the St. Louis newspaper and inquire
about the possibilities with them.

It was a thought. Just a thought.

Two afternoons later, when Rachel again came to read, he
took her out in the boat.

He didn't so much want to write as just to enjoy the day, he
said. He'd made corn pones from meal he had bought in Brush
Lane, and he'd gone hunting for a wild turkey, had killed one,
cleaned it, and baked it just this morning. No matter the reason
he gave for not especially wanting to write—thoughts weren't
coming to him, he couldn't seem to sit still for long—Rachel
knew that what really kept him from it was the shiner he'd
come by since the last time she'd seen him.

His right eye was purple and blue and swollen nearly shut.
He changed the subject the first time she asked him about it—
while she was helping him wrap the food in cloths and put the
bundles in a basket. He turned and mumbled something about
how she would want to take along *Glimpses of a Boyhood*
since that was the real reason she'd come.

As they started off in the boat she again asked how he'd
come by the shiner. He began talking about spring in the
Ozarks, how the trees and land had turned so green, with
splashes of other colors here and there that really livened

things up. If he were a painter, he'd have his canvas out right now. . . .

Rachel refused to be put off again. "Reckon you met with Lloyd an' Frank," she said stubbornly.

"What makes you think that?" he asked, rowing.

"Both of 'em were pretty sore the night of the Howitts' frolic."

"Yep."

"Yep, they were sore, or yep, they did that to you?"

"Maybe both."

She glared. "You don't have to be so stubborn!"

"Why do you need to know who did it? Maybe I walked into a door and—"

"A stretcher if I ever heard one," she muttered. "I figure I'm the reason, that's why I want to know."

"Like you warned the night of the frolic—neither man's been too pleasant at the mill."

"Lord, Timothy. Do you have to work there?"

"A character in my new book operates a lumber mill."

"That doesn't mean you have to work there! Couldn't you just ask questions and—"

"Make Lloyd and Frank think I'm scared of them?"

"It wouldn't be like that."

"It would."

"I've a mind to go right now to Brush Lane and tell the law."

Timothy sighed. "Rachel, you'll make the situation worse."

"Lloyd an' Frank'll be locked up," she argued. "What about Jed? Was he in on it?"

"Jed's been keeping quiet."

She watched him for a few moments, then she lay back in the boat, cushioning her head on a blanket he'd thrown in, and stared at him some more. The water lapped gently at the sides of the skiff, and the sun glittered on the river's surface. A breeze played with the branches of overhanging trees on both banks. Fish leaped a ways off in the water.

"I'm not coming back after today," Rachel said by and by.

Timothy inhaled deeply. He'd known Rachel Cameron could

test a body's patience if she was of the mind. "What, are you going to just give yourself over to those two hounds?" he demanded irritably. "Leave it alone."

She sat straight up. "That's a mean thing to say! I wouldn't."

"What do you think will happen if Lloyd and Frank think you're not seeing me anymore? Did you really think they wanted to 'walk' the night of the frolic? Sure. Walk you back to a nice bunch of bushes, where they could take turns at you!"

She drew a swift breath. "You've no call. . . . Besides, we ain't 'seeing' each other! I come to read some afternoons, is all."

"You're fooling yourself, too. I could have loaned you the book, Rachel."

She laid back again to study him from that position. "What're you saying? Why didn't you loan it to me, then?"

His gaze held hers. "Because I didn't know how often I'd see you if I did. An' I wanted to see you again. Not just one afternoon either."

Rachel felt a little thrill go through her. She told herself to ignore it—Timothy would be gone once his notes were finished and whatever writing he'd come to do was done—but she found that she couldn't. She found that the long look he gave her made the thrill grow, made catching her breath hard, made her heart pump fast.

She watched him leave both oars in favor of moving toward her, and she knew she ought to say something to stop him. Words of objection formed in her head but never reached her mouth.

He stretched out beside her. His hand on her hip turned her to face him. He brushed a stray tendril from her face, then two fingers caressed the sensitive area just below her ear.

"Rachel," he said low, in a way that made her heart beat all the faster.

She swallowed. "Lloyd an' Frank'll do their best to run you out of what they think is their territory."

"Yep, and they might find that I'm a fairly wise mountain man when I want to be. Maybe they just might fall into a trap of their own making."

His face neared hers and she held her breath, waiting. . . .

When his mouth pressed against hers, the kiss was soft and undemanding. Then his tongue urged her lips apart, slipped into her mouth, and the kiss turned sweeter than anything she'd tasted; it was as warm and enticing as apple pie just out of the oven. She thought briefly that they had sworn to each other that she would only come calling on him in the afternoons to read. But she didn't think either one of them had believed that at the time, not really. They'd only been trying to convince each other.

He ended the kiss, then lay watching her, perhaps wondering if she would be angry. She thought of asking him if he ever thought of giving up that job in Chicago, but she couldn't ask that . . . she just couldn't. They were only beginning to know each other, he'd only kissed her twice, and she couldn't expect anything of him. She couldn't expect him to commit himself to her.

His fingers touched her shoulder, then slipped to the back of her neck and gently urged her toward him. His body pressed against hers, and she felt his arousal, hard and unrelenting. She jerked back, sat up, and folded her arms across her breasts.

"You must think I'm stupid or somethin'. It's not . . ." She laughed nervously. "I mean, I know—"

"No, Rachel. Not stupid. Untouched and frightened. Sorry. I should have kept rowing."

"Please understand," she whispered. "I can't. I like the way you look at me and kiss me. The way you touch me. But, Lord! I don't want to end up like Susie. I know what you said—that you'd never leave a girl pregnant, but . . . don't hate me! Please. I couldn't stand that either."

He sat up beside her and touched a finger to her lips. "I'd never hate a gal for saying no. Like I said, I should have kept rowing."

He returned to the oars. She watched him for a bit, needing to know if he was angry. He smiled finally, and feeling reassured, she took up the book she'd placed on the wooden seat in the boat.

"I'll be careful around Lloyd and Frank," he promised.

"You do that."

The water splashed gently. Along the riverbank, squirrels chattered.

"Gramma told me to ask if you'd like to come to supper," Rachel said directly. "That ain't me askin', mind you. I wouldn't do nothing so improper and forward." A smile tugged at one corner of her mouth.

Chuckling, Timothy tossed his head, throwing the hair from his eyes. "Of course you wouldn't. I'd love to come calling for supper. In answer to your grandmother's invitation, that is. She's priceless."

"I think she's silly sometimes," Rachel confided. "Spouting superstitions an' all. Can't believe an educated man like yourself believes in some of that stuff."

"Like I said, I've seen some of it happen."

"Do you really think there'd be a terrible storm if I trimmed my or Little Ben's hair on a calm day?"

"Can't rightly say, unless you do it and a storm comes along. Why do the beliefs bother you so much?"

She sighed. "I got teased a lot at school for things like not putting my left shoe on first to avoid bad luck an' sleeping with my head to the north for good luck. Was teased about plenty of other things, too, things Gramma taught me over the years."

"I can imagine."

"So I've tried to get some of 'em out of my head, y'know. That way if I ever get to go back to school—maybe college someday—I won't be repeating things people might make fun of me for. But I don't know. . . . It hurts Gramma's feelings, I allow, that I don't believe so much anymore. I got angry with Ben one afternoon when we were fishing—he kept spitting on the bait."

Timothy laughed. "For luck."

She nodded. "I told him I didn't put stock in Gramma's superstitions, and the very next morning he told her I said that. It hurt her feelings. She didn't say so, but I could tell it did."

They were silent again for a time. Then Timothy looked off at the blue-green ridges and the slopes populated by rich foliage. "This is a different place, Rachel," he said thoughtfully. "A world all its own, with its own set of laws and ways. We're both a part of it. We always will be, no matter how far we go from it, no matter how much time we spend away, no matter how much we try to change. It calls, and we return sooner or later to find a simple people who will always be the same in heart and soul. They watch the sky and the trees and the animals and each other, and they form beliefs based on what they see, on what they've observed for years. I've been north, even east on occasion. I've seen the crowded cities and new inventions, and all the changes scare me sometimes. Sooner or later the new things will come here. They'll touch our people and change them. I guess that's why I wanted to come back, why I *needed* to come back. More than capturing the scenery—the mountains, the trees, the cabins, the mill—I want to capture the people as they are now. I don't want our world to change. But it will."

He shook his head and laughed low. The rowing of the oars slowed. "Guess what I'm saying is be proud of your heritage, because it's special—it's sweet and fresh. Be proud of what you are and don't ever hang your head when someone laughs at you or teases you. And above all, don't change inside."

"You changed," she said softly, touched by all that he'd said. Why had she ever accused him of not belonging here anymore? She felt ashamed that she had, because he obviously loved the mountains and the people so.

He nodded. "Not entirely. After a time I found that I missed home. I missed all that had made me what I was deep inside. My parents died in a train accident, my brother was killed during a bank robbery, my sister died of cholera—all within two years. I was caught up in making my dreams happen and I lost sight of who I was, *what* I was. What was really important. I went to Springfield before coming here, and I visited all the graves for the first time. I took a deep breath of the mountain air and thought, Damn, it's good to be home. I'll never lose sight of home again. It's here," he said, tapping his chest.

"Oh, Timothy," she whispered. "I didn't know about your family."

He shrugged. "It's not something I talk about much."

"Do you have other family?"

"A grandfather who moved to St. Louis some years back. I looked him up before traveling on to Springfield. Do you know when it really all hit me? That I'd let their lives just slip away while I chased after the next story or lay dreaming up characters? A few years ago a Chicago friend invited me to a supper at his home—a supper in honor of mothers in the family. Honoring mothers yearly is something that's being done more and more every May all over the country. Anyway, I realized that I'd never told my mother and either grandmother how much I really loved and appreciated them. That's something I'll always regret."

Rachel immediately thought of her own grandmother. After Ellen Cameron, Rachel's mother, had died of cancer, Gramma Cameron had stepped in to help care for the children—Rachel and Ben. And though Lydia Cameron was full of superstitions, Rachel couldn't think of another person in the world she would rather have had help raise her.

During the long nights right after Ma's death, when Rachel had had nightmares and Ben sometimes got up thinking to go snuggle against their mother, Gramma had slept in a chair in their loft room, soothing Rachel with a cool hand upon her brow and taking Ben onto her lap and letting him snuggle against her. They were two motherless children with a hardworking pap, and Gramma had come from far back in the hills where she'd lived with her husband, who had been dead for some ten years by then. Before Ellen's death, Lydia had refused to give up the cabin she'd occupied with Grampa, but for her grandchildren, she hadn't blinked at the thought of giving it up. She'd told Rachel once that moving her and Ben out to that old cabin would have been to take away something else that was familiar to them, something else they loved, and she'd never given the thought of doing that much notice—she'd just packed up and come to live in the cabin beside the river with Paul and the younguns. Soon she'd had Paul sell the land on which his parents had raised him and five other children, and soon after that was when she had started teaching Rachel to read well.

She's priceless. That's what Timothy had said about Gramma Cameron. Rachel thought—no, she *knew*—he was right. For her and Ben, and even Pap, Lydia Cameron was indeed priceless.

"Want some food?" Timothy said, again moving from the oars. They bumped against the locks, then went still. "I'm powerful hungry, Miss Rachel. I'm going to eat."

She smiled and said yes, she was hungry and would he please pass her one of those turkey legs they'd packed. He reached for the basket of food he'd placed in one corner of the boat earlier, lifted both turkey legs, and handed her one.

While eating, she told him how her mother had died and how Gramma had moved in right after the burial to take care of her and Ben and the farm whenever their father went to work at the mill.

They finished the turkey legs, and Timothy pulled out the corn pones. He and Rachel kicked back in the boat, him on one side, her on the other, their necks resting on the narrowed edges of the skiff. They talked about dime novels and superstitions and his boyhood spent hunting, fishing, and farming near Springfield. They talked about Chicago and newspaper stories he'd written and how he had finally taken the big step he'd always wanted to take and had started writing a novel that had sold within two months after he had sent it to a New York publisher.

By and by Rachel and Timothy realized that the sun was lowering a bit.

"We'll take the boat and go on to your pap's place," he said. "And hopefully your father won't meet me with a loaded shotgun."

She laughed. "He ain't like Lloyd and Frank. Worst that'll happen is that he'll peck at me a bit."

"He's gotten quieter since the frolic. He hardly says a word while we're working at the mill."

"It takes Pap a while to thaw out."

"Does he know you come to my place some afternoons?"

She didn't answer. She twisted her lips.

Timothy heaved a sigh. "He doesn't. Rachel—"

"Gramma thought it best not to say anything. Like you've found out, Pap doesn't take too well to people he thinks don't belong around here. We sure wouldn't want him thinkin' that maybe you and I are looking at each other like . . . well, you know."

He lifted both brows. "Like how?"

She finished off a corn pone, then wiped her mouth with the back of a hand. Then she laughed nervously. "Teachers at school woulda laid into me for doing that."

"Is there a napkin handy?" he asked with some humor, looking around.

She glanced up. A breeze blew strands of hair across her face, and she brushed them aside. "No napkin so far as I can see."

"Is there a handkerchief, by chance?"

"Not unless you've got one in a trouser pocket," she said, laughing.

"I'm afraid not. And you're not in St. Louis anymore, Miss Rachel."

She faked a glare. "Why do you call me that sometimes? You started it at the mill that mornin', and Lloyd, Frank, and Jed picked it right up."

"Because sometimes you act a little prissy."

"Pris—why, I've a mind to throw one of those turkey bones at you!"

He shrugged. "You asked. I can't tell a lie. I just can't."

Grinning, she drew the back of her hand across her mouth again. "You're right. I'm not in St. Louis anymore an' I suppose I do act a little prissy sometimes."

"Like how might your pap think we're looking at each other?" he asked, his voice lower now. "You avoided my question."

Sobering, she glanced down at her lap. "Don't tease so, Timothy Benton. The daisies won't be in full bloom till midsummer, and I plan to walk right by them an' never look down once they are. You're an Ozarker, certain-sure, but you're still just passing through."

He went back to the oars and began rowing. She folded the cloths in which the food had been wrapped and placed them in the baskets.

"Borrow the book, Rachel, so you don't get in trouble with your pap," he said after a time. "I'm ashamed that I didn't loan it to you in the first place."

"I'm glad you didn't," she responded. "Otherwise we wouldn't have talked so. This has been fun."

They smiled at each other as water lapped at the sides of the boat.

SIX

During supper, Paul Cameron was quiet for the most part. Of course, if he had said much, he wouldn't have been heard over Ben's chattering anyway. Ben went to school three days a week in Brush Lane and was always bursting with talk after he came home.

"Tommy Langdon said that was the biggest critter he ever did see," Ben said around a mouthful of cooked beans. "Joe, he raised it on a stick an' 'bout that time ol' Missus Slocum come chargin' outta the school house a-yellin' an' a-screamin' how Joe better put that snake down. Joe didn't care none by that time 'cause he'd already got a good look at it, an' sho had all the other boys. He dropped it, an' it headed straight through the grash at Missus Slocum, who was still chargin'. I ain't never seen nobody turn 'round so fast! She got herself a look at that thang—all twenty-odd foot of it—"

"*Twenty feet,* Ben?" Rachel interrupted skeptically.

"Yep. 'At's what Tommy said it was. Well, Missus Slocum, she went like a spinnin' wheel, zipping 'round an' tryin' to figure which way to go to get 'way from that thang. Us boys, we was laughin'. An' then the girls started to screamin' an' a-hoppin' in the grass in the direction of the schoolhouse, an' it was all commotion!"

Timothy couldn't help himself—he grinned over a biscuit he'd started working on when Ben had launched into the account. Paul was grinning, too, though both Rachel and Lydia wore frowns aimed at Ben, frowns that quickly turned on Paul and Timothy.

"Lacey Elberton, she los' part of her skirt to a tree branch—weren't no stoppin' her once she was a-moving 'way from that

271

critter," Ben said between giggles. "Mary Lawrence 'n Rose Moore ran smack into each other. 'Liza Jane went splat in the mud. Emmitt Peters was the only boy a-runnin—always has been a sissy—"

"Hush that now!" Lydia scolded. "Paul, you stop encouragin' the boy!"

"That's right," Rachel said, looking straight at Timothy.

"Hell, Ma," Paul remarked somewhat sheepishly. "That's what he is—just a boy."

"That's right," Timothy said in response to Rachel's admonishing gaze.

Lydia gave both men a thorough look of disapproval. "All the same, there'll be no more talk of Ben scarin' folks with that snake the boys found in the schoolyard. Ben, you best remember why you go to school. It sure ain't so you can upset the rest of the day for ever'body."

"It did too!" Ben boasted. "We didn't do no more cipherin' all day!"

Paul chuckled behind his coffee mug. Timothy couldn't help a snicker.

"Don't sound so proud, Ben," Rachel chided. "Poor Emmitt."

"That boy never has been too sturdy," Lydia remarked.

During Timothy's childhood, any boy who ran from the sight of a snake would have been known as a sissy. But Timothy wasn't about to say so; Rachel was watching him, as if knowing his thoughts and waiting for him to speak them.

He shook his head. "If Emmitt's going to make his way in the mountains . . ."

"He can't be no sissy," Ben finished.

"That's mean," Rachel said straightaway, glaring at Timothy. "How can you say that?"

He held up his hands in defense. "I didn't say anything about him being a sissy."

"You started to."

"I could have finished that sentence a number of ways: he's got to toughen up . . . he's got to learn to face snakes . . . he's got to learn to face trouble."

"Uh-huh. And if that snake were comin' at you, would you have just stood there?"

"What kind of snake was it, Ben?" Timothy asked.

"Don't rightly know," the boy answered.

"What did it look like?"

"Yellow bands. Chainlike, y'know. White underneath with black blotches."

"A king snake," Timothy said without hesitation. He turned back to Rachel. "I wouldn't have run, but I wouldn't have bothered it too much."

"King snakes don't get twenty foot long," Paul said. "But they're sure big enough to eat a little boy if they're hungry enough."

Ben's eyes widened. His grin faded. He swallowed hard.

"How many did he have to pick from?" his father asked, cold sober now. Or perhaps he was putting on a show for Ben's benefit.

"W-what?" Ben's mouth had apparently gone dry. He licked his lips.

"How many boys was in the schoolyard when you went to messin' with that thang?"

"Um, five, I reckon."

"Add 'bout five more to that, 'cause you always come up without about half the number. That gives us ten. I figure ol' king had ten good-lookin' boys to pick from for dinner."

Ben made a sound as if he was strangling—Timothy wasn't sure if he'd ever swallowed all of that mouthful of beans. Timothy saw humor in Paul's blue-green eyes, and he fought to keep a straight face. A king snake could probably eat an infant whole, but a child upward of three years old . . . Timothy doubted that the snake could manage that. But he kept his mouth shut and all humor from his expression because he guessed what Paul was doing.

"Don't be playin' with snakes," Paul told Ben. "You don't always know which'll hurt you an' which won't. An' I'd just as soon you didn't find out by teasin' 'em."

"I didn't tease it! Honest Injun, Pap!"

"Sounds like you had a go at it all the same. Don't do it again. That's all we'll say about it."

"Yes, Pap."

Ben hung his head over his plate. Timothy was a little sorry to see the boy's fun be taken away; there was something charming about Ben when his eyes were lit up with excitement.

Supper continued, and the conversation turned to the revival soon to come to Brush Lane. It would be attended by folks for miles around, for sure, Lydia said. Timothy smiled, remembering when he had attended a few revivals with his parents and siblings.

After eating several servings of peach preserves (Lydia eagerly told how Rachel had put them up herself), Timothy walked with the family through the orchard. Now and then he felt Paul's eyes on him, sizing him up, and several times he met the man's hard gaze. The conversation over supper had relieved the tension between them, but Timothy still felt a sense of distrust from Rachel's father.

Presently, Timothy remarked that he had to be going. His day at the mill tomorrow would come early, and the sun was setting.

As he climbed into the boat Lydia, Ben, and Rachel waved good-bye from where they stood near a large willow tree. Paul stood beside Rachel, giving Timothy another of his curious, uncertain looks. Timothy lifted the oars and prepared to head back to his cabin, all the while wondering how long it would take Paul Cameron to decide that they needed to talk about his daughter.

The next morning Rachel pulled her boots on and began lacing them. Her fingers trembled, and she paused in her task to close her hands tight and try to calm them. When she opened them seconds later, the trembling had stopped. But there seemed no way to stop the nervous flutter in her stomach.

Pap wanted her to walk with him to the mill. They usually took Little Ben along, but Pap had specifically said only

Rachel should go today. Ben had opened his mouth to yell
an objection, but Pap's hand on the seat of Ben's britches
had snapped the boy's mouth shut, and now he was outside
helping their father with chores.

Rachel finished lacing her boots. She ran a brush through
her hair several times, then tied it all back with a ribbon.
They had already eaten breakfast, and she was sure that if
she dallied around much more, Pap would come in the house
and yell up at her.

Days ago she'd placed the rabbit's foot Timothy had given
her with the one she'd had for years in a box she stored beneath
her bed. Now, thinking that Pap surely wanted to discuss
Timothy—or tell her how things would be with Timothy—
she pulled the box out, lifted its leather latch, and dropped
both good-luck charms into the pocket she'd sewn onto the
dress she now wore. Then she shut the box and pushed it back
beneath the bed. Taking the rabbit paws with her this morning
surely wouldn't hurt anything. Maybe there was something to
what Gramma said about them. Maybe there was something to
most everything Gramma said; after all, Timothy *had* kissed
her soon after she'd seen that ring of grounds in the bottom
of Pap's coffee mug.

Paul was leaning against the fence near the barn when
Rachel emerged outside. Seated on the top rail beside Pap's
elbow, Ben threw grain to the chickens, who busily clucked,
scratched, and pecked at the ground. A hog came sniffing
around, scattering the chickens, and Ben swung a leg, trying
to scare him away. The boy toppled backward, and the hog
snuffed up grain.

"Whoa, there," Pap said, righting Ben. "Just scoot down the
rail some and throw it where the chickens go."

Ben began scooting down the rail as Rachel neared the
fence.

"Ready?" Pap said, giving her a warm look. He didn't look
angry or annoyed with her.

Rachel released a breath of relief. "Ready."

He withdrew from the fence, warning, "Me an' Rachel are
headin' out now, Ben. No more smart moves. Let the boar go

if he wants the feed. You ain't big enough yet to challenge him on it."

Ben nodded but grumbled, and Paul and Rachel began walking toward the river.

"It'll be real good fishin' weather soon," Rachel's father remarked presently as they walked along the edge of the water. "You always have liked to fish."

Rachel nodded. "So does Ben."

"Yep, but he gets in the way sometimes an' scares 'em with his talk. The boy's got jumpin' beans in his britches."

"Might that snake really have eaten him?" Rachel asked.

"That king? Naw." He laughed. "Ben . . . sometimes you gotta warn him in a roundabout way. Otherwise he don't listen an' he goes off to scrounge around for more trouble—sometimes in the same place."

"Do you suppose he'll get teased if he runs from snakes now?"

"He won't run. He'll stick around to have a look but he won't handle 'em. That Joe's gonna get bit someday. He'll fetch up a coral or a copperhead on a stick, get the thing riled up, and it'll strike at him. I don't like Ben runnin' with that boy. Same as I don't like you runnin' with Benton." Paul said the last softly, looking off upriver.

Rachel jammed a hand into her skirt pocket and wrapped her fingers around both rabbit feet.

"Ain't nothin' going to come of it, Pap. Soon as Mr. Benton writes down descriptions an' things like that, he'll be heading back to Chicago."

"An' leave you with a broken heart."

She shook her head. "No. I know the rules."

"Do they ever lay down rules, Rachel? These fellers that come through for one reason or another, they don't have rules. I was a youngster once. I know what it's like to run after the gals. I reckon the foreigners ain't no different. Fact is, they're worse."

"He's not a foreigner. He's from near Springfield."

"He'll be gone just the same, like you said. Ben told me you go to his place to read books. I don't like the sound of that."

She scowled. "Ben tells everything."

"You an' yer gramma—you weren't gonna tell."

"No, we weren't," she said, refusing to feel ashamed. "You wouldn't have allowed me to go back. Just like with school, you wouldn't have cared about me being happy."

He stopped walking, took her by the shoulders, twisted her around to face him, and glared down at her. "You listen up, Rachel Sue. There ain't been one day when I haven't wanted you to be happy. I sent you to that school an' started workin' at the mill so we could pay the bill an' buy you new dresses. It ain't right, you accusin' me of not wantin' me to be happy!"

"Why did you take me out?" she asked, a little too resentfully.

"You changed in a way I didn't want you to change. I saw you growing' different from us. I traveled all the way to St. Louis to pick you up one time, an' you acted like you didn't want nothin' to do with me, like you was ashamed of me. I saw you hangin' back behind that door till all the other girls was gone. Then you came out an' got in the wagon. I thought then, It's time Rachel remembered who she is."

"I was happy there, learning an'—"

"I take it you ain't happy here?" he demanded, giving her a shake.

"I am, but—"

His hands tightened on her shoulders. "That Benton feller's given you all the happiness you have, is that it?"

"No, Pap, I—"

He shook her again. "You really been readin' or you been messin' with him?"

"Pap, stop!" she cried, tears springing to her eyes. "I wouldn't, I—"

"You listen up, Rachel Sue, an' you listen real good," he warned, his voice lower now. "I lost yer mother to cancer an' I ain't gonna lose you to that man, to that—that citified hillsman! I ain't gonna let him take you with him to Chicago. Lloyd an' Frank plan to stay right where they are, so I reckon you'd best be choosin' from one of them."

"He ain't plannin' on marrying me!" she blurted, trembling.
"Pap, let—"

"What's he plannin' on doin', then? Bangin' you up then
takin' off? I'll put a load of buckshot in 'im big enough to kill
a bear."

"Don't, Pap! Leave him alone! He's—"

"Stay away from 'im, you hear me?" he growled.

"I'll do what I want to do!"

"You'll do . . . ?"

She had time enough to register his hand rising, but not time
enough to duck what she knew was coming. He slapped her
square across the cheek, hard enough to send her sprawling.
She lay in the grass, holding her face, crying as quietly as she
could, not believing what he'd done. Aside from a spanking
now and then when she'd been much younger, he'd never
lifted a hand to her in anger.

"I ain't marryin' Lloyd or Frank," she said. "You can hit
me all you want—I ain't marryin' either of them!"

"Get on home," he said softly, looking stunned. He glanced
down at his hand, then back up at her. "Get up to the loft an'
don't come down till tonight when I get home."

She didn't move.

"Go, Rachel. Go now."

She struggled to get on her feet. "Leave him alone at the
mill today, Pap. Please. I won't be the same if anything
happens to him. I won't forgive you either."

He studied her, his jaw jutting out, his eyes glossy. Then
he turned and trudged off.

Once he was out of sight, she thought about lying in the
grass and crying. He'd never hit her!

She sniffed twice and headed for the woods. She was eighteen, old enough to choose for herself who she would marry.
And she wasn't about to spend all day in the loft as he'd told
her to.

She cut between trees and over rocks, climbing the trail
that led to the Howitts' place, not really noticing much when
branches snagged and scratched at her skirt and arms. She
tasted blood once and figured her father had busted her lip

when he'd hit her. Realizing that, she grew angrier and more defiant, and she climbed faster, hot tears rolling down her cheeks. Maybe she shouldn't have talked to him like that, in the prissy way Timothy had told her she sometimes talked, but he still shouldn't have slapped her.

She climbed on, pushing her way up, until at last she heard chickens squawk and children shout and Susie's sweet voice telling them to get back or the billy goat would kick them.

She broke into the clearing. Susie saw her and headed her way, wondering aloud what was wrong, why she was crying. Rachel could do no more at the moment than sit down on a boulder, put her face in her hands, and let the tears flow as much as they wanted to. She'd be in trouble for coming up here without telling anyone where she was going. But right now she didn't care.

At the Cameron farm, morning came and went, and Lydia began to worry about Rachel. Usually Rachel came right home after walking with Paul to the mill. But there was no sign of her. Every time Lydia walked to the river, put a hand up to shade the sun from her eyes, and took a look in the direction of the mill, she saw only trees, bushes, and water—no Rachel. Afternoon arrived, and Lydia saddled and mounted a horse behind Ben. They rode toward the mill.

She found Paul helping Timothy Benton repair a section of the milldam that had been built some fifty years ago in the river near the main wood-and-stone building. She asked both men if they'd seen Rachel—the girl hadn't been home since she'd set out with Paul this morning.

"We ain't seen her," Paul said, working his jaw the way he often did when worrying over something.

Timothy straightened slowly, wiping his wet hands on his duckin's legs. "Well, where might she be?"

"Don't know, but I'm worried," Lydia answered. "It ain't like Rachel to—"

"I reckon she's run off," Paul said, turning away. He started off up the rocks, picking his way out of the water, heading toward the back of the mill building. To walk toward her this way, he'd have to swim part of the river. Lydia figured he meant to walk around the building. All the same she didn't like him turning his back to her. And why did he reckon Rachel had run off?

"Paul Cam'ron, you turn back right now," she ordered. "Face me an' tell me why you think Rachel's run off."

He turned back all right—sweating, his eyes shifting from his boots, to her, and back. He pulled a rag from the bib of his overalls, wiped his forehead, then tucked the rag back in the bib.

"You'd better start talkin', boy, afore I come through the water after you," she warned. She'd gone after him enough times when he'd been a boy, so he knew she was serious.

"We talked this mornin'," he said finally. "Rachel . . . she didn't like what I had to say. She had a few things to say herself, an' I . . . well, I hit her, Ma."

Lydia stiffened. Timothy twisted to gawk at Paul.

"Why'd you hit her?" Lydia demanded. "What did she say that coulda made you do somethin' like that?"

"I told her to stay away from Benton here," he said, cocking a thumb Timothy's way. "Told her to choose either Lloyd or Frank an' settle down. She told me she'd do what she wanted to do."

Lydia stared at him. "The girl oughta be allowed to choose for herself."

"I ain't gonna argue with you about this, Ma."

"No . . . I ain't gonna argue either. Get up to the Howitts' an' see if she's there. Where's Frank an' Lloyd?"

"Down fixin' the rollers," he said, drawing the back of one hand across his chin.

"We'll need both of 'em if she's not found at the Howitts'."

Nodding, Paul turned to start off again.

"I'm going with you," Timothy said. "I'll go tell Mr. Stephens what's happening." Mr. Stephens was the operator.

"Only a piece of it," Paul muttered, making clear that this was personal business.

Timothy lifted his chin. "I'll tell him she's missing, then I'll catch up."

"We'll see."

"Reckon I can climb a hill as well as anyone in these parts, Mr. Cameron."

Paul grunted, then disappeared around the corner of the building. Timothy crossed the rocks and went inside the mill-house, intent on talking to Mr. Stephens.

As promised, he caught up with Paul later on the trail leading up to the Howitts'.

"I wouldn't hurt her, Mr. Cameron," Timothy said, broaching what he knew was a sore subject with the man.

Paul was silent.

Timothy scrambled around several boulders. "Whatever happens, I plan to do right by Rachel."

"She's a good girl, all in all," Cameron finally said quietly. "A bit mixed up in the head sometimes, but good in the heart. If you ain't got plans to marry her, leave her alone, stop seein' her. Get out of Taney County."

Timothy inhaled deeply. Paul looked over at him, and Timothy nodded and said, "I understand, sir."

"Good," Cameron muttered, taking the lead.

In the end, it was Lydia and Ben who found Rachel, curled up asleep, safe and sound in Timothy's boat. Lydia bowed her head and said a quick prayer, thanking the good Lord for his mercy. Then she bent and gently stroked Rachel's forehead while Ben peered over her shoulder and whispered Rachel's name.

Rachel came awake with a start. She'd left the Howitts' she didn't know how long ago, after Susie had said she ought to go home so no one would worry about her. Susie felt bad for her, but Lydia and Ben and even Paul would be concerned. Susie had said she thought Rachel's pap would be real sorry about now and would never hit her like that again. Rachel had left, but she hadn't headed for home; she'd come here and lain in the little boat she and Timothy had had such a fine time in yesterday. Consoling herself with the memory of his kisses, she'd fallen asleep. And now here was Gramma, bending over her, soothing her with a hand as she had so often after those nightmares.

"It's all right now," Gramma said.

Rachel lay back, closed her eyes, and concentrated on slowing her heartbeat. "Where's Pap?" she asked.

"He an' Mr. Benton went up to the Howitts' to look for you."

She started again. "Pap'll shoot him!"

Lydia put her hands on Rachel's shoulders and pressed the girl back down. "He ain't gonna do nothin' of the sort."

"He said he would."

"He won't. He knows I'd fetch the law after him. Let me see you," Gramma said, turning Rachel's head. She sighed. "You've got a swollen lip thar an' a little cut on the inside where your tooth must've hit. We'll go back to the house an' mix up somethin' to put on it."

Rachel started to say she didn't want to go back. But to keep running was childish, not to mention cowardly. She wasn't a child anymore and she darn sure wasn't a coward. She'd face her father, try to talk to him in a reasonable manner, and hope he'd talk in a reasonable manner back to her.

"I love you, Gramma," she said suddenly, sitting up.

Smiling, Lydia embraced her. "I know, Rachel." She withdrew and smoothed Rachel's hair. "C'mon now. Let's go home an' see if we can sort this out."

SEVEN

When Rachel climbed from the boat, Timothy and Pap were coming around the base of the hill on which Timothy's house stood. Rachel gave Timothy a worried look, wondering if her father had done anything to him. But Timothy looked fine—not a mark on him—and Gramma, seeming to know what Rachel was thinking, said not to worry, that Paul knew she'd tan his hide if anything happened to Timothy Benton.

Though Rachel knew her grandmother would take her side where Timothy was concerned, she didn't mean to ask her to. She'd thought a lot about how she had accused Pap of not wanting her to be happy. She'd considered, too, what he had revealed about how hard he'd worked to put her in the St. Louis school. She felt ashamed that she had sassed him so and she meant to apologize for doing it. After that, she wanted to make him realize somehow that he shouldn't try to force her to marry Lloyd or Frank. That Timothy was a good man.

Despite what Gramma had said about sorting out the bad situation, she refused to let Rachel and Paul speak to each other for the rest of the day. Of course by the time Rachel had climbed from the boat, all that remained was evening. Still, the hours dragged as Rachel helped her grandmother fry chicken for supper, then clean up after the meal.

"I'm sorry, Pap," Rachel said softly over breakfast the following morning. "I'm sorry I didn't tell you I was going to his place to read some afternoons. I'm sorry, too, for saying you don't want me to be happy. That was mean."

"Let's go walk in the woods an' talk, Rachel," he said, wiping his mouth with the back of a hand.

She didn't know if she wanted to do that. Like it or not, she was apprehensive after the way he'd slapped her yesterday.

He seemed to know her thoughts. "I ain't gonna do that ever again, girl. I shouldn't have in the first place. The last thang I want is for you to be afraid of me."

She nodded and rose, all the while feeling Gramma's and Little Ben's eyes on her. Her father rose, too, and held out his hand. She took it, then walked outside with him.

Located behind the apple orchard, the forest was a haven of spring freshness. Morning sun trickled between branches and leaves, forming patches of light on beds of soft grass and a multitude of shrubs, herbs, and ferns. Deer trails cut through the woods in a number of places, and the sound of rustling brush indicated the presence of small animals that scurried along in search of hiding places. Rachel and her father walked along a trail he'd forged himself a number of years back; it led to a salt lick.

"I didn't know the St. Louis school cost so much, Pap," she said by and by. "At the time I just knew I wanted to go. It was a good one, according to that man from St. Louis who came through and told Gramma all about it that one time. I never thought about what it would cost. That was selfish, I know, but . . . I never thought about why you started working at the mill either. I just took everything for granted."

"I didn't start workin' at the mill just to put you up in the school, Rachel, though the pay helped. Truth is, the money comes in handy when the apples an' other crops don't do well some years."

"Timothy . . . he's not the kind of man who'd get a girl pregnant, then run off," she said cautiously. "He's just not. An' he's real proud of where he comes from. He was telling me how he forgot who he was for a while, how he got caught up in his dreams. While he was going after them his parents, brother, and sister died. He was ashamed of who he was, too, of where he came from. Then he realized that he should be proud of being an Ozarker."

"You sure he ain't just talking fancy?"

"I'm sure. When he found out that you didn't know I was going to his place some afternoons . . . he didn't like that."

They walked on, twigs crunching beneath their boots, the trees and foliage whispering around them.

"He ain't done anything more than kiss me twice," she said. "Besides, I told him I'd never think of wastin' a daisy on him—or any man. I won't let any man worry me crazy. If he ever asks to marry me, then I'll start worrying about things that need to be worried about. Until then . . . I don't want to feel like cryin' all summer like Susie did last year. I plan to be careful."

A gray rabbit bounced across the path up ahead, then disappeared into the brush.

"I *was* ashamed, Pap, that day you came to get me from school," Rachel admitted. "As I told Timothy, the other girls teased me about the way I talked and how I followed or repeated some of the beliefs Gramma had taught me. The teachers sometimes made me feel like a fool. Nobody likes being made to feel like that, so I tried to change. But Timothy . . . he's made me see that I don't have to change *inside,* that I don't have to be ashamed of who I am. I don't think we're strange anymore 'cause of the way we talk and act here in the hills. I think we're special."

He squeezed her hand and smiled a little. Then he sobered. "I'm gonna tell you somethin', Rachel. Benton scares me 'cause I 'llow you care about him more than you say. I figure all he's got to do is ask an' you'd up an' go away with him. I watched the two of you lookin' at each other at the frolic an' at supper last night."

"Oh, Pap . . . I wouldn't run off with him. I'd never do that. I'd marry him if he asked me 'cause he'd be good to me, and I like him a lot—like you said. If I ever go away again, I'm not going to try to forget who I am, and I won't ever, ever forget the people who are important to me."

"Frank or Lloyd . . . they'd give you a good home," he said, sighing.

She shook her head. "I don't want to marry either one of them. I'd have baby after baby after baby an' I'd cook and clean an' do chores all the time. That's a fine life for some. But, Pap, that's not what I want. It's just not. I want to think about college—and I'm willing to find work to pay the bill myself."

He looked off in the distance. "I shouldn't have given you a taste of the world."

"I would have found it sooner or later. You can't stop a person from growing."

"Guess I'm learnin' out of all this, too." He shook his head. "But I don't know about him, Rachel. I just don't know."

"Give him a chance, Pap. Please. Be decent to him. If he comes for supper, talk to him—don't ignore him. Maybe he'll leave soon an' we'll never see him again. But until then we ought to at least treat him like a neighbor. We ought to treat him with the same kindness and hospitality we'd offer anyone from up here."

"You've got your gramma's goodness an' stubbornness, I reckon."

Rachel smiled. "Gramma's priceless. And that's straight from Timothy Benton's mouth."

"That she is," he agreed. "When she heard what I'd done to you, I thought she was gonna strip a willow branch and take after me. I reckon she'd still like to."

"I keep remembering how when Ma died, Gramma dropped everything, packed up, and came to help raise me an' Little Ben. I had nightmares, and she was always there. What would we have done without her, Pap? She loved that old cabin where you were raised, but she gave it all up for us."

"She never asked nothin' but for me to sell the land for her either," he said. "I don't know what we would have done. I thought about scoutin' out the possibilities of marryin' again, but thar was no one I'd have for you an' Ben."

"I've been thinking," Rachel said as she spotted the pale salt lick up ahead. "Timothy was telling me that a lot of people around the country have started honoring their mothers in May every year. Well, Gramma, she's your ma and me an' Ben's grandma *and* mother really. We could plan something. I could go to Brush Lane and get some calico from the store there and make her a new dress and maybe even a bonnet. Me an' Ben could do all the chores that day while she sits and rests. She likes to eat outdoors during warm weather. I could cook, and we could spread some quilts near the river and have a picnic."

He smiled, and sat with her on boulders near the lick. "Sounds like you've got this all thought out."

"Well, what do you think?"

"I think it's a fine idea. I might even tell her how much I appreciate all those times she came at me with a switch— I turned out the better for it."

Rachel laughed. "Judging from the stories she's told, you looked for trouble when you were a boy, just like Ben."

"I reckon I did at that. Guess that's why I have a hard time scowling so at Ben when he does things like help scare the girls with snakes. You plan the day an' when you want me to take you to Brush Lane for that calico."

"I could go on my own, Pap. I don't want to put you out."

He gave her a long look. "I 'llow you can, Rachel. Lawd, look how big you are. Look how grown up! When did it happen? You ain't a little girl anymore. It scares me sometimes. Reckon that's why I've been actin' so awful."

She smiled. "You've been sayin' I'm more than old enough to be married. That means I'm grown up."

"Yep, but girls up here . . . Hell, they get married when they're still girls. You know that. Guess that's what I expected you to do. But I ain't gonna force you. I ain't gonna put a mountain between us, Rachel Sue."

"I never meant to make trouble, Pap. Really," she said, holding his gaze.

He shook his head. "I know."

"If Timothy asks . . ."

"I reckon I'll have to give serious consideration to gettin' along with him. But one thing, girl."

She waited.

"You're my only daughter. Let me be your pap. Don't see him 'cept at our place. I was his age. I know what goes on in a boy's head."

"I won't anymore—I promise."

He slapped his knees with his open hands and stood. "Found a new cave the other day. Me an' Ben were lookin' 'round. Traces of a bear in thar. Wanna go see?"

"As long as the bear's long gone from winter."

"She's gone. An' her younguns with her. Figure she has about three, judging from the prints in the dirt."

"Don't you worry, Pap? A bear this close to our place?"

"She ain't done us no harm so far. C'mon, we'll go have a look at the cave."

Smiling at his childlike eagerness, Rachel followed him around the salt lick.

After the conversation with her father, Rachel didn't waste much time making her way to Brush Lane. The very next morning she offered to walk Ben to school. Gramma said she was tired, so she'd be glad to let her. Little Ben and Rachel set out, with him giving her funny looks the whole two miles.

"What're you up to?" he asked as they neared the schoolyard.

"If I thought you could keep a secret, I'd tell you," she said.

"I can keep a secret!"

"What a stretcher. You tell everything."

"Don't neither!"

"Do too. Now go on to school."

"Where're you goin'?" He just had to know.

"Ain't none of your concern right now."

He frowned. "If you're meetin' Mr. Benton, I'll tell Pap."

"Told you you couldn't keep a secret," she said, scowling. "Besides, I ain't meetin' Mr. Benton. I wouldn't do that. I promised. Now go on. I've got business that ain't none of *your* business just yet—like I *said*."

"I ain't going to school today. I'm goin' with you," he announced stubbornly.

She stopped walking and put her hands on her hips. "Oh, no you're not, Benjamin Cameron. You're going to school."

"I'm goin' with you, an' you cain't do nothin' to stop me!"

"No, I sure can't. But when Pap comes walking up the riverbank this evening, I'll have to tell him how you and Tommy trapped those squirrels that time and tossed the whole lot of them down Mr. Crawford's chimney."

Ben went pale. He huffed some and kicked at the dirt a bit. "You said you wouldn't tell that."

"Well, I might just have to. Maybe you shouldn't have told me. Maybe you should learn not to tell certain things."

"Me an' Tommy'll get in a powerful lot of trouble if you tell, Rachel."

"I suppose you will," she said. "I hear Mr. Crawford's still looking for the culprits. Those squirrels had the run of his place for the longest time."

Ben snickered. "He had to move out to his barn to get away from 'em."

"Pap don't think it's as funny as you do. You heard him at supper that one night: 'If Crawford ever catches those boys, I'll help him lay into them.' "

"Aw, Rachel . . ." Ben sighed, his shoulders slumping. "I just wanna know where you're going!"

"Don't be peckin' at me," she said sternly. "Go on to school, where you're supposed to be. Pay attention to the lessons and don't be looking frowsy-headed. And mind yourself—don't let Joe and Tommy talk you into messin' with snakes."

He turned and shuffled off, grumbling how he and Tommy had never meant no harm putting those squirrels down Mr. Crawford's chimney and how sometimes all *her* pecking was more than a body could stand and where *was* she going anyway and why couldn't he know—he didn't tell *every*thing. . . . He muttered and grumbled and dragged his feet all the way to the schoolhouse door, then he shot her another glare that he probably thought was fierce looking. In reality, it was cute, and Rachel turned away to hide her smile.

Once he'd disappeared beyond the door, she walked straight-away to Mr. Rafferty's shop on Main Street, passing the drugstore and the post office, which were both gray buildings with their titles painted on long slabs of wood hung over the awnings. The post office had just opened last fall, though Mr. Rafferty's shop and the drugstore, with its soda fountain, had been here for at least five years. Down the street a ways new buildings were going up, and the hammering and excited talk carried far through the dusty air.

The inside of Mr. Rafferty's shop was always cool and always smelled of licorice. At present, the storekeeper stood on a ladder before a long shelf stocked with cans wrapped in neat labels— green beans, tomatoes, Boston baked beans, and green turtle meat. There were sardines in oil and sliced peaches and even oysters. Farther down the row sat one-hundred-pound bags of sugar and salt, bottles of salad dressing, and other things. Coffee was marked fifteen cents a pound, cocoa twenty-five. Plows, tools, trinkets, bolts of material, thread, and sundry other things occupied places in the back of the store.

A rather heavyset man, Mr. Rafferty stepped carefully down from the ladder, turned, and tugged at his mustache as he greeted Rachel by name and asked how he could help her today.

"I'm after calico to stitch Gramma a new dress," she confided, smiling. "But that's a secret, Mr. Rafferty, and having Ben tell all my secrets is bothersome enough. So don't you tell."

He raised both bushy gray brows, then lowered them. "Oh, I surely wouldn't Rachel," he whispered, looking about to see if anyone else was listening. His eyes twinkled.

Rachel laughed. She and Mr. Rafferty were the only ones in the store.

"C'mon back and see what we have," he said. "While you're choosing, maybe you wouldn't mind telling what the occasion is. Lydia doesn't often sport a new dress."

"Mother's Day."

"What's that?" he asked as she followed him.

She explained that Mother's Day was a day spent honoring your mother, or the mothers in your family. As Rachel and Mr. Rafferty reached a long counter, he rounded it and pulled out at least six bolts of calico. Rachel chose one decorated with tiny blue-and-yellow flowers.

While unfolding the material she'd selected, Mr. Rafferty asked if Mother's Day was something she'd invented herself or learned up in St. Louis. She said she'd been told about it by Mr. Timothy Benton, who had rented the old Newton place for a time. He knew Mr. Benton apparently—Timothy came in from time to time for supplies and "this an' that."

"Seems like a bright feller," Mr. Rafferty observed, cutting the calico.

Rachel plucked a spool of white thread from a shelf. "He is. He's had two books published an' he's writing a third. He's worked for some big newspaper up in Chicago, too."

"But he's still a mountain boy."

She smiled. "Yes, he is, isn't he?"

He sat the bolt aside and began folding the material he'd cut. "Life here gets in your blood, and there ain't no getting it out, that's for sure."

She agreed with that, too, while watching him work. He finished folding the calico, then he pulled some crackling brown paper from a nearby roll, cut it, and began wrapping the material.

"This Mother's Day thing," he said. "That's good . . . a way of telling our mothers how much we appreciate them."

She nodded.

"That might just catch on."

"I hope so."

He fetched a roll of string from a shelf behind him, then turned back, cut a length of it, and began tying it around the package. "I might tell a few people about this Mother's Day business myself. Tell you what." He handed her the package. "You tell folks an' I'll tell folks, and surely before long we'll have the whole of Missouri setting aside one day a year to *really* prize mothers."

"A fine idea, Mr. Rafferty," she said, laughing. "Now if you'll cut me a little of that licorice that always smells so good, we'll settle the bill, then I'll run home and figure how I'm going to work on Gramma's new dress without her knowin'."

He dipped his head several times, then headed for the front of the store. "Lydia'll look mighty fine in it, I'm sure," he remarked just as he passed behind another counter. Behind this one hung a huge roll of licorice on a large spool lodged between shelves. Rachel's mouth began watering as Mr. Rafferty pulled on the end of the candy rope.

EIGHT

A week later the dress was finished and hidden away in the brown wrapper in one of Rachel's drawers.

Timothy had come calling twice—on Monday and Wednesday afternoon. He'd been talking to Mr. Rafferty, who had been talking to the parson, who'd been talking to members of the congregation. . . . There was to be a big to-do at church come Sunday morning. All mothers would be recognized, then in an after-service picnic, special prizes would be awarded for such things as having the most children present, being the oldest mother, and for being the youngest mother.

The church picnic changed Rachel's plan for having a picnic just for Gramma, but she didn't mind. Rachel loved seeing the folks from Brush Lane and from outlying hills get involved in honoring mothers, and she knew the turnout for the service would be wonderful. Word of mouth had a way of working in the hills. Everybody came by information in a timely fashion, too.

Rachel's "secret" from Gramma wasn't a secret for long, what with everyone telling everyone else about Mother's Day. But the dress was still a surprise, and when Rachel hugged Gramma early Sunday morning and handed her the package, Lydia wrinkled her brow.

"It's a gift," Little Ben said, scrambling up onto a chair and peering at the women with big eyes. He'd caught Rachel stitching late one night, and she'd confided in him that the dress was for Gramma, reminding him, of course, that if he told Gramma what the surprise was, *she* would tell Pap about him and Tommy and those squirrels. He had scowled, tucked his head back beneath the quilt, and had soon fallen sound asleep again.

"For me?" Gramma asked, truly surprised.

"Sure, Ma," Paul said. "Open it now."

"We've all been thinking about what we would have done without you after Ma died," Rachel told her. "And we don't know, except that it wouldn't have been easy, an' life wouldn't have been the same. It wouldn't have been as good." As her father provided Gramma a chair and Lydia sank down into it with the package in hand, Rachel leaned over to hug her again and say softly, "All the things you've told me over the years . . . I'm learning to believe again. There was a perfect ring in the bottom of Pap's cup one morning, an' that same day I met Timothy. I heard a dove coo, too, just before he rode up, so there still might be a chance with me an' him."

Gramma smiled, laughed a little, and whispered, "When an unmarried girl hears a dove coo . . ."

" . . . the next man who rides by will be her future husband," Rachel finished, laughing, too. "I had his an' my rabbits' feet in my skirt pocket the day I ran off, too, an' everything turned out fine. It didn't start too well, but by the next day everything was good again. Better."

"Open it, open it!" Little Ben said.

Gramma wiped at her face and mumbled about how the sun from that eastern window was making her eyes water. Rachel and Paul exchanged knowing glances. Ben, with the usual tact of an eight-year-old, said, "Ah, Gramma, that's tears! Why're you cryin'? It's just a dress!"

"Ben!" Rachel glared at her brother.

He clapped a hand over his mouth. "Don't tell, don't tell, don't tell, Rachel," he said, his voice muffled. "I didn't mean to—honest! Don't tell about me an' Tommy an' the chimbley squirrels."

"What?" their pap asked, his eyes narrowing on Ben.

Rachel shook her head sadly. "I don't have to tell, Ben. *You* did. I wasn't going to anyway. I was just trying to get you to keep your mouth shut about today and the gift."

"I'll go straightaway to Mr. Crawford an' 'pologize, Pap,"

Ben promised. "I will! Don't whup me too awful. It was Tommy's idear to begin."

"Hush now an' let yer gramma enjoy her present," Paul said. "You an' I got to have a talk out in the barn later. For now, yer gramma's goin' to have a peaceful day."

Lydia opened the gift finally and couldn't blame the sun again for the tears that swelled in her eyes as she held up the dress and bonnet. "Lord, Rachel . . . Paul, Ben. They're pretty . . . but I never expected—"

"Of course you didn't," Rachel said.

"You gonna wear 'em to service?" Ben asked.

"I surely am." Lydia placed the items in her lap and shook her head. She reached out for both grandchildren, pulling Ben from the chair, and hugged them. "I'd have never thought to do things diff'rent than how I did them. Your mother was gone an' I was needed. There ain't been one day that I've regretted." She motioned to Paul and drew him into the circle, too.

Ben soon squirmed away, always unable to stand still for long. He was just old enough that he didn't go for much hugging and kissing. But as Pap often said of late, give Ben another three or four years and he'd like it—he'd go looking for kisses and hugs as a matter of fact.

"I'm cookin' breakfast this morning," Rachel announced, giving Gramma an extra squeeze. "You go on an' spend as much time as you want getting dressed. I'll holler when everything's ready."

"You c'mon with me, Ben," Paul said. "I need help with the animals."

"I don't wanna go to the barn, Pap," he objected.

"The barn ain't gonna be the worst of it, son. Talkin' to Mr. Crawford's gonna be the worst of it."

"Aw, Pap," Ben whined. "Mr. Crawford's jus' gotta know?"

"C'mon," Pa said, giving Ben's right ear a little twist.

Ben shuffled to the door with Pap following right behind.

"That boy's better at findin' trouble than your pap was," Gramma remarked once they'd gone. She gathered her dress,

bonnet, and the brown paper and soon disappeared through
the doorway that led to her bedroom.

Rachel had just put a pan of biscuits in the oven of the old
iron stove when she glanced out one of the front windows and
saw Timothy helping Pap force a cow into the barn. Her eyes
widened. What in the world was he doing here? He'd never
called so early. Not to mention that he was supposed to have
met them at church. When she'd talked to him Wednesday
morning, that had been the plan. But here he was, a bit fancied
up in dark trousers and a clean white linen shirt, looking as
fine as a man could possibly look, hair tumbling over one
side of his forehead, his face lit with a smile. He shook the
honey-colored hair back in his usual way, then caught her
looking at him through the window.

Looking a fright. She'd thrown on an old green shirt and
skirt and had tied a brown apron on over them, only the apron
was now smudged with flour in places. As she'd worked the
biscuit dough some of her hair had fallen from its pins, and
the unruly strands now dangled sloppily along both sides of
her face.

She jerked away from the window, turned and planted her
back against the wall, and tried to slow her heartbeat. She
sure hoped she'd have time to clean herself up in the event
Timothy decided to have breakfast with them. Maybe Pap and
Ben would keep him occupied outside for a while.

She hurried around to put bacon on to fry, then she climbed
the loft ladder and changed clothes. She pulled on a beige
shirt decorated with ruffled strips that had been made from
brown cotton printed with flowers. The skirt matched the
ruffles, and two rows of lace circled it some four inches
above the hem. She plucked the pins from her hair, ran a
brush through the mess real quick, then grabbed a brown
ribbon and her apron and went back downstairs.

The biscuits were a little more done than they should have
been, but at least the bacon hadn't burned. Rachel placed the
biscuits on thick cotton pads on the table, then returned to the
stove to turn the bacon. Once that was done, she pulled her

hair to one side, braided it, and tied the tapered end off with the ribbon.

When the bacon finished cooking, Rachel began frying eggs in the hot grease. She was watching the sixth one bubble and turn white when the cabin door creaked open and Ben came inside, beaming.

"Mr. Benton's come to ask Pap if he can sit with you at service this mornin' an' *take* you next Sundy," Ben said, hooking his thumbs in the bib of his duckin's. He propped himself against the wall near the door, a smart expression on his face.

Rachel stared at him. The grease popped, drawing her attention. She flipped the egg.

"Well, ain't you got nothin' to say?" Ben asked.

She shook the spatula at him. "If you're lying, Ben Cam'ron . . ."

"I ain't."

"Honest Injun?"

He jerked a nod. "Honest Injun."

She knew when he said that that he wasn't lying. Ben wouldn't say "honest Injun" if he was. But for Timothy to sit with her today and *take* her next week . . .

"Ever'body knows that means yer his gal," Ben said. "Sittin' with you in service, that's one thing. *Takin'* you is another."

"Nobody knows yet," Rachel snapped, lifting the cooked egg from the skillet and letting it slide onto the plate she held. She placed the plate on the table and took another egg from a nearby basket. Cracking the egg on the side of the skillet, she let the yolk and white spill gently into the pan, then dropped the shell into a bucket sitting on the floor to the left of the stove.

Ben again, "They'll know soon enough."

"Maybe they won't," she muttered. "I don't know what Mr. Benton's up to—he ain't stayin' in Missouri forever as far as I know. Unless he's got something different to tell."

"What's that?"

"Nothin'."

"Pap said that'd be fine with him. But you don't know if you like the idear, do ya?"

"Did he?" she blurted, jerking her hand back when the grease popped her. "Did Pap really say that?"

"Certain-sure, he did. But, Rachel, soon as a gal goes to church with a feller, she's his. Ever'body knows that."

She spun around. "What're you doing? Teasin'? Go help Pap finish the chores! I swear, Ben, sometimes I want to stuff your durned mouth with cotton! Your ears, too. Now go on before I ruin the eggs."

"Gimme a biscuit," he said, tipping his head.

"What?"

"Fer a biscuit I won't tell nobody this mornin' that he's *takin'* you next week. You don't know if you like the idear of him takin' you, so—"

Rachel flipped the egg. "You'll get a biscuit shortly—with your breakfast."

"They smell good an' I'm hungry an' want one now. Otherwise I'll tell."

"You'd better keep your mouth shut."

He grinned. "Gimme a biscuit."

She grabbed one and threw it his way. He caught it with both hands, laughed, then turned, pulled the door open, and charged outside—straight into Pap as Rachel took the egg from the skillet.

"Here now," Pap said, taking him by the shoulders. "Where're you runnin' to with that biscuit?"

Rachel snickered.

"I didn't snitch it!" Ben objected. "Rachel gave it to me."

"Is that right, Rachel?"

She pursed her lips, then sighed. "Yeah, Pap, that's right." It was the truth, after all. She'd been forced to give it to her brother, of course, but she *had* given it.

"Go feed those chickens like I told you to," their father told Ben.

After the boy disappeared around one side of Pap, Rachel spotted Timothy grinning over her father's shoulder.

"Mornin', Miss Rachel," Timothy said. "Having a little disagreement with your brother?"

She felt her face warm. What was he doing, asking Pap if he could sit with her in service today and take her to service next Sunday? As far as she knew, he still meant to head back to Chicago in the near future, and like Ben had said—when a man took a girl to service, that was as good as claiming her for his own.

"Somethin' like that," she answered, turning back to the stove. She set the spatula down, then took another egg from the table.

"Reckon you can fix up an extra place for Mr. Benton, Rachel?" Pa asked, crossing to a far corner and the washstand that sat there.

"Yes, Pap."

Her father washed his hands while Timothy faced her and settled his bottom against the edge of the table. Soon Pap wandered off through a door near the southwest corner of the back wall of the main room, into an addition to the cabin that had once been a lean-to. His door creaked shut. Seconds later Gramma emerged from her bedroom, looking fresh and ten years younger wearing her new dress, her bonnet resting on her back. Rachel and Timothy both told her how nice she looked. She blushed while thanking them, and they both laughed because she was so cute.

"I'll set the table," she said.

Rachel gave her a playful glare. "No, you won't. Go walk by the river or in the orchard. I'll call you in ten minutes or so."

Gramma opened her mouth to object, then thought better, shut it, and headed for the front door.

"You're lookin' pretty," Timothy told Rachel after Lydia had gone.

Rachel's heart quickened. "What brings you out so early in the day, Mr. Benton?"

He grinned, and his voice dropped a notch or two. "Why, you're surely *welcome*, Miss Rachel. It ain't often I pay a gal a compliment, 'specially not with her daddy right in the next room."

She huffed. "Thank you."

He inclined his head, acknowledging the words. "Are you goin' to cook that egg you're holding?"

She cracked it, spilled the contents, dropped the shell in the bucket, then wiped her hands on her apron.

"What can I do to help?" he asked.

She looked at him as if he'd lost his mind.

He shrugged. "I'm a bachelor. I know how to do these things. I don't like eatin' bad food, which is why I learned to cook. Here, I'll serve up biscuits and bacon on these plates," he said, lifting one from the four she'd placed side by side on the table.

She walked off to fetch another one from the cupboard while he served the biscuits and bacon.

"What do you *think* brought me out?" he asked as she approached the table. His eyes came to rest on her lips. "Or should I ask *who* do you think brought me out? I've missed you."

They stared at each other for a long moment.

"The egg needs to be turned," he said softly.

She hurried to tend to it. "I—I don't understand why you asked to sit by me durin' service today. A person can't tell half the time whether or not Ben's tellin' the truth except when he says 'honest Injun.' He told me you asked Pap if you could sit with me this mornin'."

"I did. I figured we'd best do this your father's way. I don't want to cause trouble in your family, Rachel."

"But church, Timothy! Everybody'll start wonderin'. Then if you *take* me next week, believe me, that means . . . well, that means I'm . . ." She let the egg slide onto the plate she'd brought from the cupboard.

"That means you're my girl," he said, reaching for the plate. He held one side of it, and she held the other. They regarded each other intensely over the dish.

He asked softly, "You don't wanna be my girl?"

"Lord," she whispered. "You know I do! But . . . why're you playin' with my head? It won't mean anything, not really—not to you. An' I ain't willing to play around at somethin' so serious."

"How do you know it won't mean anything to me?"
She swallowed. "Will it?"

"It just might."

"That's no promise."

"I can't promise you anything."

Her father's door creaked slightly. She let go of the plate;
Timothy turned, placed it on the table, and put two biscuits
and several strips of bacon on it.

"Breakfast ready, Rachel?" Pap asked.

"Yes. Would you mind hollerin' at Gramma and Ben? She
went to walk either by the river or in the orchard."

"Surely. You all right?"

She smiled and nodded at him over her shoulder. His gaze
shifted between her and Timothy. "I'm fine, Pap. Really."

"Reckon after Mr. Benton faced down Lloyd at the mill the
other mornin', he's entitled to a few minutes alone with you,"
her father said, starting for the cabin door.

Rachel glanced from him to Timothy. "Lloyd? What happened with Lloyd?"

"It was nothing," Timothy said quickly.

Paul snorted and turned back. "Oh, it was *somethin'* all
right, somethin' like I ain't never seen. I can still imagine
him wakin' up on that sluice."

"The sluice? You put him on the sluice?" Rachel demanded
of Timothy.

"He sure did." Paul laughed in disbelief. "Tied him up,
not tight, mind you, an' put him right up thar with the logs.
'Course, that was after Lloyd an' Frank tried to arrange a little
accident with him and the rollers. Frank talked him over,
wantin' help. Lloyd come up behind, meanin' to give Mr.
Benton a push an' set the rollers goin'."

Rachel gasped. "How do you know what they were
plannin'?"

"I heard 'em talkin' earlier in the day."

"Pap, you didn't *do* anything? You didn't try to stop them?"

"Up here a man fights his own battles, Rachel," Timothy
said, looking rather uncomfortable. His shifted from one boot
to the other and wiped his splayed hands on his thighs. "If he

has kin, they help. But my kin are dead an' buried."

Her father nodded. "Not that you need your kin, but that's
the long an' short of it. If he hadn't fought 'em, Rachel,
they'da kept after him. He gave Lloyd an elbow in the nose
that sent that boy sprawlin' against a rock. Lloyd was out
fer a while. Frank jumped Timothy, an' then it was all hell.
Timothy set to work. Gave Frank a beatin' Frank ain't gonna forget. Stephens an' the others . . . they'd known it was
brewin'. Ever'body did, I reckon."

"Everyone just stood an' watched?" she demanded, horrified. "Timothy, I told you I should have fetched the law that
day! Now maybe you need the law fetched on you, too. 'Gave
Frank a beating?' How bad? What does he look like? God . . .
Is he still *alive*?"

Timothy and her father exchanged glances. "Mr. Cameron,
I just did what I knew needed done," Timothy said softly.
"There's no need for Rachel to—"

"Hell, I know that. But I was powerful proud."

"An' impressed, " Rachel remarked dryly. "Go get Ben an'
Gramma, both of you. I don't want your help, Mr. Benton,
and I don't care to sit by you in service."

Both men stared at her.

"C'mon now, Rachel," her father pleaded. "Those boys were
gonna *kill* him in those rollers. Or else hurt him somethin'
fierce."

"Not to mention that they'd already jumped me from behind
once," Timothy said. "What the hell was I supposed to do?"

She turned away. "I don't want to hear any more of this.
I'm worried about Frank. Go on, both of you."

Paul shrugged at Timothy. Timothy rubbed his jaw, feeling
as though he'd been slapped, not physically but mentally. He
joined Rachel's father at the door.

She was herself again over breakfast, but Timothy figured
her light behavior was merely for show so Lydia wouldn't
sense trouble and the day wouldn't be ruined. Ben blabbed
that Timothy had asked to sit by Rachel in service and
take her to service next Sunday. Lydia looked delighted—
she turned a sparkling gaze on Rachel and said how she was

certain Rachel meant to accept Timothy's proposition. Paul coughed and opened his mouth to speak, but Timothy gave him a little nudge with a boot beneath the table. A quick jerk of Timothy's head made Paul snap his mouth shut. Timothy caught a glare from Rachel and reckoned there was no way in hell she would sit with him in service later.

NINE

Rachel sat with him, albeit stiffly and primly, her hands folded in her lap, her chin up, her eyes fastened on the parson who stood behind the pulpit.

She was the epitome of the prissy lady.

Feeling irritated, Timothy reached for her hand, knowing hand-holding with the opposite sex wasn't permitted during service. Ozarkers might make moonshine on the sly, the men might tomcat around, the women might gossip from sunup to sundown when the occasion arose, but all in all the mountain people took religion seriously, and there were unspoken rules that folks respected.

She jerked her hand away as he knew she would.

He reached for it again. He might be tossed out of church for doing it, but holding her hand, even for a second, was worth being tossed out for.

They were seated on a bench behind her family. The Howitts were seated behind and around them, and Mr. Rafferty sat with his wife and four children to Timothy's left.

"Stop," Rachel whispered through clenched teeth, again pulling her hand back.

"Don't be mad, Miss Rachel," he whispered back. He eased his hand over both of hers this time; she'd clasped them in her lap again.

She pursed her lips. "Would you quit? You'll get us both thrown out!"

"I only want to hold your hand."

"And I'm only sittin' by you so Gramma won't be disappointed!"

"You're soft."

"Stop!"

The parson interrupted telling about various biblical mothers and the important roles they had played, to scold "the youngsters in the sixth pew there." Rachel turned nearly as red as a beet. Behind Timothy, Susie Howitt giggled. Mr. Rafferty leaned over and said, "Aw, let 'im hold your hand. You're soft, after all."

Timothy grinned. Susie giggled again, and this time others joined her. Rachel stared straight ahead at the minister. Another warning sounded from the parson—the *last,* he said. A group of elderly people had turned austere stares on the sixth pew. Even Frank and Lloyd were present with their families, and surprisingly, they grinned from the third bench.

Finally relenting, Rachel turned her hand palm up and let Timothy slide his fingers between hers.

The little meetinghouse quieted again. All heads turned back to the minister, and the sermon continued. Afterward, bevel-plated hand mirrors Mr. Rafferty had ordered some time ago from the latest Sears, Roebuck and Company catalog and had donated for today's event were given to the oldest and youngest mothers present, and to the one with the most children present.

Once the service broke up and everyone dispersed outside, Timothy expected Rachel to set after him with some pretty scathing words. But she seemed determined not to talk to him. Every time he tried to start a conversation, she cut him off and wandered away, between quilts spread on the ground, to visit with friends she hadn't seen because not everyone came to service every week—and that included the Camerons.

Once he spotted Lloyd and Frank watching him from where they stood talking to a group of girls. They didn't look at him in too friendly a manner, but Timothy would wager everything he owned that they'd keep their distance from him from now on. They'd keep their distance from Rachel, too. The entire conflict between himself and Lloyd and Frank had been over whether or not he had the right to court her, and he'd won the battle by beating them both at once. They might be pretty sore, but even wolves as mean as those two knew when to cower away and not approach again.

By and by, after most picnic dinners had been eaten and chicken bones and empty dishes were all that were left, Timothy approached Rachel from behind. She was talking and laughing with Susie and a few other girls near one corner of the church. Timothy leaned over Rachel's shoulder and asked, "Care to walk with me?"

"As a matter of fact I—"

"Now, before you say no, Miss Rachel, think about how I'll feel, that my heart will be absolutely broken, torn in shreds . . . I don't know how I'd ever put it back together."

Her friends giggled. She couldn't help a smile. "Don't be silly," she said.

"*Silly?* You don't know how hurt I was when you wouldn't hold my hand."

"You shouldn't have been tryin' to do that."

"Oh, but you're so *soft,*" Susie teased, laughing. "Go walk with the poor man."

"Yes, do walk with the poor man," he coaxed.

Rachel gripped both sides of her skirt and turned away with a jerk, a swish of material, and a toss of her head. "All right, I'll walk with you. But don't think this means I plan to let you court me."

He wanted to laugh aloud in frustration at her sauciness. He gave Susie a grateful nod, and Susie whispered that Rachel liked him a *whole lot*; she was just being *difficult*. Then Timothy hurried to catch up to Rachel.

He walked three or four paces behind her for a time as she passed between trees, moving farther and farther from the church, putting distance between them and the small crowd. He couldn't help but feel she was doing so intentionally, that she was teasing him. There was a little more sway to her hips than what was normal, and now and then she gave a toss of her head and a little glance over her shoulder—just to see if he was still behind her.

She lifted her skirt and stepped over a fallen log. Then she passed between two tall, thick oaks, wandered around one, halted, and peered at him from what she obviously considered a safe position; she stood nigh to the far side of the trunk with one hand touching the bark, prepared to bolt behind the tree if he came too close. Her lips were parted slightly, her breasts rising and falling gently. He stopped walking and rocked back on the heels of his boots.

"If you'da let me fetch the law that day, Lloyd an' Frank would never have tried to jump you from behind again," she said.

"And I'd be known as the sissy of the county," he responded. "Just because the law's here doesn't mean anyone uses the law."

"That's stupid."

"Maybe so, but you learn to live by the rules if you want to live at all. You weren't at the mill the other mornin', Rachel. You didn't see what went on. You're wrong to stand in judgment. Don't tilt your chin an' look down your nose at me."

She stared at him, her eyes flashing. "God, Timothy, Frank looks awful! For the one shiner they gave you, you gave him two and a broken nose an' arm!"

"Yep, an' now he'll leave you an' me alone. Lloyd will, too."

"I hate the way men fight sometimes. You might've killed him!"

"I didn't set out to do that. I knew what they were up to when Frank called me over to have a look at the rollers. I saw Lloyd's shadow coming from around the corner of the building. *They* might've killed *me*."

She looked off at distant trees, then her gaze returned, soft and tempting, to him. Birds chirped from where they perched on branches. A dog barked from afar.

Timothy approached Rachel, halting once the distance of the thick tree separated them. "Why'd you tease me out here . . . *Miss Rachel?*" he asked in a low voice. Sunlight made her hair shimmer.

She lowered her lashes, then glanced at him from beneath them. Excitement rushed through his veins.

"Maybe that wasn't right of me," she said quietly. "I don't know what gets into my head lately. I'm not too sure about it all, that is. One minute I think I wanna be with you, an' the next I'm thinkin' that would be stupid, that I'd regret everything we did if we were to, you know, really be together."

She turned away and planted her back to the tree, where he could see only one side of her. He put an open hand on his side of the trunk and tapped the bark with his fingers.

"Take me to Chicago with you," she said.

He laughed. "Your daddy would skin me alive. Besides—'

"Then stay here. There's plenty of land to be had. You could write your books. We could keep a farm together, cook together . . . do all sorts of things together."

He smiled. " 'All sorts of things . . . ' That's interesting."

"I'm being serious." She sounded offended again.

He sighed. "Rachel, part of me is a big-city newspaperman. I love journalism. It's in my blood."

"Start a paper in Brush Lane."

"I said big city."

"So we'll be together, an' then you'll leave."

He swore under his breath. "Why argue about this? Why do you keep expecting me to prove that I'm not like Susie's artist?"

Silence. "That's not what I'm expectin'."

He ran a hand over his mouth, then rounded the tree an' looked her straight in the eye. "Yes, it is. Don't."

Her braid draped over her shoulder, ending some four inches below her right breast. Timothy fingered the plait beginning near her chin. She uttered no objection when he wrapped his hand around it and began a slow descent over her shoulder and the tempting curve of her breast. He twirled the tapered, feathery end up into a loop and brushed it lightly across where he knew her nipple pressed against her shirt.

She gasped and started, but he leaned forward and placed a hand on the tree just above her shoulder, his head just over the other shoulder.

"I'm tired of having to prove myself to people around here, so listen good, Rachel," he said gruffly. "Do you know what integrity is?"

Breathing rapidly, she nodded.

"Well, I'm mighty proud to say that it's one of my better characteristics. So don't try to shoot me down with words anymore and don't give me suspicious looks from the corner of your eye. Take me for what I am or tell me to leave an' never come back. Somethin' else . . . if we're ever 'really together,' it won't be something you regret afterward. I asked you in a roundabout way if you'd be my girl. That means I'm trying to make plans, that means I'm serious about what I'm doing. Don't play with me. Don't lead me around like I'm a goat on a line, swishing your skirt and teasing. That wouldn't be a wise thing to do with any man."

She stared at his chest, at the ground, at anything but his face.

"Do you have anything more to say?" he asked.

She shook her head.

"Good." He withdrew from the tree. "I'm going back to the church now to beg some cold lemonade from one of the ladies. I reckon you can find your own way."

He walked off.

Rachel stood in stunned disbelief, his words ringing over and over in her ears: *Don't lead me around anymore . . . swishing your skirt and teasing. Don't shoot me down with words . . . don't give me suspicious looks from the corner of your eyes. I'm trying to make plans . . . I'm serious about what I'm doing.*

She *had* led him around—she couldn't deny that. She got so close to letting him touch her, really touch her, and then a distrustful part of her wanted to pull away.

She'd lose him entirely if she didn't start trusting him, if she didn't believe that he was trying to make plans, that he really wanted her and was nothing like Susie's artist. There was no problem with Pap objecting to Timothy anymore; her father seemed to trust Timothy more now than she did. Or at least he admired the way he'd handled Lloyd and Frank. He thought Timothy worthy.

She loved Timothy. Oh, Lord, how had this happened? She'd told herself it wouldn't, but it had, and she was frightened.

She tipped her head back against the tree, wishing, despite what she'd vowed to Timothy, that she had a daisy in her hand.

He didn't come around for five days. She counted the first four as they passed with horrible slowness. One evening while sitting on a chair before the house, Gramma thought aloud that Mr. Benton surely must be busy these days. And while Rachel was gathering eggs the following morning, Pap walked into the henhouse, wiped sweat from his brow as he leaned back against the door frame, and said he reckoned her and Benton had had a falling-out, but if she ever got of the mind, he'd be glad to take her to go talk to him.

"Thank you, Pap," she responded. "I'll walk to the mill with you in the morning and talk to him there."

Which is exactly what she did. He was behind the mill building, shirtless, perspiration beading on his skin as he worked with some other men at lifting logs onto the sluice for shipment upriver to Springfield, where they'd be shipped east and west by rail. He was bending to grab one end of a log when he saw her. He straightened, staring at her, and Paul walked over to take his place.

Timothy approached Rachel, stopping some six inches in front of her. "Howdy," he greeted.

She smiled nervously. "I just came to say I'm sorry. I *have* been comparin' you to Susie's artist an' I know I shouldn't. Things got more serious than either one of us really counted on—though I shoulda known. It ain't ever'day a girl sees a perfect ring of coffee grounds in the bottom of a cup and hears a dove coo close by."

He returned the smile, rubbing the toe of a boot in a patch of dirt. "A perfect ring of grounds, huh?"

She nodded. "Perfect. I was shocked."

"I bet." He reached out and gave her lower arm a light squeeze. "Seen one today?"

"Wha . . . ? A ring? No." She shook her head and said more slowly, "No, I'm afraid not."

"I'll look in all the cups lying around here."

She lifted a hand to her lips, remembering his kisses in the boat that afternoon.

"I'm glad to see you," he murmured. "I wanna kiss you right here, right now."

She wished he would—and if he did, she wouldn't care a fig that there were ten or so men working not fifty feet away. "Come by tomorrow?" she asked breathlessly.

He jerked a nod.

"For supper?"

"I'll be there."

She smiled again, then turned away.

When the next evening finally arrived and she heard hoofbeats, she had to restrain herself to keep from racing outside and throwing herself into his arms. She'd donned her best clothes—a rose shirtwaist with a high collar, tucking, and pleats, and a skirt of Manchester cloth bound with velvet around the hem. She had tried to curl and pin her hair in a way one of the girls at school had shown her, but it wouldn't cooperate, and frustrated, she had given up on the task and simply let her hair fall free.

"Reckon he'll be wantin' to marry you next," her father said, standing near the table. Ben was still upstairs, changing into clean clothes. Gramma was at the stove.

Rachel's breath caught in her throat. "Oh, Pap . . . He asked?"

"Not in so many words. But he'll do right by you, gal. He promised, an' I believe him."

A knock sounded on the door. She jumped.

"Simmer down," Paul said, grinning. "It's just a feller."

"Pap!" she whispered. "He ain't just any ol' fellow!"

He laughed. "You look perty."

In the end, Pap was the one who walked over, opened the door, and invited Timothy inside.

Dressed in dark trousers and a white shirt, Timothy nodded greetings to Paul and to Lydia, who said the beef and potatoes were about ready. Timothy turned a soft gaze on Rachel. She greeted him with a smile then hurried over to help her grandmother.

TEN

Rachel and Timothy went walking along the river later, with the moon glowing softly overhead and locusts and crickets singing in the trees and scrub. Branches whispered, and silver ribbons danced on the river. Their boots brushed the damp grass. Her hand felt warm, enclosed in his.

"There'll be rain soon," she remarked. "Pap's been worried about the apple crop 'cause we ain't had much rain this year."

"Why, Miss Rachel, are you making that prediction based on that circle around the moon?" Timothy asked. "One with no stars in it, at that."

He was teasing her. She tilted her head. "I'm learnin' not to be so skeptical. And I'm tryin' not to be prissy. Besides, I've *seen* rain come soon after a haze like that around the moon."

"Don't get rid of all your prissiness. It's one of the things I love about you. But it's like cream on strawberries—a little is good. Too much and I don't want to eat them."

Rachel's heart seemed to leap up into her throat. Had he said that? Had he said *It's one of the things I love about you*? She wanted to ask him to say it again, just to be sure. But she wouldn't. She'd told herself that she would be patient and not make demands.

"I finished your book this mornin'," she said instead.

"Finally?" he teased.

"I know. It's taken me a while. Chores an' other distractions."

He nodded, his eyes shimmering in the moonlight. "I know about those other distractions."

"I couldn't believe when they got frozen in. And when Henry walked out onto the ice to help Captain Manning an' the ice broke an' Henry went down! I was holding my breath, I swear. That was mean. Why'd you have to write that in?"

"Because it was part of the story, part of Henry's adventures that year. It was part of his maturity."

"It didn't have to go like that."

"It happened."

"You made it up."

He grinned. "That could be debated."

"And when they signed on that stranger in Milwaukee. I knew there was something odd about him. He talked strange, you know, like somethin' from centuries before."

"And lo! He was."

"You could really scare a person from here with that. We're told about ha'nts early on."

"Did I scare you? Did Mr. Chapman's sudden appearances and disappearances frighten you?" He made a low sound, like that of a ghost.

She laughed a bit nervously. "Stop that before you have to hold me."

He *oohed* again, louder and longer this time. She pulled her hand from his and walked ahead, tipping her chin but smiling. She shivered, too, but she wouldn't let on that she was scared. The scene where Mr. Chapman had suddenly appeared behind Henry, and Henry had turned and blinked, swearing he could look right *through* the man for a few seconds there . . . it had frightened her, and Timothy's teasing brought it all back— how she'd spent hours looking around after every sound in the house. With the trees casting shadows everywhere out here and all the little noises coming from different places . . . Outside at night was no place for a frightened person to be. An owl hooted from nearby, and she jumped.

Timothy chuckled. "Aw, c'mere, Miss Rachel. I'll hold ya. Shame on that feller who scared you. But I'll be glad to comfort ya. Certain-sure."

She turned around and walked backward. "You rascal! Don't." Something splashed in the river, and she jerked that way, tripping over the hem of her skirt.

His hand lashed out to catch her around the waist, and then they both tumbled to the grass. The collision with the ground knocked the breath out of her. The moon seemed to circle the sky, then Timothy was there, hovering over her, concern narrowing his eyes.

"Rachel?" He pushed hair from her face. "Rachel, are you all right?"

"No, I . . ." She took a deep breath and fought a smile. Tease her into such a frightened state, would he? Well, she meant to have a little fun of her own. "My leg . . . It twisted pretty awful. I don't know."

"Which one?"

"The left."

He touched her left thigh, shifted his body, and moved down. His hand traveled the length of her limb, feeling for a break in the bone. As he probed she was reminded of how good his touch had felt that afternoon aboard his boat. It had been a more intimate touch, one she hadn't forgotten, one she'd wanted to feel again.

He'd reached her ankle. He unlaced her boot and pulled it off, then touched her joint lightly, his fingertips sending a shiver up her leg. "Maybe you just sprained something. There's no break."

"Timothy," she murmured. His gentle inspection stirred her in a physical way that only he could rouse.

He glanced up. He stared at her for a moment, then shook the unruly hair back from his brow. "If I didn't know better, I'd think you were trickin' me. But you wouldn't do that, now, would you, Miss Rachel?"

She smiled.

He watched her a little longer, shadows dancing on his face. Then he began touching her leg again, working his way up, never taking his gaze from hers.

"Maybe I should, uh, examine you all over, just to be sure," he said, his voice low and thick. "You know, sometimes a person feels pain where there ain't really pain. The pain is somewhere else, and the whole body has to be checked."

Her smile faded. She closed her eyes, tipped her head back, and inhaled.

His hand reached her hip, and she felt his body move up, felt his thigh and then his groin touch her leg. He shifted, and she opened her eyes and found him stretched out beside her, his head propped on an elbow as he looked down on her. All the tension that had been building for weeks and weeks . . . she knew it was about to rush together.

"This can't happen, Rachel," he whispered. "Someone could—"

She pressed two fingertips to his lips to silence him. Then she slipped her hand to the back of his neck and urged his head to hers. "I love you, Timothy Benton. For all your ha'nts and your teasin', for all the things you make me feel. For making me proud to be who I am."

She kissed him lightly, then traced one side of his mouth with a forefinger. She moved her body closer against his and kissed him again, tasting his salty lips with her tongue.

Groaning, he took control, raising up, easing her flat onto the grass, shifting to slip a leg between her thighs. He pushed hair from her face, then lowered his head to kiss her deeply, parting her lips, drinking of her, savoring. His hand eased up over one of her breasts, and she arched up to the touch, moaning, unable to remember when anything had felt so good, so achingly sweet.

He began unfastening her shirt buttons. She felt a tremble go through him as he worked, and she marveled that he seemed as nervous as she was. She didn't think for a minute that this was the first time he'd been with a girl, but he was nervous all the same, whether he was nervous about making love to her or about where they were. She didn't know . . . but she smiled as he tugged impatiently at the buttons.

"I can't get the last two," he said breathlessly. "An' you're laughin' at me. C'mon, Rachel—help."

"All right," she said emphatically. She pushed him away, sat up, unfastened the last two buttons at her neck, then parted the shirt.

His hands touched her shoulders from behind, and he slid the shirt down her arms and off her hands. Then he reverently touched her shoulders, kissing one, fingering the ruffled sleeve of her muslin chemise, then easing his hands down and under her arms, making his way to the front clasps on her corset.

The corset soon slipped away, then Timothy pushed the chemise sleeves down, over her breasts and off her arms. The garment lay bunched around her waist. She had only a few seconds to feel self-conscious about her nakedness, to raise her arms to cover herself, then he urged her back onto the cool grass again, dipped his head, nudged her hands aside, and began kissing her swollen breasts. She gasped when his hot mouth covered a nipple.

His hips moved against her thigh again, and she felt him as she'd only felt him once before, his length hard and straining against his binding trousers. His hand moved down, over her stomach and hips, then her skirt was being pulled up.

A slice of apprehension went through her, and she gave half a thought to objecting, to pushing his hand away. But the ache that had been building and building deep in her belly had become a dull throb between her legs, and shamelessly, she wanted his touch there; she wanted *him* there.

He lifted his head and whispered, "Are you sure, Rachel? Tell me soon, or else I can't stop. . . ."

In answer, she splayed her hands on his chest. She unbuttoned his shirt, then took a deep breath of courage and reached down to unbutton his trousers.

He laughed low in disbelief.

She jerked her hand back, afraid she'd offended him.

"No," he said, catching her hand. "Don't be afraid to touch, Rachel. I didn't mean to scare you—not this time anyway. Touch me, see how much I want you."

Unsure how far that breath of courage would take her, she didn't move.

He guided her hand down, down, to the waistband of his trousers, then lower. Her knuckles brushed his hardened length, and she gasped again, feeling the throb in her private place flare into fire. She turned her hand over and cupped him fully, marveling, feeling a surge of confidence when he squeezed his eyes shut and groaned with pleasure. She massaged with her fingers, caressing and memorizing the feel and shape of him.

He groaned again, then became desperate . . . frantic. He pulled at the lower half of her chemise, and she lifted her hips to accommodate him. He raised the garment up, gripped her drawers, and pushed them down to her knees. She stopped him long enough to unlace and kick off her remaining boot— while he worked at his trousers—then she reached for him, grasped his upper arms, and urged him to settle between her open legs.

He covered her mouth with his and thrust with his hips at the same time, drinking her whimper of pain. He felt too large, too hard, too *unsuited,* and she panicked, squirming beneath him, trying to get away. It wasn't like what she'd thought. It hurt and it wasn't right and—

"No, Rachel," he murmured, pleaded. "Don't say no now. We've gone too far. Lie still. It won't hurt for long. Spread your legs. Lift your hips. *Trust.*"

Through the blur of pain, she heard his last word more clearly than the others and she forced herself to do as he said, to spread her legs and lift her hips. The movements eased the pain, and he settled in more deeply, pushing her knees up slightly and slipping his hands beneath her hips to lift her to him.

He began moving in and out, and the pain died more with each gentle plunge. A sweet pleasure replaced it, growing, building, sweeping every reservation and fear aside. She heard only his heavy breathing, smelled the saltiness of his perspiration, felt the strength of him, the tightening and relaxing of his every muscle.

He lowered his head to kiss her, and the plunges became thrusts, deep and exquisite. Her hands circled his waist, then his hips, boldly pressing against his buttocks, urging him on. A storm built around them, the kind that often blackens a lush summer sky and builds in intensity until finally—oh, finally!—it explodes in sweet fury.

They cried out at nearly the same time, their bodies going rigid.

Rachel watched pleasure contort his face, and she reached up and drew his head down to her breast.

"Are you angry?" he asked from the haven of her breast.

She smiled. "Are you scared I might be?"

"You know I am."

"I know," she said, stroking his soft hair. "No, I'm not angry. It just . . . hurt. I knew it would—I've heard talk—but I didn't know it would be that bad at first."

"Then it went away?"

She nodded, feeling her face warm. "Yes. I did what you said, I trusted you, and it got better."

He raised his head. "I want to marry you, Rachel Sue Cameron. But I don't want to take you away from where you belong."

"Did it ever occur to you that maybe I *want* to see Chicago and places like that?" she said, smiling again.

"I'm not sure I can leave the Missouri mountains yet, that I'll ever want to live in another place again. I'm home, Rachel. God, I'm home . . . and it feels good."

She couldn't help a giggle. "Well, I surely am glad you feel at home, Mr. Benton," she said, wriggling her hips against his. "Home's a good place to be when it's so warm and—"

"Wet." He grinned. "I can't believe you. You're shameless."

She blushed to her roots. "I couldn't resist."

"I'm glad you're not beating me off of you."

"Lawd," she said, employing a heavy Ozark accent. "Now jes' why would a gal do that?"

"You would have before tonight."

She turned serious. "I wasn't ready before tonight. The thing with Susie and the artist—that scared me bad. People . . . outsiders . . . come up here, having heard about the mountains. They stay awhile, make friends if possible, sometimes make real good friends with the girls—after all, most girls from the hills are a little free about certain things—then they up and leave."

"I told you I wouldn't."

"I've seen tomcatters. They try to say all the right things."

He twirled a strand of her hair around his fingertip. "I bet your pap and gramma are wonderin' if I mean to return you tonight."

"I can't believe Pap—how he's changed toward you. He didn't like or trust you at all. Now . . ." She laughed incredulously.

"Now he'll say yes the second I ask to marry you. He probably knows exactly what we're doing out here, too."

"He doesn't!"

"Do you think he's never wooed a girl out into the moonlight? He knows."

"Are you goin' to ask his permission to marry me?" she ventured.

"Of course I am," he said, bending to kiss the upper swell of one breast.

"What about bein' a big-city newspaperman?"

"I wrote to the editor of the *Springfield Journal* a few weeks ago."

"And?" She waited, holding her breath.

"And . . . he'd like me to join his staff."

She yelped. She couldn't help herself. She tapped the backs of her heels against the ground and hugged him tight. "That's not so far. That's not so far at all! Forty miles at that."

He laughed. "I don't think you really want to leave home either."

"Not to live. You're right about that. I wanna see Chicago and Henry's Lake Michigan, but I'm an Ozark girl, through and through."

"And damn proud of it?"

She laughed. "That's right—damn proud of it."

He sobered. "Here comes that rain."

"How do you know?" she asked, frowning.

"I felt a drop on my backside, that's how."

She clapped a hand over her mouth to smother a snicker.

"Funny for you," he said, withdrawing. "Up, Miss Rachel, and get dressed. I'll smooth the wrinkles in your clothes so your pap doesn't come after me with a shotgun."

"He wouldn't!"

"He might," Timothy teased. "Just to hurry things along a bit." He sat up and tugged at his trousers.

She stretched and smiled. "You wouldn't be sorry."

He paused in dressing to smile back and run a hand up the inside of one of her thighs. "No, I wouldn't be sorry. Now get dressed, like I said."

A few more drops fell, on her face this time. She sat up, pushed her chemise down, pulled the bodice up over her breasts, and slipped an arm into one sleeve just as rain began pelting down. She yelped again. Laughing, Timothy stood and snatched up the rest of her clothing. He grabbed her hand, pulled her to her feet, and they headed for a cluster of trees.

ELEVEN

"He quit at the mill las' Mondy mornin'. I don't think he'd do that unless . . . y'know . . . he was thinkin' of leavin'."

Rachel was standing near the barn fence, watching the chickens and hogs. Gramma had sent her out to pick a bird for the afternoon kettle. The sour smell of the pigs drifted up. The birds clucked and scratched at the ground, wandering in and out of the nearby henhouse.

Rachel shut her eyes, feeling dizzy suddenly, not wanting to hear what Pap was telling her. It was now nearly the end of June, and she and Timothy were supposed to be married tomorrow. They'd planned the date around the full moon so they'd have happiness and good fortune. Only she hadn't seen him in nearly two weeks.

She bowed her head, resting it on the top rail. "Why didn't you tell me before, Pap?"

"I, uh, couldn't much believe it m'self," he mumbled behind her. "Didn't want to. Didn't . . . y'know, wanna see you hurt."

"Have Lloyd an' Frank bothered him anymore?"

"Naw. They wouldn't."

Silence.

"Listen," he said. "I really 'llowed he was diff'rent, Rachel. I believed him when he promised he'd do right by you. I'd go load up m'gun an' hunt him down if I thought it'd do any good. But that bus'ness with you, girl . . . that taught me somethin'. If a grown person's dug their hooves in an' jes' don't wanna do somethin', thar's no sense in tryin' to make 'em. They get mad an' you get mad an' thar jes' ain't no sense in it 'tall."

One of the hogs snorted around, scattering chickens in a flurry of fluttering wings and loud squawks.

What had happened?

Rachel thought back to the last time she'd seen Timothy. He'd shouted to her from the river, from his boat. Her chores were all done for the morning, so prompted by a nod of Gramma's head, she'd gathered her skirt and raced to the water. Timothy had helped her into the boat, and they'd lain back and spent the afternoon drifting and talking. They'd found a place near the bank where the trees drooped over, and they had moored the skiff beneath its massive branches. Feeling well hidden despite daylight, they'd made love, and the time together had been incredible, as always.

He had said nothing to indicate that he was unhappy, that he was having second thoughts. But then, a body couldn't always know what was going on in another person's mind. . . .

Pap came to stand beside her at the rail. "Thought I'd go up an' have a talk with him, friendlylike, y'know."

If he's still there.

"I ain't gonna demand nothin', I ain't gonna try to force—"

"No, Pap," she said, lifting her head. "I'll go."

She met his soft gaze. He worked his mouth one way for a minute, then the other. "Wish thar was somethin' I could do."

She reached down, squeezed his hand, and managed a smile. "I love you."

He embraced her. She didn't want to let go. She suddenly wanted to be a little girl again, safe in either his or Gramma's arms, ignorant of the world, untouched by anything outside the farm. She wanted to climb high up in a tree and sit there, hidden by well-dressed branches.

She couldn't. She wouldn't. She wasn't a little girl anymore, and while an embrace and the sanctuary of a tree might comfort her for a while, nothing could protect her from the pain and disbelief that clenched her heart. She was surrounded by a loving family, but this was a problem she had to face alone.

Pap withdrew first and smoothed back the hair on one side

of her face. "I'm here if you need anything. I'll saddle you a horse."

She nodded, then they headed for the barn.

She found the old Newton cabin virtually empty.

Empty, that is, of Timothy's belongings.

Rachel forced herself to walk inside, to draw nigh to the now empty shelves he had built to protect his books. She remembered the sloppy arrangement of them. Oh, some had stood in a neat file, but others had sat atop those, some had been pushed into any available space, and still others had been piled on a nearby table. A table that was now bare and dusty. She approached it, wrote his first name in the powder, and made a sound deep in her throat.

He'd run off. He'd packed everything, had quit his job at the mill, and now he was gone.

She should have known.

She had. Then he'd made her believe in him.

A creak sounded from somewhere outside. She whipped around. A breeze swept inside the open door and caressed her face, and she closed her eyes again and tipped her head, imagining that the breeze was his touch, his fingers lightly skimming her cheek, her jaw, her neck, dropping down to her breast. . . .

"Found us a nice house in Springfield," he said.

Stupid Rachel. Imagining him saying such a thing! She was dreaming again, of a future that wouldn't be. That *couldn't* be because he was gone. Like Susie's artist, he'd come through, snatched up her heart, and now he was gone.

"Thought your pap told you not to come up here anymore," he said. "Stubborn gal. You'll get yourself in a heap of trouble someday."

His voice sounded so *real*. She shook her head. Then she forced her eyes open. She had to look, just had to—

He was leaning against the door frame, his arms folded across his chest, his honey hair falling over one brow, his turquoise eyes glowing softly in the sunlight peeking in through the doorway and through the windows. He wore duckin's and a pair of dusty boots. A piece of straw twisted in one corner of his mouth, and his ankles were crossed. He looked comfortable and relaxed, and she wanted to *kill* him for scaring her so!

"Blame it all, Timothy Benton! Where the blazes have you been?"

Grinning, he reached up, plucked the straw from his mouth, and tossed it aside. "Havin' a little problem with trust again?"

She gripped the sides of her skirt and whirled away, turning her back to him. She was so mad she could breathe fire. And she was so relieved she might rush into his arms if she turned back. So she'd keep her back to him, make him pay for scaring her so.

She heard his boots brush against the puncheons. She smelled straw and sweat and horse manure. . . . The dust in the cabin made her nose itch and her throat go dry.

His large hands touched her shoulders, and he leaned over to kiss her hair. She tossed her head aside. "If you think—"

"Saucy Miss Rachel . . . I wanted the house all ready by the time we were married," he said in a husky voice. "A man can't take his bride into an ol' run-down place such as this. Figure we'll head out tomorrow afternoon an' be in Springfield by night. There's a nice big bed up there an'—"

"Thar," she whispered.

He chuckled.

"Why didn't you tell me where you were goin'? What you were plannin'?"

"I wanted it to be a surprise, an' I didn't think arrangin' to buy the house would take so long. Besides," he said, "I ain't the kind to tell plans till they're all laid out nice an' smooth."

"I'm so mad, I jus' might not marry you after all!" she said in a huff.

He laughed again, then pulled her back against him. "Gonna say howdy, Miss Rachel? Somethin's sure got your dander up t'day. Wouldn't be that feller you took up with, would it? That citified hillsman? 'Course, you don't have to *say* nothin'."

She turned, meaning to smack him good on the chest. Instead she kissed him.